LORI HOLMES

The Last Kamaali

First edition

ISBN: 9798372398986

This book was professionally typeset on Reedsy.
Find out more at reedsy.com

Contents

Dedication

To Frank, for kick-starting my love of everything sci-fi and fantasy, and ultimately storytelling, by always providing an endless supply of Star Trek series and Star Wars books from when I was a little girl. And for walking me down the aisle at my wedding. Forever thankful.

Prologue - Slave Race

400,000 years BCE

"The Igigi have rebelled!"

Lord Enlil's voice reverberated through the research bay. Both Ninmah and Enki glanced up in alarm as the leader of their council stalked through the gleaming space; his reflection curling along the polished walls. Enlil's golden skin was bleached with rage, his full mouth mashed into a line of anger.

Beside her, Ninmah felt Enki founder. His shock at the news that the Igigi would dare to rebel against their betters was palpable. Ninmah's own mouth went dry. "Surely not, Enlil—" An explosion from somewhere outside their complex shook the research bay, forcing Ninmah to catch her weight on a nearby console.

"It cannot be!" Fear shredded Enki's usually sibilant tones as he found his voice at last.

"They have destroyed their equipment!" Enlil shrieked, his glowing blue eyes incandescent. "Mining for the element is no longer possible."

Ninmah gripped her console until bone showed through her knuckles. All three of them knew what this meant, and the weight of that knowledge fell like a shroud upon the room. The thought of their homeworld choking into nothingness as the atmosphere leaked away was too much to bear. They needed the element, or Nibiru would die.

Enlil's long fingers closed into a fist that he slammed down onto a reflective worktop, rattling the instruments lying there. "I will not have disorder! I will make them obey me!"

"Enlil, please consider," Enki reasoned with his brother. "We are only nine. The Igigi outnumber us a fifty to one. We have no way of bringing reinforcements from Nibiru in time to restore control."

"Then what do you suggest?" Enlil rounded on him. "That we give up? Forget the sacrifices we all made to find this world and turn our backs on our home? If the Igigi will not obey, then Nibiru is doomed!"

Ninmah flinched as the words lashed through the air like a laser-drill, designed as they were to quell Enki. To Ninmah's dismay, they had the opposite effect. She felt the first stirrings of defiance as Enki faced Enlil. Panic shot through her as she discerned the direction of his thoughts.

Don't, she thought at him. *We don't know what—*

Enki's blue eyes flared in her direction. *We have to try. The Igigi are lost. Nibiru's existence is worth anything he might do to us.*

Before Ninmah could formulate another counter thought, Enki spoke: "What if we didn't need the Igigi? What if we had another, more obedient workforce?"

Enlil growled. "There is no such thing. Speak your meaning, Enki. I am running out of patience."

Enki met Ninmah's pleading gaze for a fraction of a second, but ignored the warning flick of her head.

"Ninmah and I have been working on a... personal

research project. Our experiments have yielded a result beyond anything we could ever have imagined. One that could be the very solution we need to appease the Igigi and continue the labours they have abandoned without need for bloodshed."

"Research?" Lord Enlil demanded. "I did not authorise any research. What have you been doing, Enki?"

Only Ninmah discerned the quick breath that her spouse took before laying their freedoms, perhaps even their lives, on the line. "If you would follow me."

Without a hint of hesitation, Enki swept over to the inner chamber of their research bay. The green beams of light criss-crossing the entrance would kill anyone other than Ninmah or Enki should they try to enter without permission. Detecting Enki's distinct signature, the glow of lasers melted back, permitting his entrance.

Enlil did not move to follow. Instead, he turned his penetrating azure gaze upon Ninmah. She straightened her back, attempting to emulate Enki's confidence, but the small scales of her skin rippled under his scrutiny as she raised one arm, indicating that Enlil should go after Enki. There was nothing else she could do now. Enki had tipped their hand.

Emitting a hiss in the face of her equal lack of explanation, Enlil turned on his heel and stepped through to the inner chamber. Ninmah considered fleeing to the other side of the complex to avoid the dangerous fallout she knew was inevitable. Enki's quick decision to reveal their unsanctioned experiment brought home to Ninmah the seriousness of the situation facing Nibiru now the Igigi had shirked their duty to their betters.

The lingering shock of the announcement at last gave way to anger. *How* dare *they put us in this situation,* Ninmah thought to herself. *How could they risk Nibiru? Surely saving our home is worth any hardship.*

Any hardship... The thought stiffened Ninmah's spine. Instead of fleeing, she shadowed the leader of their council through the disarmed doorway over to where Enki waited. At his side, a swathe of metallic grey cloth concealed a large horizontal cylinder. Instruments whirred on the various work-stations and fluids dripped softly in their tubes.

"What is *that?*" Lord Enlil jabbed a finger across the sterile chamber to where a hairy creature with a flat, naked face was cuffed by its four limbs in an upright position against the wall. The five-fingered hands, hairless like the face, hung limp from disproportionately long arms.

"A primitive creature native to this world," Enki answered.

"And you brought the filthy beast into our base?" Enlil's scales rippled.

"There is no need for alarm. It is dead."

Ninmah tensed. If Enlil was furious at them simply for bringing an animal onboard...

But if Enki feared what was to come next, her spouse did not show it. His face was steady. "That creature was the basis of our research. It had potential. Ninmah and I decided to find out what would happen if such a creature was given a... push in the right direction."

Enlil's nostrils flared. "A push? Enki, what have you *done?*"

"I have saved us all!" Enki declared and ripped the glimmering grey cloth from the cylinder beside him, revealing the results of their slumbering experiment in all its naked glory.

"Great An!" Enlil shrieked, falling back away from the stasis pod. "What blasphemy is this?"

"Exactly what you see before you." Enki was unrepentant. "We have created a clone using that creature as a base and infused it with our own living code. Ninmah herself carried the resulting embryo to term."

There was a beat of shocked silence before Enlil's outrage exploded through the room. Ninmah cowered back, horrified, as Enlil grabbed her spouse by the insulating cloth at his chest. "You gave a primitive creature from a backwater rock the divine blood of the Anunnaki themselves?" Enlil's eyes bugged. "What gave you the audacity to—to—?"

"Curiosity. And now, need." Enki gripped Enlil's wrists. "We *need* this creature, Lord Enlil! It is intelligent. It is biddable. It is the perfect slave. The Igigi will no longer..."

"Destroy it!" Enlil hissed. "Destroy the abomination or I will kill you right here as a punishment for your vile transgression."

"No." The word was out of Ninmah's mouth before she was even aware of formulating it. Her fear melted before the protective fire now burning in her chest. She stepped up beside the pod. "If you destroy this being, Enlil, the Council will hear of it. They will hear how you snuffed out the one hope of saving our home because of your fear and pride. You will be no better than the Igigi."

"I lead the Council!" Enlil snarled, his hands still curled into fists at Enki's chest.

Ninmah gripped the sleeves of her robe as she sought the courage to say what needed to be said. "But you are not its only voice, Lord Enlil. Summon the Nine. Allow Enki to put his findings before them, and we will vote. If this creature we have created could save Nibiru, the others deserve a hand in its fate. That is not for you alone to decide."

Enlil's eyes flickered back and forth, taking in both Ninmah's defensive stance over the pod and Enki's cold, hard resolve. Ninmah was glad she had stood by her partner and not fled. She watched as the realisation he could not fight both of them settled over Enlil's face.

"Very well," their leader said in a voice that was more deadly for its softness. "I will summon the Council, and you will admit before them all the heresy you have committed here. Should the vote go against you, death will be too lenient a punishment. I will see that you will live painfully in Irkalla, regretting your trespass until the end of your days."

Enlil threw Enki to the ground and tore out of the room, the oppressive weight of his fury trailing him like a dark cloak.

For several drawn-out moments, all Ninmah could hear was the sound of the whirring instruments and the drip, drip of fluids; indifferent as they were to the council leader's rage until Enki's soft laugh broke the near silence. Shaking herself back to her senses, Ninmah extended a hand to help him from the polished floor.

"That went better than I thought," he said as he straightened his tall, polished headdress. "Well done."

"He will have your head, Enki!" Ninmah's body tingled as her scales rippled. "If the vote goes against you—"

"It will not," Enki said. "The Nine will not see Nibiru waste away into nothingness for a matter of pride now that the Igigi have burned their tools. Our brothers and sisters are not as pious as Lord Enlil."

"You are putting a lot of faith in them making the right decision over something they have never faced before."

Enki tilted his head in a shrug. "Faith is all I have, Ninmah. If the others are so blind as to vote against us, our beloved homeworld will cease to support life and I will not care what happens to me if that comes to pass."

Ninmah pressed her full lips together as Enki put the situation into perspective. Yes, what did living matter if Nibiru ceased to be?

Ninmah laid her hands on the stasis tube that held all of their hopes within its thrumming frame, gazing down upon the creature lying so blissfully unaware of the storm brewing around him. Eron, she had named him. Her eyes travelled over the naked, muscular body, noting once again with fascination the differences from the primitive animal across the room. The skin was paler, taking on the golden tone of the Anunnaki blood infused into his genetics. Sparse hair curled along the smooth flesh, thickening only at the groin and the top of the head. The legs were longer, straighter, while the arm length was reduced. The hands were a balanced mix between the shape of her own and the base creature. Strong, dexterous and capable.

Ninmah's attention finally settled upon the face, studying the smooth, hybrid features. There was still too much of the KI creature present for her taste, the jaw and brow too prominent. With the eyes closed, the broad, protruding nose was the only notable difference. Ninmah tilted her head. This was only their first attempt. There was room for improvement yet.

If the Council voted the right way.

They must! Ninmah thought fiercely. *They will! We*

will make them see sense. Shedding her remaining doubts, Ninmah asked: "What shall we name our new slave race?"

In her periphery, Ninmah saw Enki smile. His answer came on a breath.

"Lullu Amelu, One That is Mixed. Human beings."

* * *

1

A Vision Realised

38,000 years BCE

The sound of birdsong pulled Juaan from his sleep. A soft breeze blew across his face, bringing with it the scent of the approaching morning. He kept his eyes closed, willing his mind to sink back into oblivion. The slumbering presence of the girl lying beside him, pressed against his latent senses. Hers was a presence that had always been a balm to his soul, a power it had still somehow possessed even when he had not remembered who she was.

Now, even that one beacon of light in all his wretched life had become a torture. A torment. Her presence a stark reminder of the evil he had become.

Juaan could not see the lifting of darkness behind the shelter of his eyelids, but the sound of Nyriaana's breathing altered. She was waking as she always did with the rise of Utu, of Ninmah, whichever name the burning ball of fire in the sky chose to go by.

Juaan hunched his shoulders, ignoring the pain the motion caused. The wounds Eldrax had dealt during his failed Challenge were healed thanks to the skills of the woman who had saved his life, but the pain of them continued to twist his scarred innards.

Nyri groaned. From the sound of shifting pebbles, Juaan surmised she had pushed herself into a sitting position. He could feel the burn of her eyes upon his back. There was no point in pretending. She would sense that he wasn't asleep, but Juaan could not bring himself to turn and look her in the face.

Her sigh of frustration echoed through the cave, but she did not attempt to call for his attention and Juaan was grateful for that small mercy.

More scraping sounded, then came the soft pad of her feet moving away from him. It took Juaan a moment to realise she was heading towards the cave's mouth and the naked world beyond. His heart skipped a beat.

"Where are you going?" he asked without turning, his voice rough from disuse. There was no need for her to venture out. They still had the rations Halima had given them upon their escape from camp. An underground stream breaching the surface at the rear of the cave provided them with all the water they needed.

"To find forage," she said, her voice a mere intonation.

"What forage?"

"I don't know, a root, a mouldy nut. Anything! I cannot bear one more bite of dried flesh."

"Nyriaana," Juaan reproved, and flinched as he heard a bite of his former self in his tone, of Khalvir.

"It's been days, Juaan. I need... clean air."

To get away from you. Juaan's mind supplied her true

2

meaning between the spoken words.

"I won't go far, and I will know if anyone approaches."

Juaan could almost picture her finger tapping her fore-head as she reassured him, and before he could raise another protest, the crunch of thawing snow signalled her exit from the cave.

Silence.

The torment of Juaan's thoughts grew louder, as if finding it necessary to fill the void. Juaan tightened his fist around the symbolic spearhead resting in his palm. Carved with the image of a wolf, it was one of the many trinkets he had kept in the now destroyed leaf-leather pouch gifted to him by his mother. *Keep it with you and remember. Remember the people who have loved you and sacrificed themselves for you.*

It was the promise his mother had exacted from him over this very object. Juaan screwed his eyes shut and squeezed his fingers around the carved spearhead until the edges cut into his skin. Fresh blood spilled forth to mingle with the crusted remains of his own dead father's. He had betrayed his mother. He had betrayed them all.

Rebaa's dying face, glowing with misplaced trust and boundless love, swam in the void behind his closed lids. Her sacrifice had been in vain. She had been wrong. *I'm sorry, mother,* Juaan thought to the vision. *You should have lived. You should have let me die...*

Tears welled and Juaan could no longer hold them back as he clutched the tattered remains of the leaf leather pouch to his chest with his free hand. It was a long time before he regained enough control to force the tears away and release his hold on the spearhead.

The silence inside the cave reigned, unrelenting.

3

Nyri. Juaan glanced up, realising with a kick to his gut that Utu was now above the horizon and Nyriaana had not returned. Fear for her thrilled through his limbs, driving back the sucking grip of despair and self-loathing. "Nyri?" he called as loud as he dared. She had said she was not going far. If she was right outside the cave, she would have heard his call.

Had she finally tired of looking upon the face of the man who had destroyed her life and left? Juaan would not blame her if she had. He was out of danger now, and she no longer needed to care for him. Her obligation was at an end.

Though the thought of separation pained Juaan above all else, he should let her go. And he would let her go, but first he needed to ensure she was safe. Much as he respected her skills with the creatures of KI, she still did not fully understand the dangers of this savage world beyond her forests. If another human should come upon her…

Juaan staggered to his feet, wincing as his mangled tissues tugged. "Nyri." His heart thudded harder when silence remained his only answer. Frustrated with the continued weakness that pulled at his steps, Juaan limped from the cave. "Nyriaana!"

The wind whipped at his hair as he emerged onto the open landscape. They had followed the river south, away from the Mountains of the Nine Gods, away from Hunting Bear and Eagle territory, putting as much distance between them and Eldrax's hunters as they could manage. Juaan's injuries had slowed them down, but Nyri had refused to leave him, no matter how much he had begged, or tried to push her away in the first grip of madness that had overcome him as his old identity closed over his soul.

4

The Mountains of the Nine Gods dominated the skyline far to the north, looming over the foothills and the Southern Plains. Winter's icy grip continued to clutch greedily at the vast lands that should by now be flushed with new life.

At least the lingering snow cover was a friend to Juaan now. Not that bare rock would have stopped him tracking her, but it eased his task. He needed to teach her the art of covering her trail.

Nyri's bold footprints led away from their refuge, moving in a direction leading back towards the foothills and the Mountains. Why would she go that way? Juaan shifted into a jog, ignoring his body's protest. They had evaded Eldrax's hunters for now, but that did not mean the dread Chief would have given up on them.

Juaan knew Eldrax. He would not break hunt until he had run down his quarry. Accepting defeat was not in his nature. Neither was forgiveness. Eldrax would pursue them to the ends of the earth. He would not be satisfied until he had Juaan's hide strung over his dwelling as a warning to all, while he made Nyri his own within.

"Nyriaana!" Juaan shouted, throwing caution to the wind as his fear for her consumed all else. If Eldrax had come upon them at last—

There! A lone figure was sitting huddled on an outcropping of rock facing away towards the distant Mountains. The sight of her slight frame swallowed by the vast emptiness of the Plains squeezed Juaan's heart afresh. She did not belong here. She belonged in the arms of the trees, kissed by the gentle dappled light filtering down through the protective canopy of home.

A home he had deprived her of.

Gritting his teeth, Juaan stepped up to her side. He was in her eye line now, but Nyri did not turn to him. She did not even appear to be aware of his presence. Her indigo eyes remained locked, unblinking, upon the distant snowy peaks in a way that was unsettling.

"Nyri?"

No response, but a frown of distress slashed her brows, creasing the purple tattoo marking her honey skin. Then her eyes rolled back and she let out a keening whimper of denial.

"Nyri?" Juaan grabbed her shoulder. "Nyriaana!"

She flinched, crying out in alarm as awareness flooded back to her face. "Juaan," she gasped, clutching at his arm.

"What happened?" He caught her by the other shoulder as he studied her face.

"I don't... I... Nothing." She straightened her back, smoothing her features into an impassive mask. But her skin had taken on a pale cast, betraying her.

"The Mountains?" Even Juaan could feel their ever-present tug against his senses, calling to the terrifying energy that existed within him. He shuddered. The further away they got from those heights and the powerful River Line that lay beneath, the better. Then the monster inside would remain trapped.

Nyri shrugged in his grip and didn't answer. The distance between them since they had escaped was growing wider with each passing day. Juaan was conscious of the warmth of her hand seeping through the furs on his arm, aching as he remembered the way she had held him when she had wrenched him back from the jaws of death, the feel of her lips on his when she had kissed him in a rush of relief. He longed to take her back into his arms, but he could not. He did not deserve her affection. As gently as he could, he let go and twisted his arm out of her grip.

A flash of hurt crossed her face, before her features settled back into an expression as frosty as the surrounding landscape. "So, you can move, then?" She eyed him as he stood next to her.

Juaan ignored the jab. "I didn't know where you had gone. I feared…" he trailed off.

"Well, as you can see, I'm safe. You needn't have worried." She folded her rejected hand against her body.

"We need to get back under cover." Juaan kept to the essentials. "It is not wise to be out in the open. We are on high ground here."

Nyri grunted but rose to her feet and set off in the cave's direction without another word. Juaan followed in her wake, disguising her clumsy tracks as he went. Now was not the time to begin his lessons. He caught up to Nyri inside the cave. She was sitting on the ground, chewing sourly on a piece of dried meat.

Juaan lowered himself against the far wall, leaning back against the rocks. "We cannot remain here much longer." They had already risked too much by staying in one place for as long as they had. The need to continue putting as much distance as possible between Eldrax and Nyriaana beat upon Juaan's skull. The only way he could protect her was to stay one step ahead.

"And where will we go?" she asked without looking up. "As you once pointed out to me; other clans will as likely kill you as take you in, and I will become nothing more than a contested prize for those savage enough to Claim me."

7

Juaan flinched at the accusation in her words and cast his eyes to the rocky ceiling. Indeed, where could they go? Where would she be safe? Such a state did not exist for her, but he did know of at least one place where she would not be fought over like a piece of meat.

"To the shin'ar forests. I will take you home, Nyri, where you belong."

There was a beat of silence before it was broken by a bitter laugh. "That is your answer?"

Juaan dropped his gaze to hers. Faced with his grave expression, she sobered, raising her eyebrows. "That was another life, Juaan. I am so changed from what I once was. You think I can just go back and be who I was before?"

"I-I don't know."

She rubbed her eyes and sighed. "Well, I can't. I… do not know who I am, or where I belong anymore."

It was too painful to look at her. Juaan tipped his head back again. "I am sorry," he whispered. "You have no idea how much I wish I could go back and undo the evil I have done you."

Juaan heard her teeth clench together. "And what about you?" she demanded. "Where do you fit into this plan of yours? *I* might have changed, but my People won't have, if they still exist at all. Do you think they'd let you live any longer than another Cro clan that Eldrax has wronged?"

Juaan shrugged. "Does it matter?"

"Yes, it mat—!" Her words cut off in a harsh sigh. "Never mind. We're not going back to the forests, Juaan. I cannot go home. Not yet."

"Then where can I take you?" Juaan's own frustration flared, driven by his helplessness. "We cannot run forever."

"I don't know!" Nyri threw her hands up. "I don't know." She rose to her feet. Juaan knew where she was going: into the shadows at the back of the cave, where the babble of the underground stream would hide the sound of her tears from him.

You did this, Juaan thought. *You caused her this pain.*

A sudden clatter drew Juaan's attention down from the rocky ceiling. In her haste, Nyri had brushed against an object leaning against the cave wall, overbalancing it and sending it to the ground. She paused for a moment, as though considering lifting it back into place, but then just as quickly ignored it, fleeing to her favoured spot without a word.

Juaan stared at the fallen spear. Another gift from his mother. A gift from his *tarhe,* whoever she had been. All Juaan knew of the mysterious figure who had fashioned this weapon was that she had been a Thal who had sheltered his mother in her greatest time of need, pledging her life to his when he had been born.

Another life wasted on him. Another life Eldrax had destroyed.

Juaan pushed himself upright and stepped over to the weapon. It had come to rest beside a puddle on the ground. Fingers hovering over the haft, Juaan studied the familiar carvings below the razor sharp tip.

The vision flashed out of nowhere. It was the same one that had come to him as a boy, in the very moment he had first looked upon this weapon: the ghost of a dark and grizzled warrior. He had not known all those countless seasons ago how his mother had not seen the green-eyed apparition standing beside her when she had offered him the spear. Juaan had seen him. He had seen the killer in the midst of their home. Those same hard eyes stared back at him now, reflected in the puddle of water.

Juaan shuddered, touching his face, feeling the solid flesh beneath his fingers, a ghost no longer.

The monster now walked in the light of day. A vision realised.

* * *

2

Fears

The baby was crying.

Kyaati awoke, sweeping her son up against her chest before her eyes were fully open. Out of habit, she looked to the furs beside her, where Galahir's sleeping form should be. But the space lay empty. Her mate had not yet returned from the hunt Eldrax had sent him on.

The hunt for Nyriaana.

Nyri. Ice slipped through Kyaati's gut as she clutched Elhaari closer. Galahir had promised her that Khalvir was more than skilled enough to evade the men Eldrax had sent after him, but her mate's forced confidence had done nothing to reassure her.

Recovering from the aftermath of Elhaari's traumatic birth, Kyaati had not witnessed Khalvir's efforts to save Nyriaana from the Chief's clutches, but from the horrific tales she had heard whispered around camp, Kyaati understood that Khalvir had been dealt a mortal blow. No matter Nyri's skill in healing, Khalvir would be all-but useless. It would be a Ninmah-sent miracle if he survived at all. Could she really rely on that Forbidden to keep her tribe-sister safe?

That Forbidden. Kyaati snorted to herself and turned her attention to her new son. Her heart glowed at the sight of him as she brushed her fingers over his downy cheek. So much had changed in her life so quickly. Not in her wildest dreams had Kyaati imagined that defying Ninmah would bring her so much joy.

Enough joy to keep any lingering fears she still harboured in committing the Forbidden at bay. Habitual fears, she told herself. The Cro had been willfully committing the Forbidden for generations, and yet they had become the strongest People on the Plains. That knowledge had been enough to give Kyaati the courage to turn her back on the lies at last; on the gods that had turned their backs on them.

If they had ever existed at all.

Elhaari fussed, already rooting for his breakfast. As he suckled, Kyaati lifted her face towards the outside world. She did not need to be able to see past the thick hide walls of her shelter in order to sense the pall of tension and fear brewing like a storm cloud on the other side.

When Galahir had first admitted to Kyaati what he had done to save Nyriaana from Eldrax's advances, admiration and fury had warred for dominance inside her. He had protected Nyri from a brutal fate; but in striking the Chief unconscious, he had placed their new family and the rest of the clan in mortal danger. Galahir had assured Kyaati that Eldrax had not seen his attacker, occupied as he had been with Nyri, but his words had offered Kyaati little comfort.

The Chief's rage upon waking and finding Nyriaana gone

had been terrible to behold. Just as Kyaati had feared, Eldrax swore to hunt out the traitor in his camp, threatening that all would suffer until he had the responsible man's heart dripping in his fist.

Kyaati had been prepared to flee. The knowledge that her mate was Khalvir's closest friend was no secret. Galahir would be the first Eldrax came for. And he would have, had it not been for one man.

Kyaati's lips twisted as she thought of Lorhir. She did not want to owe anything to that ruthless jackal, but she could not deny she had him to thank for Galahir's life, if nothing else.

At the crest of the Chief's rage at finding Nyriaana gone, Lorhir had appeared, dragging a body behind him. The face of the corpse had been battered and bloodied beyond recognition, but an Eagle totem had dangled boldly from the dead man's throat. Kyaati recalled how Lorhir had dumped the carcass at Eldrax's feet, claiming it to be that of an enemy infiltrator he had caught fleeing from the camp. Lorhir told of how he had given chase and killed Yatal's cowardly assassin for daring to assault his Chief in his moment of triumph.

If Lorhir had expected thanks, he did not receive it. Kyaati recalled Eldrax backhanding the warrior to the ground, cursing him for taking the kill that should have been his. But, though Lorhir had taken a bruising for his trouble, the intervention had done its work. Eldrax was swayed from suspicion of his own clan.

That, however, was the only positive Lorhir's deception had achieved. Eldrax's madness had not abated. Foaming like a rabid wolf, the Red Bear swore to eradicate the Eagle

Clan, raving before his horror-struck followers that he would kill every man, woman, and child before Yatal's eyes. No one would be spared.

Kyaati swallowed back the bile in her throat. Lorhir had saved her family, but how many more had he now condemned? Hunting Bear and Eagle alike in the fight that was to come.

The only reason Eldrax had not yet marched his forces into the foothills to exterminate Yatal's clan was because his obsession to repossess Nyri surpassed even his thirst for vengeance. Half the men had been sent to hunt Nyriaana and Juaan down.

Nyriaana... Kyaati closed her eyes and cast a prayer to whatever deity may exist that her tribe-sister was still safe. The thought of Eldrax catching up to her made Kyaati twitch with anxiety. Her imaginings ran wild until she could no longer remain within the shelter, alone with her fears.

Bundling Elhaari up, Kyaati shot to her feet. Ninmah was only just rising over the eastern foothills outside, but Kyaati was sure Halima would be awake and already rousing her charges.

The wind outside whipped through Kyaati's silver hair as she ducked out of her dwelling. The icy breath on her cheeks made her shiver, but it lacked the savage bite it had once had. The Fury was relinquishing its grip at last. Kyaati breathed deep, scenting the traces of the Blooming on the air. Despite her cares, she could not help but feel a brief, instinctive flash of hope.

"Should you really be exposing your son to the cold, Kyaati?"

Any sense of wellbeing Kyaati felt evaporated at the sound

of the unwelcome voice. Shoulders rigid, she turned to face Selima. *Traitorous snake!* Here before her stood the reason Kyaati may never see Nyriaana again.

The red-haired girl was regarding her with haughty disapproval. "You want to be careful. My father will not be... pleased if the only witch-child in the clan perishes because of your carelessness. Especially now he has been denied the chance of fathering his own."

Kyaati's lips peeled back off her teeth, resisting the very Cro-like urge to fly at Selima and gouge her eyes out. "I have no doubt he will be informed of every move I make with *my* son. Why don't you scurry along to him now, Selima? Get out of my sight."

A spasm of panic contracted over Selima's features as her dark eyes flickered in the direction of the Chief's dwelling. Even Eldrax's own daughter feared being within arm's reach of the Red Bear in his current madness. She recovered quickly, and a smile curled across the pale, broad face. "You want to speak more carefully, Kyaati. You are the only she-elf in my father's possession now Nyriaana has deserted the clan. You surprised him with your strength. The thought might not have crossed his mind yet, vexed as he is, but one whisper from me, and he may just decide to take you for himself instead."

Kyaati's breath caught. "No!" she hissed. "He cannot. It is against your customs. Galahir Claimed me before the whole clan."

"Well," Selima's smile grew wider as she succeeded in breaking Kyaati's composure. "Accidents can happen. My father is the Chief and no one would dare stand against him in the mood he is in. He will take what he wants to soothe

15

his disappointment, and the clan would be glad of it."

"You," Kyaati took a step forward.

"Selima!" Halima's voice cracked through the air. "Johaquin is searching for you. See to your duties, girl! I have need of Kyaati."

Selima graced the matriarch with a disdainful sneer. Kyaati wondered if she dared to speak against Halima, but after a moment, she clearly thought better of it and walked away with her head held high. Kyaati heard Halima growl low in her throat, a frown slashing her dark brow. "And I thought she was unbearable before she gained her father's favour."

Kyaati drew a quick, deep breath, tempering the panic that had flared to life at Selima's unexpected threat, and lifted her chin. The wretched girl was just trying to get under her skin. Kyaati had learned enough about the Cro to understand that even Eldrax was not above the tenets of tradition. If he started taking what rightfully belonged to another man, he would lose the trust and support of his clan entirely.

He wouldn't do it. He wouldn't dare. Would he? She pictured the fevered craze she had witnessed in the Chief's eyes and a shiver of doubt slithered through Kyaati's resolve. Selima was right, Galahir losing his mate might seem a small compromise to the clan if it calmed the Chief. She ground her teeth together. She hated feeling unsure about her own judgement.

"How are you and the babe?" Halima broke into Kyaati's musings as she led the way back towards the Dwelling of the Unclaimed; the large shelter where Halima presided over the young women yet to find a mate and the old crones whose men had long since perished. Other members of the clan scurried about their duties as they passed, keen to get back to their shelters should Eldrax decide to appear.

"We are well." Kyaati mustered a proud smile for her son. "Elhaari is as strong as an ox. Just like his father."

"Feeds like one too, I would imagine." Halima's lips twitched.

Kyaati gave a small shrug in return; she could not argue.

"Hmmm. You look pale. Let me find you something more to eat."

"No, Halima, you don't—"

"Silence," Halima cut her off and, without another word, disappeared into the shelter.

Kyaati was left to follow. Despite the drain on her energy that Elhaari presented, she knew it wasn't hunger sapping the colour from her cheeks. She needed more from Halima than food. As soon as the thick, protective hides of the Dwelling of the Unclaimed had fallen back into place behind her, Kyaati could no longer hold back. "Is there any word, Halima?"

The already tense muscles in the matriarch's back tightened as she paused by the central fire and the hapless animal spitted over the flames. Kyaati made herself hold firm in the face of its dead, empty eye sockets and the cooked lips peeling back over the blunt teeth.

"Two more of the hunting groups Eldrax sent out have returned," Halima said. "Both empty handed."

Kyaati let out a small, silent breath of relief.

"They are managing to stay one step ahead, Kyaati."

"Yes, but for how much longer, Halima?" Kyaati spilled her deepest fear. "Am I to spend every waking moment

17

living in fear that the next group will be the one to carry Nyriaana back into camp and straight into the clutches of the Chief? They can't stay one step ahead forever. They were doomed from the start." Kyaati cut herself off as she felt her throat close, despair threatening to overcome her. "They have nowhere to go."

"Hush," Halima admonished. "What the gods wish will be, but Khalvir is no fool. If anyone can keep Nyriaana from Eldrax, it is him."

Kyaati wanted to point out that it was Khalvir who had brought Nyriaana into Eldrax's clutches in the first place, but held her tongue with an effort as Halima carved her a piece of seared flesh from the animal on the spit and gifted it to her.

The taste of meat still did not appeal to Kyaati, but as her stomach rumbled, she thought little of the heavy flavour or the rough texture as she wolfed down the extra ration. Food in any form kept her baby strong, and that was all that mattered.

"Thank you." Kyaati made sure Halima heard the heartfelt gratitude in her words and read it in her expression, since the matriarch was unable to sense it in her soul. These were lean times. The Fury had gone on longer than any in living memory, and the herds were slow to return north from their winter grazing. But Eldrax had still refused to break camp to find a richer territory. He wanted to keep Yatal trapped in the foothills, even if it meant driving his own clan to near starvation to do so. Everyone had endured a shortage of rations. Even the Chief. Kyaati snorted, remembering the snatches of unrest she'd heard around the camp. Kyaati did not complain. She had known far worse.

18

For a brief moment, Kyaati's thoughts broke loose from her careful control and flickered to her tribe, her family, far away to the south. She was quick to bring her mind to order. She could not think of them. The blind fools had made their choice. Their fates were in the gods' hands.

"Where is Kikima?" Kyaati asked once she had swallowed the last bite of her meal, gazing around at the near empty shelter. Only a couple of elder women dozed in a far corner.

Halima's lips turned down. "With the Chief."

"Ah." Kyaati tasted bile again. Following Nyriaana's escape, the Chief had taken it upon himself to Claim a new mate to ease the disappointment of his loss. Kikima.

Kikima was strong, just like her mentor, and she faced her duty stolidly as Halima had taught her. But behind her stoic mask, Kyaati had not failed to taste the despair running beneath the surface. This was not the future Kikima had wanted for herself. The prestige of being a Chief's Claimed did not make up for Eldrax's notorious reputation with the women that he chose. And now he was more dangerous than ever. Kyaati feared for her friend. One displeasing move and—

The direction of her thoughts brought a question burning to Kyaati's lips; it had bothered her for days, and now she found she could no longer refrain from asking it. "Halima, what made you save Nyriaana? Eldrax has Claimed many girls and you teach them to accept; that fighting against the way of things will only bring them more pain. Why did you jeopardise everything to save her? A girl you barely knew."

Halima paused for a long moment, so long that Kyaati thought she would not answer, but then she said: "For Khalvir."

"Khalvir?" This was the last thing Kyaati had expected to hear, and the shock made her voice sharper than she intended. She had never thought of Halima and Khalvir as close. The encounters she had witnessed had been waspish at best.

Halima smiled, reading her expression. Kyaati had not realised her face had become so easy to decipher. She had lived among the Cro so long now, showing her emotions outwardly had become habit without her even realising it.

"Yes, I know, we stepped on each other's toes," Halima explained, "but I can never forget the sacrifices Khalvir has made for the safety of this clan. Perhaps even more than Rannac ever made. I watched him grow from a frightened but stubborn boy with no name, no story, into a brave and loyal man. The clan owes him more than they will ever know. When Eldrax," Halima broke off, taking a moment to compose herself, and Kyaati knew she was reliving the horrors of the fight in her mind. "I could not bear to let him die. Neither could Kikima. As we stood watching his life slip away, she revealed to me the miracle Nyriaana performed to save you, and I knew I had to act. Galahir did not hesitate, of course."

"Of course," Kyaati sighed.

"I am sorry for putting your family at risk, Kyaati. Forgive me. But I could not see another way."

Kyaati reached out and caught the older woman's dark hand. "There is nothing to forgive, Halima. If I had been faced with such a choice, I would have done the same."

Halima flexed her fingers, returning Kyaati's grip. "Thank you. But I'm afraid there is everything to forgive. In saving one man's life, what have I done, Kyaati? Innocents will suffer because of my actions."

"*You* were not the one who placed the blame on the Eagle Clan, Halima," Kyaati growled.

"And you cannot resent Lorhir, either, Kyaati. Digging up that Eagle raider's body and throwing it before Eldrax was the only thing he could do to stop the Chief tearing through this entire clan."

Kyaati ground her teeth together, still unable to bring herself to feel gratitude.

Halima's lips twitched. "Never an easy one to like."

Kyaati snorted, the memory of being dragged through the undergrowth by that man, unable to fight, unable to escape, flashed through her mind. Only Galahir's intervention had saved her that day. She shuddered as she felt her mate's absence all the more keenly. Although she knew she was as safe as she could be with Halima, and had come to know and trust most of the Cro within this clan, Kyaati still felt a sense of vulnerability without Galahir's solid presence at her side. He had been her first protector in this new life of hers.

"Can I hold him?" Halima asked, breaking into Kyaati's musings as she extended her arms towards Elhaari.

Kyaati knew the wave of anxiety she felt in allowing any space to open between her and her most precious bundle was irrational, but it still took her a few moments to relinquish her grip. Halima waited, wisely not pushing until Kyaati placed Elhaari into her waiting arms.

"Such a blessing for both you and Galahir," Halima murmured as she gazed down into Elhaari's round face, her hollow expression lifting. "A reward from the gods for your past losses."

"Yes," Kyaati whispered, blinking quickly. It was all in the past now, and she had learned not to look back. Before her was a living and breathing son. It was more than Kyaati could ever have hoped for. It was all that mattered.

"Eyes like the grassy Plain," Halima's smile was wondering as she brushed Elhaari's soft cheek. "I've never seen such eyes in anyone but Khalvir."

"No?" Kyaati experienced a beat of surprise. Her brow pinched together as she recalled every face she had seen since her journey began and realised Halima was right. Since leaving her own People, Kyaati had seen many eyes; those the colour of the clear blue sky, like Galahir; eyes like storm clouds; those that matched the leaves that tumbled in the Fall and eyes the colour of the dark earth like Halima's. But never the colour of grass or fresh leaves. Those had belonged to Khalvir alone. Until now. *Huh,* Kyaati turned this new realisation over in her mind.

"Do I get a hold?" a rich voice broke in.

Kyaati looked up to see Kikima enter the dwelling, her bright amber eyes blinking until they adjusted to the dimness within. The half-Deni woman ducked her head under a low beam as she approached. Tall for a female and strong, she possessed every trait Eldrax looked for in a mate. Kyaati did not envy her friend.

Then she recalled Selima's threat, and was reminded that physical strength was not the only gift the Chief coveted. Kyaati shuddered. *He wouldn't dare take me from Galahir,* she told herself again.

Halima handed Elhaari to Kikima as the younger woman folded herself down in their company.

"What's that?" Kyaati moved to brush at a blooming bruise

under Kikima's high cheekbone.

"It's nothing." Kikima evaded her touch.

"It doesn't look like nothing."

"Kyaati." There was a bite of warning in Halima's voice.

Kyaati bit her tongue, only managing to do so because she sensed the pain flickering through Kikima as she drew attention to the wound marring her golden-toned skin. Kyaati frowned, detecting another emotion simmering beneath the hurt and indignity. Fury.

"What is it, Kikima?" Halima asked before Kyaati could form the words. The matriarch did not need higher senses to understand that something was wrong with her protégé.

Kikima gave up on pretending to be engrossed in Elhaari and handed him back to Kyaati. "I cannot bear it," she whispered.

"Kikima," Halima said gently. "Just do as he pleases, as I have told you, and—"

"No! He is a monster, Halima!" Kikima's outburst cut her off. "He is possessed. With each passing day, and the return of each empty handed hunting group, he gets worse. He is plotting to attack the Eagle clan with all the men before the snows lift. He will not wait any longer. He wants his revenge on Yatal now." Kikima's eyes beseeched her mentor. "The men are not ready. They are weak from the long winter and ceaselessly patrolling the borders of the foothills for signs of Yatal trying to escape. He will leave us defenceless again. Perhaps permanently this time. This is more than a show of strength to protect our clan. This is evil. How can I face lying with a man who plots to kill women and children? How can I bear *his* children? What have we done, Halima? Not only have we condemned the Eagle Clan, but

23

our own as well."

Halima's stolid expression flickered; for a moment she appeared afraid.

Kyaati gripped Elhaari closer. "Surely the Eagle clan won't pose much of a threat? Not after starving in the foothills of the Mountains for the entire Fury."

Halima shook her head. "Never underestimate Yatal. She is a cunning and determined woman. She guided a broken handful of women and children from the brink of oblivion to being a force even Eldrax has to reckon with. Our own men have lost their best leaders in Rannac and Khalvir. I have witnessed the Chief maddened by hate once before, a long time ago. If he goes after Yatal now," Halima shook her head. "I cannot be sure of the outcome."

A cold sweat broke out over Kyaati's skin as she looked down into Elhaari's dozing face, remembering the terrible night when Tamuk, the Eagle's lead raknari warrior and Khalvir's old rival, had attacked the camp in force while Eldrax had led all the men away on a hunt for a wolf. Eldrax could leave Elhaari vulnerable, fatherless…

"What can we *do*, Halima?"

Halima's face was a mask of infinite sadness steeped in memories. She was opening her mouth to reply when Kyaati's senses quivered. The situation had not changed, but she felt her fears receding as she let out the breath she felt she had been holding for days. "Galahir!"

Without waiting for the others to react, she leaped to her feet, barely noticing Elhaari's cry of protest at being jostled from his sleep as she swept from the shelter. Kyaati was momentarily blinded by the brightness outside the tent, but her stride did not falter. She knew the direction to take.

As she wove between the shelters, Kyaati could hear the commotion ahead, voices raised as other clan members moved to greet her mate, clamouring for news. Had they found the witch? Would the Chief be appeased at last?

Despite the burning need to be reunited with Galahir, Kyaati's stride faltered, fearing the sight that might await her. She could not sense Nyriaana, and that meant either her tribe-sister was not present, or—

Kyaati rounded the last shelter before she lost courage. Hiding from what might be was pointless.

Galahir was the first figure she saw. Her mate was wading through the small crowd that had formed around him, but it may as well have been invisible for all the attention he paid to his fellow clan members. His blue eyes swept over their heads, searching until they found her. His troubled expression cleared.

"Galahir." Kyaati threw herself forwards as Galahir's powerful arms reached out to envelop her. She buried her face in his chest and, for just a moment, she did not let herself concentrate on anything but the familiarity of his scent and the warmth of his furs underneath her cheek.

"I have missed you both," he breathed in her ear, his voice rough. Kyaati did not answer, only gripped him tighter, and for a while it seemed Galahir felt as she did and simply wanted to exist in this moment of reunion and not face what awaited in the next. With a sinking heart, Kyaati realised she could feel the same sense of foreboding in her mate as she had picked up in Kikima.

Elhaari cooed between them as he recognised his father and Galahir disentangled himself from Kyaati just enough to gaze down at their son. The pale skin around his eyes crinkled as he tickled Elhaari's belly through his wrappings. The sight of the huge warrior doting over a tiny baby always melted Kyaati's heart, but this time, she could not muster her usual smile. Though Galahir was happy to see his son, his expression was leaden. Her mate was avoiding her gaze.

Kyaati glanced around and realised with a jolt that her mate was alone on his return.

"Galahir. Where are the rest of your hunting group?"

Halima and Kikima caught up as Galahir faced her at last. His broad face was lined with defeat, pale as snow under his flaxen hair.

"I-I'm sorry, Kyaati. I tried everything I could, but it wasn't enough. They sent me back to deliver word to the Chief. They knew it would be too hard for me." Galahir's voice broke upon the last.

Kyaati's lips were numb as she forced out the question. "What would be too hard for you, Galahir?"

His hands trembled as they grasped hers. "Khalvir and Nyri—I tried to conceal it, but Ekundir saw and once he did, I was powerless."

"What did Ekundir see, Galahir?"

"An undeniable trail. Traces of blood and a Hunting Bear flint. Signs that could only have been left by them. Ekundir is on the hunt, Kyaati. In two days, Khalvir and Nyri will be his."

* * *

26

3

Defeat

Ariyaana stared at her across the craggy ground, outlined against the dark, steaming pool behind her.

"Find me," she commanded.

"How?" Nyriaana asked. The wind whipped at her words, trying to tear them away. "Please, I do not know how!"

"You know the path. You hear the call of KI. Heed it, Nyriaana."

Nyri quailed as the memory of glowing blue eyes and double rows of gnashing teeth burned across her memory. The Watchers reaching for her in the dark. "I-I can't. It is impossible!"

"If you don't, all will be lost!"

"No. Please! There must be another way!"

"Nyriaana!" The vision tilted, shifting like water. Nyri's stomach lurched with the sensation of falling, tumbling into the abyss. The sound of Ariyaana's voice morphed into an inhuman snarl and a pair of terrible violet eyes flashed across Nyri's vision, blinding her to all else. "Nyriaana!"

"Nyriaana!"

Nyri awoke as the scream broke loose from her throat. She shook her head, trying to dispel the vision, but the flaming violet eyes continued to overlay her sight, like an after-effect from the rays of Ninmah; accusing and inescapable. This presence inside her head was new, and it terrified her more than any other.

Juaan's hand clasped her shoulder. He was shaking her. Nyri reached for him, needing something, anything to ground her in reality, but Juaan pulled his hand away before she could touch him.

The pain of his rejection was almost more than she could bear. Tears sprang to her eyes, and she dashed them away before he could see. When Juaan's memories had returned, the joy she felt had been overwhelming. For the briefest of moments, the world had righted itself. But it had not taken Nyriaana long to realise nothing had changed. Her friend had not returned to her. His memories were not enough to bridge the distance between them, and the chasm in their relationship remained as great as ever.

Juaan was always careful to keep his thoughts and feelings from her, but Nyri could guess the reason for his rejection. She had betrayed him. She had revealed her true powers to Eldrax despite his warnings, and because of that, Juaan had almost lost his life. It was all her fault they were out here alone in this barren wasteland, facing either death or capture.

A wave of defensive, petulant anger gripped Nyri's heart. How could he blame her for what she had done? Had he really expected her to sacrifice Kyaati's life just to avoid attracting Eldrax's attention? If he had expected that, he really did not know her at all.

Nyri scrubbed her face with her hands, too tired and careworn to hold on to her anger and frustration. She looked up into his guarded green eyes. He was ready to pull away further should she continue to reach for him.

What was left between them now? Here they were, both unable to forgive the other for past choices. Had they both done so much damage to the other that their friendship could never be repaired?

"Juaan, I…" Nyri reached out her hand, yearning to close the gap, to be near him, but as she expected, Juaan straightened up and stepped back, neatly answering her thoughts.

Very well. Nyri nodded to herself, accepting. They were simply two lost souls who had to survive together as long as possible. That was all.

"Nyri, what is happening to you?" he asked. "Tell me, please. These lapses are getting worse."

Nyri gritted her teeth together. "I told you, it's—"

"It's not nothing!" Juaan snapped, and she felt his frustration sear beyond his control to lash against her senses. "Stop telling me blind stories!"

Nyri turned her face away. How could she explain to him that every time she closed her eyes, she saw a girl she did not know, in a place she had never seen, calling out to her? Visions of a dead Kamaali beseeching her to keep her promise and save her People from extinction? That the future of mankind depended upon it. And now there was this new visitation. A being with glowing violet eyes, whose distant presence was enough to stun her psyche? And it *was* getting worse. That knowledge was the most terrifying of all.

29

It had been two days since they had ventured from the cave that had sheltered them while Juaan took the rest he needed to recover his strength, and the further they moved south away from the Mountains of the Nine Gods, the stronger the pull of the Great Spirit became, the more frequent and intense the visions that plagued her. KI tugged upon Nyri's every step, begging her to return, making every stride she took away from the Mountains a torment.

But she could not go back. She had obeyed the call before and, in doing so, had brought both herself and Kyaati face to face with the most terrifying creatures imaginable.

Most of the monsters still lurked in the black forests they had left behind, but one existed beside her even now, caged within the body of the man awaiting an answer. How could she go back and face such horrors again? Only death awaited her on that path. Nyri knew this as certainly as she knew her own name. If she ever returned, she would die.

Juaan was not backing down. His jaw was set in a way Nyri knew well. He would not let her move until he had an answer. She would have to tell him just enough to keep him from asking further questions. They did not have the luxury of time for a test of wills. "KI is calling to me. He wants me to return to the Mountains. It's... getting harder to ignore." Nyri rubbed at her temples and rolled her eyes back against the headache that was forming from the effort it took to resist. She had never fought against KI openly before and it was *painful*.

A frown slashed Juaan's brow. "Why?"

"I don't know," Nyri said through her teeth. She had revealed enough. What did he care, anyway? "Can we please just keep moving?"

It was clear the answer was not to Juaan's satisfaction. He wanted to press further, but the frown on his forehead shifted into a worried crease as he glanced over her shoulder, back in the direction they had come. He was imagining Eldrax's hunters getting nearer with every moment they wasted. His fear of his former Chief overcame his concern for what was happening in Nyri's mind. Without another word, he set off, choosing his path carefully as he ranged over the thawing earth, ever mindful not to touch the clinging areas of snow. He did not look back, his every line spoke of his displeasure.

Growling low in her throat, Nyri used the long spear she carried to push herself to her feet. The duty of bearing their only weapon had fallen to her now. Since they had left the cave, Juaan had refused to touch it, claiming he had used it to lean on for long enough.

There was more to his reluctance than he was admitting, but he was as reticent to talk to her about his fears as she was to him, and so they had just carried on, two beings forced together in a game of survival.

Girding herself for another gruelling trek until nightfall, Nyri followed in Juaan's wake, habitually mimicking his every move so as not to leave a trace for those who would seek to do them harm.

Nyri guessed they had now turned in a south-westerly direction. The surrounding landscape was rolling and rugged, marked here and there with sparse clumps of trees and outcroppings of rock. Such surroundings had become familiar to Nyri; the open ground no longer made her feel naked, and endless skies above no longer terrified her. Nevertheless, there was a part of her that still longed to be surrounded by a forest, to feel the protective trees at her shoulder, to sleep above ground and be at ease.

Nyriaana. The ache behind her eyes flared. *Nyriaana, stop!*

Leave me alone! She screamed silently in reply.

Go back.

Find me...

Nyriaana!

The violet eyes flared across her vision again and a pain akin to lightning cracked across her mind. Stunned, Nyri's foot caught on a rock. Unable to regain her balance, she crashed to her knees. Dropping the spear, she caught herself on her hands, dimly aware of something skittering across the ground away from her. The rough stones grazed her palms, tearing her skin, but she barely noticed as she gasped against the aftershocks of the attack on her mind.

Nyri braced herself for Juaan's reaction. But it never came. Forcing her watering eyes to focus, she saw to her relief that for once Juaan was not paying attention to her. Twenty paces ahead, he was examining the ground at his feet. Her relief fled when an expletive slipped past his lips. Something was wrong. Nyri forced herself back to her feet, stumbling towards him.

"What is it?" she breathed. She could see scuff marks and splintered remains of a bone. These signs meant little to her, but they obviously spoke a stark warning to Juaan.

"Thals," he hissed. "This kill is less than a day old. We need to get out of here right now."

"Let me guess. Yet another People who will kill you on sight because of your past deeds?" Nyri regretted the words as soon as they were out of her mouth, driven as they had been by fatigue and frustration. She felt as well as saw the pain contract over Juaan's face as he spoke.

"More than likely. Let me take that." Before she could protest, Juaan removed the sling containing their rations from Nyri's shoulders and draped it over his own. Leaving the spear with her, he set off at a ground-covering lope. "Come, Nyriaana. Quickly."

Nyri almost wept with the effort it took to keep up with him, but she forced her body to obey her will. She would not give him a reason to carry her. Not only would her pride not allow it, but she wasn't sure Juaan was capable. The wounds Eldrax had inflicted had taken their toll. He no longer moved with the smooth grace that he once had. He tried not to show it, but he was still hurting.

The landscape blurred by as Ninmah moved slowly across the sky. Nyri forced herself to think of nothing but the ground ahead, and soon the exhaustion was enough to numb her mind to everything except keeping one foot moving in front of the other. She was almost grateful, for it stifled the voices.

Ninmah was setting on the far horizon when Juaan at last came to a halt outside of a large copse of trees. His ragged breath steamed on the rapidly cooling air, and Nyri saw him wince as he held his hand to his midsection.

"In here," he rasped. "We will shelter in here for the night."

"The Thals?" Nyri choked, not recognising her own voice as she leaned heavily upon the spear. Her legs trembled, threatening to give out.

Juaan shook his head. "I saw no further signs after we passed that tall outcropping of rocks. With any luck, we have left their territory behind."

Nyri jerked her chin in acknowledgment, refraining from remarking on their "luck" thus far. She was too exhausted to even suggest continuing their flight. She could not imagine forcing her body to carry her for one more step.

Hobbling on blistered feet, Nyri moved past Juaan into the cover of the trees. She flinched at the sudden crackle of leaves underfoot. After so long moving in muffled silence over bare ground, the sharp noise was startling. It saddened her further that a sound that had once been a part of her daily life was now alarming to her ears. Another sign of the wholly different person she had become.

But the deeper Nyri moved into the trees, the more relaxed she began to feel. The solid trunks were a barrier between her and her enemies, protecting her in their embrace. Sore as she was, she did not stop until she reached the very centre of the large copse. She could hear Juaan's soft tread behind her as he let her choose their place of rest.

One trunk of a tree had been hollowed out and Nyri lowered herself down against it with a soft groan of relief, stretching her abused feet out in front of her. She winced as the grazes on her palms made their stinging presence known. Giving them a cursory examination, Nyri extended a slight effort to block the throbbing pain of the cuts.

The light grew dim above the spidery canopy of the trees, and Nyri listened to the wind singing softly through the branches as Juaan prowled around the perimeter, scanning for signs of a threat.

No matter what lay between them, even though she was running for her life in an unfamiliar place, the sight of him still made her feel grounded. Home. Nyri longed to offer him some small comfort in return.

"Rest, Juaan," she bade him. The lines on his face and the stoop of his shoulders screamed of his exhaustion. "There is nothing dangerous within range. Trust me."

A tired smile twitched over his face as he conceded to her superior senses and he collapsed into a seated position across from her. Nyri half expected a small remark; she could almost hear Khalvir speaking: *you are useful to have around sometimes, witch.* But he was not Khalvir anymore. Nyri no longer knew who this aloof being was before her.

Did *he* even know? Guilt jolted through her chest. She had been so wrapped up in her frustrations with his behaviour and her own hurt, Nyri had not stopped to consider what Juaan must be feeling. He had lived almost his entire life believing himself to be someone other, and now… everything he had known had turned into a lie.

Nyri could partly empathise with what such a revelation felt like and how lost Juaan must feel. She berated herself for her selfishness. She should be helping Juaan remember who he was, not lashing out at him.

The voices continued to whisper in her mind, demanding her attention, but Nyri bent all of her focus upon the man before her. Juaan was studying the leaves upon the ground. It was quite apparent that he wanted to avoid her gaze.

Drawing a deep breath and attempting to keep her voice light, Nyri broke the uncomfortable silence. "Did you know this was one of my first dreams as a child?"

The green eyes came up, and Nyri found herself thrown back to another time, standing upon the edge of a Pit, looking down on the newly returned Juaan as he stared back, questioning her sanity.

"This was your childhood wish? Us, running for our lives

from a bloodthirsty Chief with no hope, no shelter, and nowhere to go?"

Nyri flinched at the harshness of his words, but made herself hold strong. "Not exactly," she said. "More, the two of us, alone, away from judging eyes, exploring beyond the trees, seeing all the places and the People you told me about in your stories."

Nyri saw the shudder move through Juaan's frame, his brow pinching together as his features worked to hold their composure, but he could not hide the gleam of moisture that sprang to his eyes.

"Oh, Juaan." Nyri pushed herself to her burning feet and limped to his side, fully intending to soothe away his pain, to let him know he wasn't alone, that she was there. But her fingers had barely brushed the furs at his shoulder when Juaan thrust himself away from her.

"No!"

More flashbacks from the Pit exploded through Nyri's mind as she fell back from him, stunned by his anger and desperation. "Juaan! Please! I understand. I know what it's like to find out your whole life has been a lie. Let me help." Nyri reached for him again.

"You don't know," Juaan shook her off. "How could you, *you*, have any idea? Do not try to know me, Nyriaana. I don't even know myself. I should not even *be* here."

Invisible flint blades lanced through Nyri's heart. He did not even want to be with her. "Leave me, then!" Nyri lashed back, wounded. "Go, if that is what you want."

"It's not wh—" Juaan dropped his arms and faced her, smoothing his features. "That's not what I meant. I will stay and protect you, Nyri. I will do so until you are safe or until my death. Whichever comes first. I owe you that much. But I cannot be anything more to you. I cannot be the friend you remember. Please, for my sake, understand that and leave me be."

Nyri closed her fists as her cheeks flamed. She was shaking, both from the pain of the rejection and the cold. The sweat from the gruelling day was cooling on her body, chilling her skin. Against her control, her teeth chattered.

The hard expression on Juaan's face wavered for a single moment and the fingers of one hand twitched towards her. The motion was diverted quickly. Juaan raised his arm to remove the sling carrying their supplies from his shoulders. "I'll set a fire."

"But?" Nyri glanced towards the outer edge of the wood.

"The trees will provide enough cover to hide the light. The dark will hide the smoke."

The promise of warmth overcame Nyri's caution. "I'll… fetch some wood." She turned to flee from him, but then Juaan's voice flew out, low and urgent, catching her in her tracks.

"Nyri, where is the flint?" He was digging through the hide sling, his motions becoming more and more frantic as the rock continued to elude him.

"It was on top of the meat. I checked it at dawn."

Losing patience, Juaan upended the sling, spilling the contents on the ground. Nyri threw herself to her knees beside him, pawing through the strips of meat, but the flint Halima had provided them with was nowhere to be found.

The memory of stone skittering over rock sounded in Nyriaana's mind as the answer came to her. "I-it must have fallen out."

Juaan stiffened. "When?"

"When I fell, I—" Nyri threw her arms out to the sides helplessly. Juaan's eyes widened. His hands flashed to catch her by the wrists, revealing her bloodied palms. "You cut these on the ground?"

"Y-yes."

Another curse slipped from Juaan's lips as he released her and began throwing their rations back into the sling. "We have to move."

"B-but—"

"Now, Nyriaana!"

Nyri snatched up the spear from where she had left it as Juaan shouldered their supplies. His expression was grim. "Here." He handed her a strip of their dried meat supply. "We'll eat on the run."

"But, Juaan—"

"Your blood and the flint will give them all they need. They'll know now which direction we took."

"How will they know it was us?" Nyriaana asked. "Anyone could have dropped that flint. You said yourself. Thals are in the area."

Juaan shook his head. "Thals use a different technique for knapping their stone. Technique varies even from Cro clan to Cro clan. Those hunting for us will know where that flint came from. Our only hope now is to run and run hard."

Nyri swallowed, a sick feeling settling in the pit of her stomach. "I'm sorry, Juaan."

"It is too late for that now. Do everything that I do. I still know a few tricks that might throw them off."

Nyri followed him out into the darkening evening. The

shadows lengthened over the ground as Ninmah set in a blood-red haze behind the low, rolling hills. Nyri's palm was slick on the haft of the spear as she laboured along in Juaan's wake. Despite the fact that he was recovering from mortal injuries, his endurance still far surpassed hers when running over open ground. Juaan was mindful of her needs and allowed her to rest whenever her legs threatened to give out from beneath her, but he would not allow her to rest longer than it took her to recover her wind, to eat and to sip some water.

Occasionally, he would leave her to travel a short distance away in order to leave a false trail. Nyri could tell he didn't hold out much hope such diversions would fool his former clan brothers, but such was his desperation he would try anything.

They did not speak. Even if she'd had the breath to spare, Nyri could think of nothing to say as Ninsiku's night gave way once more to Ninmah. This was her fault. The visions had made her careless and now she had as good as handed them back to Eldrax. Her weary legs almost buckled as she imagined what would happen if the Red Bear's hunters caught them. She knew the fate that awaited her back at the Hunting Bear camp, but what horrors would Eldrax exact upon Juaan?

Merciless black eyes floated before her vision, the madness simmering beneath the surface, flaring forth at the slightest provocation. Just the rumour of the Hunting Bear chief's brutality was enough to keep most other clans at bay. It was perverse that this was the one reason his clan fell into line around him. Fear was power out on the Plains. As long as Eldrax remained in place, they were safe.

39

Nyri decided right in that moment that she was not willing to trade her freedom for such protection. She gripped the small skinning knife tucked into her furs. Should Eldrax's hunters catch up to them, she promised herself she would not hesitate. A quick death was preferable to a slow and painful demise. She just hoped she would have the courage if it came to it.

And she would have to find that courage soon. Nyri's heart screamed a denial as the presence of several beings flickered to life upon the very edges of her awareness. The flavour of the intruders was faint, like a distant scent wafting upon the breeze, but Nyri could still taste the distinct essence of Cro.

"Juaan." It was the only word she spoke. She didn't need to say more. He took one look at her face, and the last glimmer of hope died in his eyes.

"How many?"

"I-it's hard to tell. Five. Maybe six."

He jerked his chin once in acknowledgment.

Nyri brushed at the knife tucked into her furs again, gathering her resolve. "Let me go back," she said. "Let me go back to them. If they have me, perhaps that will satisfy them enough to stop hunting you."

An expression of horror froze upon Juaan's face as the words parted ways with Nyri's lips. Then he was snarling. "If you think I am going to let you sacrifice yourself to that monster for me after everything, Nyriaana—"

"Juaan, please!"

"No!" And then, just as if she was a child again, Nyri found herself off the ground, Juaan flying into the shadows with the beasts chasing on their tail.

It was a doomed last effort. No matter how hard Juaan ran, the hunters gained on them with every step. Any moment now, Nyri knew she would see their figures looming on the top of the last rise behind them, swift and tenacious as wolves on the scent.

They were beside a cluster of standing rocks when Juaan stumbled to his knees, his depleted strength giving out. He tried to rise again, but his legs refused to hold them.

"Juaan, stop." Nyri struggled free of his grip with frighteningly little effort. "Please. Let me go."

Shrill whistles broke the stillness behind them. The anticipation of a successful hunt almost at its end rang in their calls. Juaan's head bowed to the ground before he lifted his face and focused on the cluster of tall rocks. Nyri did not know where he found the strength as he lifted her again and set her down in the centre, hidden from sight. Dragging the sling of rations over his head, he thrust it at her.

"Juaan, what are you doing?"

"Stay here. Hide yourself."

"No! Juaan—"

"Nyri. There is no time." Juaan caught her wrists. His green eyes bored into hers as though he were trying to convey everything in that single moment. Everything.

"Juaan, I—"

"Nyriaana, I—"

Another shrill whistle, closer still.

Juaan's face settled into a mask of resolve that Nyri knew all too well.

"N-n—"

His hands were warm on her cheeks, silencing her protest,

as he kissed her fiercely on the brow. "Survive for me." And then he was gone, disappearing before Nyri could regain her wits. The bodiless voices in her head screamed out in a deafening cacophony of denial.

"Juaan!" It was her childhood nightmare all over again. Nyri closed her fists as the panicked breaths fought to be free of her throat. It was only then that she realised she was still holding the spear. Juaan had gone off to face their enemies completely defenceless.

He did not plan to come out of the confrontation alive.

"No," she swore, scrambling to her feet. "Not again. I will not lose you again!" If he was going to die, then she had no interest in facing this cruel wilderness alone.

Ignoring the frantic voices in her head and Juaan's last admonishment for her to hide herself and survive, Nyri leapt from concealment. She did not need to read the ground to know which direction Juaan had travelled in; she could feel his presence flickering like a signal fire up ahead.

Along with the auras of the six others, closing in.

Nyriaana drove herself as fast as she could, but she was no Cro. No matter how fast she ran, her targets were widening the gap between them. A howl of frustration tore from between her lips. But then, abruptly, they stopped.

There was only one reason for them to do that.

The hunters had run down their quarry.

"No, no," Nyri panted, tripping and stumbling over the ground in her need to reach them. Her legs were trembling with exhaustion when the last small rise separating her from Juaan rose before her.

"You have… led… hunt, Khalvir." A voice drifted in and

42

out of her hearing as the breeze tugged it this way and that, but Nyri recognised it in an instant. Ekundir. Gritting her teeth, Nyri stole up the hill, then lay on her belly as she looked down on the scene, a mere handful of strides distant, stifling her ragged breath against her arm.

Juaan was standing amid Eldrax's men. Besides Ekundir, Nyri recognised two other raknari warriors among the hunters. There was no chance that Juaan could best all of them unarmed. Even so, there was an undercurrent of unease in the way the men flexed their hands upon their weapons and in the cautious shift of their feet. It was like witnessing a pack of wolves testing a large *grishnaa* cat in their midst. They might outnumber him, but they still feared the damage he might inflict before they brought him down.

This was the man who, until only a few days ago, had been their leader. This was the man who, when last they saw him, had been a heartbeat from death; now here he stood, very much alive, defiance radiating from his every line. It unnerved them.

"The Chief sent us to reclaim what you stole from him," Ekundir jabbed his antler-tipped arshu at Juaan. "Where is Eldrax's witch, Khalvir?"

Nyri saw Juaan flinch at the name before he responded. "The Red Bear had no right to her!"

"He had every right! The Chief Claimed the witch in ritual combat. He bested you. By our customs, she belongs to him. Or have you already forgotten what makes us strong, *brother?*"

Juaan's fists clenched. "I forget nothing." Nyri felt the monstrous power that lay hidden at Juaan's centre flare, responding to his turmoil, but it remained trapped, caged within mortal flesh. They were far from the Mountains and the powerful River Line of KI that lay beneath. Juaan could not release it and vanquish his enemies as he had when facing the Watcher in the forest.

"Then return the witch to us and the Chief may yet grant you the mercy of a quick death."

"No," Juaan said. "I no longer recognise Eldrax as my Chief."

The six hunters let out a collective snarl of outrage, shifting their weapons to a ready position. Ekundir took a step closer to Juaan. "Think carefully about what you say now, deserter. Eldrax ordered me to bring you back alive, but he said nothing about bringing you back in one piece. All he desires is to look you in the eye when he kills you; properly this time. "

Juaan's lips gave a humourless twitch. "That doesn't give me much of a reason to want to return with breath in my body, now, does it, Ekundir?"

In a motion so fast that Nyri barely saw it, Juaan's arm flicked out. A handful of grit cascaded out to hit Ekundir in the face. The raknari warrior grunted in surprise, making a blind swipe with his weapon. Before he could recover his sight, Juaan had swept his legs out from under him. Ekundir landed heavily, the air whooshing from his lungs.

But that was as far as the surprise attack got him. These were hardened warriors, conditioned to fight for the survival of their clan. Nyri gated a cry between her teeth as an arshu struck out, whistling towards Juaan's legs in an attempt to cripple him. Juaan danced backwards, the deadly prongs missing his flesh by a mere breath of wind.

Same as it had been in the fight with Eldrax, Nyri could not tear her horrified gaze away from the scene playing out before her as the six armed men attempted to bring Juaan down. He dodged between their blows, twisting and ducking, evading their efforts. But not once did he try to fight back.

It was only a matter of time before Juaan made a fatal wrong step. Already, she could see the pain flash across his face whenever his speed wasn't enough and an antler tip would graze his skin. "Fight back," she pleaded. "Why don't you fight *back*?"

A blow went wide, the hunter behind the clumsy strike stumbled off balance. It would have been easy for Juaan to grab his weapon for his own, but he let the opportunity pass. It was then that Nyri realised Juaan did not want to fight back. He had truly come here to die. His resistance was merely a delay, giving Nyri enough time to put as much distance between her and the hunters as possible.

A delay that had already gone on for as long as it could. As a tiring Juaan twisted to avoid a scything strike to the shoulder, his eyes widened, his face draining of all colour as his hand flew to his side. The motion had been too much for his scarred innards. His attacker was quick to take advantage and backhanded Juaan to the ground with a meaty fist.

Juaan landed upon the rocks, spitting blood. Ekundir was on him in an instant, his arshu poised, ready to strike. Knowing he was defeated, Juaan lay back and gazed up into the other man's face.

Ekundir's eyes were streaming from the dust Juaan had thrown, his nose bloody from striking the ground. "Eldrax wants you alive," he hissed. "And I will obey his wish. But I'm sure as Ea going to have my fun first." With that, he lifted his arshu, fully preparing to bring the sharpened prongs down into Juaan's spear arm.

"No!" Nyri leapt out of concealment. In the space of two heartbeats, the tip of her spear was digging into Ekundir's back. "Stop, Ekundir! Leave him alone!"

"Nyri," Juaan moaned, dropping his head back in despair at the sight of her.

The other five Cro stood, frozen into stillness by her sudden appearance. Their eyes went to Ekundir, awaiting direction.

The raknari leader was the first to recover. Nyri felt his throaty chuckle vibrate through the spear in her hands. "And what are you going to do to make me, little witch?"

"I'll kill you," Nyri snarled through her teeth with as much force as she could muster.

"Go on, then," he challenged.

Nyri caught her breath. She had never killed before. She tightened her grip on the oversized haft.

The brief hesitation was all Ekundir had needed. Before Nyri could twitch, he twisted, yanking the weapon from her grip with enough force to pull her off her feet. Nyri landed hard on the ground as Ekundir threw the spear away. It came to earth with a clatter of finality among the distant rocks.

The Cro warrior's laugh grated against her ears. "Eldrax will favour me above all others for this." Pain lanced through Nyri's scalp as Ekundir twisted his fingers into her hair and dragged her from the ground. "I will return with both his she-elf and the deserter."

Juaan made a dive for Ekundir's legs, but the other man saw him coming and kicked him square in the side, directly above his healed wounds, sending him rolling back against the ground. Nyri heard the quiet cry of agony escape between his teeth.

"You see, elf-witch," Ekundir said. "This is where a weak man leads you."

Nyri spat in his face.

The Cro warrior wiped his fur-covered arm across his cheek, then, without so much as a flicker of emotion, backhanded Nyri across the face. The force of the blow exploded through her head. Her vision blurred as her eyes watered. "Consider yourself lucky, witch. It is only because you are the Claimed of a more powerful man than I, that I will not snap your scrawny neck for that. It is beyond time you learned the order of things!"

Ears ringing, Nyri struggled against his hold on her hair, but it was in vain. Two of the other Cro yanked Juaan from the ground, quickly twisting his arms behind his back before he could muster a rebellion.

"Move out!" The air vibrated with Ekundir's triumph as the five Cro fell into line behind their leader.

The time had come. There was no other escape. No other way. Nyri closed down. She did not let herself feel; she did not let herself think as she reached for the knife concealed within her furs. *I will not go back to him.* Her hand closed around the horn hilt.

A loud hooting shattered the quiet of the landscape, freezing Nyri's hand in place.

Ekundir tensed, his alarm washing across Nyri's senses as he floundered, head swivelling this way and that.

47

But only for a moment. The raknari leader recovered his wits and gave one terse order. His men obeyed without question, forming a defensive circle; backs to their brothers while their weapons bristled outwards. They thrust Nyri and Juaan to the centre.

Nyri shifted closer to Juaan. He pulled her into his side as the hooting grew louder, coming from all around them.

"Adamu above!" one of the Cro swore.

Shadowy figures loomed out of the landscape, entrapping Ekundir's force before coming to a halt, staring down the Cro band in their midst.

The hooting ceased.

"Thals," Ekundir snarled into the ensuing silence.

* * *

4

Whispers of Rebellion

Two days. It had been two days. Kyaati paced her shelter as she opened and closed her fists, palms slick with sweat. Her stomach growled. Since Galahir had brought the news of her tribe-sister's doom, she had barely eaten. Any day now, Ekundir would return triumphant with Nyriaana as his prisoner.

No. Kyaati spun on her heel, waves of helpless frustration rolling from her body.

Elhaari's cry from the corner of the shelter checked her stride.

"Shh, shh," Galahir soothed. He looked up from where he sat with Elhaari cradled in his arms. The baby dropped the carved mammoth he had been clutching to the floor and cried again. "Kyaati…"

Kyaati read the plea in her mate's tired eyes. Galahir looked vastly older than when they had first met. She felt the weariness she saw in his gaze fall over her own shoulders and she collapsed down beside him, letting her head fall against his shoulder.

"Nyriaana," she breathed into the stillness. The familiar name on her lips and the lifetime of memories it evoked finally broke Kyaati's tenuous control. She squeezed her eyes shut, but the tears escaped to roll down her cheeks.

Galahir shifted his hold on Elhaari and wrapped his free arm around Kyaati's shoulders. He did not speak, there was nothing he could say. He sat with her through her grief.

"Galahir." Lorhir's voice sounded on the other side of the hide walls. Kyaati stiffened and Galahir's fingers flexed upon her shoulder in silent support. The draping skins at the entrance of their dwelling parted, permitting a cool breeze that diluted the heavy scent of furs inside the shelter. Lorhir's head appeared in the gap.

His dark eyes took in the scene before him. His proud face was impassive, but Kyaati could discern a faint whiff of displeasure and a deeper concern lurking beneath the surface. "The Chief has summoned us to his dwelling," the raknari warrior said.

Galahir handed Elhaari to Kyaati and rose without question, but Kyaati snatched a hold of his furs, halting him before he could move further. "Why?"

Lorhir's features tightened at her demand. She could almost hear *none of a woman's business* sing out across the space between them. Kyaati's chin jerked up.

"Ekundir is bringing the other witch. All the other hunting groups have returned. The Red Bear will wait no more. He is ready to exact punishment upon Yatal for her trespasses. He believes it will... sweeten his triumph when he returns to his prize."

Kyaati blanched; not only would she have to witness Nyri's recapture, she would also have to watch as Eldrax led her mate away to fight merciless and desperate enemies on their own ground. It was too much. "No. He can't!" she blurted.

"The Chief will do as he sees fit, she-witch. Or are you going to be the one to stop him?"

Kyaati closed her mouth, simmering.

"Come, Galahir." The hides fell back into place as Lorhir left without another word.

"Galahir," Kyaati glared up at her mate. "Do not go. You are not a murderer. And if Eldrax fails... Do you want Elhaari to end up like Akito? Do not leave this clan undefended for the thirst of a madman!"

Agony lashed across Kyaati's senses as Galahir's pale face twisted. "I have no choice, Kyaati," he whispered. "If I stand against Eldrax openly... that would seal your fate more certainly than any battle."

"Galahir..."

He silenced her by placing his calloused fingers against her lips. "I may not be quick of wit, but I am not blind. I have seen the way the Red Bear looks at you now. If he had any excuse to be rid of me..." he trailed off.

Kyaati gasped, Selima's all-but-forgotten threat ringing loudly in her head. Her hand fell away from Galahir's arm, releasing him.

"I'm sorry," he whispered, dropping a kiss on her brow before disappearing from their home.

Kyaati sat in the silence he left behind, feeling the weight of it pressing down on her shoulders. Not since she had become Galahir's Claimed had she felt so powerless. She had found happiness at last and now she would have to stand by and watch as it was all torn away from her. All because of the whim of one man.

Just. One. Man.

Are you going to stop him? Lorhir's challenge echoed around her head, taunting her.

Kyaati balled her free hand into a fist. One man. She had faced worse odds. Her thoughts began to race. Everything rested upon Eldrax holding power. If he was gone, then the men would not be sent into the barren foothills, risking their lives against a wily foe to slaughter innocents. If Eldrax was gone, he could not threaten to take her from Galahir. If Eldrax was gone, Nyriaana would be safe.

The answer seemed so easy. Eldrax had to go. And she *would* be the one to stop him if she had to. To protect her family, Kyaati would risk anything.

But she would need help. She leaped to her feet, only one destination in mind. What she was about to do was extremely reckless, but Kyaati charged from her shelter and raced through the camp before doubt could weaken her resolve. Surely deposing Eldrax would be in everyone's best interest. Her ideas were only just forming, but there was no time for more thought. Eldrax was already laying his plans.

"Halima!" she called before she had even finished pushing through the draping entrance of the Dwelling of the UnClaimed. "Halima! We need to—"

"Shhh!" The older woman swept from where she had been sitting to meet Kyaati halfway across the floor. "What is it, child?"

"Is the babe sick?" a voice croaked from behind Halima. Panic shot through Kyaati. She had been so caught up in her ambition, she had not thought to check who else might have been present within the matriarch's domain. Halima had been sitting with the ancient Cro healer woman, Johaquin, and next to her crippled form, squatted Selima. "Speak up, girl!" Johaquin demanded. "Do I need to examine him?" a gnarled hand reached out.

"No!" Kyaati rolled her body, shielding her son from the old crone's beady, mismatched eyes.

"Then why the urgency, Kyaati?" Selima's face was intent, and Kyaati knew her moment of panic had not been lost on the red-haired girl. Suspicion curled across the air. "Is there something you wish to share with us?"

Kyaati bared her teeth, her temper and impatience making her careless. "I came to see the matriarch, not a lowly herb mixer."

A sharp movement in the corner of her eye caught Kyaati's attention. Kikima was sitting in a far corner of the shelter. The half-Deni girl shook her head once in warning. Kyaati ignored her, keeping her eyes fixed on Selima, having the satisfaction of seeing Eldrax's traitorous daughter stiffen.

"Enough!" Halima commanded before Selima could strike back. "Johaquin, you may choose from the young girls. Take as many as you need to teach in the art of healing."

Healing. Kyaati could not hold back a derisive snort. These Cro did not know the meaning of the word.

"Thank you, Halima." The old crone inclined her head and struggled back to her twisted feet. "Girl, help me home."

Selima's black eyes did not leave Kyaati's as she took her mentor's arm without a word and led her none too gently from the Dwelling of the Unclaimed.

"You need to be more careful with her," Halima admonished once Johaquin and her charge had departed.

Kyaati blew out a breath. "I know." She was a fool to let

her pride and temper get the better of her, but controlling such things had never been her strongest talent.

"What is your purpose here, Kyaati?" Halima raised an eyebrow.

Kyaati hesitated. She trusted Halima, but now that she faced the forbidding Cro matriarch, she found herself at a loss. How did one go about asking the Chief's prime mate for help in bringing down said Chief? She clutched onto Elhaari and forced herself to think of Galahir being sent off into the maze of the foothills to face the Eagle Clan in their home territory, to murder children. The memory of the last time he had faced the rival clan flooded her mind. He had almost lost his life then. Kyaati would not risk his life a second time. She could not lose another mate.

"Eldrax is readying the men to face Yatal's warriors as we speak."

Halima's composed expression did not shift. As Kyaati had guessed, the matriarch already knew of her mate's plans.

"We cannot allow it, Halima."

Halima sighed. "There is nothing we can do, child."

"Yes, there is!" Kyaati threw caution to the wind. "A Chief only holds power if his clan deems him fit to lead. I have heard the whispering as keenly as you, Halima. The clan is becoming discontent with Eldrax's leadership. His thirst for revenge has brought everyone to the brink of starvation. If we gave them a nudge, if we could persuade them to stand united…"

Halima was already shaking her head. "It is not enough, Kyaati. One hungry winter will not move the clan enough to overthrow Eldrax as leader. It would take—"

"So we kill him!" Kyaati's declaration echoed into the

stunned silence that followed. She had stunned herself, but now the words were out, she knew she meant them. If the clan was too cowardly to stand up to their leader, then the only answer was to eliminate him entirely.

"Kyaati!" Halima snapped. "Do not speak of such a thing."

"Why?" Kyaati challenged. "You all hate him. No one has any love for that monster."

Halima sighed. "It's not a matter of love. You have lived among us for so short a time, Kyaati. You cannot be expected to understand. Before Eldrax, our clan was weak, preyed upon by others, pushed to the brink. When the Red Bear became Chief and recovered from the madness of losing that first elf-witch, all of that changed. He matured, he made us strong by punishing those who dared try to hurt us. He learned as a child that to be weak is to suffer. And that learning has served our clan well. Times may be hard right now, but remove Eldrax and our family will perish."

"But he is going to kill us anyway!" Kyaati burst out. "He is no longer in his right mind."

"She's right, Halima," a soft voice broke in, and Kyaati sensed Kikima was now standing at her shoulder. "Eldrax is no longer a worthy Chief. I, for one, will not see the women and children of this clan thrown to the wolves by him again. Nor will I see other innocents slaughtered. Eldrax is breaching the laws of the Plains. He needs to die."

"Quiet!" Halima's dark face flushed. "You are playing with your lives!"

Kyaati stepped forward. "Halima. I may have only lived with you a short time, but it has already been long enough to witness the Chief's thirst for revenge almost destroy this clan once. We have to do something."

"None of the men will risk their lives in such an attempt. Battle offers a quick death. Eldrax will not."

"The men are not the only power here, Halima," Kyaati hissed. "Eldrax will watch for an attack from a man. But what of a woman? We should not have to live in fear of Eldrax any longer. It is time for it to end. I will protect Galahir. I will protect Nyri, even if you won't. And what of Khalvir? You did what you did to save him, Halima. Now Ekundir is about to bring him back. What do you think Eldrax will do to him this time?"

Halima's brow mashed together as she bit her bottom lip. Kyaati had never seen the indomitable matriarch appear so unsure, so fearful. Not even in the face of a horde of invading Eagle warriors. It brought home to Kyaati the enormity of the risk she was asking these women to take.

"Halima, please. I know you will not be able to live with yourself if we just stand by and do nothing."

"Halima?" All three women flinched as Akito appeared like a ghost at the matriarch's elbow. Kyaati swallowed at the sight of the young boy's ruined face as it turned upwards to meet the matriarch's gaze. A habitual motion, for Akito could no longer see Halima's face. An Eagle warrior's weapon had stolen his sight from him forever. Kyaati clutched Elhaari closer to her chest, her determination to see Eldrax gone intensifying.

"What are you doing here?" Halima demanded, though her voice lacked its usual bite.

"Forgive me," the boy ducked his head. "Please, I want to help."

"With what, boy?" Halimas's tone hardened.

"With stopping the Chief," Akito whispered, his smooth

cheeks flushing at his own daring. "I don't want to be in a fight again, Halima. Please don't let him make us fight."

It surprised Kyaati to see Halima's lips tremble.

"I can help," the boy continued into the silence with a sniff. "The Dugnamtar bids me to listen, and I have listened well. Nobody notices me, you see. I hear things. The clan does not want another battle. They would be glad to see Eldrax gone."

"All of them?"

Akito's mouth closed, and he scuffed his feet on the ground.

"And if we stood united, who would lead us?" Halima threw her hands up. "Rannac is dead. Khalvir is gone, running for his life. Even if we could unify the clan against Eldrax's leadership, even if we killed him, there is no one left who the entire clan would support to take his place. We would be splintered between competing males, vulnerable, easy prey for rivals, who would not hesitate to put the men to death and take the women as their own. Is that what you all want?"

Kyaati's mouth snapped shut. Fury rolled through her at the impossibility of the situation. "There has to be a way!" she cried.

"There is," Kikima said. "Kyaati said it herself. Khalvir is no longer on the run. Ekundir has found them. The clan would support a claim of leadership from Khalvir."

"Yes," Akito agreed, hope rekindling his spirit. "Yes, they would."

Kyaati's own heart leapt. "Then it needs to be done before Ekundir returns. Before Eldrax can order Khalvir's death."

"This is madness," Halima flared.

"I will do it," Kikima growled, fingering her skinning knife.

"How?" Halima rounded on her. "Eldrax is a warrior and a hunter. Skills that have honed his senses and reflexes far beyond yours."

"I will wait for him to sleep. You know as well as I do he sleeps like a hog after taking his pleasure."

"Are you forgetting his sentries, Kikima? He has not slept without his most trusted men keeping guard since Galahir knocked him senseless. You know that."

"I do," Kikima said. "But I am fast enough to cut his throat before they reach me. They won't suspect until it is too late."

"And what then? They'd kill you, Kikima! Please, stop this foolishness. I cannot bear it."

"What is one life when it can save many others?" Kikima whispered.

A tear spilled down Halima's cheek and Kyaati sat back. She had not thought through the consequences of her hasty plan. She had not thought to cause Halima pain. "Halima, I..."

"I can distract the sentries," Akito spoke. "If Kikima gives me a signal, I will get them out of the way."

"It will still be obvious who killed him," Halima barked an incredulous laugh. "Lorhir can't invent another convenient Eagle assassin."

"But it would give me a chance to flee," Kikima said. "The clan will be in chaos with Eldrax dead and Khalvir's return. I will find another clan. Strong females are coveted. It will not be hard."

"Your place is here," Halima said.

"It was," Kikima whispered to her mentor. "But I have to

58

do this. We have to be free of him. I need to be free of him. I cannot go on as his mate, Halima. I am sorry. I am not as strong as you."

Kyaati felt something break inside the matriarch as she cast her dark eyes to the hides above. "Alright," she whispered. "If this is want you truly want. But you will not be the one to murder the Chief."

"Halima!" Kikima protested.

"It has to be me," Halima brought her gaze down. "I will be the one to kill the Red Bear."

* * *

5

Bahari

"Thals," Ekundir snarled, facing the force that entrapped his own.

"Ekundir, be still," Juaan hissed next to Nyri's ear. "All of you, put your weapons down, now."

But Ekundir was not listening to his former leader. He laughed disdainfully. "If the brutes want a fight then I will give them one." Nyriaana could feel his drunken pride, his drive to prove himself, as he raised his spear in challenge.

"No! Ekundir!" Nyri watched as Juaan made a grab for the Cro leader. But it was too late. The Thals' reaction to Ekundir's show of hostility was swift and brutal.

"Get down!" Nyri only had a fleeting moment to register his words before Juaan pulled her to the ground, throwing himself on top of her as the unmistakable thud of spears striking flesh sounded over her head.

"Juaan!" Nyri could see nothing, only feel the charged, desperate energy rolling all around her.

"Be still! Be still!" he hissed.

With the weight of Juaan's body pinning her to the ground,

Nyri had no choice but to obey. Her whole being thrummed with the need to flee, her scalp prickling as the earth vibrated with proximity of pounding feet. Closing her eyes, she focused on the rhythm of Juaan's breath rushing past her ear, hoping to block out the sounds of slaughter, to not feel the lives being snuffed violently from existence and escape the knowledge that her own death could find her at any moment.

Ekundir's last howl of defiance twisted Nyri's gut before it cut off in a wet gurgle. Another heavy thud and then silence. The only sound that remained was the surge of blood in her own ears.

"Juaan?" she forced out between dry lips, her voice splintered with fear.

He did not answer. Long fingers flexed once upon her arms before he released her, his weight lifting away. Her muscles tensed, still anticipating the sting of a blade slicing through her skin at any moment. Soft grunts broke out all around. Nyri cracked her eyes open as she raised her cheek from the gravel.

Juaan's fur-wrap boots blocked most of her immediate vision, but she could see the similarly wrapped feet of another man approaching. A long knife dangled from a gloved hand next to the stranger's thigh. Fresh blood slid from its flint blade to splash on the ground. The stranger came to a halt three long strides from Juaan and a voice, rolling in an unfamiliar cadence, called out. "On your knees, Cro, or I will do to you what I did to him." The knife flicked.

Nyri followed the blade's direction and regretted it. A body lay close by, its throat opened to the air. Ekundir. Nyri quickly turned her face away as her stomach rolled and pushed herself up into a crouched position. A quick glance told her she and Juaan were the only survivors of the Thal attack. The bodies of Ekundir's hunting group lay in bloody heaps around her.

A strange emotion curled through Nyri's gut. They might have become enemies, but these were men she had lived with for an entire turn of the seasons, eaten with, hunted and celebrated alongside. Now, here they lay, cooling upon the ground, never to hunt or listen to stories beneath the light of Ninsiku again. Her throat closed, and she bowed her head, muttering a prayer to Ninmah before pushing her confused emotions aside. She and Juaan were now at the Thals' mercy. Nyri rose to her feet to face what awaited.

She felt more than heard the collective gasp of shock that went around the strange group. Everywhere she looked a Thal face stared back at her, their bulky, fur-wrapped frames poised as they kept their spears in a ready position.

"Dryad!" Juaan still blocked Nyri's full view of the one who spoke.

"Stay back," Juaan warned, but made no move. He kept his hands lowered and in full view of the other man. "We are no threat to you. Leave us in peace."

"You do not give orders to Eron's *magiri*, Cro. We decide who is threat. On knees. Now."

Juaan remained an immobile rock before her. Nyri reached out to tug at the fur of his waist. She did not like the way the Thals were now glaring at her companion.

"Wait." The tone of the speaker's rich voice shifted.

Nyri peered around Juaan to finally see the speaker for herself and rocked back in surprise. He was not Thal. He was a Cro man. Young and tall, his face was dark-skinned beneath a mane of braided black hair. His keen grey eyes raked over Juaan, taking in his paler complexion and finer features. "You not Cro. You *ikkibu*. How Cro say? *Forbidden.*" He spat on the ground. Nyri felt Juaan shift his weight accordingly as the strange man lifted his spear and took another step closer, eyes narrowing as he studied Juaan's face. The dark skin paled as he hissed. "You eyes! I know you from stories. You the Red Bear's *gistukul*. Traitor. False friend." The Cro's strong fingers twitched on the spear levelled at Juaan's throat. "Jade Killer."

"That is not who I am." Juaan's response was low. "Not anymore."

The spear did not waver as the Cro man turned his head to the waiting Thals and spoke in a torrent of guttural words, supplementing them with a series of complex hand gestures. The sounds created no pictures of understanding in Nyri's mind, but it was clear he was revealing Juaan's identity to his followers. Nyri quivered as a wave of murderous energy swept through the Thal ranks. A hulking Thal male standing closest to the Cro speaker grumbled and pointed an accusing finger at Juaan.

"Ngathe!" The Cro man made a cutting motion with the blade of his right hand. "Runuk gistukul."

"If they want to kill me, then that is their right," Juaan spoke over the exchange. "Just spare the girl. She is innocent."

The Thal let out a snarl of outrage at the sound of Juaan's voice and struck out with his spear. Its flint tip grazed across Juaan's upper arm, tearing through his furs. Blood sprayed in its wake.

"No!" Nyri cried at the same time the Cro leader bellowed.

"Ngathe!"

"Juaan!" Nyri reached for him as his hand went to his wounded arm, wincing.

"Runuk! Not move, Dryad."

Nyri faced the new Cro with a hiss.

"Nyriaana," Juaan murmured. "Don't. They don't have a reason to hurt you, and so they won't. Let them do what they will with me. I deserve it."

Nyri's inarticulate hiss turned into a snarl as she turned her fury upon her companion.

"He right, Dryad. Remain peaceful, and you will not be harmed." His voice right above her head. The strange Cro had closed the distance between them. Nyri's hand twitched towards her concealed skinning knife as she glared up into his face. The movement was not lost on the Cro and his full lips twitched. "I would not," he said.

All amusement then drained away as he lifted his gaze to Juaan. "I Bahari, *magiri* of the great Sag Du of these lands. I take you to him now. He should have pleasure deciding the punishment for your acts of savagery against the Children of Eron."

The Cro named Bahari signalled to his Thal followers. Nyri tried to plant herself between them and Juaan, but Bahari's broad hand flashed out and caught her by the arm. His grip was not cruel, but Nyri could not fight against his strength as he drew her away.

There was nothing gentle in the Thal's handling as they kicked Juaan in the back of the legs, sending him to his knees. One Thal unwound loops of twisted rope he had carried over his brawny shoulders.

"Those bindings for bringing home prey," Bahari said,

"But they do for you."

Juaan grimaced as the Thals wrenched his arms behind his back and binding his wrists so tightly the ropes cut into his skin.

Nyri struggled against Bahari's grip. "Leave him alone! He won't hurt you."

"I take no chances with the Jade Killer," Bahari said. "Others have done so and they speak no more." He made a gesture with his hand against his mouth.

"I promise, he won't fight you." Hot tears of helpless rage pricked in Nyriaana's eyes. "Please, just let us go. We will leave your range. You won't ever see us again. We need to get far from here."

Bahari gazed down at her, a frown creasing his dark brow. "I sorry, Dryad, I cannot. He spilled too much of my kin's blood. Responsible for much sorrow. Eron demands penance. He must answer to the Sag Du."

"Bahari," Juaan beseeched. "Heed me. Destroy these bodies." His words broke off in a grunt as one Thal kicked him down onto his side. Unable to catch himself, he landed heavily, splitting his lip on a rock. He coughed once at the force of the impact, then sought Bahari's gaze once more. "If Eldrax finds them, he will know your tribe is responsible. He wants her desperately." He flicked his chin towards Nyriaana. "If he has even the slightest suspicion she is in your possession, he will hunt you to the ends of the earth. There will be no rock you can cower behind." His words cut off again. One of the Thals jammed a wad of hide into his mouth, silencing him, before another strip of hide was bound around his eyes.

"*Magiri* do not cower," Bahari said, but Nyri did not miss

the quiver of uncertainty trickle through the Cro at her back. Glancing up to see his face, Nyri saw him stare grudgingly at the Cro corpses. A few more unintelligible orders were given and two Thal hunters broke away from the group, drawing out long hunting knives and stone axes as they approached the bodies of the fallen Cro. Guessing what was about to happen, Nyri turned her face away.

"We scatter the remains," Bahari said over the thuds of the axes and wet slicing of flesh. "These plains crawl with spitters at night. Hungry time. They be glad of the gift." He turned to Nyri again, his stern expression relaxing. "You innocent of crime, Dryad. You walk away free, if wish."

"I go where he goes." Nyri said, as she jabbed a finger at Juaan's bound and blindfolded form.

The Cro frowned again, but Nyri sensed it was more a gesture of puzzlement than annoyance. Nyri did not know what she would do if he refused her, but he tipped his head in acknowledgment and did not protest. "Tsk, tsk!" The sharp clicking hiss was clearly a command. The Thal butchers cleaned and re-sheathed their weapons, dividing the dismembered remains of the Cro between them before falling into line behind their Cro leader. The burliest Thal gripped the end of the rope binding Juaan's wrists and yanked him up onto his feet, forcing him to walk blindly ahead of him at spear point: just another piece of meat to be delivered to their chief for judgement.

Nyri could not bear it, she would not let it happen. A long pole of wood poking out from among the rocks caught her eye. Without a second thought, she seized Juaan's fallen spear and turned it upon the Thal holding the ropes. She would not hesitate this time. She would not allow them to take Juaan from her.

The blow came out of nowhere, colliding with her head and knocking Nyri to the ground. The strike had been open-handed, but such was the strength of the Thal it may as well have been a closed fist. Lights sparked behind Nyri's eyes, the breath leaving her body as the spear flew from her grip and clattered to the ground for a second time. As the world spun, Nyri saw a furred foot come to rest on the haft, preventing it from rolling further.

"That not wise, Dryad." Bahari plucked the spear from the ground, holding it up before him in cursory study. His grey eyes widened. "By face of Eron," he breathed, before casting a black glare at Juaan. "Where you get this?" But Juaan could not see to answer his question, nor speak with the wad of hide jammed in his mouth. Letting out a hiss of frustration, Bahari shouldered the weapon and turned back to Nyri.

She protested, struggling as the Cro caught her by her furs, but her flailing hands were as ineffectual as gnats against an ox and Bahari hefted her over his shoulder. Hearing the sounds of her distress, Juaan pulled on his bonds, fighting against the Thal's hold. An angry hooting went up and the rest of the Thals converged upon him, unslinging more ropes from around their thick shoulders.

Nyri fell silent at once. Her resistance was only going to make things worse. "Juaan!" she called out as his face turned this way and that. "Stop. I'm unharmed" the lie tripped from her tongue even as her ears continued to ring from the blow the Thal had dealt her. "Please don't fight."

Bahari grunted. "If you wish to travel with us, Dryad, you stay with me now. If what Jade Killer says true, it best you not leave tracks. And I not allow you to attack my brothers."

Nyri remained silent as Bahari set off again. She promised herself that this was a temporary surrender. Better to survive the moment and live to fight another day. She had learned that much.

Nyri glanced around. There were nine Thals in Bahari's force, and they had demonstrated a fearsome fighting prowess in their slaughter of the Cro. Bahari had killed Ekundir himself. If they got free, their only hope lay in running for their lives. Nyri doubted a Thal could keep up with Juaan over distance. Only Bahari might prove a threat there. Would he risk leaving his advantage of numbers behind to face Juaan alone if it came to pursuit?

Nyri doubted it. The strange Cro appeared to be well aware of Juaan's skill as a warrior. He had not permitted Juaan to keep the use of his arms, despite being blindfolded and overwhelmed by superior numbers. That told Nyri just how much Bahari feared him.

"Where are you taking us?" she asked. The shadows were growing longer over the ground as Ninmah slid towards the western horizon. *How much time do I have to figure a way out of this?*

Bahari paused, and Nyri sensed he was weighing up the risks of revealing anything to her. In the end, it appeared he considered their travel plans of no consequence now that Juaan had been neutralised.

"The *etuti sagkal* lies within the broken lands." Bahari's shoulder shifted beneath her, and Nyri strained to turn her head. Bahari was pointing at the beginnings of the rocky foothills on the northern horizon, rising out of the rolling plains like jagged, grey teeth. "We reach there before *Gisnu* brings light twice more."

Nyri assumed he meant another day's travel. "Will you travel through the night?"

Bahari gave a soft laugh. "Ngathe, Dryad. What do Cro teach you? Spitters stalk these lands in the dark-time. We rest with rocks against our backs."

Nyri retreated into her thoughts. So, there was at least another day's travel before reaching Bahari's *Sag Du* and the Thals would rest for the night . Good. Darkness would provide cover when she made her attempt to free Juaan. In the night, it would be so much easier to evade Bahari and his Thals as they ran.

"Why you risk life for Jade Killer?" Bahari asked, breaking into her thoughts. "In our stories, Dryad hate Cro. Hate everyone."

"I am not telling my story to you," Nyri snapped. She was bone weary from lack of sleep, days of hard travel, and the shock she had just suffered at the swift turn in their fate. Her head felt clouded as the adrenaline slowly seeped from her limbs. She did not need Bahari's added distraction. She needed to think.

Nyri detected a curl of hurt at her harsh words, but they achieved the effect she wanted and the Cro man fell silent, striding on into the deepening shadows. He appeared to have a specific destination in mind, and just as the last rays of Ninmah's light were dipping below the horizon, the Thal band reached an outcropping of rocks atop a large swell in the Plains.

Bahari crested the rise first, and Nyri saw that the chosen site gave an unparalleled view of the surrounding landscape. No threat could move on the Plain below without the Thals being aware of it.

Bahari placed Nyri on the ground as the Thal leading Juaan hauled him up to the nearest standing rock, forced him to sit with his back against it, and then bound him tightly, winding the excess rope around and around both Juaan's torso and the immovable. Nyri bared her teeth. "He can't go anywhere," she snarled at the Thal. "Why do you need to do that?"

The Thal blinked at her, understanding her tone if not her words, before huffing in dismissal. The rest of his brethren, moving with the ease of those familiar with their surroundings, were already preparing for the night. Many stole glances at Nyri as they passed by. Others who had finished their preparations squatted on the ground and outright gaped.

"What are they staring at?" Nyri demanded, shifting under the scrutiny.

Bahari chuckled. "Forgive them. Not see Dryad before. Many believe you People just a tale for children. No believe true." His smile faded. "Do not move from here." He hooked two fingers in a gesture that resembled fangs. "Spitters stalk. Not safe alone. Stay within protection." His arm swept out to encompass the camp.

Nyri did not favour him with a response and she heard a soft sigh as the Cro man moved away. As soon as he did, she rushed to Juaan's side.

"Ngathe!" A powerful hand caught her shoulder.

"Get off me!" The energy of the Great Spirit rushed through Nyri in a defensive wave and the Thal fell back with a yelp, stung. Confusion pinched across the coarse face as the Thal studied his hand, searching for the thorns that must surely litter his skin. When his search came up empty, he eyed Nyri warily.

"Stay away from Jade Killer." Bahari's presence radiated behind her as he spoke.

Nyri bowed her head. She could not fight all of them if they tried to stop her. For all her anger at the Cro man, Nyri sensed Bahari was not a cruel being. She met his clear grey eyes. "At least let me take the hide from his mouth. He is at your mercy. Please, he needs water." Juaan's bloodied lips were cracked and parched, the hide drying his tongue even further.

Bahari hesitated.

"Are the Thals so cowardly they will not grant a tied man a small mercy?" Nyri challenged.

Bahari shook his head, a knowing smile playing on his full lips. "You not among Cro now, Dryad—"

"Nyriaana! My name is Nyriaana. And I know that." Nyri was floundering. She did not know what motivated a Thal.

"Nyriaana." Bahari tested the name on his tongue. "You cannot insult us as Cro… but we are also not the monsters *his* kind are, even to killers like him." With that, the Cro man drew forth a full skin from the folds of his thick fur coverings, dipping his head. "He may drink."

"Thank you," Nyri emulated his head bow. She did not know if that was the customary response, but it couldn't hurt.

She felt Bahari's watchful eyes on her back as she closed the remaining gap between herself and Juaan, but the Thal leader did not interfere. "It's me," she soothed as she reached for Juaan's face, wiping the blood from his chin before struggling with the knotted hide binding the gag into his mouth.

Juaan gasped as it came loose, drawing gulps of fresh air over his tongue.

Before anyone could stop her, Nyri also yanked the blindfold free from his head. Juaan flinched against the evening light before his green eyes focused on her. "Nyri."

"Shhh, I'm here." Her voice cracked as she reached out to stroke the marks the bindings had left on his face. It eased her heart when he did not pull away from her touch, but leaned into her hand as they each drew comfort from the other. Juaan's gaze roved softly over her features until his eyes fell upon her cheek, and a frown marred his brow. Nyri grew conscious of the bruise that must now be blooming across her skin opposite the one Enkundir had already given her. She raised a hand to it, wincing. Juaan's regard shifted to glare over her shoulder, and Nyri guessed it was directed at Bahari.

She did not wish to give the Thal leader an excuse to rescind his small concession or increase the watch, and so she blurted. "Juaan. It was my own fault. I tried to put a spear in one of them."

Juaan's attention diverted back to her, his brows raising in alarm.

"It seems I've been spending too much time around the Cro," she said as lightly as she could.

But the words did not draw a smile. To her dismay, Nyri felt the walls between them slam back into place. "So it would seem." Juaan closed his eyes and tipped his head back against the rock behind him, his disapproval saturating the air around them.

"Did you expect me to sit by and let them take you without

a fight?" she demanded, irked.

"Yes." He half opened his eyes to regard her. "As long as you remain unarmed, the Thals will not harm you. For my sake, Nyriaana, do not be foolish."

"I won't let them hurt you," Nyri swore stubbornly, grabbing one of his bound hands where it rested behind his back. His fingers were as cold as stone. She turned on Bahari. "These bonds are too tight! Let me loosen them."

"I'm afraid I cannot do that."

"He could lose his hands!"

"That may be his fate, anyway."

"*What?*"

"Nyri." Juaan's voice called her around. "Don't."

"But—"

He shook his head, stilling her. "I have known worse discomfort," He offered a wan smile. Now he was the one trying to soothe her as her heart raced. Nyri swallowed, before realising the fingers she had twisted around Juaan's were now soaked with a warm liquid. She let go of his hand and lifted hers before her, flinching when she beheld the dripping red.

"Your wound." Regaining her senses, she yanked aside the slashed furs on his upper arm. She had forgotten about the injury the Thal spear had dealt in all that had happened since. Blood was sliding down Juaan's skin and pooling upon the ground behind him. Her eyes travelled over his body, seeing for the first time the scattering of wounds beneath his torn furs left by Ekundir's attack.

"To Ninsiku with all the savages under Ninmah." Taking a deep breath, Nyri pinched together the sliced tissues of Juaan's arm and concentrated, drawing the strength of KI to her. Despite her fear and anger, Nyri drank in the sensation of the Great Spirit flowing willingly through her every fibre, letting it steady her. How she had missed this calming assurance, this part of her being.

The slash to Juaan's arm was clean. It required only a small amount of concentration to fully seal the wound. As Nyri released the Great Spirit, she wiped the blood from the now-perfect skin beneath.

"Thank you," Juaan murmured. "It seems like you're always putting me back together."

"An old habit." The corners of Nyri's mouth twitched.

"*Bekar*, Eron!" Bahari's exclamation jolted them from the moment. Nyri had forgotten the Cro man was watching. He loomed over her shoulder, staring down at Juaan's arm. Appearing to forget himself, the leader of the Thals reached out with a trembling finger to touch the place where the spear wound had been only moments before.

Juaan glared, trying to lean away, but his bonds did not permit escape. Nyri knocked Bahari's hand aside on his behalf. "Leave him alone."

A tense muttering broke out around them. Many of the Thals had also witnessed the healing and were now converging on Nyri's position. A cold sweat broke out on her body and she reached for her concealed skinning knife. Did they now see her as a threat? Were such skills a heresy in Thal tradition? She should have been more careful.

But before she could draw the knife in panic, Bahari raised his hands in a non-threatening gesture and stepped back, calming Nyri enough for her to listen to what her senses were telling her. There was no sharp tang of fear or anger in the air, only the thrum of disbelief and reverent wonder.

"A miracle," Bahari said, his face alight. "A miracle has been sent to the Children of Eron."

* * *

6

The Watchers

200,000 years BCE

Ninmah watched from the viewing station of her healing bay.
Far below, under this world's blistering sun, Enki's creations
toiled. The latest form of their Lullu Amelu experiments, the
Adamu, *was proving superior to its predecessors. Ingenious, for*
a mortal level of understanding, eager to learn and to please.
Effortlessly, the members of the new Adamu race mastered any
tool put into their hands. Enki's gamble had paid off. He had
been right to reveal to Enlil their creation of a new life form on
this invaluable little island in the stars. The treacherous Igigi
were no longer needed to mine these gold-rich lands.

Nibiru would be saved thanks to these new slaves.

Slaves. *Ninmah's full mouth turned down at the corners. She*
had carried many of these new hybrid creatures herself, nurtured
and taught them as she would a child. Essentially, they were
her children. She and Enki had created them all; they carried
the DNA of the Anunnaki themselves. They were half divine.
Slaves? Ninmah snorted. They could be so much more.

The burn of resentment that existed in Ninmah's chest flared at the thought of Enlil and his cold decrees.

The soft whir of a door sounded over the faint tinkling of instruments, interrupting Ninmah's thoughts. She shifted her weight, rustling the silver cloth draped over her lean body. Enki had entered her healing bay. The bright lights overhead gleamed upon the same silver garments clinging to his tall frame. The metal-wrought adornment covering his long, elegant head almost brushed the ceiling, scattering prisms of colour, but the weight of concern marred the regality of his face.

Ninmah guessed she was about to discover the reason he had summoned her here from the deep forests of the East where her own personal projects were developing. But Enki did not speak. He fixed his blue eyes upon the viewing station beyond Ninmah, looking down upon the activity below. He flexed his long-fingered hands.

"What troubles you?" Ninmah ventured after long minutes of this world's time had passed.

They work gladly, do they not? *Enki's sibilant voice echoed softly in her mind. Ninmah could not miss the tenderness in her spouse's eyes as he gazed down upon the Adamu. It was no longer the gaze of a clinical scientist. He, too, had grown to care for these wide-eyed children reared to serve them.* They take our learning and our resources and thirst for more knowledge. Their boundless curiosity never ceases to amaze me. What more I could teach them if only it was permitted. Such a waste of potential.

Do not let Enlil hear you speak so, *Ninmah thought back.* They are slaves. Nothing more. Tell me, what business had you bring me here?

Enki's face lifted into a smile, though the expression did not entirely dispel the gloom that hung about him. Eager to get back to your own little curiosities, eh?

Ninmah blew the sterile air out through her nostrils. She knew what Enki thought of her Ninsar form; a batch of creations spliced with a different strain of Anunnaki blood. Their smaller size, however, had disappointed Enki, and he had decreed them unfit for the work they had been created for. Too weak.

But Ninmah had sensed something in them and spared them from destruction. Relocating them to the forested East, she had worked to develop their unique abilities. Like so many of the previous experiments before she and Enki had perfected the Adamu form, the Ninkuraa were not creative thinkers. Just like the primitive creatures that provided the basis of their DNA, they were set in their ways. But their telepathic and empathic abilities were close to her own. What intrigued Ninmah the most was how the DNA of the primitive KI creature had influenced and morphed these powers; somehow connecting the abilities of the Ninkuraa to this world and the flow of its energy in a symbiotic union.

These creatures might not have the physical might of the Eron or the Adamu forms, but they were powerful in their own right. One day, she would surprise Enki with what she had discovered. But not now. Something had happened, and she was getting impatient to find out what.

"You did not answer my question."

Enki glowered down at the mining structures below. "Enlil," he spoke aloud for the first time. He lifted his eyes to hers, his face apologetic.

Ninmah curled her fingers. Whatever Enlil had demanded, Enki knew she would not like it. "What does he want?"

"The work is not progressing as fast as he would like. Nibiru

needs more of the element if it is to continue to support life."

Ninmah hissed. "We can ask no more of the slaves. They are working as hard as their bodies will allow. Does Enlil seek another rebellion?"

"No." Enki shook his head. "He wants more slaves."

Ninmah's hands flew to her abdomen as though to protect the cradle of life that lay within. "No!" she declared. "I vowed to carry no more. So did Damkina! No, Enki. I refuse."

Enki raised his hands. "I know. I heard your vow and I respect your decision. Since Enlil came to me, I have laboured on finding an alternative solution. If you do not wish to create more slaves yourself, then... I see no other option. We must make the clones themselves fertile."

Ninmah gasped. "Impossible!"

"Maybe not. Ningishizidda believes he has isolated the markers that would enable them to breed. Such a modification would allow them to increase their population exponentially, at a much faster rate than we can create them ourselves. There would be no further shortages of workers. Nibiru would be saved."

"If he did not want a shortage of workers, he should not have ordered us to shorten their lifespans and make them susceptible to disease!" Ninmah snapped.

"Agreeing to that was the only way we could get him and the Council to sanction their creation in the first place. They wanted them perishable so that the issue of their existence would be resolved once we leave this planet. The natural evolutionary course restored, as if we had never interfered."

"In that case, what makes you think Enlil will agree to giving them the ability to breed?" Ninmah growled. "That would wholly defeat the idea of them dying out once we stop creating them."

"Who said anything about Enlil agreeing to anything?" Enki's

glowing eyes were steady. "He rarely descends. If we don't tell him, how would he know?"

"Go behind his back again?" Ninmah gasped. "But..."

Enki's attention had returned to the work being carried out far below. "Do you not agree they deserve such a gift?" he asked. "They are so much more than we ever dreamed or intended, Ninmah. In time, they could be a match for us. They have the potential to join us in the greater cosmos, beyond this tiny island in the stars."

Ninmah pressed her lips together. She could not deny the affection she felt for these beings she, Enki, and Ningishizidda had created. She had grown especially close to her Ninkuraa, but if Enlil ever found out...

Enki read her reluctance. "Our desires aside, Nibiru must survive, Ninmah. If you and the other carriers refuse to incubate more clones, what choice do we have? Allowing the creations themselves to breed solves our predicament and technically obeys Enlil's wishes."

Ninmah's mouth twitched. "You always know how to twist things to get your own way, you old snake."

Enki was silent, awaiting her agreement.

She sighed. "Allowing them to breed among themselves will sully our research. We cannot predict what might be created if we lose control over their bloodlines. It's dangerous. Enlil will surely be alerted. You are playing with fire, Enki."

Enki rubbed at his golden face. "We will keep the nine existing forms separate," he said. "I will give the order that the act of childbearing must only take place within their own forms, on pain of destruction. We will keep the batches pure, if that is your wish."

Ninmah nodded. A wise course, if they wished for this new

feature to remain secret. And, though she trembled at the thought of Enlil's wrath if he discovered what Enki was planning to set loose, the scientist within Ninmah rubbed her hands in glee. This was her chance to discover what her Ninkuraa could achieve if given the ability to procreate. Already, part of her mind was planning. She would select the most talented among them... Perhaps she could finally prove to Enki that her little side project was not such a folly after all.

"Do I have your support, Ninmah?"

"Yes," she said, the chance of discovery overwhelming her caution. Her mind was already thinking ahead. "The females will need modification to accommodate bearing children. It will never be easy for them, to do what they were never initially designed for, but it will be possible. Tell Ningishizidda to proceed."

Enki's face brightened and his headdress flashed as he swept towards the door.

"But Enki," Ninmah's voice called him around. "Do this, on your own head be it."

For the first time, she witnessed a flicker of fear pass through his glowing eyes before it was quashed. Indeed, if Enlil discovered him, Enki's own head might just be the price. Her spouse acknowledged Ninmah's warning with a dip of his head before disappearing into the corridor beyond.

As the door swished closed behind him, Ninmah closed her eyes, praying to the Great Father, An, that she had not set Enki on the path to oblivion.

* * *

38,000 BCE

The first rocks of the foothills closed behind Galahir and the small band who accompanied him. To Galahir, it felt like the closing of a predator's jaws.

Eldrax had ordered them to scout for Yatal's whereabouts, assess the strength of their enemy, and return. Kyaati had raged against his departure, appearing much like a falcon whose nest had been threatened.

Galahir's brow pinched together, anxiety rippling through his chest as he thought of his mate. A fierce and dark determination had appeared in Kyaati's eyes ever since Eldrax had summoned the raknari in order to lay down the preparations for the slaughter of the Eagle Clan. Galahir knew Kyaati well enough now to know that such an expression did not bode well. The fire in her eyes had burned all the brighter when Galahir told her he was departing for the foothills. He had feared leaving her alone, but under Eldrax's orders, he'd had no other choice.

"Don't frown like that, Galahir," Lorhir drawled. "It makes you look more witless than normal."

Galahir shook himself back to the present. For once, he did not feel the sting of Lorhir's verbal jab. They were walking into enemy territory. He needed to be alert. He had promised Kyaati he would come back to her and Elhaari alive, and Galahir intended to fulfil that promise. Shifting his grip on the arshu staff in his hand, he kept his eyes on his surroundings, scanning every shadow and crag. There was no telling where the Eagle clan may be. All Galahir and the rest knew was that the rival clan had not come out of the hills to travel south with the herds. Eldrax had made sure of that.

"Are they even alive?" Tanag muttered as they wound their way further into the maze of rocks. The Mountains of the Nine Gods loomed above their heads, the dark forests curling around the base of the foothills to the east.

"I doubt it," Lorhir sniffed. "Any game to be found in this forsaken wasteland would have been hunted down long ago. Unless a bunch of mainly half-Thal brutes found a way to live on rocks and water alone."

Galahir was aware of his companions' eyes flicking to his face in anticipation of his reaction, but he ignored Lorhir's veiled insults once again. He could not start trouble. The scouting group needed their sharpest leader right now, and that was not him.

The stark smell of cold stone leached the scent of earth from the air. Galahir could not help but shudder as the chill seeped from the rock and into his bones. He could not imagine living in this place. No wonder Yatal was so bitter.

"I am surprised we survived thanks to the *Chief* insisting we winter in the north," Ayel, the fourth and youngest member of their group, grumbled, his voice twisting in disdain.

Before Galahir could blink, Tanag's flint blade was at Ayel's throat. "Are you questioning our Chief?"

Ayel's eyes bulged. "I-I," he stammered.

"Tanag," Galahir stepped up to the other man's side, placing a hand on the hilt of the blade.

Tanag stiffened in shock at Galahir's daring. His lips peeled back off his teeth and he made to strike Galahir's hand away, but Lorhir was already at Galahir's side.

"Galahir is right, Tanag," Lorhir said in an equally threatening tone to the one Tanag had used. "We need to find Yatal and get out of these hills. Fight it out later, if that is your wish."

Faced with all three of his companions, Tanag ripped his arm back with a snarl. "You better stay out of my way, Ayel," he said as a parting shot. "Or the Red Bear might just hear of your *displeasure* with his leadership."

Ayel's face turned ashen under his dark skin as Tanag stalked away. "H-he wouldn't?" he stammered.

"How would I know? Just watch your tongue from now on," Lorhir snapped as he walked away. "I will not stretch my neck out for you again."

Galahir pressed Ayel's shoulder before hefting their group's meager supplies on his broad shoulder and continuing on. He was surprised to catch up to Lorhir in just a few strides. The other man appeared to have been waiting for him. Galahir eyed his brother-in-arms warily as Lorhir fell into step at his side, keeping his dark gaze riveted on Tanag's back.

"You might want to give the same advice to that witch mate of yours, Galahir," he warned in a low voice that would not carry on the air.

"Why?" Galahir started defensively. "Kyaati has done nothing."

Lorhir gave him a pitying stare. "She makes her opinion of the Chief clear. I doubt Eldrax will bring himself to harm your mate, as she is the only witch left to him. That is her only protection. But he does not tolerate dissent. He will punish somebody, and that somebody will most likely be you."

"She cannot help it," Galahir argued. His need to defend

the mother of his child made him bold. "Ayel is right. The Chief has weakened the clan in his lust for vengeance. He is putting us in jeopardy; that is hard for the mother of a newborn babe to tolerate." Galahir's voice dropped to a mere breath. "Even Rannac questioned the Red Bear towards the end."

"And Rannac is dead."

Galahir winced and fell silent. As they wound deeper into the maze of the foothills, he dwelt on the moment he had beaten Eldrax about the head to save Nyriaana. In the heat of the moment, he had left the Red Bear alive for the sake of the clan. But now Galahir wondered if he had done the right thing.

A smarter man than he might have the answer. Galahir longed for Khalvir's presence. He had always known what to do. Galahir eyed Lorhir. Could he confide his worries to his oldest rival?

A low warning whistle scattered his thoughts. Ahead of them, Tanag had come to a halt, his shoulders tense as his head swivelled this way and that. Galahir shared one glance with Lorhir before they dodged forward to cover Tanag's flanks, weapons at the ready.

"What is it?" Lorhir breathed.

"I don't know. I thought I heard something on the breeze. Not an animal tread. It has stopped now, but I don't like it. I don't like it."

Galahir scanned the surrounding rocks along with his brethren. He knew what Tanag meant. The hairs on the back of his neck prickled. In that moment, he knew for certain they were being watched.

"We should get out of here," Ayel hissed. "Tanag, uh—!"

A dull thud and a bubbling gurgle cut the younger scout's words short.

"Ayel!" Galahir caught the other man before he hit the ground, blood spilling over his hands from the spear protruding from Ayel's neck.

"Overhead!" Tanag cried, just as another spear struck the ground at his feet. Galahir looked up to see Eagle warriors lining the ridges of the hills all around them, roaring out their challenge to the intruders below.

Yatal had survived.

"Go!" Tanag screamed as a hail of spears rained down. Galahir flinched as the flint tip of one weapon scythed across his upper arm.

Galahir dropped Ayel's body; there was nothing more he could do for him. With Lorhir and Tanag at his side, he sprinted from the jaws of the trap, dodging and twisting this way and that like a hunted antelope to avoid the barrage of spears falling on their heels. Despite his best efforts, he felt the sting of another spear wounding his left leg.

At last the sound of spears striking rock ceased and Galahir knew they had made it out of range. But the relief was short-lived.

"They're giving chase!" Tanag huffed, increasing his pace as the sound of pounding feet replaced that of spears. The Eagles were not satisfied with warning them off. They wanted blood. Galahir groaned. This was the second time he had had to fight for his life against Eagle warriors in these forsaken hills.

"Back to the Plains!" Lorhir launched himself down the path they had followed from open ground to the point of ambush. It was the most direct route home. Galahir struggled to keep up with the other two Cro men. What advantage he held in strength, he sorely lacked in speed.

It was a disadvantage that proved to be his saviour. Lagging behind gave Galahir vital moments to see the movement on the ridges above the narrow gully they were about to pass through.

"Look out!" He grabbed Lorhir and Tanag by their furs, yanking them back just in time as the boulders came crashing down. All three men threw themselves to the ground, shielding their heads as the onslaught of the avalanche rumbled and crashed before them, drowning out the hoots of triumph from above. When Galahir dared to raise his head again, a wall of immovable rubble was all he could see. Their passage home was blocked.

"Ea, preserve us," Tanag choked, staggering back to his feet.

There was no time to take in the turn of events, no time to dwell on the fact that they were now cut off from the Plains. They needed to get away before the clouds of dust settled and the Eagles realised they had missed. Trying not to cough, Galahir leaped to his feet. "Get up," he urged Lorhir, catching his fellow raknari by the scruff of the neck, and dragging him along beside him until Lorhir's legs rediscovered their strength and the other man twisted loose.

Galahir sprinted back down the path with the other two on his heels. Cries of dismay followed them as they emerged from the dust cloud. Galahir cast his eyes about. They had to get off this trail before their pursuers routed them, trapping them between the boulders and insurmountable numbers.

But he wasn't fast enough. The Eagles were swift and

knew this range well. A warrior appeared at the head of the path, a triumphant smile playing over his lips as he barred their way.

No!

The man was alone, having outpaced the rest of his group. Galahir gritted his teeth and charged the enemy warrior, barrelling into him with all of his strength. Unprepared, their enemy flew backwards, hitting a rock face before crumpling to the ground.

"You shouldn't have left your clan behind," Galahir panted as he ran on, acutely aware that the rest of them would arrive at any moment. Escaping the blocked trail, Galahir chose a different path leading away from their enemies. His mind flew through their options as he pounded along, his footfalls echoing off the surrounding rock faces. Their options were lacking. They were tiring, outnumbered, and the Eagles knew this range far better than they did. For all Galahir knew, he, Lorhir and Tanag could, in that very moment, be heading into yet another trap. He kept his attention on the ridges above, watching for more Eagle warriors intent on bringing rocks down on their heads.

The triumphant hunting calls continued behind them. They were getting louder.

"What in Ea's name have they been living on all this time?" Tanag panted. "Eldrax had all passages out of these hills watched."

"Turn around and ask them if you want!" Lorhir spat. "I'm sure our hides will be on a spit when they catch us."

Kyaati, Kyaati, I'm sorry, Galahir thought as he continued to sprint. He had promised her he would return. Promised. *Great Ea, what can I do? Where can we go?* He wanted to see

Elhaari grow. As they scrambled around a bend in the path, an answer revealed itself in the form of the dark line visible in the near distance.

"The forest!" Galahir pointed ahead. "We need to get to the forest!"

"No!" Tanag cried, just as a spear flew past his head and smashed into the rocks.

"I'm not arguing!" Galahir shouted with a force of will that surprised him. "Follow me or not." Gathering his remaining strength, he threw himself ahead, straining every sinew to reach the ever-nearing line of black ahead. He was aware of the other two faltering for a moment, but the sound of more spears decided their path for them and then they were racing at his flanks once more.

The thought of entering the trees filled Galahir with a terror he had rarely felt, but if he did not, he would never see his mate or child again. The unknown was better than certain death at this moment.

It still took every ounce of his courage to continue forward when the first twisted branches reached out to ensnare him. The smell of damp and rotten death assaulted his senses, firing warnings off in his brain. Rock gave way to sucking black earth beneath his reluctant feet as the air fell dead around them.

Galahir tried to force from his thoughts all the stories he had heard about this place, but the unnamed horrors continued to dance at the edges of his mind's eye, sucking at his courage like the mud at his feet. The hair on his scalp lifted, and Galahir wondered whether he would rather turn tail and face the hoard of murderous Eagle warriors than take another step into the trees.

"They've stopped," Lorhir hissed just as the hunting calls turned to cries of disbelief and dismay. Gasping for air, Galahir came to a halt and turned to face their enemies. Terror shone in their eyes as they stood at the edge of the forest. They did not hold their position long before they turned and fled, disappearing back into their rocky maze.

"They don't want to be the next helping when the monsters are through with us," Tanag muttered, his voice sounding strange and hollow to Galahir in the thick atmosphere.

"At least we're alive," Galahir struggled to make the best of their situation as the adrenaline pulsed through his body in cold waves.

"But for how long?" Tanag's voice was icy as the air. "You have no idea what you have brought us into, you lumbering fool. I do. I have seen the horrors that walk this forest with my own eyes. We had better pray that the eyes of the Watchers remain closed to our trespass."

All colour had drained from Lorhir's dark skin. Like Galahir, it appeared to be taking all of his courage to remain standing in the midst of the trees.

"We should move," Galahir whispered without responding to Tanag's chilling words. "Keep low. If we head south, we should make it out of here and back to camp before nightfall." He felt strange instructing the others on their next action, but it had been his idea to flee into this nightmare. It was now his responsibility to get them out of it.

"Lead on, then." Galahir ignored the mockery in Tanag's voice, taking a moment to smear some of the camouflaging black mud over his pale skin and hair before getting his bearings and striking out.

The twisted trees leered down, catching his furs and clawing at his face with their fleshless fingers. The smell left a sick taste at the back of his throat. Galahir tried to breathe in as little as possible.

The phase of day could only be guessed at as they crept through the Forest of the Nine Gods, every sense straining into the eerie silence. A half light overlaid everything, the dense canopy cutting off any sign of Utu. Galahir soon lost track of how long they had been inside the trees. It might have been a day, it could have been five days. The light never seemed to change. Claustrophobia began to claw at his throat, making him want to bolt for open spaces and clean air. He had thought the *shin'ar* forests of the elf-witches had been bad. Now the memory of them was as welcome as home.

It was the stench that thickened before Galahir detected the first movement.

"What was that?" Tanag flinched as the sound of branches snapping under force shattered the silence. Galahir stopped dead in his tracks. The smell of old blood and rotting flesh overpowered his senses. Galahir clamped a hand over his nose and mouth before he gagged. Only a lifetime of conditioning as a raknari warrior held him in place. The snapping sound echoed back and forth through the trees, making it impossible to pinpoint where the source was coming from. Fleeing in panic would only result in their death.

The sound stopped as suddenly as it had started and silence reigned once again. The smell, however, did not dissipate. Breathless, they waited as infinite moments passed, but nothing moved.

Holding his breath, Galahir took a step forward.

"What are you doing?" Lorhir hissed.

"Going home," Galahir answered. "We can't just stand here."

Galahir could tell Lorhir wanted to argue, but there was nothing he could say. They had to get out of this forest and the only way to do that was to go forward.

Bent almost double, Galahir wove around the gnarled tree trunks, trying to keep his attention everywhere at once. There came the occasional crackle of leaves, but each time he ignored the leap in his heart and kept his pace measured. *Don't run, don't run,* he chanted over and over to himself. Only prey ran.

Surely the treeline must be close. There had to be an end to this. Had he chosen the wrong direction? A new fear took hold of Galahir's heart. If he had chosen the wrong path, they could wander forever lost within this nightmare. Where was Utu to guide him? Galahir turned his face towards the canopy, but the branches overhead curled and twisted together in many layers without break, blocking out the sky.

"Gah!" The breath left Galahir's lungs as he stepped forward and the ground failed to meet him. He grabbed at a branch, trying to save himself, but the rotten limb disintegrated in his grip and Galahir fell away, tumbling down the slope he had failed to see, so desperate had he been for a glimpse of Utu. Over and over he rolled, lashed and battered by the trees he struck until, with a last gut-wrenching drop, Galahir was dumped, bruised and bloodied, into the wet mud.

For a few heartbeats he lay panting, spitting the dank leaf

mould from his tongue, before realising his wasn't the only breath he could hear rushing in his ears.

Something big awaited just out of his line of sight.

Ea, preserve me. Galahir rolled into a crouch just as Lorhir came skidding down the slope to his side.

"You—!"

Galahir clamped a hand over Lorhir's mouth and pointed. Just through the trees in front of them, a clearing had opened out. He felt Lorhir go rigid beneath his palm as the shadows moved.

Even Galahir's darkest nightmare could never have conceived such a beast as the one he was beholding now. A Watcher of the Sky Gods. It could be nothing else. He had only ever heard his clan's campfire stories of these creatures and he wished with all his might that were still so. He would never again purge the reality from his mind.

The Watcher shouldered its way into the clearing. Uncured animal pelts draped from its massive shoulders, the height of three men above the ground. The thick arms and legs bristled with broken and jagged bones, worn in the same fashion as Galahir and his fellow raknari when going into battle or setting out on a raid.

Eldrax had come face to face with the Watchers before becoming Chief. Galahir wondered if this was where the Hunting Bear tradition of wearing bone armour for intimidation and offence had sprung. The bloody skull of an ox dangled from one long-fingered hand, much like the one Galahir himself favoured to protect his head and face.

Flies buzzed around the elongated head, but the giant did not appear to notice. Blue eyes glowed from hollow sockets, intent on a point at the centre of the clearing where a grisly monument stood; a tower of broken tree trunks upon which the impaled bodies of animals and human remains hung.

A loud crack ricocheting through the air next to him almost had Galahir leaving his own flesh behind. Lorhir had taken a step back at the sight of the monster and brought his heel down on a branch.

The gaze of the Watcher snapped up. Galahir could not have moved, even if he had wanted to. All he could do was hold his breath as the Watcher stared eerily without blinking into the trees towards him. Galahir felt as though his very soul was being pierced.

"Ngathe!" A cry broke the standoff. The Watcher's face turned away as a second creature entered the clearing. What little blood remained in Galahir's face drained from his cheeks. The newcomer carried a thrashing Thal woman under one arm. "Ngathe!" she screamed again, clawing at the Watcher's pallid flesh, punching and kicking with all her might. Blood dripped from the wounds where she had dashed herself against the jagged bone coverings in her desperation.

The Watcher paid no more attention to her struggles than it did the flies swarming around its rotten garments.

Galahir watched as the two monsters lumbered to the grisly monument of wood and bodies at the centre of the clearing. Placing the terrified Thal on the ground, the second Watcher stooped to help the first lift an enormous stone from the ground in front of the monument. Released from the creature's grip, the Thal woman scrambled away. It was a doomed attempt. The second Watcher saw her and, with a frustrated grunt, brought its great foot down on her legs. The sound of snapping bone was almost enough to drown out her cry of agony.

Fury surged through Galahir at the sight of the Watcher breaking her legs with no more emotion than if it had stepped on a tree branch.

Their sobbing prey immobilised, the two creatures continued their effort to lift the stone away from the ground. Lorhir's sharp intake of breath sounded next to Galahir's ear as a golden light flashed forth. It was like a ray of Utu, but filling the air from the earth rather than the sky. Galahir rocked back at the unnaturalness of what he was witnessing. How could Utu be coming from the ground?

A soft hum filled the air. It rose and fell in a somehow familiar rhythm. The Watchers stooped over the source of the golden light, listening intently.

"We have to get out of here," Lorhir whispered. "Now, Galahir, while they're distracted. I can see light. The tree line is not far. If we're quick, we can make it."

But Galahir did not move. His eyes were still on the unearthly golden light emitting from the ground. Lorhir yanked on his furs. "Let's go!"

Galahir shook himself. Keeping the thought of Kyaati and his new son firmly in his thoughts, he crept forward through the trees. He skirted the clearing with Lorhir, keeping one eye on the Watchers' turned backs as they remained intent on the strange hum.

"Almost there," Lorhir breathed as the far side of the clearing and escape neared.

But they didn't make it. "Yanna!" The cry went up. "Yanna!" Galahir spun to face the wide, beseeching eyes of the Thal woman staring right at them. "Yanna!" *Mercy!*

"She's given us away!" Lorhir snarled. "Run, Galahir!"

But Galahir could not leave. All he could see was Kyaati lying there on the ground, about to be sacrificed to gods only knew what. Before he was aware of it, Galahir was tearing into the clearing, sprinting to the Thal woman's side even as the Watchers turned, roused from their apparent trance by the commotion. Now that he was closer, Galahir could hear the hum more clearly. It was a voice. A voice coming from the very bowels of the earth. It was raised in anger. Galahir got the terrifying impression that the disembodied voice knew he was there.

The Watchers bellowed at the sight of him. The sound of their voices shook Galahir's bones. Acting on instinct and nothing more, Galahir snatched the wounded woman from the ground and fled towards the faint light of day he could just make out ahead of him.

Lorhir was already sprinting ahead. Then Tanag was there. "This way!" he screamed at them. "Follow me, this way!"

A chilling, wailing call went up behind him, and the vibrations in the ground told Galahir that the Watchers had given chase. He dared not look back. He kept his eyes focused on Tanag and the direction he was leading them in, driven faster by the splintering of tree trunks as their monstrous pursuers thrust them aside behind him. Galahir knew it was only the trees' hindrance to their giant enemies that was keeping them alive right now.

The Thal woman yelped and moaned as his motion jolted her broken legs, but he could do nothing to ease her pain. It was all he could do just to keep them out of death's reach.

"I always knew you were a fool, Galahir!" Lorhir hissed as he ran. "But not enough of one to poke a stick into the eye of the gods themselves! I was leaving that to Eldrax's madness."

Galahir had no breath to answer. The woman he carried was becoming a boulder weight in his arms. Gasping, he used his very last reserves of strength to launch himself at the approaching tree line. The freedom of the Plains beckoned beyond. The Watchers would not follow them into the open once they had chased their quarry from their lair.

But as the last trees melted away, the sounds of crashing did not abate behind him. "They're still coming! Why are they still coming?"

"Because you took *her*!" Lorhir snapped. "You have doomed us, Galahir!"

"I'm sorry!" Galahir burst onto the Plains with Tanag and Lorhir before him. Now the freedom of the open ground was not a comfort. It was a death sentence. As soon as those beasts shook free of the trees, they would have them in just a few strides. Galahir closed his eyes briefly. *I'm sorry, Kyaati.* Fool that he was, he had made the wrong choice. He only hoped the Watchers would be appeased with their deaths in payment for the trespass and theft of their sacrifice.

"Ea be blessed!" Galahir's eyes snapped back open at Lorhir's exclamation and his heart leaped.

Eldrax, with all the clan's remaining men standing armoured and armed at his back, was waiting at a distance across the open ground. Waiting in just the right place to meet their foe.

"How?" Lorhir panted. "How?"

Galahir saw a flash of silver at the back of the Hunting Bear force and had his answer. "Kyaati!" Her glorious eyes were terrified, but fierce. She had come to protect him.

Along with the other two men, Galahir pounded towards his clan, but under his load and on open ground, there never had been a hope that he would reach safety in time. The Thal woman screamed as the first Watcher burst from the forest and Galahir knew that it was over for him. Across the space between them, he met Kyaati's eyes, hoping she could feel everything he wanted to say, before launching the Thal woman as far out of reach as he could.

A hand closed around his leg and the world whirled as the monster swung Galahir up and around until all that filled his vision was the Watcher's mouth as it bellowed in his face, double rows of teeth gnashing behind cracked lips.

Another hand caught hold of his arms, and Galahir grunted as the Watcher pulled, fully intent on ripping him in two.

"No!"

It took Galahir a moment to realise the piercing screech had not come from his own lips. And then the air was filled with the buffeting of ferocious wings. Feathers blocked the view of the Watcher's face and the monster roared in pain. The air left Galahir's body as it dropped him to the ground below. Winded, he lay where he had fallen for a handful of heartbeats, staring up in dazed horror as he watched the great bird clawing at the Watcher's face with talons as long as his hands.

"Galahir! Get out of there!"

Galahir recovered his breath as the Watcher staggered in its struggle with the Dalku eagle. Over and over he rolled, escaping the trampling feet by a mere hair's breadth.

The Watcher freed itself from its attacker as Galahir

leapt upright. The eagle twisted in the air, avoiding the giant's clumsy swipes and rose into the sky, shrilling its fury. Galahir thought he caught a note of Kyaati's voice in its anger.

The Watcher moaned. Galahir's stomach turned over. Bloody, gaping holes were all that remained of the glowing blue eyes. Blinded, the creature stumbled, groping at the ground, still trying to find its prey, not realising Galahir had already escaped to a safe distance.

Instead, the searching hands fell upon the Thal woman he had rescued with a voiceless bellow of triumph. Before Galahir could move, the giant swung its helpless victim from the ground and threw her with tremendous force back at the tree line. In a blur of motion, she glanced off the head of the Watcher's emerging companion, rebounded, and then, with a sickening crack, hit a gnarled trunk and fell to the ground, dead.

Galahir snarled in fury as the second Watcher shoved its staggering companion out of the way, cruel blue eyes fixing upon the lone man before it. Galahir braced himself, ready to go down fighting. Out of the corner of his eye, he saw Eldrax's arm sweep forward, and five of the men led by Tanag advanced towards the Watcher.

"Here!" Tanag cried. "Here!" A hail of spears followed. Most bounced off the Watcher's jutting bone coverings, but one struck true, embedding itself in a patch of exposed flesh.

With a piercing howl that curdled Galahir's blood, the creature whirled on Tanag's advance force. It ripped the spear from its body and snapped it between its fingers like a twig before charging the men in a blood-maddened rage. There was no possibility that Tanag and four others could stand against such a beast.

Eldrax had sent them to their deaths.

But to Galahir's surprise, a triumphant grin split Tanag's face. Putting his fingers to his lips, Tanag let loose the whistle for retreat. As one, he and his men turned and fled before the monster, leading it on a path straight towards...

"Kyaati!" She was still standing at the back of Eldrax's fighting force. The sight of the Watcher bearing down upon her was more than Galahir could bear. "Kyaati!" he cried again, giving chase. What was Eldrax doing? Not even all the men combined would be a match against what was approaching. The Red Bear had brought Galahir's mate into the middle of the slaughter field.

"Here!" he cried at the Watcher's back, sweeping rocks up as he ran and launching them at the beast. He had to get its attention back on him. He would lead it back into the forest. "Here!"

His efforts were futile. The beast's focus remained on the fleeing men who had drawn its blood. Its massive strides ate up the ground, gaining on Tanag. At any moment, the Watcher would have them.

"Here!" Galahir screamed again, hurling another rock with all his might as the long arms reached for the first victim.

A spear's throw away from the Red Bear, Tanag's piercing whistle sounded again, and the men separated at that precise moment, peeling off in two directions just as a giant hand swiped out.

The Watcher ground to a halt at the point where Tanag's force had split in two. The five men continued to run until they rejoined the rest, spinning back to face their confused foe behind their fiery-haired leader.

Galahir sprinted along, fighting to catch up as Eldrax glared up at the Watcher weaving uncertainly just three of its giant strides from the Cro leader.

"Come on!" Eldrax bellowed in challenge, beating his free fist against his chest as he brandished his bone-spiked club in the other. "Come and face me at last!"

He was mad. Kyaati was right. Their Chief had lost his mind. Galahir gritted his teeth as the sweat poured down his face. The camouflaging mud he had smeared on his pale skin dripped into his eyes, but he could not blink, could not take his attention off the scene unfolding before him as the Watcher snarled in response to Eldrax's challenge.

Still, it appeared reluctant to take another step towards the waiting Cro. It glanced down at the ground before its feet, then back at Eldrax. Confusion swamped Galahir. He did not understand. Three strides and that thing could fall amongst the men and rip them apart with barely the flicker of an eyelid.

"Come to me!" Eldrax roared. "Hit it again!" The men let a second hail of spears fly, striking and cutting at the Watcher.

The shriek that tore from the creature's throat this time was beyond reason. It shifted, preparing to lunge.

But the beast's hesitation had given Galahir the time he had needed to catch up. Yanking his hand-arshu loose, he swung with all his force and embedded the antler tips deep into the leg of his enemy.

The Watcher let loose an inhuman howl of pain, stagger-ing back and away from the assembled men.

Eldrax's shriek of denial was almost as anguished as the

creature's as the Watcher swung around in the opposite direction, seeking the one responsible for its latest injury.

Eldrax screamed more orders, but Galahir could not make out the words as he ducked the first swipe the Watcher made in his direction. Blood seeped from several spear wounds to its face as the giant's crazed eyes fixed upon him. Galahir had its full attention now.

"That's it," he breathed. "Follow me." He did not know what would happen when he got the creature back into its lair. No doubt his life would end with him in pieces, but Galahir could not allow himself to think about that. All he knew was that he had to get the creature as far from the mother of his child as possible.

Praying to the gods for the speed to stay ahead, Galahir ran, the dark tree line his only focus.

Eldrax's fist came out of nowhere, colliding with the side of his face and shattering the bone in his nose. Galahir's sight exploded with light and blood as the blow sent him crashing to the ground.

"You fool!" Eldrax bellowed down at him, red hair wild around his fury-twisted expression.

Galahir lay stunned as the world spun. Blinking through the tears that blinded him, he could just make out the figures of his brothers as they rushed to reform their ranks in front of the Watcher, cutting off its return to the forest.

"Drive it back!" Eldrax was snarling. "Send it down!"

"Kyaati!" Galahir could not see her in the chaos unfolding in front of him. The men jabbed and feigned at the Watcher. It swiped at them with a bare hand, and several dodged, but Eldrax held firm, only moving enough to let the crushing blow pass harmlessly over his head.

"Spears! Aim for the face!"

Weapons scythed through the air and the Watcher roared, staggering back a step as it brought its arms up to protect its vulnerable eyes. An ominous snapping sounded at the monster's heel.

"Again!" Eldrax ordered, as the barrage ceased and the great arms lowered. "Again!"

"There are no more spears!" Tanag cried. "Eldrax, we have failed. We must flee!"

"No!" Lifting his bristling club high over his head, Eldrax charged the Watcher single-handed, ducking and dodging with a speed that belied his great frame as the creature tried to smash him to the side. The Hunting Bear Chief struck at the monster's legs with his weapon, trying to drive it back, his face a mask of crazed fury.

"Protect the Chief!" Tanag cried, rallying the other men behind him. The whites of their eyes flashed, but they charged to the defence of the Red Bear. Screams went up as the Watcher seized a rock in its massive hand and swung it through the ranks of Cro, knocking several into the air.

"Kyaati!" Galahir cried again as Eldrax continued to swing at the Watcher's shins.

"I'm here!" Small hands caught hold of his.

"Kyaati, get out of here!" Galahir fought to get the words past a mouthful of blood.

But Kyaati wasn't paying attention. Her eyes were on the Watcher. "It won't go back," she hissed. "It has to go back. Not enough. Not enough."

Galahir did not know what his mate was talking about. He fought to rise. The blow Eldrax had dealt was still ringing in his head.

Then it happened. A wail of dismay went up from the Cro men as the Watcher caught their leader with a glancing blow. Even that was enough to send Eldrax flying, rolling over the ground until he landed in a battered heap.

The Watcher let out a triumphant howl, its glowing eyes fixing on the remaining men.

"No." Kyaati pulled her hands away from Galahir. Planting herself in front of him, she faced their monstrous enemy. To his horror, Galahir saw Elhaari was bound in a sling on her back as Kyaati crouched, digging in her fingers into the ground. As she did so, a keening shriek answered that of the Watcher, and a great black form once again fell from the sky like a spear. This time, a swarm of smaller falcons swooped at its sides.

Wings beat the air, battering against the Watcher's face, clawing and gouging, trying to reach the Watcher's blue orbs.

Under the persistent assault, the Watcher staggered back another step, trying to open a space between it and the hail of talons. "Yes!" Tanag cried. Heartened by the reinforcements, the men regrouped to double the efforts of the birds, striking at the Watcher's shins with renewed ferocity.

The creature's hands flashed out. This time, the Dalku eagle was not quick enough, and the Watcher caught hold of one wing, eliciting a cry of denial from Kyaati. But her concentration did not waver and the giant bird continued its attack under her influence, striking at the pallid face with beak and talon. Blood sprayed out. The Watcher howled and stumbled back again. Shouts of triumph from the attacking men drowned out the shrill cries of the birds as the ground beneath their enemy's feet cracked, crumbling away to reveal a gaping maw in the earth.

The Watcher threw the eagle from its grip, snatching at the air in a futile attempt to save itself as it tumbled away into the waiting depths. Galahir heard a thud and the monster's screams cut off in a bloody gurgle.

A holler of victory went up as the men danced around the pit into which the Watcher had fallen. Galahir cast around quickly for the other creature, but the blinded Watcher was nowhere to be seen, only a trail of blood revealed itself, leading back into the forest.

A hitching sob from Kyaati pulled his attention back to the immediate. Ignoring the celebrations, his mate had rushed over to where the Dalku eagle had come to rest. Galahir's mind was whirling. Everything had happened so fast, but he staggered to his feet, letting out a hiss between his teeth. The leg the Watcher had caught hold of was badly strained. He blocked out the pain and limped after Kyaati. She needed him now.

Tears were streaming down his mate's face as she sank to her knees beside the felled bird. Galahir could see its wing was shattered, crushed by the grip of the Watcher. He sighed. There was no hope for it.

One great golden eye fixed upon Kyaati, and Galahir could have sworn the animal was pleading with her. Kyaati sniffed and wiped an arm across her face, dashing away the tears. Straightening her back, she put one hand on the animal's breast. "Go, Son of KI. Fly free with the rest of your kin who have gone before."

Galahir couldn't rightly say what happened next, but as he watched, Kyaati's hand contracted in the thick black feathers and the great body sank to the ground. The light drained from the fierce golden eye. The Dalku eagle moved no more.

"Lonely creature," Kyaati sighed. "He was the last of his kind."

Galahir wasn't sure how to respond and so he simply pulled her against his chest and held her. He looked toward the gaping pit into which the Watcher had disappeared and at last understood what the plan had been all along. In his ignorance, he had almost thwarted his brothers. A wave of intense guilt washed over him. He was the reason his mate was now weeping over this hapless mass of feathers. "I'm sorry, Kyaati," he murmured. "I'm such a fool."

Kyaati brought her hand up to grip his fingers in a gesture of forgiveness as she turned her own gaze upon the pit. A soft snuffling cry reminded Galahir of Elhaari's presence, and he remembered he was not the only fool. He had not expected such an action from Kyaati. She had been reckless to come here herself, but to bring their newborn son… For the first time, Galahir was angry with his mate.

"What were you thinking, Kyaati?" he demanded, snatching Elhaari from the sling and holding him protectively against his chest.

Kyaati bared her teeth. "He made me!" she spat. "He forced me to bring our son, 'for motivation.'"

Galahir did not need to ask of whom she spoke. Fury blazed through his chest as Kyaati pulled Elhaari back to her, checking over him, a frown between her brows.

"What's the matter? Is he hurt?" Galahir's eyes darted over the tiny bundle.

"No," Kyaati said, "but he did something. I was not the

one who brought the eagle. He was too far away for me to reach, but then Elhaari…" she broke off, seeming at a loss for words, and nodded to the place where she had sunk her fingers into the ground. Galahir's eyes widened. A circle of blackened land now existed where they had stood.

"He did that?"

Kyaati jerked her chin, her face pale. "Just like Khalvir."

"Khalvir?"

But his mate just shook her head. She didn't appear capable of more speech. Pushing herself from the ground, she left the body of the Dalku eagle behind and joined the rest of the Cro standing upon the edge of the pit. Galahir followed.

At the very bottom, at a depth of three men, the Watcher lay, its giant body pierced by an array of sharpened stakes. Its dead eyes glared up at them, frightening even in death.

A sudden bark of laughter made Galahir flinch. Eldrax, his face bloodied from the blow the Watcher had dealt, limped back to the pit. His black eyes burned as he turned them upon Elhaari in his mother's arms. "I was right," he rasped. "I knew the witch-children were the answer."

Galahir grabbed Kyaati's arm as she took a step towards the Red Bear, hissing between her teeth. Fortunately, Eldrax had already looked away.

"Tanag," he barked. "Bring me the beast's head."

"What are you doing?" Kyaati demanded, as Tanag and several others clambered down into the hole.

"Sending a message," Eldrax growled. "One that the gods will hear. The time has passed for the petty bickering between clans. Now is the time for mankind to take their revenge."

* * *

7

Etuti Sagkal

Nyriaana was growing desperate. The night had come and gone and she had not succeeded in freeing Juaan from the Thals' clutches. Since healing Juaan's wound, Bahari had not taken his eyes off her, quashing any hope she might have had of escape. Now, after nearly another full day's travel towards the Thal's home in the foothills, they were no closer to regaining their freedom. Nyri cursed herself for being so hasty in healing Juaan's wound. She should have waited until they were free. Now, because of her thoughtlessness, she had gained their captors' undivided attention.

The day waned and Ninmah dipped below the horizon as the Thals halted their march to make camp for a second time. Nyri sensed an undercurrent of frustration as several of them glanced longingly at the foothills in the near distance. Nyri took a small satisfaction in their discomfort. She had done everything she could to slow their travel and delay their return. Now they had to spend an unplanned night on the plains. She hoped her play for more time would reap a reward. Bahari had spent the whole of the previous night awake. Surely this night he would have to break his vigil and rest.

The group found another raised vantage point upon which to make camp. Juaan was tied, and the Thals settled down to rest in a circle. But, to Nyri's utter dismay, Bahari did not join them. Just as before, the Cro man took up his unwavering vigil over her, staring as though she was Ninmah herself come to earth. Nyri could have howled with frustration. No matter what she did now, they would reach the Thal camp the next morning. She cast about in desperation, her mind racing, trying to conceive a way she might evade Bahari and cut Juaan's bindings, but it was futile. She was trapped.

"Can all of your People mend hurts as you do?" Bahari's voice slipped through the shadows. Since witnessing her healing powers, the Cro man had seemed too overawed by her to speak. He appeared to have overcome that now.

Nyri gritted her teeth and considered ignoring him for a moment, but perhaps if she quenched his curiosity, he would lose interest and sleep. "No." Unbidden, her mind went to her old teacher, Baarias, cut down by a Wove spear, and her breathing hitched. The memory of his killing ripped through her heart as savagely as if it were still unfolding before her eyes. She had never really had time to absorb his loss, the man who had been a father to her since the day Juaan had been taken. "I am probably the last with the true skill."

She sensed, rather than saw, Bahari's frown in the darkness. "But you all have magic, just as the stories say?" There was a tone of innocent wonder in his voice that might have been endearing had the situation been different.

Nyri snorted. "It's not magic."

Bahari laughed. "Perhaps not to you, who see it every day. But to my eyes… Eron send miracle."

"Eron?"

"Thal maker, from Sky Path." Bahari gestured to the thick purplish line of glimmering spirits overhead.

"Ah." Ninmah, Ea, Nunamnir, Ninhursag, Ninsiku, now Eron. So many names. How to know which was the truth? Nyri sighed, her eyes wandering towards the Mountains outlined against Ninsiku's silver light. The pull was still there, drawing her towards those peaks like a moth to a flame. But the agonised pleas that had crippled her mind since leaving the Hunting Bear camp had fallen silent. Nyri fancied there was a quiet satisfaction to the energy around her. She was now heading in the direction the voices wanted. Nyri let a long sigh hiss out between her teeth.

"Yes." Bahari seemed to have guessed the direction of her focus. His voice was sad. "Eron gone into Mountains. No Thal seen him since the earliest stories."

"Just like in the tales of the Hunting Bear," Nyri murmured.

She felt Bahari bristle at the comparison. "Hunting Bear—"

A snarl in the darkness beyond the circle of sleeping Thals cut off the rest of his words. Twin points of green light flickered in and out of existence as they caught the faint light of Ninsiku's half-open eye.

Beside Nyri, Juaan tensed, pulling out of the light doze he had fallen into.

"Spitters." Bahari rose to his feet, drawing his spear close.

Now Nyri understood Bahari's meaning. *Grinshnaa.* She could feel the smooth feline presences slinking through the darkness. Two, no, three, invisible presences circled the camp slowly, assessing the strength of the Thal band and the potential for a meal. Nyri balled her fists as their disappointment washed against her own. There were not enough of them for her to use against the armed and defensively positioned Thals.

"Don't worry," Nyri said to Bahari. "They're not hungry enough to risk an attack. They don't have the numbers."

"How you know that?"

"Magic," Nyri sighed.

"By Eron," Bahari swore.

Yowls and angry hissing sounded in the distance. A scuffle had broken out between pride members. The primal lust for food flared against Nyri's mind. She guessed they had found the last of Ekundir and his followers' scattered remains. The three cats circling the camp took off into the deeper darkness, the scent of blood drawing them to the feast.

"At least your friends were good for one thing," Bahari told Juaan grimly.

"They were not my friends," Juaan responded. "Not anymore."

Nyri's eyes darted to his shadowed face. To see the Cro men lying dead following the battle with the Thals had caused a storm of mixed emotions for her. She had known them for only a short time; and she had viewed them as enemies for far longer than she had considered them allies. But, for Juaan, these were men he had passed into manhood with, led into battle, shared the spoils of the hunt with, celebrated with. What must he be experiencing? Once again, his emotions were as unreadable as his features. He was closing her out.

Bahari grunted, unimpressed by Juaan's words. "Here." He handed Nyri several strips of cold, dried meat. The Thals had not lit a fire. The high vantage point gave them the luxury of far sight, but would also make any light they made a beacon to enemies closer than the farthest horizon.

Nyri made a face as she accepted the offering. Ignoring Bahari's rumble of disapproval, she held a piece of the gifted flesh to Juaan's mouth first, which he accepted between his teeth. Nyri then chewed on her own unappetising morsel.

Her fingers itched towards her skinning knife. Juaan's bindings were so tauntingly close. But she could feel Bahari's eyes on her in the dark, alert to her every move.

His regard was not threatening. It was a gentle attention, but it left her with no chance of severing the tough ropes before the Cro man stopped her. And Bahari still possessed their only significant weapon. Juaan's spear. Her small knife would not be enough if it came down to a fight. Nyri dropped her head back against the rock behind her as she worked through one futile plan, then another. She did not sleep.

All too soon, the first light of Ninmah began to warm the eastern horizon. Nyri blinked gritty eyes. Her time was up. All around her, the Thals were rising, grunting as they stretched their heavy limbs and passed water skins around to their brethren.

Bahari approached Nyri, offering his arms. "We reach *etuti sagkal* today."

Nyri waved him away. "I'll walk. I have had enough of being thrown across a Cro's shoulders."

Bahari dipped his chin, but his gaze flickered towards Juaan and Nyri did not need her higher senses to perceive his concern. He would honour her with the freedom of her own movement, but he could not risk any foolhardy attempts at escape. "You walk with me," he said pointedly. Nyri scowled but gave her agreement.

The wind was gathering strength as Bahari's group set out once more over the Plains, combing through the sparse tufts of grass and whistling through the rocks. Shadows played across the ground as the white clouds chased before Ninmah's countenance.

The Thals pulled Juaan along in their wake, his blindfold firmly back in place. From her position at the head of the group, Nyri kept a close eye on his treatment as the group moved stoically behind their Cro leader, watchful of their surroundings as the land became ever-more rugged the closer they got to the birth of the foothills.

"Where you from?"

Nyri glanced up to see Bahari regarding her solemnly as she walked at his side. She was not finding it a challenge to keep pace with him and realised the Cro man had moderated the length of his strides to match hers, taking into account her smaller stature. No Cro had ever shown her such consideration before. With the Hunting Bear, it had always been keep up or die.

"From the forests to the south," she murmured. "The Hunting Bear named them the *shin'ar* forests."

Bahari tensed at her mention of Eldrax's clan. Nyri didn't have to stretch her imagination to understand why.

"What they like?" That overwhelming sense of childlike curiosity was back and Nyri felt a pang. It was almost like

114

walking alongside a larger version of Akito. For a moment, she let herself wonder how the wounded boy was before reminding herself that Bahari was awaiting an answer.

She shrugged. "Like nothing that exists out here." How could she describe the might and beauty of an *eshaara* tree, the song of the wind as it played through a sheltering canopy? How could she conjure for him an image of golden light dancing through the undergrowth and the rich smell of sap rising in the air? She closed her eyes against the moisture that threatened to turn into tears of loss.

"I'm sorry." Bahari reached out to touch her cheek. Nyri flinched away, caught unaware by such a physical display of empathy from a Cro. Bahari dropped his hand. "I mean no harm," he said. "You miss home?"

"Yes." The admission tore from Nyriaana's throat. "Every waking moment."

A wave of agonised pain had Nyri's head whipping around in alarm. *Juaan.* But he was unharmed, still walking along with his captor with no outward signs of distress. She frowned.

"Why you not go back?" Bahari brought her attention back to him. "You are free now. I free you from Jade Killer and followers."

Nyri blinked. Bahari thought he had freed her from imprisonment. In his mind, he had rescued her. The fact that she had not taken her freedom and fled into the distance to return to her People must have perplexed him deeply. Nyri shook her head, recalling other, less happy memories; those of slow decay, despair, hunger. "My home is dead," she whispered, more tears threatening in her eyes. Sefaan had thought she could save her tribe, made her promise.

115

She had betrayed the old Kamaali.

A sudden gust of wind battered against Nyri's body, exploiting the weaknesses in her coverings, making her shiver. Without a word, Bahari loosened the thick, brown fur that draped from his broad shoulders and cast it about Nyri's own. The end of the cloak dragged along the ground behind her, but Nyri was instantly warmed.

The wave of gratitude she felt towards their captor caught Nyri by surprise. Her experiences of the world beyond her birthplace had made Nyri hard and mistrustful, but despite her best efforts, she was finding it more and more difficult to dislike Bahari. He was unlike any Cro she had ever met. His was a soft presence of the kind that was slow to anger and quick to care.

She glanced about at his men. The Thals' treatment of Juaan upset her, but had their situation been reversed, would she have behaved any differently towards a hated enemy? An enemy who had killed her brethren and may do so again, given the opportunity? She already knew the answer to that. If she had not recognised Juaan when he had tumbled back into her life, if she had continued to believe him to be nothing more than a demon Wove, she would have left him to suffer a slow and painful death, starving at the bottom of the Pit.

Her People would kill any stranger not of their own kind on sight without question.

Nyri pulled the gifted cloak more securely about her shoulders, shamed. She was a stranger to Bahari, but a stranger who had caused no harm, and therefore, she was treated with care and respect. Was this a Thal custom? Nyri stole another glance at Juaan. Perhaps fighting the Thals for their freedom wasn't the answer. Fighting was a Cro solution. As Bahari had pointed out, the Thals weren't Cro. She felt she was beginning to see the full truth of that.

Perhaps if she could just make Bahari understand, gain enough of his trust to convince him that Juaan was not a threat, there was a chance he would let Juaan go peacefully. They had blindfolded him, concealing the location of their home from an enemy. Would they have bothered to do so if there wasn't some possibility that their Sag Du might let Juaan walk free? *But in what condition?* a small frightened voice whispered, recalling Bahari's allusion to removing Juaan's hands.

She *had* to convince Bahari of Juaan's innocence before they reached his leader. It might be her only hope.

"How...?" she hesitated, self-conscious as she considered her words. "Tell me, how did a Cro man end up leading a company of Thals?"

Bahari tensed, and Nyri instantly regretted speaking. After all, she had been harsh in refusing to share her own story with him just a couple of days before. The Cro man's grey eyes fixed upon the ground, his mouth turned down at the corners. Nyri feared she had offended him and dashed any hope of friendship in its infancy. But after a moment's pause, Bahari spoke.

"I was just a child when Hunting Bear came for clan. Man with hair that burned led them. My *ama* and *adda* made me run. Hide." Bahari lifted his gaze from the earth and Nyri's breath caught at the desolation on his face. "I no want to go, but I obeyed. I hid for whole day, waiting for *ama* to find me, but she never came. When I go back," Bahari shook his head. "*Etuti* burned. *Ama* and *adda* gone. All clan, gone.

117

Only dead remained."

Nyri took a breath, trying not to drown in the grief rolling from the Cro man as the memories played behind his eyes. "I'm sorry," she said. "I lost my home to Eldrax, too."

The lines of grief on Bahari's face hardened. "Red Bear take many things, ruin many lives."

"Yes."

In an absentminded motion, Bahari twisted Juaan's spear around in a skilful display. "I searched for family, but never find them. I survived scavenging kills. One day, hunger made me careless. I scavenged spitter kill. Spitter still hiding nearby." Bahari pushed aside the furs covering his right arm, exposing five long parallel scars along his bicep. "I was prepared to die. Then Thals found me. They chased away spitter and carried me back to their *etuti sagkal.*" At these words, Bahari crossed his wrists and held them over his head in what appeared to be a habitual gesture.

"They took you in? The child of an enemy?"

Bahari smiled. "Thal not Cro, Nyriaana. I do no wrong. Wise *azu* healed me and I adopted by great Sag Du." He swelled with pride. "I am his *magiri* defender."

"Sag Du?" Nyri tested the words. "Is that Thal speak for *Chief*?"

Bahari shrugged. "Close enough." Nyri felt him appraise her. "You ready to share your story now?"

Nyri wasn't. Despite her initial hatred having drained away, Bahari was still a stranger to her and the man holding her against her will. But if sharing her story could help gain his trust and Juaan his freedom, then she had to let him in, if only a little.

"How Dryad come to speak Cro and be in the company

of Jade Killer?" Bahari pressed.

"He's not a killer!" Nyri flared. Bahari recoiled and Nyri sucked in a breath, clawing back the pieces of her fragile temper. She needed him on her side. "Not anymore. Bahari, please—"

Bahari's arm shot out across her chest, blocking her advance as he came to a sudden halt, a hoot of warning leaving his lips. Alarmed, Nyri threw out her higher senses as he elbowed her back, taking up a defensive position.

Three presences lurked among the crags ahead. Nyri knew from their flavour that they were Thal. A string of hoots and whistles flowed over the air towards Bahari's band in a complex pattern.

Bahari relaxed, a grin splitting across his face. His arm dropped from Nyri's chest and he replied with another series of sounds before turning to her. "No fear, Nyriaana." Her name still sounded awkward on his lips. "My kin. Sag Du sent them to watch. We're late."

The newcomers broke cover and came loping over the remaining ground between Bahari's group and the beginnings of the foothills. They ground to a halt, several strides away as their dark eyes came to rest upon Nyri standing in Bahari's shadow. They stood so still in their astonishment, only the hairs on their loose-fitting garments stirred in the breeze.

"Dryad!" One found his voice at last, pointing a thick finger. He shot a stream of sounds that Nyri could not follow at the Cro man beside her, gesturing with his large hands. Nyri concentrated and picked up the flickering of images flowing through his mind.

Bahari responded, his tone eager as his hands swept

through the air. He ended by clapping a hand to his opposite arm. In his thoughts, Nyri could pick out the defined memories of her healing Juaan's injury.

"Bekar, Eron!" the newcomer exclaimed. Before Nyri could react, the three Thals surrounded her in a rush, touching, scenting, catching hold of her chin to study her face.

Nyri gave a low cry and tried to escape. The all-too-fresh memory of another heavy body pressing in on her sent panic shooting through her limbs. *You are mine now, witch... it is time for the Claim.* "Get away!" she cried, but they did not understand and continued to crowd her. She was drowning. "Get away, *please.*"

Then Bahari was there, gently restoring order to his brothers. "Ngathe," he said, then gestured with a fist against his chest before flicking his fingers open and shaking his hand. *Afraid,* the meaning radiated from his thoughts.

The three Thals stepped away, tipping their own hands in what appeared to be an apologetic gesture. Nyri took a half step behind Bahari as she fought to get her racing heart under control. Eldrax was far away. He could not harm her. But the ghost of his hands stroked over her quivering flesh. She almost wished she could tear her skin away. The symbolic ochre marks of a Claimed Cro female still curled over her body under her coverings. She could not see them, but they burned there.

Trying to quell the nausea roiling in her stomach, Nyri forced herself to pay attention to what was happening around her. The new Thals were now gesturing at Juaan and, this time their eyes were flat with hate. Nyri held a shaking hand over her knife, her heart leaping as one of the

Thals drew theirs.

"Alok nibiti," Bahari said, his tone firm. The newcomers grumbled unhappily, but touched their sloping foreheads in acceptance and the knife was re-sheathed. Gracing Juaan with one last murderous glower, they set off, leading the way back towards the crags of the rising hills.

Reassured that Juaan was in no immediate danger, Nyri shuffled along in Bahari's wake, folding herself down into the heavy cloak he had gifted her like a defensive skin.

"They meant no harm," Bahari said. "Forgive curiosity."

Nyri nodded but did not look up, not trusting herself to speak. Bahari seemed to sense her renewed reticence and left her be. Shame and hate seethed through her. Eldrax had haunted her life since she was a child. Now he had given her a whole new set of nightmares. Worse, for these reached out for her in the light of Ninmah. Inescapable. Her flesh crawled.

Nyri was almost grateful when the foothills rose around them. In her exhausted state, keeping her feet over the rough terrain demanded her full attention, banishing all else from her mind.

The Thal band picked their way unerringly through the twisting maze of pathways as the rocks rose higher on all sides. Nyri soon became hopelessly disorientated. Everything appeared the same to her eyes. She could not see Ninmah behind the walls of rock to give her a direction. Had they been going in circles, she would not have noticed.

She was reminded of her first trip through terrain such as this, a prisoner of the Cro, on her way to meet Eldrax. The memory made her breath grow short. Who was this Sag Du that awaited at the end of this stony journey? Of the two chiefs she had met since leaving her home, one had sentenced her to death by stoning, the other had tried to do much worse.

But before her bleak imagining of the Thal chief could gain in strength, a vibration against her senses drew Nyri's face forwards. A large group of individual presences lay ahead of them. A hum of voices followed, a shriek of laughter.

They had reached the Thal camp.

No, no, she needed more time. Nyri's step faltered and Bahari caught her by the arm. She glanced up at him in time to see his reassuring smile break into a joyous grin as he let loose a distinctive howl.

The voices quieted, then answering howls broke out, rising over the rock faces that separated them from Bahari's band.

"Come!" Bahari propelled Nyri along with him as he rushed forward, taking the last couple of turns in the path at a near sprint. Nyri twisted her wrist free as she stumbled into a large expanse of open ground walled between the maze of craggy rises. The mouths of several caves yawned from the surrounding stone faces, stocky Thal figures outlined on the thresholds. A blazing fire burned at the centre of the open space. The heat reached out to waft across Nyri's frozen cheeks.

"Nyriaana," Bahari announced. "Welcome to *etuti sagkal* of the Children of Eron."

"Bahari!" There was a rush as the Thal tribe converged on Bahari's returning band, a mass of red and black hair, pale faces and dark eyes. Most of the faces were female, with a couple of stockier male figures and smaller children mixed in. Hands reached out, touching the returning hunters in welcome.

Many of the Thals reacted to the sight of Nyri as their brethren had out on the Plains, and there were some outright exclamations of shock. Keeping close to Bahari to avoid curious hands, Nyri kept watch on Juaan as hisses of anger broke out around him. Juaan was keeping still, but Nyri could taste his apprehension. He was bound and blindfolded, surrounded by a People who would like nothing better than to spill his blood. Tension mounted as more and more of the Thals turned their attention from her to the former Hunting Bear warrior in their midst. One wrong move could trigger an attack. Nyri could not breathe.

Bahari thrust himself between the crowd and his prisoner, speaking in urgent tones to the nearest Thal man who had come to greet them. The man replied by gesturing towards one of the many paths leading out of this clearing of rock and into the surrounding hills. Bahari nodded his understanding before addressing Nyri.

"The great Sag Du gone to walk with the *genii*. He'll not return for another two rises of *gisnu*. We hold Jade Killer until then." The Cro man signalled to the Thal holding Juaan's rope, pointing towards the far end of the settlement. The Thal tugged Juaan in the direction indicated to the accompaniment of further hisses from the angry locals. Nyri started to follow, but Bahari caught her arm. "You stay with women as guest," he pointed to the largest cave. "More comfort. Get warm."

"No. I stay with him." Nyri ripped her arm free. She was not letting Juaan out of her sight. Her failure to free him thudded through her.

Bahari drew himself up, her continued attachment perplexing and disappointing him. He looked like he might argue, but the set of her jaw appeared to convince him he would not dissuade her. The Cro man sighed. "Go for now. I bring you warmer garments to fit."

Nyri inclined her head in thanks and followed after Juaan.

"Nyriaana." Bahari's voice pulled her back around. He was holding his hand out with an almost apologetic expression. "If go with him. Give knife."

Nyri hesitated. Her skinning knife was her only physical weapon, but she knew she would only be allowed to stay with Juaan if there was no risk of her trying anything foolish while Bahari's back was turned. Hissing through her teeth, she took out her knife and placed it in his hand.

The guard leading Juaan had reached the point Bahari had indicated. Nyri caught up just as the Thal gave a sharp whistle. Two other Thal males approached. Nyri blanched, already regretting sacrificing her weapon, but the other men simply hefted two great rocks, the muscles in their thick forearms popping from the effort, and set them atop the rope binding Juaan's wrists, tethering him to the earth. Their deep-set eyes flicked to Nyri several times. They appeared to want to speak, but she glared at them and any words they might have spoken died upon their lips. Instead, they paced a few strides away to take up guarding positions around their prisoner.

Nyri waited for a few moments until their attention was elsewhere and then gave an experimental tug on the end of Juaan's rope. A futile effort. The rocks were too heavy. Even a Cro would not match the feat of strength the Thals had just displayed. She dropped the rope in disgust before

124

reaching out to pull the blindfold and gag loose from Juaan's face.

This time, his eyes did not search for hers as he regained his vision. There was no sweet relief at the knowledge that they were still together. Instead, he surveyed the Thal settlement with the practiced attention of a hunter, taking in every detail, then cast his gaze to the ground.

"I promise I will get you free," Nyri murmured. "I won't let them hurt you."

He did not look up. "Why do you do this?" he asked, catching Nyri off guard with the rancour in his voice.

"Do what?" Nyri reached out for his hand behind his back. She had a moment to feel the frigidity of his skin before he curled his fingers away from her. "Juaan?" The sudden bitterness confused Nyri, but she did not have time to press the issue. Bahari was approaching. Several strides behind him was a black-haired Thal female bearing several small furs in her gnarled hands. Nyri couldn't help but notice that the female's own loose-fitting furs were adorned with a variety of objects. Thin strings looped about her neck and wrists, tinkling with intricately carved ivory and translucent green beads that appeared to be a type of stone.

"Here." Bahari motioned the Thal female forward. "These keep you warm in hills."

The female Thal stepped around the Cro man and placed the small furs next to Nyri. Nyri gave them a cursory study. Taking the cloak Bahari had gifted to her from around her shoulders, she handed it back to the Cro man. "What about him?" she asked, gesturing at Juaan.

Bahari's expression closed. It was akin to watching clouds pass before the face of Ninmah. "He remain tied until Sag

Du decide upon punishment."

"At least let me undo his bindings for a time," Nyri beseeched.

"No."

"Bahari, if the ropes aren't loosed he *will* lose his hands. By your words, his punishment is yet to be decided. I beg you. He is not so foolish as to fight your whole clan. Please."

"Ah, Eron, *vag nitu!*" It sounded like an expletive. Bahari gave a sharp whistle. Three Thal men armed with clubs and axes appeared at his side. He spoke to them rapidly. Grim-faced, they fanned out around Juaan, weapons poised above his head in a ready position.

"Wait!" Nyri panicked. "What are you doing?"

"*Shalanaki*, Nyriaana." Bahari motioned with his hand before kneeling down beside Juaan. Juaan did not react to him, still brooding into the ground. Nyri could taste Bahari's tension. He was mistaking Juaan's removed gaze for concentration, expecting his dangerous enemy to spring at any moment. Very slowly, he worked the knots loose and then unwound the ropes from Juaan's wrists. Juaan did not so much as twitch a finger, remaining rock still under the blades of his twitchy guards, but Nyri perceived a breath of relief leaving his body as the tight bindings fell away, releasing his taut shoulders.

She was at Juaan's side as soon as Bahari stepped back a pace, motioning for the guards to do the same. Lifting his nearest hand in hers, Nyri massaged the skin of Juaan's forearm, her fingers travelling over the depressions the tight bindings had left as she helped the blood flow back into his fingers. She spared a small amount of concentration to ease the jabbing discomfort she knew Juaan must be feeling. A frown twitched across his brow. He was aware of what she was doing.

"Juaan, look at me," she pleaded. "I promise I won't let anything happen to you."

"That is for the Sag Du to decide," he responded. "And I do not doubt he will possess better judgment than you. He will not so easily forgive my sins."

"Stop it!" Nyri gave his arm a shake. "You are not Khalvir anymore. You are Juaan."

"Nyri," Juaan brought his gaze from the ground to stare her full in the face, "they are one and the same. These hands," he lifted them before her, "Juaan or Khalvir, these hands are bathed in the blood. They tore you away from your home. I took everything from you and made you into this. Please, do not give me your pity, for it only makes it worse to bear."

Nyri rocked back. "Is that what your problem is?"

"What more could there possibly be?"

"You're not angry with me?"

"Why would I be angry with you, Nyriaana?"

Nyri swallowed, the words coming out in a rush. "For breaking my word. For revealing my skills to Eldrax and forcing you to have to…" she broke off, trying to block the memory of Eldrax's weapon erupting through Juaan's body. "For forcing you to leave your clan and most likely die running." Nyri dropped her gaze as her own shame rose to choke her. "That's my fault. I should have been more careful. I shouldn't have trusted—"

Cool fingers caught hold of her chin, forcing her face up. "Nyriaana." Her breath caught as she looked into his eyes, his breath brushing past her cheek. "The Hunting Bear was never my clan. I would do it all again in a heartbeat. Seeing you safe and free from that monster is all that mattered to me. For my sake, do not burden yourself with guilt over whatever happens now. I sealed my own fate here long ago, Nyriaana. You are blameless."

"Juaan." Nyri tried to catch hold of his hand, but the three Thal guards had returned. They pushed Nyri back as they worked to rebind Juaan's wrists.

"Not so tight, please!"

"Nyriaana," Bahari's voice pulled her around. "Yini will take you now."

Nyri eyed the dark-haired Thal woman. "Where?"

"To cave with the women. You rest there for the dark time. Warm and safe, befitting a guest of the Spitter *Imrua*."

"No," Nyri shook her head. "I told you, I'm staying here."

Bahari sighed. "I give word no harm come to Jade Killer while you are gone."

"And why should I trust you?" Nyri challenged, her upset choking her as Yini came forward to take a gentle hold of her arm. Nyri shook her off, drawing an offended glare.

"Nyri, go." Juaan's voice came from behind her.

"No." She turned on him.

"Go. I will be alright here." A ghost of a reassuring smile traced across his lips.

"But—"

"A Thal's word is sacred to him. I will be safe for the time being. Go."

Nyri was about to point out Bahari was not a Thal, but Yini had taken hold of her arm again and there was no arguing with her grip this time.

"Go," Juaan whispered, then his eyes fixed on a point over her head and hardened into flint. "Take care of her."

Bahari responded with a derisive snort as he and the Thal woman led Nyri from Juaan's side. Nyri barely noticed where she was going. Despite her burgeoning confidence in Bahari, it frightened her to let Juaan out of her sight. She had trusted someone once, and that had almost cost Juaan his life. She would not be so trusting again. Juaan's eyes followed her and it did not help to see the reassuring expression had faded to be replaced by one of pain.

Tutting, Yini propelled Nyri towards a cave on the far side of the settlement. As they neared, a fierce hissing broke out. The sound was originating from several sources concealed within the shadows of the cave. Bahari halted abruptly and Nyri pulled back against Yini's guiding hold, seeking the Cro man's gaze.

Yini clucked her tongue and tugged on her arm as Bahari waved her forward. "No fear. Go."

Nyri gritted her teeth, wishing more than ever that she had not given up her knife as the black-haired Thal dragged her into the darkness.

8

Children of Eron

Nyri's higher senses swept out as her eyes were momentarily robbed of sight, preparing for the attack. None came. The hostile hisses melted away to be replaced by an excited babble that echoed off the rock walls. Four female presences converged on her and Yini as soon as they crossed the threshold. Nyri could see herself in their minds, a strange and other worldly being; a make-believe creature walking out of an elder's tale. Had the circumstances been different, she would have found their reaction amusing.

Then they were on her; hands brushed at her hair, pulled on her clothes, faces pressed in close to take a deep sniff.

The same panic she had experienced out on the Plains sluiced over her. "No!" Nyri twisted loose of Yini's grip, slapping away their advances as she fought to free herself of the pressing crowd of heavy bodies.

Shock rippled through the women. They parted, and Nyri fell to the hard ground, gasping. Hyper-aware of every thought and emotional vibration, Nyri again saw herself reflected in the Thals' minds. This time, she saw a very real and frightened girl with wide indigo eyes staring out of a pale and tormented face.

Pity cooled the tense vibration of indignation and hurt. Yini shooed her fellow women back a step, then held her hands up, palms outward, in a gesture to be recognised across all Peoples: *Peace. I will not harm you.*

From her position on the ground, Nyri scrambled away until her back was against one of the rock walls, watchful and shivering from a combination of the sudden panic and the cold stone she rested against. Yini's keen, deep-set eyes missed nothing. The dark-haired Thal woman gestured to her fellows, holding up her hands and wiggling her fingers while uttering the sound *is'nu.*

The women dispersed, only to return to the centre of the cave moments later, burly arms loaded with wood and fistfuls of dry grass. Sure hands piled the grass and arranged the sticks over the top, with twigs at the bottom moving to increasingly sizeable limbs above; all twisting around in a formation that came to a peak in the middle.

Once the work was done, Yini produced two pieces of flint, striking them together until a spark caught the kindling and the whole construction began to glow.

"*Is'nu,*" she said again, lifting her hands and wiggling her fingers at Nyri.

Fire.

The Thal woman then dragged a pile of furs over and placed them at Nyri's side, arranging them into what was obviously a nest for her to rest upon.

"Uh, thank you," Nyri muttered.

To her surprise, Yini flinched and drew back. Nyri

assessed her tone. Had she spoken too sharply? She hadn't believed she had. Then her mind caught up, and she understood the problem at once. She had spoken in the Cro tongue. The voice of this woman's most feared enemy. Nyri closed her mouth. She did not know the sounds to make to show gratitude to a Thal; it was wiser to keep silent.

Yini and her fellow women left her alone, then. They went back to their tasks in the cave, all sitting on piles of furs while they stripped, carved, knapped, and wove pieces of sinew together to make rope.

Though they did their best to ignore her, Nyri could still feel their smouldering curiosity. Deep-set, glittering eyes stole glances at her at any given opportunity. Nyri avoided eye contact and, despite their fascination, not one of them demanded anything of her. They had realised her fear and were allowing her space.

Nyri recalled the day Juaan had handed her over to Halima upon arriving at the Hunting Bear camp. The Cro matriarch had shown no mercy, brusquely, even savagely inaugurating Kyaati and herself into their new lives. Nyri had hated her for it at first, but had come to understand that Halima cared deeply for the women in her charge; her harsh manner was a way of preparing and hardening them for the unforgiving paths they needed to travel. As with everything with the Cro, it was adapt or die.

Nyri shifted herself into the nest of furs Yini had gifted her. The soft surface welcomed her aching bones and Nyri let out a groan. Even though the fire was in its infancy and its heat had yet to reach Nyri where she huddled against the wall, the climate of the cave was still noticeably warmer than the world outside. The rocks, crouching over her head and cradling her sides, blocked the cruel winds that were a constant companion out on the Plains.

She would have welcomed the comfort had it not made her exhaustion harder to battle. More than once, Nyri caught her eyelids drooping, lulled by the softness of her resting place and the murmur of the women's voices around her. But she could not let herself rest. Juaan was still out there and in danger. One part of her mind kept a constant watch over him.

A wave of helplessness threatened to crush Nyri under its weight. They were now right in the belly of the Thal camp. Bahari had said the Thal Sag Du was due to arrive back in the camp within two rises of Ninmah. She had failed to free Juaan out on the Plains surrounded by only a handful of Thals. How could she hope to free him now and escape from under the watch of an entire clan?

Nyri buried her face in her hands and scrubbed at her tired eyes. She had not had time to gain Bahari's trust. She did not know if she would see the Cro man again. He had no doubt returned to the Plains on another hunting trip. After all, thanks to their encounter, his group had returned empty-handed.

"Dryad."

Nyri's head snapped up.

Yini was standing several strides away next to the now roaring fire. "*Ikul?*"

Nyri cocked her head, probing the Thal's mind for a meaning. The sound brought with it a sense of recognisable need, pleasure and satisfaction. *Eat. Food.* Something was cooking over the fire. Nyri did not recognise the smell, and it was not inviting.

Nevertheless, Nyri's forgotten stomach ached. She had not eaten since the night before. "Please." She spoke using her mother tongue. The sound of the word made her heart ache for an earlier time in her life. The Thal women would not understand her meaning, but Nyri did not wish to cause further offence or fear by using Cro speak.

Yini must have heard the plea in her tone, for she turned back to the fire, blocking Nyri's view of it. She worked for a moment before approaching Nyri again. In one hand, she held forth a steaming piece of flesh wrapped in leather, which she placed close to Nyri, before taking a step back again.

Nyri unwrapped the offering. Inside lay a strange piece of pale, pinkish white meat, ribbed in a way Nyri had never seen before. She gave Yini a questioning glance.

Yini grinned and put her hand out, blade-like, then swished it back and forth. "Kua."

Nyri shrugged, not caring enough to probe, and broke off a piece of the strange meat. It was soft and flaky. Placing it in her mouth, she took a tentative chew. "Ugh!" It was without question the worst thing Nyri had ever tasted.

Yini snickered and popped her own portion into her mouth. As she did, she made an exaggerated expression of revulsion. It seemed the meat was not to her liking, either. A reluctant answering smile tugged on Nyri's lips before she returned her attention to her meal. If this was all that was being offered, she would have to take it. Thoughts clouded by hunger would not help her now. Nyri wolfed the meat down as fast as possible.

Her eyes strayed to the cave entrance. Juaan would be hungry. Nyri ached to take him some nourishment, but she did not know how to ask. She eyed the fire, then shook away the idea of trying to take a portion of whatever was cooking herself. The Thal women had been welcoming thus far, but Nyri doubted they would take kindly to a stranger helping herself to their food without invitation, and she was almost certain any attempt to leave the cave would be questioned or outright blocked.

Time slipped like water through her fingers as she sat helpless in the dark, fighting to remain alert. More than once, she dug her fingernails into her palms to ward off the sleep that wanted to steal over her. She had to keep watch. Nyri occupied herself watching the Thal women work, noting the differences in technique compared to what she had been taught by Halima until the light waned and Ninmah's sleepy light glowed off the rock faces outside. This night marked the third since Nyri had last slept.

One of the Thal women, this one with bright red hair that reminded Nyri uncomfortably of Eldrax, rose to refuel the fire. A fresh wave of heat rolled out to sting Nyri's sore eyes, but the flames banished the growing night chill wafting in from the cave mouth, enveloping her in a cocoon of warmth. It was too much. The wood crackled, and the women sang softly. Nyri lost the battle against her exhaustion. Her eyes drifted closed. She would rest them for a moment.

Only for a moment.

Nyriaana...

The voice yanked Nyri back to full consciousness. She leaped into a sitting position, automatically reaching for her knife. But of course it was gone. Her eyes darted around the cave, searching for the one who had called her. Yini and her fellow Thal women were slumbering around the fire upon piles of furs. Outside the cave, the sky was a purplish colour. The angle of light was wrong for a day's end. With a thud, Nyriaana realised she had slept through the entire night. Dawn was at hand. She cursed and threw out her senses for Juaan, panicking. If anything had happened... She let out a breath when she found he was still where she had left him, his mind hazing as he dozed.

The fire blazed in the centre of the cave. One of the women must have tended to it recently, for the flames were now burning brighter than ever. Nyri fell back onto her elbows, lolling her head back as she blinked up at the rocks overhead... and gasped.

The walls of the cave were not blank, featureless rock. Carvings were etched into every surface. Creatures painted in red and golden ocher pranced in vast herds over hollows and rises of the grey plains. Everywhere Nyri looked, stories were unfolding. People travelled, hunted, celebrated. She realised she was witnessing whole lives unfolding before her, every triumph and every sorrow. Here and there, a battle was fought, won, or lost. At the end of one such scene, she caught a glimpse of what looked like a red-haired woman being chased away from the rest with rocks. A pall of collective sorrow hung over that image, and next to it, figures huddled together in grief. Others had thrown themselves upon their knees, arms flung above their heads as though seeking forgiveness from some higher power.

Nyri's gaze continued to travel up, her breath catching when her eyes came to rest upon the pinnacle of the cave roof. There, hovering among the carved pinpricks of Ninsiku's captured souls, were drawn three glowing discs with bright light arrayed around them.

Nyriaana.

The silent call brought Nyri's attention around to the entrance of the cave.

Nyriaana... The voice beckoned, seductive and wholly irresistible. Lost in the magic of the images and the clinging haze of sleep, Nyri obeyed. Rising to her feet, she winced at the stiffness of her muscles, and padded to the cave entrance. The world beyond was still in the pre-dawn. Ninsiku's silver eye had fallen below the hills, but his captured spirits twinkled overhead in the same pattern as they had been drawn within the cave. All that was missing were the three shining discs. Nyri felt a strange pang at their absence.

Nyriaana, come... The voice echoed again, more powerful than ever before.

Yes. Why had she fought so long against it?

Nyri could not see the Mountains, caught as she was within this circle of looming rock faces and harsh hills, but she knew instinctively which direction to take. The Great Spirit would not see her lost. A pathway twisting between two boulders on the far side of the Thal settlement would take her where she needed to go. A smile twitched across her lips as she set off.

"Nyriaana!"

Was that Juaan's voice calling her? It was too distant to tell, drowned out as it was by the much louder voice in her head. Nyri increased her pace, almost breaking into a jog. It felt good to give in to the call at last. She felt light, free. She was on her way at last…

"Nyriaana?" A hand caught her arm, dragging her back.

Nyri cried out and rounded on the one who had dared to

stop her with a snarl on her lips. Startled grey eyes stared down at her, shattering the spell she had fallen under.

"Bahari?" Her breath curled in the air as she panted, casting around her. How had she got out here? Hadn't she just been inside the cave? "You're still here."

"Nyriaana, you well?"

"I, y-yes. Forgive me, you startled me."

Bahari's face became reproachful, even a little hurt. "You leaving? Not a good idea to leave in dark time. Wild spitters roam the hills looking to pick off weak."

"I wasn't leaving," Nyriaana blurted, still confused and not a little bit frightened by what had just happened. "I couldn't sleep. I thought I'd explore a little."

Bahari relaxed, easily dissuaded. "I'd be honoured to guide you and keep safe," he said.

"Aren't you sleeping?"

Bahari curled a fist and shook it briskly back and forth in front of him. *No.* "Guarding this dark time."

"Oh."

Nyri noticed that he now sported similar decorations to the ones she had seen on Yini, except his were heavier, less delicate. The claws of a bird of prey swung from a thin rope around his neck in an elaborate design. Black feathers erupted from the shoulders of a new cloak and also from the back of his head at the point where his dark, waving hair was tied back from his face. Nyri blinked. She had to admit; he made an impressive sight.

Bahari offered her his arm. Nyri hesitated for one beat, then took it, letting his solid presence ground her and banish the last vestiges of the spell's control. Nyri shivered, glancing once at the path it had been trying to lead her along.

"That way leads to Mountains." Bahari had followed her gaze.

"I know," Nyri whispered.

"You pale, Nyriaana," the Cro man spoke, his voice laden with concern. "You want to return to cave? Rest?"

"No," Nyri said, then more firmly. "No." This was exactly the opportunity she feared she had lost. Time with Bahari. Her eyes sought Juaan across the camp. He was awake, his expression enigmatic, as he watched her standing close beside Bahari. There were no fresh injuries upon him. The Thals appeared to be keeping their word that no harm would befall their prisoner until their Sag Du passed his judgement. After that... Nyri tightened her grip on Bahari's forearm.

She went along willingly as the Cro man set off around the Thal camp, pointing out the different caves and dwellings as they walked, informing Nyri of who lived within and their purpose in the clan, or the *imrua* as Bahari named it; *family*.

"There were drawings in Yini's cave," Nyri interrupted his latest telling of Thal life. "Are the stories they tell true?"

"True happenings to *imrua*, yes," Bahari said.

There were many questions Nyri wanted to ask, but one image above all haunted her mind. "At the top of the cave, there were," she paused, raised a finger, and drew the approximate shape of the discs she had seen etched into the rock, "flying through the sky like birds. What are they?"

Bahari blinked and halted, giving her his full attention. "They part of our first stories. The burning seed pods from Sky Path that burst forth and birthed Eron and his brothers. They make Thal People. We first of the Sky God People." Bahari's chest swelled proudly.

Nyri frowned, trying to make sense of this new story. Giant flying seed pods? Were these Sky Gods the same ones as in the Cro stories? Eron was a new name that did not match any she had heard in her own stories or those of the Cro.

Bahari continued to talk to her as Ninmah crept higher above the foothills and the *imrua* began to wake. The Cro man introducing her to the Thals he had grown from childhood with. His most trusted brothers. They treated her graciously and Nyri found herself relaxing. Bahari's spirit was free and easy, not hesitating to share anything with her.

"Oh!" A movement caught her eye. A woman was aiding an older male out from the darkness of a nearby cave. It was clear that the man was sick, brought low by the ulcerated wounds littering his bare chest and upper left arm. The arm was mangled, clearly the result of a heavy impact.

Bahari followed Nyri's gaze, and his broad lips pulled down. "Enuk injured hunting ox," he explained. "Hunting dangerous. Nothing more wise *azu* healer can do for him. "

"Huh." Nothing a Thal or Cro healer could do, perhaps. Nyri's heart leaped as an idea struck. She might have just found the surest way to put Bahari in her debt. Nyri broke away from the Cro man and swept over to the old Thal male, studying the wounds as the elder and his female escort eyed her in wary confusion. "Can you ask him to sit for me?" Nyri asked when Bahari caught up to her.

"You can heal him?" The Cro man's brows shot towards his hairline. "These not fresh wounds."

Nyri grinned up at him. "Please tell him to hold still for me."

A light kindled in Bahari's eyes as he spoke to the old man and the woman, who was clearly his daughter. Hope lifted their wary expressions as Bahari explained to them, speaking excitedly.

Under Bahari's direction, the daughter laid furs on the ground and helped her father lie down upon them. Nyri winced, detecting the excruciating pain that flared with every motion. Waving the daughter away, she settled at the elder's side and placed her hands against his chest. Extending her energy, she familiarised herself with the inner workings of the Thal's body. She gritted her teeth. It seemed a Thal was even more blind to the energies of KI than a Cro. This would not be easy, but not impossible.

First things first. She turned her attention to the man's twisted forearm. The bones had not healed straight.

"We need to re-break this arm," she said, letting herself rise out of her focus for a moment to speak to Bahari. "Here."

"Nyriaana?" Bahari's voice was doubtful.

"Just do it, Bahari," she said. "Do not worry. I will not let him hurt."

Bahari gave some reluctant orders and a male Thal came forward with a raised rock. The injured elder balked under Nyri's hands, but with a flick of concentration, she rendered him senseless.

"Tell her he's only asleep!" Nyri blurted, as the daughter darted forward with a cry on her lips, alarmed by her father's seemingly lifeless body.

Bahari blocked the woman. "Uhu! Uhu!"

"I needed him still. Re-break the arm."

Nyri kept the pain pathways in the man's shoulder tightly pinched in her mind's eye, as the hulking Thal man brought the rock down upon the elder's twisted forearm, cracking the bone in the exact place Nyri had indicated.

"Now find as straight a branch as you can find," she said.

Bahari cast about, then grabbed the nearest spear from a fellow Thal's hand and snapped it in two, handing the lower half to Nyri.

"Perfect," she said. "Take his wrist, pull the arm straight."

He did as she asked. The Cro man pulled on the elder's arm with all his strength until Nyri could feel the bones align in the correct position.

"Bind it tightly to the spear. I will do the rest." And then she was gone again, calling the power of the Great Spirit to her and channelling it into the elder's body. Nyri lost herself in the familiar rhythm, throwing every bit of concentration she possessed into knitting the freshly aligned bones together. Once they were set and no longer causing internal harm, she turned her attention to the abused flesh, purging the curses that had prevented the old wounds from healing.

She was dimly aware of gasps and the hoots of shock and amazement coming from all around her as the elder's tormented skin sealed before their eyes, but she ignored the distraction with practiced ease.

And then it was done. Nyri released the Great Spirit before laying a hand on the elder's temples and raised him from his sleep. The Thal sucked in a breath, his eyes opening wide under his grizzled brow. He sat upright, staring at his arm.

"*Adda!*" His daughter rushed forward, prepared to help her father from the ground, but the elder waved her away and rose to his feet with the ease of a young man before the awe-struck *imrua.* The debilitating pain he had lived with for many passing of the seasons was gone. Nyri smiled in tired satisfaction as the elder swept his weeping daughter into his arms as his own tears fell. "He will need to keep the spear tied to his arm for three more passes of Ninmah until the bones return to full strength."

Bahari's eyes bugged. "Three dawns?"

Nyri chuckled at his disbelief. "Yes."

"A miracle," Bahari muttered again.

He did not have time to speak again as the Thal group pressed in around Nyri. Breathing deep against the panic, Nyri held her ground as they all tried to touch her at once, pressing their foreheads to her hands in reverence.

The last to approach her was the elder's daughter. In her hands she bore a loop of the carved green stones. "Ningba?" she said timidly, holding the loop out to Nyri. "Ningba?"

"She wishes to give a gift," Bahari translated.

"Oh," A jolt of surprise went through Nyri's chest and she swallowed. Never had she received a gift for healing before. Bowing her head appeared to be the most appropriate action and, as she did so, the Thal woman slipped the loop of stones around Nyri's neck to rest against the *enu* seed that already dangled there. "Thank you," she whispered.

"Jade stone most valued," Bahari said as Nyri ran her fingers over the water-smooth stones.

"They're beautiful," she murmured.

"Like you," Bahari said.

Nyri flushed as she looked up into his face. The corners of Bahari's eyes crinkled boyishly as he smiled down at her. Nyri smiled back. She couldn't help it.

The rest of the day passed quickly after that. After bearing witness to her skill, Nyri could not turn without meeting the pleading eyes of a Thal as they brought their sick and wounded before her in the hopes of another miracle. No matter how superficial the injury, they sought her out, bowing and holding gifts before them as they approached the *dryad*. Tired as she was, Nyri healed even the most minor of scrapes gladly.

As the day waned, Nyri discovered to her surprise that she was no longer instinctively watching her back. The peaceful aura that permeated through the *imrua* soothed her senses. In less than a one cycle of Ninmah, she felt more at ease among the Thals than she ever had among the Cro. This was a generous and caring People, like no other Nyri had yet known. Ninmah waned towards the west, and Nyri could hardly move for the bracelets and necklaces adorning her neck and wrists, while rich feathers waved in her hair.

A smile played across her face as she ran her fingers over one intricate carving, then her eyes lighted upon Juaan, and she was brought sharply back to reality. She could not forget the main reason for striving to gain the Thals' trust. Throughout the day, Juaan had remained bound to the rock. His expression had remained unreadable as he followed her movements around the camp, though at times he appeared to be deep in thought, his eyes speculative as he watched her interactions with the Thals. She wondered if it was safe yet to ask Bahari for his freedom.

Ninmah sank below the protective rock walls and the Thals' thoughts turned to food and rest. One by one, they drifted away towards their dwellings, leaving her alone with Bahari. Nyri shifted uncomfortably, deliberating. The timing of her request needed to be right, but she was painfully aware that the Sag Du was soon to return. She may not have the luxury of waiting for the perfect moment.

"Bahari," she began, her mouth dry.

"Come with me, show you something" he interrupted her, beckoning Nyri towards a path that led out of the encampment and into the surrounding hills. The Cro man wanted her to leave the camp with him. Nyri shot a glance at Juaan. There was a tension about his shoulders that had not been there before as his eyes went between them. The rope pinned down by the rocks was now pulled taut. It was clear he did not want her to leave his sight alone with Bahari. One of the Thal guards was eyeing their captive, his hand tightening on his stone axe.

I'm safe, Nyri sent the thought to him, unsure if he would hear her or not, but needing him to be still all the same. She could not have him jeopardise all her efforts by resisting the Thals now. To her relief, he must have sensed something in the air, for the tension on the rope eased. *I'm safe.*

Nyri hoped she wasn't lying to him. Bahari had slipped beneath her defences. She couldn't deny it any longer. She had grown fond of this young Cro. No ill will lurked beneath the surface of his spirit, only the hope for friendship. But the same had been true of Selima. The memory of her former friend had Nyri hesitating as Bahari set off towards the trail. But if she was to make her plea for Juaan's freedom, she really had no choice but to accompany the Cro man. She would not get another opportunity. Balling her fists, Nyri set off after him.

"I thank you for today, Nyriaana," Bahari said as she caught up. He pointed to the dark line of the vast Mountains in the distance. "You give my People hope. Hope they not had for many passes of life. Sky Gods leave us long ago. Gone to live in Mountains inside mighty *Ekur,* where no man can tread. But maybe Eron not ignoring if he sent you to us. Send us a sign."

Nyri hummed a wordless acknowledgment as the path they followed climbed higher into the surrounding hills. If he wanted to believe some Thal deity had sent her to them, she would not argue. Such a belief could only help her cause.

The route Bahari chose took them on a well-worn circular path around the encampment below. Nyri paid close attention to him as he pointed out branching trails, informing her which paths led back to the Plains and which ones led deeper into the foothills and eventually met the Mountains.

A clear patch of ground overlooking the settlement opened up before them and Bahari folded himself down, beckoning for Nyri to sit beside him. Leaving an arm's length of space between them, she perched herself upon a rock, her new adornments jingling softly together as she moved.

"Look." Bahari threw his arms out before him.

Nyri gasped. Ninmah was setting in a blaze of glory over the peaks and valleys of the foothills, lighting the stark landscape with golden flames. Bahari smiled at her reaction and for a handful of heartbeats, they sat in companionable silence, watching as Ninmah descended, drawing with her a cloak of many colours.

Nyriaana. Nyri turned. From this higher vantage point, the Mountains appeared closer than ever, their dark outlines stark and everlasting against the array of Ninsiku's waking spirits. Their draw sucked at her mind, pulling at her, sucking her under. *Come...*

Nyri began to rise.

"You never told me your story," Bahari's voice broke into her thoughts, shattering the spell.

"Wh-what?"

"You never told me how you ended up prisoner of Cro. Why do you care so much for Jade Killer?" The Cro man jabbed a finger down towards the point where Juaan was tied.

"He's not a killer!" she snapped as she had before. She had to alter this perception of Bahari's now, or all hope was lost. "He is my dearest friend." Such words did not begin to define what Juaan was to her, but she could find no better way to explain. Bahari rocked back. Nyri glowered. "Don't look at me like that. You do not know him."

"He is the Red Bear's spearhead," Bahari said flatly. "He killed many. Many women know sorrow because of Jade Killer."

"It wasn't his fault," Nyri argued. "It was Eldrax, it was all Eldrax. He is the monster. Juaan saved me!"

"Saved you?" A frown pinched his dark brows together in confusion. "Why?"

Nyri composed herself with an effort. Where did she even start? "Juaan is like you," she said, suddenly realising the truth of that. "No, please listen. He was not born to the People who raised him, except he was not blessed with being found by the Thals. Juaan's mother was a Ninkuraa." Nyri pointed to herself to make her meaning clear.

"Dryad?"

"Yes, dryad," Nyri shrugged. "She was captured by Cro and lived among them. When the Cro clan was destroyed, she returned to our People with Juaan as a baby."

"Cro committed the Forbidden upon her?" Bahari spat away into the rocks.

"Yes," Nyri bit out. "Juaan was first raised as a... dryad."

"That how you know him?"

Nyri dipped her chin. "When my parents perished in a Cro raid, Juaan and I were... everything to each other. Then Eldrax came. He burned my home. Juaan sacrificed himself so that I could escape. I thought him dead. His loss almost broke me, Bahari.

"But then the Great Spirit of KI sent me a miracle. Juaan returned. The Cro kept him alive, raised him to fight. Eldrax sent him to raid my home."

"*He* betrayed you to Red Bear?"

"No! He did not mean to. He did not know who he was. He did not know who I was." The words tumbled out as Bahari lifted his eyes to the heavens. "Eldrax wounded him as a boy. He lost his memories, and Eldrax twisted his mind with lies and hate. The man who took me from my home, the Jade Killer who you claim has stolen so many lives, was not Juaan. Not really."

Bahari snorted softly. "And... he remember now?"

"Yes. The Red Bear tried to Claim me as his. Juaan fought him."

"He beat Red Bear?" Nyri heard a note of disbelief in Bahari's voice.

"No," she said. "Juaan has almost lost his life to the Red Bear twice now because of me. He is not your Jade Killer. He is as much a victim of Eldrax as you or I. I don't think anyone has suffered more. You are wrong to cause him more pain. Without him, I would have died as a child. Without him, I would be dead by Eldrax's hand, and I would not be here now."

Bahari stared down into the camp below, his expression unreadable in the faint light of the camp fires.

"Please, Bahari. I know I am almost a stranger to you and you have no reason to believe me, but you must grant me this one gift. That man down there is not your enemy. Please let him go."

Bahari was silent for a long moment. "I'm sorry, Nyriaana. I cannot, I am not leader. He must face Sag Du."

Nyri buried her face in her hands as a sob shuddered through her. Her last hope dashed. Bahari's distress and sense of helplessness in the face of her despair radiated between them. "But I will honour you by speaking your story," he promised, gripping her shoulder. "Sag Du anger for Jade Killer is strong, Nyriaana, but I do my best for you if not for him."

"I understand," Nyri said, lifting her head. "But you must understand, I will do everything in my power to protect him. I owe him my life."

Bahari's mouth turned down at the corners in the face of her vow. "Let get back," he said. "You are tired, need rest."

"Will your Sag Du return at dawn?"

Bahari tilted a hand. "The path of the *genii* is unpredictable."

Nyri rose to her feet and set off along the trail that would lead back down to the Thal settlement, her limbs heavy with defeat. Bahari followed silently in her wake.

When they reentered the camp, the main area was all but deserted. The Thals were settled within their dwellings, caves, and hide shelters alike. Fires burned to keep the cold and predators at bay.

A sudden threatening hiss made Nyri start. It was the same noise Yini and her companions had made on the previous night when she had first approached their cave. It was out of place against the peaceful atmosphere of the camp. Nyri cast around for the source and her eyes finally lighted on a pair of women peering out of the shelter she was passing. Nyri quickly ascertained that their attention was not directed at her, but at Bahari. Nyri frowned. Bahari appeared oblivious. When several other women made the same noise, Nyri could no longer resist asking: "Why are they hissing at you?"

Bahari blinked and glanced over at the nearest female standing in the entranceway to her home, as though only just noticing her. "Oh. Women warn me away from their *etuti.*"

"*Etuti?*" She had heard this word several times now.

Bahari pitched his hands together in a sheltering motion, his brow pinching as he struggled to find the Cro word. "Home. I Sag Du's adopted son, honoured, but I not Thal man. Women must make clear they reject one like me. Cannot risk suspicion of committing Forbidden."

"Ah," Nyri jerked her head once in understanding. "I see." The Thals were as fearful of insulting their Sky Gods as her own People had been, which begged another question. "What about the children?"

Bahari tilted his head.

"I mean, are the children of the tribe healthy?" This group of Thals was not large, and all had a familial similarity about their features.

"Yes," Bahari responded slowly as he pondered the direction of her words. "But not many. Not many born now. A sorrow for mated pairs and worry for *imrua*."

"Why do you think that is?" Nyri already knew what the answer would be. She had already heard it so many times before.

"Sickness spread when Cro came. *Nabu* elders believe curse by Eron. Cro commit Forbidden with us. Not permitted by Sky Gods. We suffer for Cro sin."

Nyri huffed. She would not counter his thoughts with the Cro beliefs. Her own doubts still gnawed inside her soul between right and wrong, the beliefs ingrained at her core and the realities she had witnessed.

Juaan was awake and waiting for her as she came back into sight. His neutral expression did not waver but his relief washed over the air.

"Can I go to him?" Nyri asked.

Bahari pressed his lips together reluctantly, but turned and disappeared into the nearest shelter. He returned moments later with a couple of small pieces of the same meat Nyri had been given the night before.

"Thank you," Nyri said as she accepted the offerings. Bahari did not accompany her as she made her way towards Juaan. He must have signalled the three guards, however, for they let her pass without question.

"I brought you something," Nyri said as she sank down next to Juaan. She held up the pieces of flesh for him to see. "I do not know what it is. But it's awful."

"Fish!" Juaan's brows rose. "Where…?" he cut himself off with a stiff shrug, as though deciding he didn't care enough to ask.

Nyri held the first morsel up to his lips for him to take.

He chewed, the frown that had become a permanent fixture on his face marring his brow.

"The Thal Sag Du will return by morning," Nyri murmured. "I'm sorry, Juaan, I have failed you. I tried to make Bahari see, but he cannot go against his leader. If you have seen a way to get out of here, tell me now."

Juaan swallowed the last of the food she had brought, but did not answer. The pensive expression that she had spied throughout the day was present again. "Nyri... how do you feel about these Thals?"

"I-I don't know." The question threw her.

He waited.

"They're a good People," she stammered, "peaceful. Not what I expected. Why?"

"I think you should stay."

Nyri drew back. "Juaan—"

"No, listen to me. Eldrax will not be looking for you here. If he expects you to go anywhere, it will be home. The adopted Cro likes you, you have proven what you can do for his People. He will persuade the Sag Du to take you in, if that is your wish. With your skill, he will not refuse. You've seen firsthand the results of their hunting methods. You give them the advantage Eldrax has sought all his life. And they, in turn, will shelter and protect you. Here is a People who will not war over you or violate you. It goes against their deepest beliefs. This," his eyes roved around the camp, "is the best haven I could ever have hoped to find for you."

"But what if it is not the haven I want?" Nyri said. "Why should you decide what is best for me?"

"Nyri..."

"No!"

152

"Sag Du!" The cry of a sentinel cut short their debate. "Sag Du!"

Nyri's head whipped around, her heart in her throat. The camp was suddenly alive with movement. Forgetting all ideas of sleep, the Thals rushed towards a point on the far side of the camp. "Sag Du!" They called in greeting.

No. She had thought they had at least until dawn. She caught hold of Juaan's rope and tugged with all her might, but it would not budge. Panting, Nyri spun and crouched before Juaan, readying herself to do what she must.

At first, she could see nothing beyond the press of adoring bodies, but then the Thal Sag Du came into sight, bathed in the light of the campfires.

He broke through the crowd like an island in water. Rich furs adorned the broad shoulders, arrayed with black feathers which enhanced the Thal leader's stature. Greying black hair crowned a broad and powerful face, lined with age. But the sagging skin did not take away from his majestic presence, rather, it gave the Sag Du an air of hard won wisdom.

The Sag Du was not the only presence that had the People moving aside. Nyri gasped as the two large tan-coloured *grishnaa* cats prowled out of the shadows on the Thal chief's heels. Their golden eyes sharpened as Bahari rushed to intercept his adopted father. He blocked the Sag Du's progression along with his view of the spot where Nyri waited. He was speaking rapidly. Nyri got the impression he was trying to prepare his father for what he was about to reveal, to cool his reaction. It was to no avail.

The Sag Du shouldered Bahari aside and the black eyes fell upon Juaan. The Thal leader hooted in outrage. Bahari continued to beseech him, but a blind hate had descended over the proud face, shuttering out reason. A sharp whistle erupted from his broad lips even as Bahari snatched a hold on his arm, "Ngathe!"

The Sag Du threw him to the side as the two *grishnaa* burst from their master's shadow, scenting the odour of an enemy in their midst. Their lips peeled back from their knife-like teeth.

Another whistle and the predators charged, intent on ripping Juaan to pieces. Cries of denial went up from the surrounding Thals as they saw Nyri crouched in death's path.

But Nyri was ready. This was not the day she or Juaan would die. She leaped to her feet, planting herself in front of the charging cats as the Great Spirit of KI seared through her veins. "No."

Her utterance was barely audible, but the power of her command carried through the air on the force of her will. The cats' claws flexed as they slewed to a halt at Nyri's feet, golden eyes wide as they fell back on their haunches. Nyri raised her hands, and at once they lowered their great heads, quiescent as deer fawns as they bowed before her.

Nyri stepped between them and levelled her gaze at the great Thal Sag Du of the Children of Eron.

9

Trade

The Sag Du's stunned gaze went from Nyriaana to his fierce *grishnaa* cats bowed at her feet, and back to Nyri again. Nyri lifted her chin, daring the Thal leader to make another move.

Bahari was back at his chief's elbow, talking and gesturing. This time, the Sag Du heard him, pulling his gaze away from Nyri. Stiff lipped, he jerked his head towards the largest cave opening in the circle of rugged cliff faces. Emitting a strange mewling cry, the Thal leader called to his cats. They obeyed, rising from their crouched positions to follow their master as he disappeared into the cave.

Many of the clan did the same, leaving Nyri and Juaan alone with the three guards outside. Without letting her guard down, Nyri sank to her haunches at Juaan's side. He did not speak; he appeared resigned to whatever fate awaited. Nyri ground her teeth together in frustration.

Shifting her weight, she eyed the bindings around Juaan's hands. There were just three guards. If she could free Juaan's bonds, she was sure together they could overpower them. But without her knife, she knew she had no chance of loosening the knot before the guards stopped her. A warning grunt confirmed the thought. The nearest guard was eyeing her, guessing the direction of her thoughts. Nyri scowled and shifted away from the ropes. Without Juaan, there was no chance of silencing the guards alone. As soon as she got to one, the other two would subdue her, and she did not have the power to drop three at once.

Nyri chewed restlessly on a fingernail, staring across at the path that would lead into the foothills and a chance at escape. It was only a handful of strides away, and yet the whole unbroken expanse of the Plains may as well have stood between her and the salvation the trail offered.

Nyri grew restless as Ninsiku's half-lidded eye passed overhead. Prowling back and forth, she kept her eyes fixed on the empty cave entrance into which the Thal clan had disappeared. A range of emotions buffeted across her senses; none of them comforting. Fear, anger, uncertainty, a flare of hurt and rage. Grief.

She needed a blade. The hilt of a hunting knife poked from the furs of the nearest Thal guard. He was no longer watching her. His dark gaze was fixed on the cave where his brethren sat in debate. Was she fast enough to swipe the weapon from the warrior and sever Juaan's bonds before he caught her?

There was only one way to find out. Nyri had run out of options. Feeling her Thal gifts slide over her skin, she felt a pang of remorse for betraying the trust she had gained, but she had warned Bahari, she would do anything to save Juaan. Gathering the Great Spirit, Nyri drew a cloak about herself, pushing the Thal's attention away from her presence as much as she could. If she had been still, she knew she could have evaded his notice effortlessly; but she was moving, and the flicker of movement caught in the corner of an eye instinctively drew the attention of all living creatures. Survival depended upon it.

Juaan's unease spiked behind her. She heard his breath catch as he fought the urge to call her back, knowing that doing so would only reveal her. Nyri ignored him, focusing on her target. Two strides. One. She reached for the knife hilt.

"Gyat!" Bahari's voice rang out. Nyri fell back, biting down on a cry of denial as the Cro man emerged from the cave. He strode across the camp to converse with the guard before his eyes fell upon Nyri. "The Sag Du will meet with you now," he said. His raised eyebrow told her he was well aware of what she had been trying to do.

The guards hefted the boulder pinning Juaan's bindings to the ground. Then, with one holding the rope and the other two flanking, they moved Juaan at spear point towards the cave of the Sag Du.

Bahari gestured to Nyri, indicating that she should walk at his side. She had no choice other than to comply.

"What has your Sag Du decided?" The words almost lodged in her throat and she tried to moisten her dry mouth.

"I... not know," Bahari responded. "I tried to tell him your story as promised, but Sag Du stubborn man. Proud. He not share his thinking with me."

Nyri pressed her lips together, moving as close to Juaan as his guard would allow. She blinked against the dimness of the cave as they crossed the threshold. It took a couple of moments for her eyes to adjust, but she could feel the weight of many gazes upon her, quiet breaths muffled in the shadows, anticipating what was to come. Hands reached out to touch her in support.

The cave was the largest Nyri had yet seen. It was the height of several trees above her head; solid rock dripped down from the ceiling like water, glimmering in the light thrown by several torches. There was a somber majesty to this place. Nyri felt it creep up her spine as her eyes fell on the Sag Du seated at the far end of his dwelling, the great cats lying upon either side of him. His deep-set eyes gleamed as he watched them approach.

Precisely three strides from the Thal leader, the guards yanked Juaan to a halt, poking the butts of their thick spears into the back of his knees to put him in a kneeling position. Bahari caught hold of Nyri's arm, keeping her close at his side as they halted beside Juaan.

The Sag Du regarded Nyri for a long moment. "I am Sag Du Alok," he spoke in a voice that sounded like rock being dragged over gravel, rough and ancient and in the Cro tongue. "You are Dryad of the southern forests." It was not a question and so Nyri simply dipped her head.

A mirthless smile touched the thick lips of the chief as he stroked the tawny head of the *grishnaa* on his right. "It would take such creature of legend to tame my cats as you did." His black gaze intensified. "My son tells me the Jade Killer took you from your home and brought you north to the clan of the Red Bear."

Nyri cast an anxious glance at Juaan. "Yes, he did, but—"

The Sag Du held up a silencing hand. "With you came other Dryad with pale hair?"

Nyri stiffened. How did this stranger know of Kyaati?

"Y-yes."

A toothy grin broke out over the pale face as the Sag Du barked a laugh. "The *genii* were right. Eron has indeed sent a gift of great value to save us."

Nyri frowned up at Bahari, but the Cro warrior did not elaborate on his adopted father's meaning and the Sag Du was no longer regarding her. His eyes had now fallen upon Juaan, his upper lip curled back in disdain.

"I never thought to have Jade Killer kneeling in my presence," he rumbled. "The taker of so many Thal lives." Alok held out a hand and the Thal closest to his side handed him a spear. Nyri recognised it instantly as Juaan's. A weapon that was both Cro and Thal, etched with strange carvings.

Before Nyri could react, Alok leaped across the space separating him from Juaan, the razor-sharp tip of the spear lancing out like a viper strike. It sliced the skin on Juaan's cheek, drawing blood. Nyri tried to dart between them, but Bahari's grip prevented her.

"Don't hurt him!" she begged.

The flint was now pressing against the pulse at Juaan's throat as he and Alok locked eyes.

"Where did you get this weapon?" Alok snarled in Juaan's face.

Juaan did not respond, just continued to regard the Sag Du silently.

"Answer!" The weapon flicked again, drawing more blood on the other side of Juaan's face. "Who did you murder for this? Where you leave her?"

Her? "He didn't murder anyone!" Nyri tried to twist free of Bahari's hold.

Alok acted as though she had not spoken. The thick fingers of his free hand flashed out and caught Juaan around the throat. "Answer me."

"My mother," Juaan fought to get the words past Alok's grip. "She gave it to me."

"Liar! Hunting Bear *ikkibu*. Your mother not Thal!" Alok's fingers flexed. Such a hand could snap Juaan's neck with one minor misjudgment.

"He's telling the truth!" Nyri shouted. "She was not Thal, she was Ninkuraaja, she was of my People. His father was Chief of the Black Wolf clan. He bears their totem. He is nothing of the Hunting Bear." Nyri did not know if her words were getting through to the seething Thal chief. Something about the weapon had snapped his control. He was beyond reason. She had to act now. She had no plan, no idea of how to escape this cave alive, but she had to do something before the Thal chief killed Juaan in front of her eyes. Bahari's life force pulsed against her arm. He needed to be her first target. *I'm sorry,* she thought at him as she drew on the power of KI and reached for his heart.

No!

The bodiless voice pulled Nyri up short. The Great Spirit of KI swirled around her, a wind that could not be seen or sensed by mortal touch. But she felt it. And somehow, Alok did too. The Thal chief stiffened as though someone unexpected had called his name. His eyes went to his shoulder, and it appeared to Nyri that he was expecting to see a hand resting there.

The wind of the Great Spirit gathered again, and this time Nyri did see it as a handful of dust lifted up and swirled around the spear in Alok's hand.

The Thal chief's black eyes widened. Nyri could not name the emotion that was passing through him, the sloping forehead pinched and smoothed as Alok battled whatever torment he was experiencing.

"Nen," he whispered, and his face crumpled. His hand dropped from Juaan's throat, and the great chief fell back between his two great cats. He appeared to age before Nyri's eyes, the weight of time hanging from bones that were no longer strong enough to bear the load.

"*Adda?*" Bahari abandoned Nyri's side to go to his adoptive father.

Alok raised a hand, and Bahari closed his mouth. Along with the rest of the Thal clan, Nyri waited for the Sag Du to regain his composure and speak again.

When the grizzled head finally came up, Alok's eyes burned with anger layered by pain as they regarded Juaan. "And who gave this spear to your mother, *ikkibu?*"

"I did not know her," Juaan answered. "But my mother named her my *tarhe.*"

Gasps ran around the cave at the word and a buzz of hushed murmuring broke out. Alok silenced his followers with a cutting gesture. His jaw flexed. "Under such protection, by Thal lore, I cannot harm you, Jade Killer," Alok ground out.

It took Nyri an entire moment to absorb the meaning of the Sag Du's words. Then the breath she had been holding left her lungs. Casting her face to the unseen heavens above, Nyri let out a silent laugh of relief. Juaan was safe. The vow of an unknown Thal woman had made him so. *Thank you,* she thought to the invisible spirit.

Alok handed the spear to Bahari. Nyri got the impression

it was too painful for the Thal chief to hold. "But because of sorrows you caused my People, I not let your evil go free." The words brought Nyri crashing back to earth. A malicious glint appeared in the Sag Du's dark eyes. "I pass judgment onto another not bound by constraint. I know now what *genii* try to show me. The curse of your presence is a gift. Our saviour. As is hers." A thick finger flicked towards Nyri, who bristled. "Bahari, gather strongest fighters. I wish you to carry terms to our *kataru*. I offer these two wanderers in trade. Their value is greater than all the jade *dudittu* we can offer."

"Ngathe!" Bahari protested, rushing back to Nyri's side and gripping her shoulders. His support brought her small comfort. "*Adda.*"

"Great Alok," Juaan broke in, surprising Nyriaana. Instead of staring apathetically at the ground as he had been, he was now giving the Sag Du his undivided attention. "I beg you, keep Nyriaana under your protection. She can serve your people well. Let her remain and I promise you will not regret it."

"Juaan, no!" Nyri protested just as one of the Thal guards jabbed him in the ribs with the butt of his spear, cutting him off.

"Your promises mean nothing to me, *ikkibu!*" the Sag Du spat. "Dryad travel with and protect Killer. Therefore, she is an enemy with no place here. Bahari, take them."

Bahari did not move. "Ngathe, *adda.*" But Alok silenced him with a withering glare.

"Return with no less than full understanding to share in the bounties of their lake until herds return north."

"*Runuk*," Bahari spoke out, lifting his chin.

"Cro speak, Bahari," Alok commanded. "The practice serve you well with our neighbours."

"No, *adda*, Jade Killer right," Bahari's jaw worked around the admittance. "Keep the Dryad. She is a gift from Eron for his Children. I saw her power. She can mend hunters better than the wise *azu*. The stories are true!"

"What good are hunters if there no food to eat, my son?" Alok reasoned. "Can she banish the empty time and conjure herds with her magic?"

"I—"

"Ngathe!" Alok's voice echoed through the cave. "Herds not return north when they should. Food is what our *imrua* needs more than any Dryad magic. Take them. That is my order. May Eron give you skill to speak well for our *imrua*." He stroked the head of the larger of his two cats and then made a hissing sound in the back of his throat. The grishnaa rose and stretched out her claws before padding to Bahari's side. "Take Nisaru."

Bahari gripped the spear in his hand until his dark knuckles paled, but under scrutiny of the Thal clan, he bowed to his leader. Nyri seethed. She should have known better than to trust their fate to the Cro man.

Bahari motioned to the three guards. They pulled Juaan back to his feet as Bahari took Nyri's arm and led her from the cave. Nisaru stalked in their wake. Nyri could hear the great cat's breath at her back. Bahari spoke not a word.

"What does he mean 'trade'?" Nyri demanded as soon as they were free of the Sag Du's cave. Ninsiku gazed lazily upon the horizon as his stolen spirits winked overhead. Dawn had yet to break.

Bahari blew a breath through his broad nose. "He means

to gift you and Jade Killer in return for fishing honours in our *kataru*—our ally's-territory. They hold only constant source of food in empty time."

"Gift? I am nobody's to gift, Bahari! If you want the territory, why don't you just fight to take it as your own?"

Bahari's face darkened. "You know Cro too long. Why fight and cause many sorrow when a peaceful agreement gets what we need?"

"I—" Nyri fell silent. Fear overcame her indignity. She and Juaan were to be given over to an unknown tribe. She swallowed. "Where are you taking us?"

"Deeper into the foothills where our *kataru etuti* lies."

"But, Bahari," Nyri started.

The Cro man laid a hand on her shoulder. "I am sorry, Nyriaana, Dryad of forest. I want you to stay, but the Sag Du has spoken." He fell silent as a couple of Thal women approached with woven slings filled with dried meat, skins of water and burning brands to see by as they travelled. Bahari and the guards each took a share in the load. There looked to be at least a day's supply.

"Bahari," Juaan spoke. "You *must* go back to your father, beg him to reconsider."

Bahari's grey eyes turned flat at the sound of his name on Juaan's lips. "Even if I change Sag Du's mind, what makes you think she stay here, Jade Killer?" he jerked his chin at Nyri. "She already made her feeling on separation clear, and you *not* staying here." He turned his back, gave one sharp whistle and two more men emerged, armed and similarly equipped for a day's travel. As soon as they were in place along the group's flanks, Bahari spearheaded his small band, the tamed *grishnaa* cat on his heels, and set off towards the trail leading directly north, deeper into the foothills and ever closer to the Mountains that Nyri had tried so hard to escape.

She settled into stride beside Juaan as the guards tugged him forward at spear point.

"I'm sorry, Nyri," he murmured.

"For what?" Her tone was clipped.

"I thought I had found you a haven. I was wrong."

Nyri growled low in her throat. "You have known me since I was a baby, Juaan. Bahari has known me for only a few passes of Ninmah, and yet he already appears to understand me better than you."

With that, Nyri stalked ahead. Once again, they were heading into the unknown, and there was nothing she could do now but accept it and face the danger head on. She thought distantly that Halima would be proud. Bahari's clan. Another clan. What did it matter? Perhaps she would have more luck in persuading the leader of this unknown tribe, the Sag Du, or whatever he wanted to call himself, to let them go free.

Nyri was aware that every step she took back north was a step closer to Eldrax. She and Juaan would be a danger to anyone who had them in their possession. Any wise leader who wanted to protect their People should understand that and want them gone. Nyri cast a prayer to Ninmah that she was headed to meet such a leader. She reassured herself that any chief who would rather *trade* than kill for gain couldn't be completely unreasonable.

Alok was such a leader, her inner thoughts reminded her.

He didn't kill us, Nyri countered, trying to quell her unease as they wound deeper and deeper into the foothills.

Something about the meeting with Alok still bothered her. Nyri increased her pace until she was moving in Bahari's shadow. "How did Alok know about my tribe sister and how we came north together? I did not tell you about Kyaati."

Bahari glanced over his shoulder. "Alok knows many things," he shrugged. "Very wise leader who speaks with the *genii*, spirits who passed into *La'Atzu*."

Genii. Nyri thought of the presence that had stirred in the cave, preventing Alok from killing Juaan in a blind rage, and frowned. KI worked in ways beyond her comprehension. Only a Kamaali could come close to divining the meaning in the Great Spirit's plan. Nyri took comfort in the fact that KI must not want Juaan dead. Sefaan had always surmised as much.

The need for this trade must have been great, for the Thal group did not stop to rest, eating and drinking on the move. Nyri was proud that she was able to keep up over the rough and winding terrain. If she had been the same Ninkuraa she had been when Juaan had first dragged her from her home, she would have been slung exhausted across Bahari's shoulders long before now. Instead, she felt... strong.

Nyriaana... Nyri gasped as the voice echoed through her mind, wrenching aside her thoughts as the invisible presence sought to rob her of her senses.

No, not now! She thought desperately.

Her skin tingled as the Great Spirit swirled around her, tugging, growing in strength. Her eyes went to the peaks of the Mountains looming in the distance. Sweat broke out on her brow with the effort it took to resist. Beseeching stares flashed across her mind's eye: green, lavender, black, violet—

"Ah!" The cresting wave of the Great Spirit broke over her and she stumbled to her knees. Blackness.

"Nyriaana!" Juaan's voice sounded muffled, distorted, as though it was coming from underwater. She was dimly aware of the sound of a struggle. "Let me go to her!"

Nyri opened her eyes. She was on the ground, the sharp gravel biting into her cheek. Juaan was resisting the hold of the Thal guard, fighting to get to her side. His green eyes burned as he glared at Bahari, who was kneeling beside her. "Leave her alone," Juaan snarled with the most malice Nyri had heard since he had regained his memories.

Bahari ignored him. "Nyriaana?"

She had lost consciousness. Nyri knocked his supporting hand away, pushing herself up on shaking arms. "It's nothing."

Bahari pressed his lips together. "It is the *genii.* I know look well. Alok is *nabu.*"

"Nabu?" Her head was pounding, blood rushing in her ears. She pinched the bridge of her nose, drawing deep breaths.

"Seer in Cro speak. But Alok usually has to drink of the fire water before *genii* talk to him. Powerful Dryad need no fire water, I see." The Cro man tilted his head.

Nyri grunted. She felt sick. This was all his fault. The initial hatred she had held for Bahari flared back to life. He had pretended to care. She had given him her trust, helped him, and he had betrayed her. He had done nothing to save them. If he hadn't captured them, she would not be here. She could be far south by now and perhaps free of the voices beckoning her towards her doom.

If he hadn't captured you, you would be back in Eldrax's

bedding, her inner voice reminded her. She silenced it viciously.

"Can you stand?" Bahari was hovering. Nyri could almost hear Juaan's teeth grinding behind her.

"Yes." Nyri shoved his hand away again and staggered back to her feet, careful to keep her gaze away from the Mountains above. "Let's move on. I would not want you to miss out on this *trade* of yours."

Bahari flinched at the accusation in her tone, but Nyri was past caring about his feelings. Their survival no longer depended upon them.

"I will make sure our *kataru* treat you well," Bahari promised. "I tell them what great healer you are."

"Much good it did me with your clan." She jabbed a finger at Juaan. "And him?"

Bahari shook his head. "That is for Eron to decide now. If he is a good man like you say, Eron help him."

Nyri snorted derisively and turned her face away.

"Come," Bahari said. "We be there before *Gisnu* rises."

They had arrived at a fork; the trail splitting in two around a rocky hill. Bahari turned towards the left fork and strode on at the head of his band of Thals, Nisaru padding like a ghost in his shadow. Nyri followed as the Thals surrounding Juaan moved up behind her.

"Nyri?"

Nyri glanced over her shoulder to see him regarding her with a pinched brow. He knew it was the proximity of the Mountains causing her plight. And she was not the only one. If she looked more closely, she could detect the signs of strain etched into his proud features. Every step brought them closer to the powerful River Line of KI that ran beneath. And the closer they got, the stronger the monster lurking within Juaan became, the impediments binding it in place no longer able to contain it.

Nyri fell back a step until she could slip her fingers into Juaan's bound hands, radiating soothing energy, calming his turmoil and bolstering his control. She heard his sigh sound in the cool air as his fingers returned her grip, and for a moment it felt like there was no distance between them. Everything was as it should be. Nyri set her jaw, fresh determination lending her strength. As long as they were together, they would overcome.

The light of dawn was creeping into the sky above as they approached yet another fork in the path. Bahari was choosing the left trail, when Juaan stiffened, yanking Nyri to an abrupt halt.

"Bahari!" His voice was sharp. "To which tribe are you taking us?"

The sudden, inexplicable anger pulsing through his rangy frame caught Nyri by surprise. She stared around at the surrounding rocks and hills, searching for the source of his distress. It all looked the same to her, but a prickle of unease crept along her spine, raising the hairs on her neck, as though her mind had already worked out what her eyes had failed to recognise.

Bahari paused. He was considering whether he should deign to answer his enemy. Nyri felt the monster beside her flex within its loosening bindings.

"Answer him!" she demanded.

"To Cro. Eagle Clan," Bahari spoke only to her.

The world became detached as Nyri's knees buckled. Memories assailed her, memories of being bound while a pack of Cro bayed for her death. The bloody rock between two trees. The pounding of stones. "Yatal," she gasped.

Juaan was already in motion. He leaped over his bindings, bringing his hands around to the front, scything the ropes along the blade of a flint axe resting on an unprepared Thal's shoulder, bursting them asunder. In the flicker of an eye, he had the rope around the Thal guard's neck, yanking it backward and cutting off the man's airway.

You could've done that the whole time? A part of Nyri's mind screamed in frustration as Bahari's spear whistled, swinging into attack position. Nisaru snarled at his side, her ears flattening against her head, poised for her master's command to strike.

"Let Nyri go free and I will spare his life." Juaan stared the Cro man down.

"I cannot." Bahari set his jaw.

Juaan tightened his hold and the Thal's eyes bugged as he clawed at the rope sinking into his throat. "Let her go, Bahari! If you do this, Nyri's blood will be on your hands!"

The spear tip wavered. "Blood?"

Even though her throat had closed like she was the one being throttled, everything fell into place with a snap in Nyri's mind. *This* was how Alok had known of Kyaati. He was friends with Yatal!

Juaan and Bahari continued to stare one another down.

"Yatal is fair leader," the Cro man said. "You try to trick me."

"No," Juaan snarled. "Yatal thirsts for Nyri's blood as much as she does mine!"

Bahari's eyes flicked to Nyri.

"H-he's right," she rasped. "She'll kill me."

Bahari's weight shifted, betraying the conflict he was feeling.

"Bahari, please, I beg you." Nyri's voice came in no more than a hoarse whisper, but the sight of her bloodless face was finally enough to convince the Thal leader. Bahari lowered his spear. Restless, he paced back and forth. "I did not know this, did not know." His head came up and all the uncertainty had vanished. He had made his decision. "Ulu," he signalled one of the Thal warriors and spoke to him in urgent tones, gesturing at Nyri. The black-haired Thal hesitated, then bowed his head to Bahari. "Ulu will get you out of here."

Nyri stepped back. "No!" She was mortally afraid of Yatal, but she could not leave Juaan. If they were parted now, she knew she would never see him again.

"Nyriaana!" Juaan's words bit at her. "Go!"

Ulu took a step towards her, clearly intent on taking her from this place, regardless of whether she wanted to go.

Nyri was assessing her chances when a piercing whistle froze every one of them in place. The shrill, challenging call came from overhead and Nyri looked up in time to see the faces appearing on the rock ledges above, spears bristling. The totem of the Eagle clan dangled from the lethal tips.

"Welcome, Bahari," a husky female voice called out.

Nyri saw Bahari pale beneath his dark skin. "Sakal."

"It surprised us to see you in our territory again so soon after our usual trading, but I see you have something more than ornaments with you on this journey."

Nyri's eyes fell upon the speaker. Straggling black hair tumbled down around a pale, heavy-featured face. The clearly half-Thal woman was leering down at Juaan. Her wide lips pursed, sounding another piercing whistle. The Eagle warriors leapt down from their perches, landing neatly to surround Bahari's smaller group. Nisaru rumbled uncertainly in her throat as she crouched. Bahari quieted her with a gesture as five of the Eagles levelled their spears at Juaan's throat.

"You're lucky we found you when we did, Bahari," Sakal said as she added her own spear to the bristling array. "Holding Eldrax's Spear Cat with so few men was a deadly mistake, as you were about to find out. Drop the rope!" the half-Thal woman hissed the last at Juaan.

With six flint tips pressing in on him, Juaan released his hold on his Thal guard, slowly raising his hands to where the Eagle warriors could see them.

"I bring Jade Killer as gift to Yatal," Bahari said, "but the Dryad is not for trade. She belongs to me."

Sakal's attention flickered over to where Nyri stood, immobilised with fear. Her black eyes widened, her mouth falling open at the sight of Nyriaana. "By Ea," she whispered, and then a cold smile slid across her face. Nyri's flesh quivered. "We will see about that," Sakal said to Bahari. "The Chieftess will honour your clan greatly for that witch. Unless you wish to violate our understanding, Bahari?"

The edge of a threat dripping from Sakal's voice was unmistakable. Nyri saw Bahari glance around at the superior Eagle numbers and his shoulders bowed.

"No, Sakal," he said. "We honour our *kataru*."

The Eagle leader responded with a satisfied nod. "Bind him more securely," she barked at her followers, jabbing her spear dangerously close to Juaan's face. "*I* will take no chances with him." The Eagle warriors rushed to obey as

Sakal turned her broad face towards Nyri, the chilling smile widening. "Yatal awaits your company, elf-witch."

* * *

10

Arisen

They had spiked the severed head of the Watcher on the edges of the Forest of the Nine Gods, just as he had ordered. Eldrax circled it, taking in every detail. At last, after all this time, he had proven himself against a Watcher.

And judging by the size of the feet of this monster, it was far bigger than the one Juran of the Black Wolf had killed all those long seasons ago. Before Eldrax's father had fallen, before he had become Chief, before he had dispatched his...

Red hair and black eyes flashed before his vision, distorted by the swirling snow of the blackest night. *My Eldrax...*

"Leave me be, mother!" Eldrax snarled to the empty air.

He could not allow her ghost to befuddle and confuse him now. He paced around and around the Watcher's head. *Now we will see who fears who,* he thought at the grimacing countenance. In killing this beast, he had taken the long awaited first step towards freeing mankind from the tyranny of the gods. His destiny. *I am the power here. Me! I bow to no one. I fear no one.*

With Rannac's help, he had ensured that when he finally confronted the Watchers, it would be they who fled before him. The name of the Red Bear would strike fear into their souls, just as they had once made him suffer such shame. Now it was time. He had sent Tanag to gather the forces he had prepared in anticipation of this day.

He did not know why the rest of the mad fools had resisted him so, why they resented his leadership. In fighting him, they had wasted lives. Lives he had had better use for. He intended to free them all. Couldn't they understand that? This unnaturally long winter was yet another punishment laid down by the gods to make mankind suffer, to snuff out the light they had created. *No more. No more,* Eldrax chanted in his mind. He would not cower in fear. The rest of the Peoples would see the wisdom of his actions in the end.

That oaf Galahir had tipped his hand sooner than Eldrax would have liked. He had hoped to have a following of witch-children when he came to face the gods. The elf-witches, the blindest, most foolish creatures of them all, would never fight for him, but had he been able to sire his own children upon the most powerful of them... children that would grow loyal to him...

A roar ripped from his chest, and Eldrax planted his fist into the side of the Watcher's face. He had had her! He had finally inflicted his vengeance upon Juran's useless son, taken what was most precious to him right before his dying eyes. A victory made all the sweeter when the object of his enemy's desire was an elf-witch finally worthy of his attentions! What a witch-child he could have sired upon her!

The crags of the distant foothills fell under his gaze. Yatal. He should have finished her long ago. He had been a blind fool to leave her and the other Eagle women alive. She would suffer…

No. The forest loomed. What was that half-Thal filth now when he had the chance to make the gods themselves tremble? And he would make them tremble! It was not the force he had imagined, but he had a witch-child and a pure witch at his command, attached to the fate of his clan by her babe and her half-wit mate.

Galahir. He may be a witless oaf, but Eldrax would forever be indebted to Rannac for persuading him to take Chief Rikal's son from the Eagles instead of just slaughtering the half-Thal infant with the rest of his male brethren. Even Rannac could not have foretold how useful he would become.

The silver-haired witch's Claiming by Galahir had proven she had strength beyond Eldrax's expectations, and gained her loyalty to the Hunting Bear. The fool had sired upon her an undamaged witch-child with the power Khalvir had failed to give him. Perhaps… perhaps this was the child he had been waiting for.

But the knowledge that he had overlooked this witch and let her slip through his own fingers rankled. Selima, in her incessant, pathetic need to gain his favour, had spoken the truth that festered in the back of Eldrax's mind. He was *Chief*, the one destined to free mankind from the bindings of the gods. He should have the best. And since the more powerful witch had temporarily eluded him, the silver-haired she-elf should be his.

And she would be.

But not now.

Eldrax was not fool enough to believe she would fight for him if he murdered her mate, and he needed all his warriors for the fight against the Watchers when they came. And they would come. This totem of his making would ensure their wrath. But afterwards… afterwards, he would rid himself of Galahir and make the silver witch his own, along with her elusive tribe-sister. It was only a matter of time before one of his hunting groups returned with his prize and the traitor.

Eldrax amused himself by deciding which he would prefer, skinning Khalvir alive before or after he completed his Claiming of the dark-haired witch. Perhaps he would order both at the same time, visual entertainment while he satisfied his desire at last. His body responded to such delicious thoughts, and he turned to face the camp away in the distance. His new mate, Kikima, was no elf-witch, but, like Halima before her, the half-Deni girl made a worthy partner until he could play out his fantasy for real. She would provide him with a strong son to carry on his bloodline after he rid the land of the gods' curse once and for all.

A flash of red against the landscape startled Eldrax into stillness. *Mother?* Then he growled. He considered snapping Selima's neck as she came into full view. One minor act and he would be free from this unwanted spawn, this unwanted reminder of the woman who had birthed and abandoned him. The similarities between them continued to catch him off guard.

But the girl had proven herself to be not quite such a useless burden in the past days. It was her, after all, who had been clever enough to befriend the elf-witches, to gain their trust enough for the dark-haired she-elf to reveal she was everything Eldrax had waited for. And so he held still; only the twitching of his fingers betrayed his desire to dispatch the girl.

She beamed up at him. Eldrax quelled the expression of welcome with a scowl. She might have proven useful, but did she really believe he felt any *affection* for her? His lip curled. He could not bear the sight of the girl's dark eyes. *Her* eyes, returned to haunt him from the grave.

"Father."

Eldrax closed his fists as the twitching of his fingers increased and breathed through his nose. "What is it?"

"I have come to warn you," she spoke hastily. "Halima intend to kill you, father."

Eldrax raised an eyebrow. "Really?"

Selima jerked her chin. "I suspected the elf-witch could not be trusted after what happened to her tribe sister. I have been following her, and I was right to do so. She has turned our matriarch against us. They do not believe in your vision. They mean to kill you before the Watchers arrive. To save the clan from your… madness."

Eldrax barked out a laugh, the sound making Selima flinch. "Do they, now?"

The girl appeared nonplussed by his response. "You are not surprised by this?"

Eldrax curled his lip. "You are not the only one who knows things, whelp. You think yourself invaluable to me? Tanag has guarded my back long before you were spawned."

He watched as his words lashed against her, deflating her pride, and she recoiled, her bottom lip trembling before she drew a breath and straightened. "What are you going to do?"

"Nothing. A handful of women are no threat to me. I am the only one who can keep them safe. Any traitors who lose faith will soon understand that."

"But—"

Eldrax's hand shot out, catching Selima by the throat. Her eyes bulged as he lifted her off the ground. "Do you think I have become the most powerful man among the clans by having my judgment questioned, you little fool?" He squeezed his fingers as she fought for air, ensuring she would be left with bruises; a reminder of where insolence got her. "I need the she-elf. I do not need you. Only my gratitude for your recent usefulness is keeping you alive, and that gratitude is wearing thin." He growled the last in her face before casting her to the ground. The girl's hands went to her tortured neck as she sucked air into her starved lungs.

"Get up." Eldrax kicked at her with his foot. "Make yourself useful. Go back to camp. Find Kikima. Tell her I want her in the Chief's shelter by the time I return." He had won a battle, and that always gave him an appetite.

Selima scrambled to her feet without meeting his eyes, her flushed cheeks glistening. Eldrax planted his foot in her rump as she fled, speeding her on her way.

With one last lingering glance at the Watcher's severed head, Eldrax walked away at his leisure, giving the dark treeline his back. He did not hurry. Even at full speed, Selima was only halfway back to the first ring of shelters.

Come for me when you want, he thought boldly. *I am ready.*

Utu was sinking towards the west when Eldrax returned

to camp. He took a brief pleasure in the sight of a group of children scurrying out of his path, their eyes lowered in submission. Upon reaching his shelter at the very centre of his domain, Eldrax was pleased to see the useless spawn had not let him down. Pushing through the hide curtains, he found Kikima waiting for him on the inside. A smile curled over his face as a flash of tightening heat curled in his loins. "Halima has done well," he crooned his approval.

Kikima had already shed her furs, her smooth golden skin bare as she knelt naked among his furs, her eyes downcast towards her breasts, puckered in the cool air billowing in from the entrance.

Letting out a feral growl, Eldrax tore his own coverings aside, freeing his already straining manhood. He had killed a Watcher. He had defied the gods and he would soon have what he had lost returned by his hunters. Throwing the girl over before him, Eldrax grabbed her hips and thrust himself all the way inside her in one savage movement. He let out a throaty groan of pleasure as she flinched upon the impalement. How this would have felt had he been allowed to mount the witch in this way!

The burn of resentment in Kikima's golden eyes and the flush of anger down her strong back only fed his desire. Catching her around the back of the neck, he slammed into her, once, twice. He was distantly aware of her groping around in the furs before her and he pinned her arm with his free hand. Eldrax took his time, enjoying the heat and her mewlings under his body, the pleasure building in his belly like a tightening rope as he yanked on her hair.

Her scream was less of a distraction than it was encouragement, and Eldrax knew, despite his restraint, he would not last much longer.

He snarled in warning as she tensed and tried to rise beneath him, her head swivelling.

"No, my Chief," she choked. "Listen! S-something is w-wrong!"

Eldrax ignored her.

"My Chief—"

"Enough!" Eldrax slammed her face into the furs, silencing her irritating voice as he pounded on. Then Eldrax arched as he released his seed inside the struggling body before him.

Spent, he collapsed upon her as his body convulsed with the aftershocks. He hoped he had put a strong offspring in her belly.

"Chief Eldrax!"

Tanag's voice burned against his ears, and his vision flashed red. Tearing himself from Kikima, he leaped to his feet and rounded on the other man. Tanag knew better. "Tanag," he spat, glaring at the warrior. "It had better be the gods themselves who have sent you here. Why aren't you—"

Tanag opened his mouth, but it fell slack. He didn't appear capable of speech. His skin was pallid beneath its earthy tones. He pointed with his spear towards the outside, the flint tip trembling upon the air. That was when the sound of screams and running feet beyond the hide walls filtered through Eldrax's awareness.

"What now?" Eldrax threw his furs around his shoulders and grabbed his club. The cries outside were filled with terror and despair. Eldrax knew the sound of battle would soon follow in their wake.

But the noise of destruction and the bloodthirsty roar

181

of invaders never came. Instead, the wails of despair were eerily out of place against a backdrop of silence. The hairs on the back of Eldrax's neck rose in response.

"Stay here," he commanded Kikima, as he thrust past Tanag's trembling form.

"I don't think so," Kikima muttered, already dressed. She dug about in the bedding furs and pulled out a concealed knife. Eldrax's eyebrows shot up, but another scream outside demanded his attention. He would deal with Kikima later.

Turning on his heel, Eldrax burst from his shelter, ready to fight the nameless threat. But there was none to be seen. He halted, confusion twisting through his mind as he beheld the scene before him.

Most of the clan were outside their shelters, their eyes fixed on the distant horizon. Many had prostrated themselves upon the ground, hands raised in supplication. Eldrax's irritation at such a display of weakness turned to anger as he heard their wails for forgiveness. Glowering, Eldrax let his eyes follow their collective gaze towards the sky above the Mountains in the distance.

For the smallest passage of time, Eldrax's anger deserted him, and he felt very small and insignificant against the vastness of the sky above. What was he against such immortal might? His knees turned to water. He wanted to throw himself on the ground next to his followers and beg for forgiveness. What else could he do?

But it was only for a moment, a moment of weakness that brought all of his anger and hatred scalding to the surface and Eldrax roared in defiance at the three balls of glowing blue light that were dancing through the air over the soaring white peaks, flaring brightly against the grey wash of clouds above.

This was what he had wanted. This was what he had waited for.

His challenge had been answered.

A flash of silver on the ground drew his attention. The elf-witch was cowering next to the boy Akito. But she was not bowed in supplication like the rest, instead she was convulsing in what appeared to be pain as her witch-child wailed against her breast.

Eldrax could not have that. He needed her now in the fight that was at hand. Leaning down, he caught her by the shoulders, irritated by how frail they felt, and raised her to her feet. "Stand strong, elf-witch," he growled in her ear. "The gods have arisen."

* * *

11

Old Enemies

"Bind him!" Sakal jabbed her spear at Juaan again. You are mine now, Spear-cat," she gloated. "You escaped me once. But there'll be no death defying leap to freedom this time. It'll ease my old Chieftess' heart to have Red Bear's greatest killer removed from the Plains."

Held tightly in the clutches of a hulking Eagle warrior, Nyriaana watched Juaan flinch at her words. The Thals shifted unhappily, sensing the unfavourable turn of events, as their deep-set eyes flicked towards their leader.

Outnumbered though he was, Bahari levelled his gaze at Sakal. "The Jade Killer is ours to offer in trade to Chieftess Yatal. Make sure she knows that, Sakal."

"Yes, yes," Sakal dismissed him with a wave of her hand, then turned her attention upon Nyri. "No matter. This one's return will rival even his in bringing Yatal solace," she grinned. "We have unfinished business, elf-witch." Somehow, a rock materialised in her hand and the half-Thal warrior bounced it in her palm. Bile rose in Nyri's throat.

A soft snarl sounded and Nyri looked beyond Sakal to see Juaan pull against his restraints. "Let her go, Sakal! She can cause no harm to you or your clan."

"Tell that to Yatal's granddaughter," Sakal sneered.

Juaan pulled harder. "Please! Let her go."

Sakal's eyes widened as his voice degenerated into a plea. Her gaze moved between Juaan and Nyri before she let out a bark of delighted laughter. "What's this? The great and feared Khalvir cares for an elf-witch?" She laughed again. Then, quicker than a striking snake, Sakal grabbed Nyri by her hair, wrenching her head back as far as it would go to expose her throat. Nyri gasped against the feel of cold, sharp flint running over her shrinking flesh.

"Sakal!" Nyri heard Bahari's protest, but the sounds of struggle coming from Juaan's direction ceased.

"How amusing! Now, on your knees," the Eagle warrior crooned against Nyri's ear, her cruel delight at her discovery saturating the air. "Know that Yatal would not care if I bring this one back whole or presented her with just the head. Either way, my Chieftess would rest better knowing vengeance for her granddaughter had been served."

Nyri's neck ached as Sakal strained her head further, bowing her back, but she refused to make a sound. She would not make things worse for Juaan by letting him hear her pain. She pressed her lips firmly together as she stared at the sky above.

Just as she thought she could bear the discomfort no more, Sakal released her. Eyes watering, Nyri immediately sought Juaan. He was now lying on the ground, his arms wrenched back unnaturally far to the point of breaking, bound from elbow to wrist. His legs were similarly tied, rendering him immobile and unable to walk. It was clear the Eagle warriors meant to drag him back to their camp. They had not bound his eyes.

Sobbing, Nyri tried to run to his side.

"Nyri, no!" Juaan warned just as Sakal's laugh sounded and the Eagle leader batted her to the ground with one blow. Momentarily stunned, Nyri righted herself and made another attempt to get to Juaan, but this time a firm hand caught her by the arm. Her eyes flew up to meet Bahari's. The Cro man looked back at her and gave a slight shake of his head. *Don't.*

Nyri hissed at him and wrenched her arm free, but he caught the back of her furs, continuing to prevent her from making any more foolish attempts to get to Juaan.

"I will keep watch on the Dryad," Bahari told Sakal, drawing Nyri back against him.

Sakal's gaze travelled over her warriors surrounding Bahari's own small force and shrugged indifferently. "As you wish. But know that if she escapes, our understanding is at an end, *magiri.*"

Nyri felt Bahari's fist tighten in her furs as a burn of resentment curled through the bright waters of his soul. But he said nothing.

"Move out!" Sakal ordered, and her entire force set off along the winding crag of a trail, keeping Bahari and his Thals in their midst. Only Bahari's grip on her furs kept Nyri upright. She tried to look back at Juaan, but Bahari deftly blocked her view, keeping her moving ahead where she could not see.

"I am sorry, Nyriaana," Bahari murmured. "I not know."

Nyri's mouth was too dry to answer, her fear too great to

allow coherent thought. Her death loomed before her like an inescapable maw.

Nyriaana! The solid rocks before her gaze dissolved and the bodiless violet eyes flashed before her vision. The voice, a blend of male and female, demanded obedience. To fight against it, to try to block it out, was to cause physical pain. Nyri was aware of the whimper passing through her lips. *Nyriaana.*

The energy of the earth shifted abruptly beneath her feet. It amazed Nyri that the rocks did not crack at the strength of it. Distantly, she heard Nisaru yowling in distress. The great cat, a Daughter of the Great Spirit, sensed the disturbance as keenly as Nyri. The vision of the eyes vanished to be replaced by another. Nyri flinched back from the monstrous face of a Watcher and its bared double rows of teeth. But the cold blue eyes were dead. Blood dripped from a severed neck. The image was filled with a sense of dismay that was not her own. *Too late, too late,* the irresistible voice chanted. *He awakes.* The gruesome face disappeared and three balls of light exploded into a dark grey sky. A challenge. A warning. Nyri choked on the overwhelming sense of despair that filled her.

"Nyriaana!" Someone was shaking her. "Nyriaana!"

She was on the ground, balled into a fetal position, her hands over her face in a futile attempt to block the vision she could not escape. She ignored Bahari as she peeked through her fingers into the brooding sky above, expecting to see the terrifying lights that had flown before her mind's eye. The sky was empty, indifferent as always, but the Great Spirit pulsed through the earth, restless, quivering, convulsing. Nyri's stomach rolled in time to the unseen motion.

"It is the *genii* again," Bahari said with certainty. "They visit you."

"Something is wrong," Nyri panted. "Something has changed. Something is very wrong." She managed to look past Bahari to Juaan, lying bound among the rocks. His face was drawn tight. The trapped monster awakening in response to the upheaval.

It's alright, she mouthed to him, and she did not know which of them she was trying to soothe in that instant as the nausea rolled on.

Nisaru was pacing, her tawny fur bristling along her back. Confusion where once there was only certainty of purpose roiled inside the cat. Bahari reached out to soothe Nisaru, but wisely drew back his hand when she curled her lips at him.

"What's wrong?" Sakal snarled, stepping to Nyri's side. "Get her up."

"The spirits visit her," Bahari spoke in a hushed voice.

"Get her up, I said." Sakal's voice had a nervous edge to it. Perhaps even she, blind to the Great Spirit as she was, could feel the shift, the new edge to the atmosphere around her.

Nyri tried to rise, but her knees shook. She felt off balance, almost like the world had been turned upside down. She clamped her mouth shut against the fresh roll of nausea.

Strong arms pushed their way underneath her, and Nyri was lifted from the ground. She made a small noise of protest in the back of her throat, but could not find it in herself to fight as Bahari held her securely against his chest. She focused on the steady sound of his heart beneath her ear, allowing it to ground her.

"Nisaru," Bahari called. The great cat ignored him,

continuing to pace, until Bahari let out a shrill whistle. Head low, Nisaru came reluctantly to heel. Nyri closed her eyes, trying to make sense of the onslaught of sensation. Never before had she experienced anything like this. It was as though the very fabric of the earth was being torn apart by some greater power.

Only the rocking motion of the man carrying her told Nyri that she was continuing on her way. But her way to where? The voices continued to echo dully inside her head as she drew ever closer to the Mountains of the Nine Gods. A sense of inevitability sank into her heart. She was destined to go to them. A path that had been set ever since Sefaan showed her that very first vision and burdened her with the task of finding Ariyaana. The Last Kamaali, the one destined to save them.

Why me? Nyri lashed out at the unseen faces, unseen but expectant. Wanting the impossible. *You can't have seen very clearly, Sefaan, because I am about to die. How did that fit into your little plan?*

"I will do what I can to protect you, Nyriaana," Bahari murmured. His voice was steady, out of place against the turmoil unfolding around him. Nyri envied his blindness in that moment. "And, for you, the Jade Killer. You have my pledge."

Nyri took a shuddering breath, trying to close out her connection to the Great Spirit and keep her mind in the physical moment. "I don't think there is anything you can do now, Bahari," she whispered. "Yatal believes I killed her granddaughter. In her eyes, I ended her family."

"Did you?"

Nyri's gaze shot up. Bahari was looking down at her

189

warily. She felt a ripple of hurt. "Of course not! The girl was dying. I tried." Nyri closed her eyes again as the Great Spirit continued to writhe in the back of her mind. "I tried."

"Then we will make her understand that." Bahari's voice was full of grim determination.

Nyri gave a mirthless laugh. "She will not listen."

A muffled grunt had Nyri shooting up in Bahari's arms before he could prevent her, looking over the Cro man's shoulder. Two of Sakal's warriors were dragging Juaan along the ground in their wake. They had chosen a route strewn with sharp rocks over the smooth, well-trodden trail. Nyri could feel their cruel amusement as they purposely yanked Juaan against the larger rocks, snickering as the edges cut his skin.

"Stop that!" Nyri struggled in Bahari's grip. "Stop hurting him!"

"Halt!" Sakal called from the head of the company. The half-Thal warrior marched back to Bahari's side to look Nyri dead in the eye. Bahari's arms tightened. "You do not give the orders around here, she-witch," the Eagle warrior snapped, then hefted her spear and was at Juaan's side in two strides. "You think a few rocks are bad?"

"No, please!" Nyri screamed as Sakal brought her weapon down, jamming the spearhead deep into Juaan's thigh. His pain lashed through Nyri as if it were her own. She thrashed in Bahari's arms in a sudden, blind haze of hate. The Cro man grunted and spasmed as he held on to her, but Nyri was too distressed to care what discomfort she was causing him.

Juaan's teeth were locked together as Sakal gave the spear a malicious twist before withdrawing it from his leg. The

Eagle woman returned to Nyri's side. "Eldrax's Spear Cat deserves much more, believe me, witch," she said, wiping the tip of her weapon against Nyri's cheek and smearing her skin with Juaan's blood. "And I promise you, Yatal will make sure that he gets it." The last came out in a snarl. "Now keep quiet unless you want that punishment to start right now."

Nyri lunged at the hated face that was so close to her own, but Bahari's strong arms pulled her back, preventing her from doing anything she'd regret.

Sakal snorted at her and returned to the front to lead her company on as if nothing had happened. Hot tears of pain and anger streamed down Nyri's cheeks to mingle with Juaan's blood. She wanted to look back again as the Eagle men jeered, taunting their prisoner, but Bahari prevented her with a broad palm on the top of her head.

"No, Nyriaana. There nothing you can do now. Wait."

Nyri gripped his furs, gritting her teeth as the tears continued to flow. *Help us, help us, anybody*, she thought in desperation.

But there was no answer. Nyri raged at the voices in her head, they that demanded so much and yet stood back and let her face this terror alone. It was only a matter of time now. Her only comfort lay in her knowledge that, no matter what, she and Juaan would soon be free of this world of horror and death. Her only fear was how much pain they would have to endure first. She doubted Yatal would grant them the mercy of a quick death. She wondered if she could get close enough to Juaan to be able to stop his heart, to grant him a painless escape before Yatal possessed him.

She shuddered away from the thought, unsure, even in such circumstances, that she could bring herself to end

Juaan's life.

A loud whistle made her flinch, and a moan of denial made its way out against Bahari's furs. Sakal was announcing her presence to Yatal's scouts, a note of triumph ringing through the tone. They had arrived at the Eagle camp. Hoots and low whistles sounded in response, welcoming the hunting group home.

Nyri trembled as Bahari carried her through the camp. She kept her eyes closed, not wanting to look upon this dreaded place. She thought she had escaped her doom here, but it had only sat, patiently awaiting her return. Baleful eyes crawled over her back. Low hisses of hatred grated across her ears.

A muffled grunt and the familiar clatter of a stone rolling over rocky ground had Nyri's heart leaping to her throat. Were they going to stone Juaan to death before they even made it to Yatal?

Bahari's voice rumbled in his chest against her ear as he spoke a command, and Nyri dared to peek one eye around his arm to see his Thal warriors forming a tight barrier around Juaan as he was dragged over the ground by Sakal's men, effectively shielding him from further abuse. They glowered from under their heavy brows at the surrounding Eagle clan. Warning snarls from the still bristling Nisaru had the would-be attackers thinking twice.

"Th-thank you," Nyri forced the words between her chattering teeth.

"The Jade Killer still belongs to me," Bahari said. "And no honour in harming a defenceless man." Disapproval saturated the Cro man's voice. His arms tightened around her. "We approach Yatal's shelter."

Nyri closed her eyes again. Moments later, the air shifted, and they passed into the confines of the chieftess' dwelling. The smell was the first thing that hit Nyri. She had smelled it before. Only now it was more acute. The stench of rotting flesh and the promise of death.

Yatal.

"My Chieftess," Sakal's voice had a different quality on the deadened air. "The honour-son of the Sag Du Alok presents you with gifts."

There came an apathetic grunt. "We have already traded for this season," Yatal rasped and Nyri's shoulders hunched at the sound of it. "I have no further need of trinkets. Tell him to leave. I am weary."

"My Chieftess. It is not trinkets Alok honours you with. He has sent the most coveted of offerings."

"Is it the Red Bear's head? For that is the only gift that would comfort me before the cursed gods strip me of my final breath."

Nyri felt Sakal's discomfort and the shift of the Eagle warrior's feet was loud in the all but silent shelter.

"Not the Red Bear, Chieftess, but two gifts of almost equal value. Bring him forward!" Sakal's voice snapped in command.

Nyri lifted her face away from Bahari's furs in time to see Sakal's hunters haul Juaan forward and kick him roughly towards the base of a heap of furs piled in the centre of the expansive dwelling.

"I lay Eldrax's Spear Cat at your feet, my Chieftess."

The furs shifted, rustling as Yatal emerged from the shapeless heap, pushing herself around from where she had been lying with her back to her audience.

Nyri recoiled at the sight of the layered, ancient face. Sallow skin hung from Yatal's bones, shrunken and wasted. Her heavy-lidded eyes fell upon Juaan lying bound before her. The colourless cheeks flushed as she hauled herself upright, blinking as though unsure if her fading sight was deceiving her.

There was a long pause, and then a wheezing laugh bubbled from her throat. "I never thought to have the mighty Khalvir brought so low before me," she rasped. "It brings pleasure to my old heart indeed. How did Alok manage a feat such as this?"

"Unknown, my Chieftess, but I suspect it has to do with Alok's next gift. The heart is nothing but a weakness after all," Sakal sneered as she turned to Bahari, beckoning to him. Nyri tasted the Cro man's misery as he stepped forward and set her down beside Juaan. He was careful to keep his hand firmly on her shoulder, however.

The colour that had risen drained once again from the Eagle Chieftess' face. "You!" she snarled.

Juaan rolled up onto his knees, wincing as the blood flowed from the deep wound Sakal had dealt to his thigh, and shouldered Nyri behind him. "Yatal, I will pay for her life with my blood. Please, spare her."

"No!" Nyri threw herself forward, trying to put herself between Juaan and Yatal, fighting against Bahari's grip.

"Oh, you will pay with your blood, Khalvir," Yatal hissed. "But no amount of it will absolve her of her crime. No amount of your pain would ease mine for what she did. Only when I send the head of Eldrax's most coveted prize back to him will the soul of my beloved granddaughter find rest."

"I did not kill your granddaughter," Nyri whispered between dry lips.

"Silence!" Yatal shrieked, shocking Nyri with her sudden strength. The hatred pouring from the Eagle leader flowed over her, suffocating. "I heard enough of your lies last time we crossed paths, elf-witch."

Then Bahari was there. "Great Yatal, I speak for my father."

"Alok may ask for whatever he wishes for this honour," Yatal rasped, though her black eyes remained fixed on Nyri and Juaan.

"I wish to speak trade."

"Ask for what you want and go. It is yours."

Bahari's hand flexed on Nyri's shoulder. "I have condition on handing over Dryad and Jade Killer."

Yatal growled, her impatience biting, though she eyed the great grishnaa cat in Bahari's shadow. "Very well. I will spare you a short time. Take them," she jabbed a finger in Nyri's direction. "Keep them secure until I have satisfied Alok's pup. Then we will begin."

Several of the Eagle clan rushed forward, fighting to be the ones to catch hold of Juaan's bindings. Those who lost the race, however, were left facing Nyri, and they shrank back as though she were a viper capable of killing with a single bite.

"Cowards!" Yatal barked.

Bahari gave a soft word to the Thal standing closest to him, who dipped his chin before stooping and gently lifting Nyri into his burly arms. The relief from the Eagles was palpable as they dragged Juaan from the foot of their leader's resting place. Nyri's gaze touched Bahari's as she was borne from

195

the shelter. The Cro man's mouth was set in a determined line, but all hope had turned to ash in Nyri's mouth. Bahari was outnumbered in the heart of the Eagle's territory. It would be wise for him to just take what he had come for and leave with his life.

The Eagles conducted them to a small shelter beside Yatal's own, dumping Juaan with his arms still wrenched behind his back in the very centre of the space. The Thal bearing Nyri placed her on the ground next to Juaan with what sounded like a sympathetic murmur, before leaving quickly, no doubt wanting to return to protect Bahari's back as soon as possible.

"Move her away from him," one of the Eagles barked at his fellows. "I don't want any of her tricks."

"You move her away," another man challenged.

They all shifted mutinously, glaring at one another.

"Snivelling babes." The first started forward.

Nyri planted herself over Juaan and glared at the approaching Eagle. She had never once considered herself a threatening figure, small and slight as she was in this land of her People's enemies, but Yatal's warrior halted in his tracks as he beheld her face, losing nerve.

He shrugged a shoulder in an attempt to save face. "They're not getting away," he sniffed. "The Spear Cat is beaten. He reeks of defeat. And Sakal made sure he won't be moving on that leg for a while." The others muttered their quick agreement, and stood back against the walls of the shelter, their spears relaxed but held in ready positions. The one who had spoken extended his weapon enough to nudge Juaan's wounded thigh with the butt, eliciting a low hiss of pain through Juaan's teeth.

Nyri kicked the spear aside. "Don't!"

The Eagle backed off, snickering unpleasantly. "That is a dream walk compared to what Yatal will have planned for him." He fingered the hunting knife at his waist as though longing to get started with whatever horror existed in his mind. His dark eyes fell upon Nyri. "But rest assured, witch, his suffering will pale compared to your own. Your crime was somewhat more… personal to the Chieftess." With that parting blow, he swept from the shelter.

Nyri's brief flare of defiance drained away, and she sagged down against Juaan. She was trembling, but couldn't really tell where her motion ended and the disturbed vibration of the Great Spirit began. The whole world continued to heave around her, gathering, gathering… for what? Her death?

It was so close now, she could feel it. Did the Great Spirit always act this way when death approached? She had faced death many times in the company of the Cro, but had never experienced such a terrible foreboding. It only reinforced the knowledge that this time there would be no escape. A half sob found its way past Nyri's lips.

Juaan's fingers closed around hers. He did not say anything as she leaned against him. The beast inside him coiled and uncoiled, flexing in response to the Great Spirit's unrest. It was fighting to be free of its bonds. Nyri recalled the times it had been loosed, the way the Watcher had dropped dead at Juaan's feet in the Forest, its heart crushed in its chest. The raw power had terrified her then, and she had wished never to see such horror again. But, if it could save Juaan's life… These Cro guards would be nothing but flies swatted by an ox's tail.

197

"Let it out," she hissed softly, knowing he would understand her meaning. "Stop fighting it, Juaan."

He grew still. "You would have me murder these men in cold blood?"

Ice slipped through Nyri's gut at the hint of betrayal in his tone, but she forged on regardless. Between Juaan's life and theirs, there could be no choice, no room to think, only to act.

"Yes," she said.

He pulled his hand from hers. "I cannot," he whispered coolly. "We are not close enough to the Great Spirit's River Line."

"But being next to the Mountain River Line is not the only time you have released your power," Nyri said. "You did it in the Pit. When I guided you, your power was freed. If I…"

"No, Nyriaana." Now the bite of anger and betrayal was plain to hear. "I will not be used as a weapon. Never again. I will not kill these men in cold blood. They only seek to protect their own, and exact what is owed to them many times over."

Frustrated tears started in Nyri's eyes. "But you are not Khalvir anymore! You don't deserve this!"

"And these men do not deserve to die."

"And what about me?" Nyri drew on her last weapon as she choked on her tears.

His fingers closed around hers once more and held tight. "You are the main reason I will not do such a thing, Nyriaana."

"I-I don't understand." Did he believe she deserved to die? Was he so repelled by what she had become? Nyri hardened her heart, preparing to do the unthinkable; to point out that it was his fault she had changed. If it wasn't for him, she would not be here. It would cause him pain beyond imagining and put such a fissure between them it would never truly be healed. But if it saved him, it would be worth it. "Juaan—"

"I can't risk you, Nyriaana." His words stopped her short. "You know what I have done. You heard my story of what happened to Nameeda. I loved her… and I killed her. What if I did that to you?"

"You wouldn't."

"You can't know that, Nyri. This thing inside me cannot be controlled. It doesn't differentiate between friend and foe. And I cannot put your life at risk. I would rather suffer every torture under Utu than know that I was the one who snuffed out your light. Please, don't ask this of me." He tilted his head to rest it on top of hers, his breath ruffling gently through her hair.

"I'm going to die, anyway."

His muscles tensed. "No, Nyriaana. I do not believe that. Bahari will fight for you and you will make Yatal see the truth. You must. You are not lost."

She barked a hollow laugh. "How?"

He chuckled. "You have powers of your own, or have you forgotten? *Make* her see."

"I-I don't know how. Nothing is right. I don't know what is happening, Juaan. Something is wrong." Fear and the building tension in the earth were scattering Nyri's connection to the Great Spirit. Waves of upheaval, of warning, pounded against her skull. Her doom was at hand. Just outside of this shelter, it waited for both of them. If

Juaan would not fight, then there was no hope. And if they were going to die, then they would do so on her terms. She would not let Juaan suffer a slow and agonising death for Yatal's pleasure. She felt his heartbeat throb against hers, so very central to her world... so very fragile.

She bit her lip. Could she stop this heart that she had only recently jolted back to life? How could she live with herself knowing she had been the one to snuff out Juaan's light? *You're not going to have to survive with the knowledge for long,* her inner voice whispered. *This will be a mercy.*

Nyri closed her eyes, the tears leaking down her cheeks, as she reached for the power of the earth. It bucked and scattered as she drew on it, the Great Spirit behaving like a wild animal cornered. Nyri grasped onto it in desperation. She needed the power of KI for this. Piece by piece, she gathered the strength she needed and clasped Juaan's hand tightly within hers, merging their life forces together.

"Nyri," Juaan warned. Misunderstanding her intentions, he tried to free his hand, fearing she was going to free the beast inside him, but his bindings prevented him from breaking loose. Nyri tightened her grip, extending her will. "Nyri, don't!" The panic in his voice almost broke her concentration.

"I am sorry," she whispered. "I can't let them hurt you." And she grasped the pulse of life within.

No! The power of multiple disembodied voices ripped through her mind and Nyri cried out as they shattered her concentration, scattering the power she had fought so hard to gather for the task.

"Stay out of this!" Nyri snarled at the unseen voices, reaching for the Great Spirit again.

"Bring the captives!" The opening to the shelter burst aside as the dark eyed Eagle warrior re-entered. "Yatal wants them now!"

Nyri cried as the other Eagles rushed forward to take hold of Juaan, lifting him away.

"Nyriaana, *show* her," he said, before his hand was torn from hers.

"No." The reluctant Cro warriors did not have to seize her and carry her from the shelter. Nyri dragged herself to her feet and staggered after the ones who had taken Juaan.

The Great Spirit broiled stronger than ever, scrambling Nyri's senses as she stumbled on, groping along. She barely noticed as she passed into Yatal's shelter, inhaling the scent of decay. There were faces all around, Cro, Cro-Thal mixes, and the faces of the true Thals who had accompanied Bahari, all staring as she followed Juaan through their midst. At the centre of the dwelling, the Eagles threw him once more at their leader's feet.

Bahari was standing close to Yatal's side, Nisaru weaving restlessly behind him, but Nyri ignored his presence, expending all her effort on maintaining her grip on reality. She focused on the immediate danger as the stooping figure of the Eagle chieftess rose to leer over them.

Yatal's breath rattled in her chest. "The trade has been agreed," she wheezed. "You are now mine to do with as I choose, Khalvir. And for the suffering you have caused, each day, I will have a piece of you delivered to the edge of Eldrax's camp, and he will know I have defeated and robbed him of his best warrior."

A sad smile tugged at the edges of Juaan's mouth. "He will not grieve the loss, Yatal. He will only be angry he was not the one to carve the flesh from my bones himself."

Yatal's lip curled back from her broken teeth. "We will see." Her gaze shifted to someone above Juaan's head. "Start with his spear hand," she commanded.

"It will be my pleasure, Chieftess." Nyri recognised Sakal's nasally voice as the warrior moved forward to take hold of Juaan's bindings.

"As for you," Yatal turned the full force of her hatred upon Nyri. "Sakal tells me you care for this butcher."

Nyri wavered, locking her knees. The Great Spirit bucked violently, rushing past her in a wave of dizzying sensation.

Nyriaana. Nyriaana!

Nyri groaned as she lost her battle to remain upright before her enemy and crashed to the ground. Bahari was at her side in the next heartbeat, his hands firm on her arms.

"Nyriaana! What?" he asked, his dark forehead creasing.

"I don't know!" Nyri forced the vomit back down her throat, but the tenor of the Great Spirit was changing and she knew it now for the warning it was. "Yatal, please, please have mercy. You are in danger. We are all in danger."

The Eagle leader grunted, unmoved. "I am wise to your tricks, witch. No more. You took the most precious thing in my life, and now I will take yours. You will remain with Eldrax's Spear Cat while Sakal works, and you will make sure he remains awake and alive for as long as your witch powers allow. And when nothing but his head remains, Sakal is to strip the skin from your flesh. That will be my last gift to the Red Bear. His greatest warrior's head wrapped in the flesh of his most desired possession." She cackled, the laugh turning to a cough. A thick hand dashed away a spray of blood.

202

"No!" Bahari's protest cut through the stale air. "That not our agreement! Dryad lives as your captive!"

"You have your right to our fish and you get to keep your lives, Alok honour-son. Deny me further, and you will lose both!"

Bahari's outrage burned through the air. Nyri sagged in the Cro man's grip, barely able to conceive the horror of what Yatal was proposing. She should have let Juaan die a quick death at the hands of Eldrax. She should have let Yatal stone her to death at their first meeting. Anything was preferable to this; keeping Juaan alive while Sakal slowly butchered him. How could anyone's hate be so powerful to pass such a judgement?

You have powers of your own. Power. Yes. Yatal thought her a murderer. *Well, then.* Nyri would give her a murderer. Through tear streaked eyes, Nyri fixed her gaze on the hated chieftess; a shrewd, cruel woman, secure in her own might. Take all that away and Yatal was nothing but an inconsequential bundle of meat and bone, so very weak.

Cold as ice, Nyri noted every vulnerable spot, every place where the slightest push would kill the Eagle leader. She just had to get to her. Only one guard stood between her and her target. Fuelled by her hatred, Nyri staggered to her feet, setting her jaw.

No! Not that way...

Nyri shook her head, trying to throw off the ghost of Sefaan's voice. But the old Kamaali made her pause for one vital moment, pushing back the thumping turmoil enough for a ray of better sense to shine through. If she killed Yatal, nothing would change. She and Juaan would still be tortured to death by the rest of the vengeful clan. *Help me!*

Show *her.*

Nyri's brow pinched together. *How?* The memory of Sefaan sharing the first vision of Ariyaana thrust itself to the forefront of her mind. Nyriaana had not been able to deny the truth of what Sefaan wanted her to see, no matter how much she had wished to deny it.

Show her.

Fighting the disorientating spin of the Great Spirit, Nyri lurched forward, reaching for the Eagle leader.

Yatal shrieked in alarm and the guard moved to block Nyri's path. In her current befuddlement, Nyri knew she could not evade him. She could barely stand as KI continued to convulse beneath her feet. But she had to get to Yatal. She had to.

"Bahari!" The cry was past her lips before she was even aware of it. He had pledged his help. She needed him now.

He did not fail her. The adopted Cro intercepted Yatal's guard before the Eagle warrior was aware of what was happening. Bahari was quick. In the time it took Nyri to lurch two strides, he had subdued the Eagle man. The other Thals rallied around their leader, gripping their weapons nervously in the midst of the Eagles. The *grishnaa* cat, Nisaru, crouched, snarling and spitting at her master's side.

Her way was free. There was no time to question whether she had the skill to do as Sefaan had. There was only time to act. Yatal tried to fight her off, but the elder was too weak to resist as Nyri planted one hand on the Eagle chieftess' head.

The Eagles in the shelter cried out, but did not dare attack for fear that one wrong move would bring an end to their Chieftess. Nyri ignored them. "Look and know the truth!"

she cried, flinging all of her energy into her thoughts and memories, projecting them into Yatal's flinching mind. The old leader had no defence against the onslaught, could not doubt the truth of what she saw.

Nyri focused on her last moments with Yatal's grand-daughter. How hard she had tried to save her, how she had almost lost herself trying to grip on to those last wisps of her life. Then she forced Yatal to feel what the girl had felt as only Nyri had known. The pain, her desperation to be free of suffering at last; her overwhelming love for her grandmother; her gratitude to Nyri for accompanying her spirit, easing her fear as she departed on her next journey.

"Oh," Yatal gave a little shuddering gasp, and Nyri knew if she opened her eyes, she would see the tears sliding down the old Chieftess' wrinkled cheeks. Her body sagged a little lower beneath Nyri's hand. The hate and rage that had kept her spirit burning within her failing body melted away, leaving nothing but the grief and despair she had kept hidden behind it.

Nyri began to release her grip, but in that moment, the Great Spirit crested, ripping through her like a lightning strike. Her hold on Yatal's mind spasmed as it rolled through her body in the strongest wave she had yet experienced.

What is happening? It was Yatal's voice, sounding small and fearful inside her mind. Unable to let go, Nyri realised the old Cro leader was experiencing KI for the first time through her connection to Nyri.

Nyriaana could not answer, for she had lost control of her own thoughts. Visions flew at her, clearer and more terrible than ever before. Old images of the very first visions Sefaan had shown her. A Ninkuraaja woman struggling through the snow, fleeing the hunters seeking her, her green-eyed Forbidden child huddled against her breast. Memories rushed by. Memories of Nyri's childhood with Juaan and the overwhelming sense of *rightness* whenever they were together. Nyri's high scream of denial overlaid the image of a young Juaan being torn from her, taken to be turned into a weapon by Eldrax. Then came the visions of the Mountains and the Forbidden girl that awaited, the enu seed of a Kamaali hanging about her neck, beckoning for Nyri to come to her. Humanity would be lost if she refused this path. The cacophony of voices began, pleading, begging, commanding. A confusion of new images. The land as she knew it turned to waste, plundered and blackened, carelessly ripped open for the offerings beneath as smoke filled the air. No trees. No water. Nothing could survive.

Why? Why? Why?

Only you can change this future, Nyriaana. My Ninkuraaja must live on or greed will reduce the world to ash.

W-who are you? Nyri's thoughts spiralled.

The answer never came, instead the next images were directed at Yatal and the disembodied voice echoed through their combined consciousness. *Prepare yourself, Daughter of Enki, for the Lord Enlil has awakened. The Lullu Amelu must no longer stand divided. He is coming in all his wrath. Destruction in his eye. He is coming...*

Nyri felt Yatal shudder as visions of the Watchers pouring from their forest under the fully open eye of Ninsiku seared through both their minds. The death and destruction of Man followed in the wake of their rampage. Overlaying the image was a face, golden skinned and beautiful, with blue eyes as cold as death.

How? Yatal's thoughts responded. *I am old. How am I to do this?*

One is coming to you. You know him. You must make peace in order to let him pass. Lord Enlil awakes...

Then the voice and its overwhelming presence vanished. Nyri lurched to the side, pain exploding behind her eyes. Her hands went to her head as she moaned in agony. The vibrations in the Great Spirit had reached fever pitch.

Yatal's hands caught her under her armpits, supporting her as the old Eagle leader staggered to her feet. "Out of the way!" she commanded the terrified onlookers as she limped towards the entrance to her shelter. "Out of the way!"

Cold air washed across Nyri's face, signalling their emergence from the shelter into the outside world. With stinging eyes, she turned her face towards the looming Mountains above, already knowing what she would see in the dark grey sky above, for the *genii* had already shown her.

Three blue orbs danced above the peaks, blinding in their spellbinding beauty.

The harbingers of death.

* * *

12

Retribution

150,000 BCE

"This is an outrage!" *Enki blustered, pacing up and down before Enlil's dais.*

Enlil smirked when his sibling turned away, enjoying his discomfort and anger. "Why is it outrageous, brother?" *he asked in a tone he knew would enrage Enki further.* "You created these abominations, forced me to accept the heresy of their existence. The Igigi needed appeasement, and the females of your experiments do please them so. We made the mistake of only enlisting male workers. The inferiors of our race cannot be allowed to dally with the elite, so I saw no reason why I should not grant them access to the slaves. It is their purpose to serve our every whim, is it not?"

"Yes," *Enki growled, but his golden skin had paled by several shades, rippling in uncontrolled distress.*

Enlil frowned, probing, but his brother was adept at shielding his thoughts. "I will not allow the Igigi to reduce the numbers of your slaves," *he sniffed.* "They will leave them alive after their *attentions," he said. "I acknowledge the sacrifice Ninmah and the other women must have made to increase the numbers as they have. Most admirable."*

Enki's scales stilled.

Enlil's eyes narrowed. "Is there any other reason why I should not permit the Igigi an outlet to their frustrations?"

Enki's pause was long and pregnant. "No," he said at last, though Enlil could see it cost him a great deal. It sickened Enlil to see how attached his brother had become to the abominations he had created.

"If there is nothing more, my Lord." Enki kept his eyes pinned to the polished floor.

"Dismissed." Enlil waved a hand, watching as his brother fled his chamber.

* * *

38,000BCE

The lights vanished from the sky, and the Great Spirit grew still. Kyaati gasped, reeling from the shock of what she had seen and felt. The Great Spirit's silence after the crescendo of sensation that had beaten her to the ground was almost a relief. Eldrax released her shoulder and disappeared.

Kyaati staggered without the support, but then Galahir was by her side. She leaned against him, her skull still pounding with the aftershocks.

"The gods." A low moaning went up around her, muttered by the voices of the clan. "The gods have arisen."

Kyaati looked around at the stricken faces and, for the

first time, saw that Halima was beside her. The matriarch's dark eyes were fixed upon the point where the lights had disappeared. "Halima," she asked. "What were they?"

Halima's voice was hushed, reflecting the pall of fear and hopelessness that held sway over the camp. "The gods," she said. "The gods have awoken."

"But the gods have gone," Kyaati argued. "They're gone!"

Nobody spoke. Kyaati could taste the terror in the air; it saturated her tongue and crept down her spine. Whatever those lights had been, one thing was clear: it was a bad omen. Kyaati's skin crawled with the sense of danger and threat that had taken hold of the Great Spirit. To stay in this place now, so close to the Mountains, was to court death. And whether it be gods or some other power, it was coming.

"We need to leave!" Kyaati declared, her voice ringing out over the murmur of nervous whispers. All eyes turned to her.

"And go where?"

Selima. Eldrax's daughter's eyes flashed as she challenged Kyaati. "You are not our leader, elf-witch. You might have tried to bewitch the clan into turning on my father, but you have no right to lead us."

Several of the clan shifted uncomfortably at Selima's words, their eyes flicking nervously between the two women.

Kyaati forged on as though Selima had not spoken. If she was going to rally the clan against Eldrax, it had to happen now. "Listen to me. We must break camp and put as much distance between ourselves and the Mountains as we can. If the gods are coming for us, we must flee."

Selima laughed. "There is nowhere far enough to evade

the reach of the gods, you fool."

To Kyaati's dismay, murmurs of assent rippled around the clan. She was losing them. This dreadful omen had thrown all her carefully laid plans to join the clan together against their savage leader to the wind. When facing danger, Selima was right. She had not earned enough of their respect to lead. "I—"

Gasps and a few quiet cheers sounded as Eldrax chose that moment to reappear in their midst. In his right hand, he gripped his battle club. Sharpened bone fragments armoured his arms and legs; and below the bear skull adorning his head, fierce lines of ochre slashed across his pale skin. Kyaati's heart sank. It was clear Eldrax's choice was not to flee. Tanag stood in his shadow, similarly dressed for battle.

"The gods have thrown down a challenge," Eldrax roared, raising his club. "I intend to answer it. They will rue the day they thought to make us cower in fear!"

Several voices rose in answer to his rally, but it eased Kyaati's heart somewhat to see that not all the clan appeared at ease with this show of force. The ancient keeper of stories, the clan's Dugnamtar stood, supported by Akito. "You have angered the gods by killing a Watcher, mighty Red Bear. Nunamnir calls for an offering to prove our continued loyalty. Such is how it always was. And so it must always be. We must appease him if we do not wish to bring his full wrath down upon us!"

A few shouts of agreement went up from the clan, opposing those gathering behind Eldrax.

Eldrax curled his lip. "Appease the gods?"

"Yes." The elder's voice was firm in his conviction. "We

must if we are to survive."

"And what appeasement would please the Great Nunamnir, storyteller?" Eldrax asked.

"What he always wanted," the Dugnamtar returned. "Children. Women. We must choose sacrifices and deliver them to the edges of the woods for the Watchers to take. We have neglected this offering for far too long."

A deep silence fell. Kyaati's mouth went dry as Galahir's arms went around both her and Elhaari, drawing them closer to him. She noticed several of the other men similarly gathering their families into protective proximity. The ranks of UnClaimed women shifted among themselves, their faces paling.

These motions were not lost on Eldrax and Kyaati watched as a triumphant smile curled across his lips.

"I will sacrifice none of our women and children, Dugnamtar!" the Red Bear snarled. "Pay penance to the gods? It is they who should pay penance to *us*!" He beat the smooth part of his weapon against his chest.

A stirring whispered through the crowd at the leader's bold words.

"I will bow to no god," Eldrax continued, pacing back and forth, his enormous presence commanding attention as he held each one of their gazes. "I will bow to no god who causes his creations to suffer!"

The soft stirring turned to murmurs of ascent.

"They do not deserve our loyalty! They do not deserve our bloodshed! They abandoned us here to die, sending winters, hunger and curses to wipe us out. They wanted us dead, and now they dare to ask for a sign of loyalty." Eldrax spat on the ground. "I say, let them come! I will not cower.

I will not hide. It is time to teach them who rules this land!"

"Yes!" Now the voice of the clan was as one.

"I have been preparing for this day. It has come sooner than we ever imagined, but I have prepared. And now we have a witch and her child ready to serve." Kyaati stiffened, her heart plummeting to her stomach as the weight of all eyes fell upon her. A cold fury seeped into her bones, causing her to shake in the circle of Galahir's arm. Eldrax intended to use her in this fight. Her and her baby.

"We are prepared." Eldrax settled into stillness. "And when I am done, I will be the one from which the gods will flee. I will banish them from this land and the winters of long suffering will be no more! Who is your Chief?"

"Red Bear! Red Bear!" The air vibrated with the fierce pride and anger that Eldrax had stirred in their souls. Kyaati tasted bile in her mouth. They were all fools.

"Galahir," she murmured, just loud enough to be heard over the din. "Please take me away from here."

His hand wasn't as steady on Kyaati's shoulder as she would have liked as he pulled her away. She was only faintly aware that Halima and Kikima were following in their footsteps, their emotions blank, thoughts wordless.

"Sacrificing women and children?" Kyaati's voice sounded sick to her own ears as the hides of Galahir's shelter fell closed behind them. She turned, her eyes seeking Halima's face. The usually commanding matriarch appeared shrunken, her eyes staring. "Halima?"

Kikima placed a hand on Halima's arm, shaking her out of the stupor that had fallen upon her.

"Such a sign has not been seen in countless generations," she said, "but our ancestors' stories tell of it from the time

213

when the gods still walked the land. The Dugnamtar is right. Nunamnir demands penance."

"Why now?"

Halima fixed her with a dark stare and it frightened Kyaati more than anything else to see the fear there. "Isn't it obvious? We killed a Watcher."

"We were defending ourselves from those creatures!"

"We are not meant to defend ourselves from the gods." Halima's smile was wan.

"I should never have gone into the Forest," Galahir moaned, breaking the silence he had held since the battle. "It's my fault. I took what was theirs. I started this."

Kyaati clutched his hand where it still rested on her shoulder.

"No, Galahir," Halima shook her head. "The Chief wanted this. He would have provoked them himself sooner or later. The Watchers have been nothing but an insult to Eldrax since he was barely out of boyhood," Halima said. "Do not blame yourself."

Galahir jerked his chin in acknowledgement, but the weight of responsibility did not lift from his shoulders. Kyaati could feel it as if it were her own.

"I wish Khalvir was here," her mate murmured to no one in particular.

Thoughts of Nyri, though not forgotten, had been far from the forefront of Kyaati's mind during the latest events. There was still no word from the final hunting groups Eldrax had sent after them.

"It would do no good if he were," Halima said. "With Eldrax still alive, he would be killed on sight. We failed to get to the Red Bear before the gods appeared, and now he is stronger than ever. Even if that were not so, what could Khalvir do against the gods' wrath?"

Kyaati shifted uncomfortably. She had witnessed what Khalvir could do. She remembered with a shiver how he had killed the Watcher in the Forest during hers and Nyri's misguided escape attempt, how he had ripped the life from the creature. His power had worked just as Elhaari's had, only with the full force of a grown man. *This* was why Eldrax had wanted her People. To use them in his vendetta against the creatures guarding the forests around the Mountains. Perhaps even against the gods themselves, if they still existed.

"I must return to my women." Halima straightened her shoulders. The shock was leaving her and Kyaati saw a ghost of her old strength returning to her face, though her eyes were still hollow. Kikima lifted her chin, her golden eyes fierce. "I'll come with you. I have no doubt the Chief will have other matters to occupy him for a time."

Kyaati almost smiled. It would take more than the threat of a god's retribution to subdue Kikima's indomitable spirit. She noted the other young woman was gripping a long hunting knife in one hand. Kyaati's smile faded. How much death was about to follow?

Kyaati flinched as fires flared to life outside their shelter. "Let us feast!" Eldrax's voice rumbled through the air as drums rolled. Kyaati hissed. The fools were actually celebrating.

Neither she nor Galahir moved to rejoin the clan, not caring if they were missed. They sat within the walls of their shelter, listening to snatches of stories as Eldrax regaled his followers with the glories of past battles. The voices of the clan became rougher and rowdier and Kyaati imagined vision water being passed from hand to hand. The atmosphere shifted as any lasting qualms or fears the men might have harboured melted away and their fervour matched that of their crazed leader. Galahir gripped her hand in his own. It was a long time before the sound of feasting and celebration filtered into silence; the clan falling into exhausted slumber as the dying fires smouldered to ash. Kyaati did not sleep. She lay awake in Galahir's arms as Ninmah crept into the sky. She knew sleep had not found her mate, and that Galahir was similarly staring up into the hides above. Only their sweetly oblivious son slept on.

A pounding of a drum shattered their contemplation and Kyaati shook herself, tightening her hold on Galahir's furs. Eldrax was summoning his raknari.

"I should go," Galahir murmured, but made no effort to shift from her side.

"Galahir." She did not want him to leave, but it would not do to provoke the Red Bear further. Her mate was already in the Chief's ill-favour for almost destroying his plans to kill the Watcher in the spiked pit.

"What do you feel?" Galahir's words caught her off guard. Her mate knew well of her abilities, but they were so strange to him. She knew they made him uncomfortable, and he rarely raised the subject.

"I-I don't know," Kyaati hesitated. "The Great Spirit of KI is quiet."

"Is that good?"

"No, not this silence." She paused, mulling over her words, thinking of how to describe what she was feeling in terms Galahir would understand. "This is like a bird falling silent before the storm."

Galahir raised up from their tangle of furs to look her full in the face. His blue eyes were serious. Kyaati's heart ached for the jovial, carefree gleam she had fallen in love with. A side of him that appeared to have died since the day Nyri and Khalvir had fled. "I promise I will let nothing happen to either of you," he said. "Whatever awaits."

Kyaati smiled wanly as she pulled her fingers gently through his wild mane of Ninmah-kissed hair. She refrained from pointing out that she and Elhaari would be more likely to be the ones protecting him.

The drums banged again, and this time, there was an insistence to their rhythm.

"I have to go." He pressed her hand where it rested against his cheek. "I will see what the Red Bear has planned."

Kyaati gritted her teeth as he planted a lingering kiss on her forehead. Galahir pulled himself away and swept from the shelter. The air felt chilly beside Kyaati in his absence. She lifted Elhaari into her arms to fill the void. He blinked his green eyes and cooed softly at her. Kyaati bit her lip. If the gods had indeed awoken, what did that mean for her Forbidden son? A fresh fissure of panic cracked through Kyaati's heart and she almost called Galahir back, ready to bolt.

Steadying herself, she took the time to wrap Elhaari in an extra layer of fur. It was no longer so cold, but a quiver in the air told Kyaati there was a storm brewing, and as she pushed out of the shelter, sure enough, dark clouds were gathering on the western horizon. The wind tugged fractiously on her furs. The air tasted electric on her tongue. She hurried to the Dwelling of the UnClaimed.

Most of the women had already gathered outside Halima's domain when Kyaati arrived. Stacked piles of bone and flint lay on the ground next to mounds of wood and hide. The boys of the clan scurried back and forth as they added to the supplies.

"We are to prepare armour and weapons for the men," a rich voice murmured close to Kyaati's side, and she tilted her head back to meet Kikima's eyes. "Halima is finding it hard to find enough tools for all the women to work with. Here," the half Deni woman handed Kyaati a knapping rock and several awls, "I saved you the best. Your work is shoddy enough without having ill-favoured tools." Kikima's full lips quirked.

Kyaati grimaced. "Thank you."

The amusement slid from Kikima's face and she squeezed Kyaati's shoulder with a large hand. Now that her friend had dropped the veneer of humour, Kyaati saw an icy dread lurking in the shadows of the other woman's eyes.

"Kikima, what's wrong?"

"It's nothing," her tall companion tried to brush her off. "Nothing we need to concern ourselves with now. We have to get to work."

"It's not nothing," Kyaati caught Kikima's hand. One touch was all it took. Kyaati wasn't Nyriaana, but she was attuned enough to detect the secret her friend was hiding. "Kikima!" Her eyes widened, though why she was so shocked, she could not guess.

Kikima scowled. "I should have known I could not hide my condition from a witch."

Kyaati ignored the slight. "Is it Eldrax's?"

Kikima gave her a pitying, sidelong stare. "You think I

would dare betray the Chief once he had Claimed me for himself?"

Kyaati grimaced. "Does Halima know?"

"No," Kikima said. "She has enough on her mind, and... I did not feel like speaking. Not yet."

Kyaati saw the warning on her friend's face and nodded, squeezing her hand. "I will not speak," she said. "Not until you are ready."

Kikima dipped her head in gratitude and led Kyaati towards a stack of flint that was only continuing to grow in size. Silence fell between them. Kyaati's heart filled with pity for Kikima. She could understand her reticence to speak of the life she now carried inside her. The child of a Chief. The child of a bloodthirsty madman preparing to plunge them all into battle against forces unknown.

Kyaati would have liked to think that if Kikima told the Chief of his unborn offspring, he might regain some sense and abandon this place. But Kyaati knew such a thought was a folly. She had felt Eldrax's crazed soul, and nothing would sway him now.

Selecting a raw piece of flint to fashion into a long blade, Kyaati settled next to Kikima to work. She studied the stone mulishly, deciding where best to strike first. Kikima was right, Kyaati was not the most skilled at fashioning the flint in ordinary circumstances and her concentration was so scattered, her fingers so tense and liable to tremble, her efforts now seemed doomed to failure. Her eyes kept straying to the Mountains and the empty space where the terrible lights had danced. Had the gods truly awoken? A shiver ran down Kyaati's spine at the thought of the purpose for which she was preparing this flint. Her fingers trembled again.

"Try it like this," Kikima said gently, taking Kyaati's small hands in her own and guiding her in the motions to split the flint apart. Akito approached them, his young arms laden with flint and wood. He listened to Kikima's instructions as Kyaati struggled to shape the blade that was forming.

"It might be better to try it like this." The blind boy reached out towards the sound of striking stone.

"I know how to make a knife!" Kikima huffed.

A smile played out over the child's face. "I know. But I know how to do it better. Galahir taught me."

"Galahir would be of more use here than I am," Kyaati muttered. She scanned the camp, feeling a curl of unease when she realised all the adult males and older boys were missing. "Where are the men?" she asked.

Kikima lifted her head and pointed away towards the distant dark line of the forest against the foot of the Mountains. "Eldrax led them."

"No!" Kyaati started rising to her feet.

Kikima caught her by the arm. "They aren't going into the Forest. Not yet. Eldrax has the men digging more pits."

"And are pits going to work?" Kyaati snapped, pulling her arm free. "Is any of this going to work? If we are facing the wrath of the gods, what good is this?" Kyaati struck the cross section of the forming knife with her knapping stone, shattering it to pieces. "Eldrax will kill us all."

Several pairs of accusing eyes turned in her direction. Kyaati met them with a raised chin.

"Sit down, Kyaati!" Kikima used her superior strength to yank her to the ground.

"You think we're going to die?" Akito's lip trembled.

"No," Kyaati hissed. "Not if I can help it."

"Quiet!" Kikima snapped, jerking her head.

Kyaati followed her gaze. Selima was approaching. Kyaati's lips peeled back off her teeth. The black eyes of Eldrax's daughter roved over the splintered shards of flint lying at Kyaati's feet. "I'd hate to be the man carrying your weapons into battle, elf-witch. Haven't you learned even that simple task, yet?" She sniffed, shifting the bundle of herbs she carried in her arms. "At least your traitorous tribe-sister was good for something. You are next to useless. It's a good thing my father only needs your—"

She never got to finish. There was a clatter of stone and Kikima's fist cracked across the red-haired girl's jaw, sending her sprawling to the ground in a shower of herbs.

"You never did learn when to keep your mouth shut," Kikima said, shaking her hand out from the force of the blow.

Dazed, Selima struggled to rise. "My father will have your head!"

Kikima laughed. "I don't think so. *I* am a valued mate, able to give him the offspring he desires. You are nothing but the unwanted spawn of an outsider. Try as you might, Selima, Eldrax cares nothing for you, and he never will."

For a moment, just for a moment, Kyaati almost felt sorry for the girl. Kikima's words tore aside the arrogance leaving Selima's face naked, and Kyaati saw she knew well what her father thought of her and it cut her to the bone.

Hiding sudden tears, Selima sprang to her feet, spitting blood in Kikima's direction, before swooping down on her spilled herbs and stalking away.

"I've been wanting to do that for many seasons," Kikima

said, rubbing her knuckles.

Kyaati frowned at the few herbs that still lay in the grass. "Be careful she doesn't try to finish you herself, Kikima," she warned.

Kikima snorted. "Selima doesn't frighten me. There are bigger concerns right now."

The cold shiver ran down Kyaati's spine again at the reminder. She scowled at the piles and piles of materials that were still being added to. For some reason, it bothered her. "Why so much?" she asked of no-one in particular. "There is enough material here to make more weapons than our men could ever carry."

"Eldrax did not inform Halima of his intentions," Kikima squatted back down to the ground, retrieving her half-formed spearhead from where she had dropped it.

Kyaati's mouth twisted as she searched for another flint.

"Perhaps you would be better making bone armour," Akito suggested, feeling around for the cracked pieces of bone he had carried over with him. "All you have to do is sharpen the ends and then thread them onto hide strips to tie around the arms and legs."

Kyaati sighed and accepted a large piece of bleached white material that appeared to be an antelope's shoulder blade. She shuddered, but got to work, her hands busy while her mind worked, hunched against the wind. Thunder rumbled in the threatening clouds above. She could not allow her son to be used in this fight Eldrax was provoking. But the clan was now united behind their leader. They would not retreat. And if she fled, Eldrax would hunt them down.

The light was dimming when Kyaati could no longer force her hands or her mind to work and she threw her tools down in exhausted frustration as the first drops of rain splashed to the dry ground.

"It is time to rest." Halima appeared at their sides, taking in Kyaati's raw fingers. "Come, we will continue at dawn."

Kyaati cast an anxious glance towards the dark line of the distant forest, almost invisible against the storm clouds, searching for Galahir. There was no sign. Her throat closed. She no longer had her busy hands to distract her from her fear.

Halima put a hand on her shoulder and guided her into the Dwelling of the UnClaimed. "He'll be back," the matriarch reassured.

Kyaati lifted one side of her mouth in acknowledgment, but said nothing. A niggle had begun in the back of her mind and she could not shake it. The rest of the women and children filed into the large shelter in ones and twos and settled around the cooking fire that Halima had set at the centre. Although she was not cold, Kyaati found herself curling nearer to the warmth and light, as though the dancing tongues could banish the darkness that was gathering like the clouds above.

The rain came faster, lashing against the skin of the shelter as the wind worried and whined around the edges. Halima and Kikima scraped together enough leftovers from the feasting night before to feed all those sheltering within. Kyaati chewed listlessly on a piece of gristle as Elhaari suckled at her breast. She had just forced herself to swallow the disgusting morsel when the flaps of the shelter pulled back to admit the hulking form of her mate.

Relief washed through Kyaati like a cool river. "Galahir." She leapt to her feet and rushed to his side. He managed a smile for her, dispelling for a moment the exhaustion lining his broad face. She took his hands; they were chafed and bloody.

Before Kyaati could say a word, the entrance to the shelter billowed again and this time Lorhir emerged dripping from the storm outside. On the slender Cro man's hip sat a small, quivering boy. Lorhir's only son. He clung to his father as his frightened eyes swept around the shelter. Lorhir's face was as tired and careworn as Galahir's, dark skin pallid.

Halima came to intercept the new arrivals. She raised a questioning eyebrow at Lorhir.

"He was afraid of staying in his shelter," Lorhir explained his presence gruffly. "I thought being here with more company would be a comfort to him."

Halima's expression softened at the sight of the frightened child and she acquiesced to another mouth to feed. "Come," she beckoned.

Kyaati stayed on the opposite side of Galahir as both her mate and Lorhir found places beside the fire. Lorhir's son took the morsel that Halima offered and chewed on it while curling into his father's side.

"Any signs?" Halima asked, her voice unusually hesitant as she squatted before the two men in her domain.

Sitting in full contact with Galahir, Kyaati felt every one of his muscles tense. His fear saturated her tongue. Kyaati was quick to realise it was not only her mate's dread she was experiencing. Lorhir was similarly stricken, though he tried not to show it in front of his child.

"No," Galahir said softly. "The Watchers are nowhere to be seen."

"But?" Halima's eyes flicked between the two men.

"There were footprints."

"How many?"

"More than we ever thought." Galahir dropped his shaggy head into his hands, hiding his face from Kyaati.

Lorhir had no such concern for preserving their feelings. "Go and play," he pointed his son toward a group of other children. The boy tightened his grip on his father's furs, but Lorhir disentangled himself and gave the child a nudge. "Go on. I'm not going anywhere."

His son regarded him for a moment, assessing the truth of his father's words, and then reluctantly shuffled off to join his age-mates.

Lorhir waited until he was engrossed, then reached into his furs, producing an object for their observation. Kyaati's arms tightened around Elhaari as the vacant sockets of a human skull stared back at her. The crown had been shattered.

"These were strewn around the borders of the forest." Lorhir's voice was devoid of emotion. "Impaled on trees. It is a promise."

"Are we prepared?" Halima swallowed, straightening her shoulders in a habitual show of strength as was befitting her position.

Lorhir's laugh was soft and mocking.

Kyaati's tone was as dead as Lorhir's. "We barely defeated two Watchers with the full might of the clan. What does Eldrax hope to do against more?" Her voice rose at the end.

Lorhir and Galahir shifted; anger simmering beneath their skins. The rain lashed harder against the shelter.

"Galahir?"

"You were right, Halima. The Red Bear planned for this

225

fight," Galahir hissed, his voice unusually harsh. "He *planned* this."

"What has he done?" Kyaati's hand found his.

"He wasn't fool enough to think the Hunting Bear Clan alone would be enough," Lorhir spoke. "He has been amassing more warriors, subjugating other clans to his rule."

There was a beat of silence. "How?" Halima's voice was sharp.

"Murder." Galahir stared into the fire. "We have been so wrong, Halima. It wasn't the fear of the Red Bear that has kept our clan safe all these many seasons. Other clans no longer exist. Not truly."

"What do you mean?"

"They are all ruled by Eldrax himself. The other Chiefs, they're gone, murdered in their sleep and replaced by Eldrax's most loyal. There was no ritual combat, they were slaughtered. He has gone against the most sacred tenets of our way of life for his own gain."

"But," Halima's voice was very small. "How? Eldrax rarely leaves the clan. Who would do such a thing?"

"Rannac." Angry tears of betrayal had started in Galahir's eyes. "Rannac killed them all on Eldrax's orders. *Rannac.* For Eldrax, he killed clan chiefs who we had no quarrel with, killed them in the most shameful of ways. The Old Wolf murdered women and children to ensure their followers remained in line..." His voice choked off. "Only Yatal resisted and remained free."

Kyaati's blood drained from her face. She had not known Rannac well, but she remembered him as an honourable man, her mate's mentor. He had saved her life. She could not reconcile the memories she had of him with the story

Galahir was now weaving. She wasn't the only one.

"How do you know this?" Halima demanded.

"Eldrax revealed his plot," Galahir went on. "He has sent men off to bring the other clans here to fight and die with us."

The reason behind the excess of weapons suddenly made sense to Kyaati.

"Why didn't Eldrax bring these other clans here before, under his direct control?" Kyaati asked.

"Too many mouths to feed," Lorhir pointed out, as though it should be obvious. "One territory can only support so many. Eldrax left them in their own territories under the leadership of his most trusted men. Those who have been with him since he became Chief."

"I should have killed him." Galahir snarled. "I should have killed him when I had the chance!" He flung a piece of wood into the fire, causing it to spit and flare.

"Quiet!" Lorhir hissed. "I've already done enough to save your sorry hide!"

Galahir faced him, fury sparking in his blue eyes. "What does it matter?" he demanded. "We're all going to die. It doesn't matter how many warriors he has under his control. You saw those footprints, Lorhir. You saw them!"

"Then what are we going to do?" Kyaati interjected. "I will not sit here waiting to die because of the whim of some madman!"

"We'll leave," Galahir declared.

"And go where? How long will we be able to survive on our own?" Halima asked.

"Longer than we will against those things," Galahir countered. "The Red Bear is distracted. We might get far enough away before he finds us gone. The loss of one warrior isn't going to draw his attention."

Lorhir snickered again. "He might not miss you, Galahir, but what about your witch and your witch-spawn? He will not let them go so easily."

All eyes turned to Kyaati. She lifted her chin. "I will play no part in that man's plan."

"You think you will have a choice?" Lorhir's mouth twisted in mock amusement. "When those things come for you, you will defend your child and your mate like you did before. Eldrax knows that, and he will keep you here. He will not risk another witch slipping through his fingers. You are being watched."

Kyaati wanted to rail against him, but knew that she could not. Every word Lorhir spoke was the truth.

"Do you think they will come for us?" Halima was staring into the fire, her features stiff.

Lorhir shrugged. "They have only ever left their Forest twice. Both times under direct provocation. First time was when Eldrax was young, and they wiped out the Black Wolf clan. Second... we just witnessed that for ourselves when Galahir here took it upon himself to steal their offering."

Galahir scowled at Lorhir. "What was I supposed to do? Leave her to be fed to whatever that was in the ground?"

"Yes!" Lorhir flared. "Now Nunamnir, or whatever that light was, is angered and we can't be sure of anything! By trying to save a stranger, you have put all our families in danger!"

"I thought we'd already established that Eldrax would have tried to pick this fight anyway," Halima interjected quietly.

"But not this soon," Lorhir shot back. "He wanted to wait for an army of witches! Or at least to possess a few more than just this one." He jerked his thumb at Kyaati.

"Well, it's no good throwing blame now, Lorhir," Halima said. "What is done is done. We should leave this place. We should have left when the winter went on too long. Eldrax is the one wants to stay and put our families at risk. Not Galahir. You'd do well to remember that."

Kyaati beamed at Halima, only just fully realising how much she loved this matriarch of the Hunting Bear clan. The niggle in the back of her mind flared again, and her smile faded. She frowned, trying to pinpoint the reason for her unease. The Great Spirit of KI was still silent, brooding since the appearance of the dancing lights.

"We should all try to get some rest," Halima bid them, though Kyaati knew from the tension on her face, Halima would get no more rest than any of them. There was too much to fear. Too much to think about. Lights in the sky. The Watchers. Eldrax's subjugation of the other clans. Kyaati rubbed her forehead. She was weary. Perhaps she would manage some sleep.

She let Galahir guide her from the Dwelling of the UnClaimed, huddling over Elhaari in his sling, sheltering him from the wind and the rain. Her eyes automatically went to the Mountains, unseen in the gloom. Nothing. No further sign of the unnatural lights. But the unnatural stillness of the Great Spirit was beginning to unnerve her. Kyaati shrugged deeper into her now-damp furs, longing to reach her shelter.

At last, Galahir swept the hides aside for her, and they ducked inside. Elhaari was sleeping soundly. Kyaati lifted

229

him carefully from his sling and nestled him into the furs beside her own, planting a lingering kiss on his soft forehead.

Before she could even turn, she found herself crushed in Galahir's embrace, his mouth possessing hers. There was a desperation in his hold that Kyaati understood immediately. Neither of them knew how much peace they had left, how much time they still had with each other. She melted into her mate's warm embrace as he ripped the coverings from both their bodies and tumbled them onto their nest of furs below.

Galahir made love to her slowly, and Kyaati let herself forget everything, focusing only on the sensations of her body for a few precious moments. She cried out softly as she found her release. Galahir was not far behind and he pulled himself away from her at the last moment to spill his seed to the air. They were both aware Kyaati would not survive carrying another child of his. Not without Nyriaana being present for the birth, at least.

Elhaari might be their only child. The thought saddened Kyaati, but she comforted herself knowing that Elhaari was more than she ever expected to have. Before becoming part of the Cro clan, she had given up hope that a healthy child could exist.

Sleepily, Galahir gathered her into his arms, his breath soft against her neck. Still keeping thoughts of the future at bay, Kyaati concentrated on Galahir's warmth and Elhaari's soft breathing close beside her. Quiescent, she drifted into sleep.

Kyaati!

"Sefaan!" Kyaati bolted upright. The call had been soft, but somehow the sound of the old Kamaali's voice still rang in her ears, impossible to ignore. Her wide eyes caught the flicker of a shadow on the far side of the shelter, and a familiar scent of herbs and earth tantalised her nostrils. Kyaati blinked, and the vision dissipated. There was no shadow and only the smell of furs and old wood smoke filled her lungs.

But the sweat, the sweat on her body was real. And the silence. The silence in the air. The silence in the Great Spirit. It pressed down on her like a shroud. Her eyes lighted on the bundle that was her son. Elhaari's green eyes were open, staring. He uttered no sound. The babe knew. He knew he needed to remain quiet; like a deer fawn before the searching wolf.

Terror crawled up Kyaati's throat.

"Galahir," she hissed, shaking her sleeping mate. "Galahir, wake up."

"Hmmm?"

Kyaati leapt to her feet, throwing her furs over her body and binding them tightly around her waist. Elhaari's sling went over her shoulders as she scooped her son from his nest and stowed him inside.

"Kyaati, what's wrong?" For once, it did not take Galahir long to catch up to her mood as he sat upright.

"Get up! Grab your weapons. We have to go. Now!"

Galahir did not hesitate. Kyaati shifted from foot to foot. Danger was coming. Every fibre of her being was screaming at her to take her mate and her child and flee. But the rest of the lives, the rest of the children in this camp, held her in place. She let out a little cry of anguish, knowing she could

231

not just leave and let them die. Not if there was the slightest chance of saving everyone.

"Eldrax," Kyaati breathed. "I have to get to Eldrax. Galahir, wake everyone you can."

"What?"

"If you want this clan to survive, just do it!" Kyaati snapped. Without waiting to see if he obeyed, she rushed from the shelter. The rain and wind had passed over, and Kyaati stumbled into the thick mist that swirled through the camp, denying her any vision beyond the length of her arm. Above, the night sky was dark. Cold as death. The warning in Kyaati's heart thudded through her body, driving her forward when all she wanted to do was freeze.

"Wake up!" she hissed as loud as she dared, thumping her fist against every shelter she passed. "Wake up!"

"Kyaati!" A hand swept out of the mist to grab her arm.

"Halima! It's happening. We leave now or we die!"

"Where are you going?"

"Eldrax." Kyaati pulled the matriarch along in her wake. "He is the only one who can convince them to run. He has to order them to run."

The shelter of the Chief was before her. Kyaati did not hesitate. She thrust herself inside with Halima a step behind. The hand of a guard shot out, blocking her. "The Chief is not to be disturbed!"

Kyaati ignored him. "Eldrax!"

"Kyaati?"

With her gloom-adjusted eyes, Kyaati could make out two figures lying on the pile of furs on the far side of the shelter. Kikima sat up and blinked at her as Eldrax gave a harsh grunt and tried to pull her back to him in his sleep.

Forcing back her loathing for the man, Kyaati struggled against the guard.

"Kikima. Get dressed. We have to go." Halima beckoned.

"What is this?" Eldrax snarled, throwing the furs from his naked body and leaping to his feet. A spear materialised in his hand, ready to dispatch the disrespectful intruder.

Kyaati did not flinch. "Eldrax. Gather your clan and get out of here." There was no more time. The knowledge of that flared ever stronger inside Kyaati. "We must flee!"

"I do not flee from anyone, witch."

"Eldrax, I am warning you." Kyaati's hand went to her head. The echo of Sefaan's voice rang through her ears. *Kyaati. Kyaati.*

"My Chief, listen to her!" Kikima was at his side.

Eldrax bellowed in her face. In the silence, the sound was deafening. Kyaati shrank down as the Red Bear caught hold of Kikima and threw her to the ground. "I am the Chief here! You think I have not taken measures? The witch is a snivelling coward, ready to jump at shadows. The sentries would have—"

"Eldrax!" Halima's voice rose above his as she twisted past the guards. "I will not allow you to condemn this clan to death! Come to your senses!"

"Enough!" In a flash, Eldrax had his arm around Halima's throat, a knife appearing in his free hand. Kyaati went cold.

"You know the penalty for disobedience, Halima," Eldrax hissed in her ear, tightening his arm. "For your lifetime of loyalty, I might have let you live. But silly little Selima informed me of your plot, of your lack of faith."

"Eldrax," Halima choked.

"Goodbye, Halima. You have served your purpose. I have

a new matriarch now. I thank you for teaching her well."

Kyaati did not know if the scream that split the air came from Kikima or her as Eldrax plunged his knife deep into Halima's gut.

He drew back, readying for another strike, when the bloodcurdling cries from beyond the shelter drowned out even Kyaati's and Kikima's wails of denial.

Eldrax was diverted. Releasing Halima, he threw a cloak of fur around his bare shoulders and seized his fighting club. Kikima was at Kyaati's side as they rushed to their matriarch.

"Halima, Halima." Kikima caught her mentor before she fell as the Red Bear barged from his shelter, leaving them alone. Kyaati fell to her knees, pressing her hands down on the bleeding stab wound. Halima hissed between her teeth. "Kyaati," Kikima hitched. "Do something!"

More howls and shrieks came from outside. Kyaati's head whipped around. They were already too late. The Hunting Bear clan's doom was upon them. Standing, she threw one of Halima's arms over her shoulder, closing out the possibility that her wound was fatal. "Let's go, Kikima! We can't do anything for her here."

Kikima seized Halima's opposite arm as their matriarch gated a moan of pain behind her teeth, but her indomitable spirit refused to bow and Halima rose to her feet, supporting her own weight as Kikima and Kyaati rushed her towards the outside.

Eldrax had stopped just beyond the entrance, sniffing the air as chaos reigned around him. The clan was in disarray, women and children barrelled out of the surrounding mist, disappearing back into it as fast as they had appeared.

"Wh-what?" Kikima began.

Something heavy thudded to the ground, rolling to a stop before the Red Bear's feet. Eldrax stooped and lifted by the hair the severed head of one of his sentries.

Body parts rained through the air, falling through the fog into the midst of the camp. The screams of panic accompanied the sound of running feet.

"Galahir," Kyaati whispered.

"To me, you fools!" Eldrax roared. "To me!"

Then time seemed to slow, the world becoming detached as Kyaati stood at the very centre, hearing and feeling every breath, every heartbeat. And out of the billowing mist, looming over the shelters, a ring of glowing blue eyes opened.

Kyaati was looking directly at Eldrax, and so she saw when the colour drained from his already milky face, before his back stiffened and he bellowed out again. "To me!"

No one heard him. A terrible voice drowned his command out. It echoed back and forth, seeming to emit from the mouths of the Watchers surrounding them. It vibrated through Kyaati's bones. "WORTHLESS SLAVES! YOU FAILED TO BOW TO YOUR MASTER, TO THE ONE WHO GRANTED YOU LIFE. ENLIL SEEKS RETRIBUTION. THE NIGHT WILL BATHE IN YOUR BLOOD AND THE LORD OF THE SKIES WILL REJOICE!"

The voice rumbled into silence.

"Move!" Somehow, Halima still had the strength to command them as the Watchers fell upon the camp. Kikima was already in motion. Kyaati knew only her friend's fierce courage saved her life in those moments as Kikima caught her by the scruff of her furs and hauled her away, forcing her weakened legs to carry her.

How many Watchers? Kyaati did not care. All she knew was that it was enough. By morning, the Hunting Bear Clan would be no more.

Tears spilled down her cheeks. She could not save them. Now there was only one thing that mattered to her. Galahir. There might still be a chance to save her own family. She would not have her mate stand behind Eldrax in this futile fight. Kyaati's eyes raked the camp as she stumbled along in Kikima and Halima's wake. But in the chaos, she could not pick out Galahir's familiar bulky outline.

Kyaati did not want to extend her higher senses. She did not want to feel the horror unfolding around her as well as see and hear it, but there was no other way to locate Galahir before it was too late.

It was worse than she imagined. Terror, anger and hopelessness whipped back and Kyaati stumbled under the force of it.

"Get down!" Kikima cried. The splintered wood of a shelter scythed through the air over their heads, before crashing into another dwelling. The ground vibrated, signalling the approach of heavy feet, but in the thick mist, they could not see from which direction the Watcher hailed. "Run!"

Kyaati bolted along on friends' heels, praying to Ninmah that they would not run straight into the beast's clutches. Red light flared against the mist as the burning brands were hurled among the shelters, igniting the hides. Shadows swirled and darted. Kyaati could still hear Eldrax rallying his men to launch a defence.

"Galahir!" He was somewhere up ahead and Kyaati almost

collided with him outside the Dwelling of the UnClaimed, evacuating the women who had called the shelter home.

"Galahir," Kyaati clutched at her mate's furs. She did not need to speak a word. He read everything in her eyes in a single glance. They had done all they could. It was time to abandon Eldrax's side and save the life of their son.

There was a single flare of denial in his blue depths before it quickly burnt out, and Galahir accepted his new reality. "With me!" he bellowed to the panicked clan members around him. "This way! With me!" No one listened.

The smoke of burning shelters thickened the already impenetrable fog and stuck in Kyaati's throat as she ran at Galahir's side, Halima supported heavily by Kikima following on their heels, driven by the screams, flashes of blue, and the roar of the unseen monsters in the night. The flames spread, highlighting the bodies and debris flying through the air. Kyaati huddled Elhaari next to her breast, no time to fear, no time to think. In that moment, all her life came down to was running.

"Lorhir!" Galahir's cry brought Kyaati's head up. A shelter had collapsed, and she could see the lithe raknari warrior pinned by the legs beneath it. A woman lay dead close beside him. In a rush, Kyaati recognised her as Lorhir's estranged mate and mother of his only son.

"Take him!" Lorhir cried out, thrusting the screaming child in Galahir's direction. "Save him!"

"I will!" Galahir rushed to his fallen brother before Kyaati could stop him. "But you're coming, too!" Without hesitation, Galahir caught hold of the heavy wooden beam pinning Lorhir to the ground, lifted it and yanked the other man free. "Let's go!" Scooping the young boy up in one arm, and slinging Lorhir's arm around his shoulders in support, Galahir continued leading them all on through the destruction and the bloodshed.

"Galahir!" They were almost to the edge of camp when Kyaati collided with the back of her mate as he slammed to a stop.

Tanag stood before them, blocking their escape. His dark face dripped with blood as the light of the flames danced over his features. His crazed eyes widened in surprise and fury as he took in Galahir and his followers and guessed at their actions. He levelled his spear at them. "Cowards! You will stand with your Chief as you are sworn to do!"

Lorhir stumbled free of Galahir's support, drawing his knife. "Eldrax has brought enough death down upon us. He does not deserve our loyalty. I am going to save my son, even if I have to go through you, Tanag. You can die here if you want, but I will not."

Tanag bared his teeth, readying his spear. "I'll enjoy impaling your sorry ski—"

And then Tanag was gone. Out of the mist, a huge hand shot out, grabbing Eldrax's longest-serving warrior by the leg, snatching him from sight. There came a sickening crunch, and Tanag's screams ended in a wet gurgle.

"Kikima, no!"

Kyaati spun around. A second Watcher, mouth drenched with Hunting Bear blood, had loomed out of the chaos behind them right next to Kikima. Before anyone else could blink, Halima used her waning strength to throw Kikima aside. The monster howled and lashed out. The wounded matriarch could not escape. The blow caught her in the chest with bone crunching force. Kyaati watched, helpless,

238

as Halima was catapulted through the air, crashing into the jagged remains of a dwelling.

"No!" Kikima screamed, "Halima!"

The beast was still coming. Kyaati watched in horror as Galahir moved to meet it. "Run!" he said, thrusting her towards the edge of the camp.

A large stone slammed into the side of the Watcher's head, quickly followed by another. The sound of rock on bone reverberated through Kyaati's body. Blood gushed from the heavy strikes as the Watcher roared in surprise and pain. In the foggy gloom, Kyaati did not see where the missiles came from, but she was forever indebted to the brave warrior who launched them.

Attention diverted from Galahir, the Watcher peeled back its lips and crashed off in the direction of the one who had dared to draw its blood. The thick swirling mist swallowed up its enormous frame as though it had never been. Only the panting of Galahir's group penetrated their little pocket of space.

"Halima." Kikima's groan of denial jolted Kyaati's heart into beating again. She rushed to her friend's side.

"No," the word spilled from her mouth. Halima lay propped against the shelter into which she had been hurled. One arm was thrown out at a crooked angle, but Kyaati could not tear her eyes away from the long splinter of wood erupting through the matriarch's chest.

"Kyaati!" Kikima's eyes turned towards her, beseeching. Looking for a miracle.

"I-I can't," Kyaati heard herself sob, "Not even Nyri..." her voice shuddered into silence.

Halima's eyes fluttered, the life draining from her as fast

239

as the blood spreading through the furs over her chest. "T-too late for me." She squeezed Kikima's hand feebly. "Go, go."

"No! I won't leave you."

Close by, the rumble of feet and a roar split the silence.

"K-Kyaati," Halima stuttered. "Please."

Somehow, Kyaati found the strength to take hold of Kikima's arm.

"No!" Kikima screamed, yanking her arm free of Kyaati's insistent grip. "Halima!"

Halima's eyes stared back at her, but she saw nothing.

"Galahir!" Kyaati called.

He was there in a heartbeat, disentangling the distraught Kikima from her dead mentor. Kikima was strong, but not as strong as Galahir. He slung her, kicking and screaming, across his thick shoulders. The pounding of heavy feet was drawing nearer.

There was no time for a backwards glance. No time for a proper farewell. Blinded by tears, Kyaati and her companions broke free of the last ring of burning shelters and fled into the protection of the shrouded night.

* * *

13

Identity

The lights vanished from over the Mountains, and Juaan thrust himself up onto his knees. He gritted his teeth as the monster clawed inside him, crawling under his flesh as it fought to be free and answer the call of the Great Spirit.

He had no time to understand what had happened. Yatal had dragged Nyri outside just before the lights had erupted from the mountainside, throwing all his senses into chaos. Now that the lights had disappeared, all that mattered to him was finding her. He did not care if the rest of the world was on fire.

The Yatal was bent on revenge. Juaan could not let the twisted old creature kill Nyriaana. He would sacrifice himself over and over again to prevent it. None of the Eagle warriors guarding him were paying attention, their horror-struck eyes still fixed on the sky over the Mountains. He swung up, grabbing a hunting knife from the waist of the nearest guard with his hands, and then sliced through the bonds of his legs with one motion.

The guard, shaken from his stupor, called out an alarm. Juaan staggered to his feet, shutting out the pain in his wounded thigh as he gathered his remaining strength, preparing to throw himself upon Yatal. If the Eagles were occupied with his attack on their leader, he might just spare Nyri enough time to make her escape. He was sure Bahari would aid her in that. The thought left a bitter taste in his mouth even as he coiled.

"Release them!" Yatal's rasping command brought Juaan up short. That moment of hesitation was all it took. The guard caught him, bringing the rope up around his throat. But Juaan did not struggle. Yatal's grip on Nyriaana was no longer the clutch of restraint, but the support of an ally. Confusion swamped Juaan as he waited for the Chieftess' next move.

Nyriaana leaned upon Yatal as though she barely had the strength to stand, her red-gold skin pallid and coated in a sheen of sweat. Her large indigo eyes sought his, helpless and panicked. "Juaan," she moaned.

There was no denying her. Juaan lurched against his guard, but the hated man kept a firm grip; the rope cutting into his windpipe. Juaan considered breaking his nose with the back of his head, but then Bahari was there, relieving the elderly Eagle Chieftess of her burden before they both collapsed. The fire that had driven Yatal from her sick bed appeared to have burnt out, and she sagged. Sakal rushed forward to catch her before she fell.

Juaan had eyes only for Nyri. Bahari had lifted her into his arms and her head fell limply against his chest. That should be him. That had always been his place until Eldrax had come along and stolen all of that away. Juaan swallowed

242

down his jealousy and his grief for that which was forever lost. He was no longer the boy who had a right to hold that girl. Bahari was a good man. Juaan was not. He only had to look around to see the hate on the faces of the Eagle clan and the Thals to know that.

"I said release him," Yatal growled at Juaan's guard as she shuffled back towards her shelter. Juaan felt the man stiffen in surprise, but a level glare from his leader had him scrambling to obey. The Eagle warrior released Juaan's neck and cut the remaining bonds. He was none too gentle about it and Juaan tried not to wince as he felt the hunting knife nick his skin on more than one occasion.

"Come," Yatal beckoned. Her black eyes were as cold as flint. Whatever had prompted the order of his release, it was easy to see it had not changed her personal feelings towards the Jade Killer.

Sakal's face was mutinous as she helped her leader back into her shelter, but she said nothing. Juaan waited, standing back and avoiding their gazes as the entire Eagle clan filed past on the heels of Yatal. They ignored him. Their emotions were flat against his latent senses. They were all in a state of shock. He was no longer their biggest concern. The lights in the sky had changed everything.

Juaan's ears were still ringing from the experience, but the beast inside had quieted, reflecting the strange silence that had fallen over the earth. The tales he had heard of such lights raced around his head. A signal from the gods themselves demanding fealty. Juaan rubbed his face, feeling lightheaded. The blood from the wound on his leg continued to flow down his skin, soaking his furs.

He lifted his gaze, suddenly realising he was alone. The

Eagle clan and their Thal guests had disappeared inside the sprawling shelter of their Chieftess. Bahari had carried Nyri inside with them. Juaan limped forward and pushed his way through the entrance.

A clamour of noise hit him. Everyone was speaking at once, panicked, questioning. Yatal had re-seated herself upon her furs, looking older and more fragile than ever. Her face was bloodless, devoid of emotion, she appeared incapable of it. Her eyes were fixed upon Nyri where she sat close beside the Eagle leader, head bowed low.

But as Juaan watched, Yatal squared her shoulders, seeming to find the strength to bear the new load that had been laid there. "Prepare!" she addressed her gathered clan.

The panicked clamouring died away.

"We have been sent a warning. Nunamnir is angered."

Confused whispers and alarmed shouts of denial swept around the clan.

"The gods?"

"They live?"

"You saw those lights as clearly as I!" Yatal snapped. "Nunamnir awakes! Through this young witch, I was given a message. He intends to destroy us, all of us."

"Why?"

"We have done nothing."

"I do not know," Yatal snapped. "But he is coming for us! When Nanna is at the brightest, he will come. If we are to survive, we must prepare."

"For what?"

"To fight." Yatal's black gaze was unwavering.

A rumble went through the shelter. Juaan noticed that Bahari's Thals were shifting uncomfortably, even angrily, from foot to foot as their leader translated Yatal's words for them. Upon hearing Yatal's declaration, several of them stormed from the dwelling, throwing black stares at the Eagles as they pushed past. Even some of the Eagles looked outraged at the idea of rebellion.

"Fight the gods? If they have returned, we should make the sacrifices, appease their anger. It was always so!"

"Silence!" Yatal wheezed, then coughed violently. "Heed me! We must fight and we cannot stand alone. I need warriors. I need those who are willing to seek out the other clans and call them together."

Sakal barked a laugh. "Have you forgotten, Yatal? Eldrax controls nearly all the other clans."

Yatal's face twisted as though her next words physically burned her mouth. "Then we must ally ourselves with the Red Bear."

Juaan winced at the volume of the clan's protest, echoing the shock reverberating through his own chest. Ally with Eldrax? Just what did Yatal believe she had seen?

Many younger members of the clan stormed from the shelter on the heels of the Thals, shoving past Juaan in their haste to leave. Juaan braced himself on a post. The ringing in his ears was getting louder, and he was finding it increasingly hard to concentrate. He locked his knees, forcing himself to focus on the radical turn of events unfolding before him.

Only respect for the leader who had brought them from the brink of annihilation to the second most powerful clan on the Plains kept the older members of the Eagle clan in place. But it was easy to see even these most loyal of Yatal's followers were questioning her sanity, wondering if the rot of old age had finally robbed her of her senses.

The sight of half her clan walking out on her appeared to diminish the Eagle leader, and fear passed through her dark eyes for the first time.

Juaan's eyes drooped, and it was a few moments before he found the strength to wrench them open again. He was dimly aware of Nyri's head snapping around in his direction.

"We cannot stand alone," Yatal beseeched her remaining followers as Juaan's vision hazed. "The Red Bear is no longer our greatest enemy. We have no—"

"Juaan!" Nyriaana's cry of alarm was the last thing Juaan heard before he hit the ground.

A cool hand laid against his cheek, breaking through the darkness, followed by the brief flutter of warm lips against his forehead.

"Nyriaana."

"Yes." Her voice sounded hoarse.

Juaan struggled to locate his eyelids as he moved to push himself upright. Thick furs cushioned and tickled his palms.

"Stay down." A gentle press against his shoulders. "You lost a lot of blood. After Eldrax, i-it was too much."

Juaan dragged his eyes open and her face filled his vision. Tear tracks marred her skin, and her eyes were red and sore. He lifted an arm, frowning at its peculiar weight, and brushed a thumb across her cheek. She was frightened. His mind swirled, threatening to return to oblivion. In this moment, he could not recall why he felt so weak nor understand why she was troubled. Habit took over. "Nyri, Nyri, Nyriaana."

"Oh, Juaan." She threw herself down upon his chest, fresh

tears flowing forth. "Juaan, I-I… What am I to do?" The words seemed to burst from her. "I have to go, but, but," her words broke off into a torrent of sobs.

Go? Juaan laid a hand on her back and felt her shudder. He swallowed down a wave of nausea brought about by the barest of movements. "I'm here," he repeated to her mindlessly. "I'll always be here, Nyriaana."

"Will you?"

Why did she sound so doubtful about that fact? Hadn't he always been? "Yes." The fog was pressing on his mind. His eyelids fluttered as she sniffed and lay on the furs next to him. A protest niggled in the back of his mind. There was a reason he should not allow this, but Juaan could not muster the will to seek the answer as her body curled around his, warm and comforting. Nothing had ever felt more right. Sighing in contentment, Juaan wound his arms around her slight body as the shroud of unconsciousness blanketed him once more.

The thud of something being dumped in front of his face woke Juaan with a start. This time, he opened his eyes with ease. The cloudiness and the strange heaviness that had overcome his mind and body were all but gone. He focused on the object before his face, coming eye to eye with a dead coney.

"That's for you," a deep voice said. The tone was less than friendly.

"Bahari?"

There was a grunt of affirmation.

Juaan lifted his eyes from the limp creature in front of him. He was inside a hide shelter, lying on a pile of furs.

Nightfall must have been close, for the light outside slanted through the billowing hides, the colour of dying fire. He began to rise but was prevented. Nyri's body was tangled with his. She stirred as he shifted, her hand winding into his furs as she mumbled unintelligibly in her sleep. "Juaan. Sefaan…"

Juaan pressed his lips together as he recalled his witless mutterings to her in his half conscious state. A headache was building behind his eyes as he lifted them to Bahari.

The other man was sitting across from him, his dark face fixed in a scowl as he beheld the way Nyriaana was curled around Juaan. Moving very gently so as not to wake her, Juaan disentangled himself and sat up.

The world spun. Grunting, he gripped the furs beneath him until his sight righted itself. When it did, he lifted the coney Bahari had dumped on the furs. Juaan was sure Nyri would not appreciate waking next to a dead animal. "Thank you," he muttered to the other man.

"I didn't do it for you. She asked it of me," Bahari said by way of explanation. "She said you would need more than *kua* to recover." He straightened. "You can cook it yourself. If the Eagles will let you. Had to trade much jade to get it."

Juaan dipped his chin, accepting the other man's quiet hostility. He doubted the Eagles would offer him so much as a splinter of flint.

"She loves you."

Juaan's heart thudded at the sudden change of subject. Bahari's eyes were resting upon Nyri's sleeping form, a protective light kindling in their depths.

"She will not leave your side for anything. I don't know what you did to deserve such a gift, Jade Killer."

Nor me. Juaan brushed the back of his hand down Nyri's warm cheek. So many tears she had shed. He traced their tracks with his fingers. How many because of him? How many left to fall?

"You love her, too."

"More than my own life."

Bahari's surprise rippled through the air at the open admission. There was no point in denying it. He could not hide it, try as he might.

"The *genii* call to her," Bahari said, a frown slashing his brow. "She fears them."

Before Juaan could answer, the hides of the shelter parted and Yatal hefted herself into view, leaning upon Sakal. The Eagle Chieftess' heavy features were grim. She and Sakal dipped their chins at Bahari, before their eyes fell upon Nyriaana's sleeping form.

Juaan bristled. This was the first true rest Nyriaana had had for days. She needed to be left free of troubles for the rest of the night. New and unknown dangers had awoken and Juaan wanted to shield her from them for as long as he could.

He opened his mouth, ready to banish the old Chieftess, but Nyri's own voice cut across him. "Yatal." Juaan looked down and saw Nyri was awake and already pushing herself into a seated position. Even in sleep, her acute senses had alerted her to the Eagle leader's intrusion.

"Are you ready?"

Nyri recoiled, fear paling her skin.

"Ready?" Bahari's eyes flicked between Yatal and the cringing girl. Juaan frowned down at Nyri. An understanding had transpired between her and the old leader that had changed everything. Juaan was impatient to know what that was and why it was causing Nyriaana such anguish.

"I… I don't know," Nyri mumbled.

Sakal hissed her disapproval. "Is that all the courage you can muster?"

Juaan growled low in his throat and a knife flicked into Sakal's hand. It was at his jugular in the blink of an eye. Juaan's fingers twitched, his mind already darting through the many ways he could put the Eagle warrior down. It was instinctual, an effect of all the conditioning Eldrax had put him through to turn him into the killer that he had become. Juaan forced his bunching muscles to relax. He would no longer be what Eldrax had created.

"Stay out of this, Khalvir, or whatever you choose to name yourself," Yatal snapped over the confrontation. "Sakal, put that away." The leader's hooded eyes turned back to Nyri. "I ask again. Are you ready?"

"I don't think I have a choice anymore." Nyri's voice was small, childlike. It tore at Juaan's heart. She lifted her gaze to Yatal, a gleam of challenge flaring to the surface. "What about you? How do you hope to gain the support of the rest of the Peoples to stand against their gods? Even your own followers have lost faith in you at the mere suggestion."

Yatal laughed without humour. What strength she'd used to come to Nyri appeared to run out, and she sank to the ground, her laugh turning into a feeble cough. "I do not know. It was a cruel path to lay before a dying woman, to make peace where none has ever existed, but it was. And it is necessary. I *felt* it." She covered her rattling chest with her hand. "We both felt the truth of it, witch." Yatal coughed again as her voice rose at the end. This time, she could not stop. Her body convulsed as she fought for every breath. Blood rolled down her chin.

Before Juaan could stop her, Nyri got to her feet and staggered to the old one's side. She took hold of one of Yatal's twisted hands and closed her eyes. After a few moments, Yatal's breathing eased. When Nyri opened her eyes, however, the look that passed between them was dark.

"Yes, yes, I know," Yatal grunted. "I will not see Nanna return to full. I have much to do in a short time."

"What of this 'one' that the vision spoke of?" Nyri tilted her head. "The *genii* said you knew him."

Yatal shrugged. "Everyone I know is already here or dead. But it makes no matter who is coming. After I am gone, another will take my place. Another who has not seen what we have seen, who has not felt the truth. You *must* go, witch, before the breath leaves my body and I no longer have control of my clan. The time for running is over, Nyriaana. You must turn and fight your battle, as I have."

Nyri bowed her head. Juaan felt the choking despair rolling from her. His fingers twitched again. This time with the need to comfort. Yatal's attention shifted to Bahari.

"The Thals must stand with us," she rasped.

Bahari recoiled. "The Thals will not fight against the holy creators," he said. "Thals not make them angry. Cro have made them angry." He glared pointedly at Sakal and Juaan. Two Forbidden beings. "Ignoring sacred teachings, ignoring signs."

"Bahari, please," Nyri beseeched him. "She is right."

"They will not stop with us, boy," Yatal croaked. "She and I both saw it. Thal or Cro. Death will find us all."

Anger tightened Bahari's face, but Juaan saw his eyes

251

flicker towards Nyri's beseeching face and he let out a harsh breath. "I will take your story to my *adda*," he said. "He will decide."

Yatal dipped her chin. "That is all I can ask. Sakal," the old leader reached for her most loyal warrior and Sakal stooped to help Yatal to her feet. But Yatal could not stand. Her legs gave way. Grunting, Sakal hefted her into her arms and carried her from the shelter. Yatal's eyes were closing even before she left Juaan's sight.

"Nyriaana?"

Juaan turned his head at the sound of Bahari's voice. Nyri was curled into a ball, her slender arms wrapped tightly around her knees, her chin tucked behind them as her large eyes stared into space.

Juaan wanted nothing more than to go to her and lift the shadows behind her eyes. It had always been his place to guard her against her fears. But now that he was in full control of his senses, he remembered why he could never again be the one to offer such comfort.

Bahari crouched before her instead. "Speak your fear, Nyriaana. Tell me."

She focused on him with an effort. "The spirits, the *genii*, or whatever power is out there, commands me to travel into the Mountains of the Nine Gods."

Bahari stiffened even as Juaan's hands curled into fists, cold dread sliding down his throat.

"The *genii* wish you to fight against the gods? Against Eron?" Bahari's face paled.

Nyriaana shook her head. "No. That is not my path. I must find someone."

"Who?"

Nyri rubbed her forehead. "I don't know! Before any of this began, our old Kamaali, my tribe's speaker for the Great Spirit himself, shared a vision. Somehow I must find a girl. A Forbidden girl. Sefaan believed she is to be the Last Kamaali of which our ancient ones spoke. The one who will guide my People and ensure our survival." Her hand shifted to the twisted thong around her neck and the large seed that dangled there. "I d-don't know how that is possible. I don't understand how a Forbidden could be a leader to my People."

Juaan flinched at the harshness that entered her tone whenever she spoke the word *Forbidden.* He knew it was not her fault. The change in her voice was entirely unconscious, a result of a lifetime of conditioning by her Elders. The child he had known had never seen him in such a way. As a heresy. That was all their doing. An old forgotten hatred filled Juaan's chest at the memory of the Elders. Aardn's face stood out from the rest. He sighed. Life had changed them both.

"I have tried running from this fate," Nyri said into her knees. "I travelled that path once, and all it did was bring me face to face with monsters I never wish to see with my waking eyes again; all for a girl who might not even exist. But Yatal is right. I cannot run any longer." She squared her narrow shoulders. "Real or not, I must somehow pass through the Forests of the Nine Gods and travel into the Mountains to find the Last Kamaali, even if doing so…" Her indigo eyes filled with tears and she buried her face in her knees.

Juaan was numb, frozen. Bahari glanced his way once before he placed a hand on Nyriaana's arm. "I will go with you," he said.

Her head came up. "Bahari, no. You cannot imagine the horrors that await. I cannot ask this of you."

"I go," he raised his chin.

"But you need to speak Yatal's message to your father."

"My men will take Yatal's words to Alok. I go with you into Mountains."

"B-But," she shook her head, then shifted her gaze to Juaan. A jolt sent heat flushing back through his deadened limbs. He knew what she was asking. "Juaan," she whispered.

"No." His denial was almost soundless.

She blanched. "Juaan, I need you with me."

"I cannot be with you, Nyriaana."

"*Why*? Do not abandon me now. To the end. You promised. You promised me that."

The beast flexed inside his chest. "Nyriaana. Even if I wanted to, you know I cannot go into those Mountains. The closer I get, the…" Juaan's throat closed as the memories strangled his mind. Nameeda lying lifeless in his arms, the tearing of life from the land.

"Juaan?" He opened eyes he had not realised he had closed. "Juaan, please."

"No!" The denial burst from him. "No, Nyriaana. I am not the one you need! I am nobody. I cannot defend you, I am not Khalvir!"

"No, you are Juaan. My Juaan!"

"No. That boy is gone. Those promises were his to keep, and he was taken from you. All that remains is a monster."

"That's not true."

"I am sorry, Nyriaana." Juaan felt cornered, unable to breathe. He could not bear to be near her a moment longer.

He had to get away before his resolve crumbled. This bond between them had to be severed now. It would only get her killed. Juaan turned on his heel and swept from the shelter, walking as fast as his healing body would allow to escape the sound of her sobs.

Sweeping through the gathering darkness, Juaan felt the murderous stares of the Eagle clan follow him from the shadows of their dwellings. He could almost hear the rasp of a blade or two being rubbed threateningly against a thumb, but none of them made any move to molest him. Whatever they thought of their Chieftess' alarming change of heart, they did not yet dare cross her orders and try to kill him.

All the same, Juaan did not push his luck and headed straight out of the Eagle's camp, quickly choosing a path that climbed into the rocks of the surrounding foothills where he would no longer offend their sight. He had no place to go, but he didn't care. All he knew was it was time to leave. Nyri had others to protect and provide for her now. That had always been the end goal. He had never planned to stay with her beyond that.

But the further he got, Juaan found his stride becoming less and less determined, his feet dragging as though they could no longer bear the weight of the stone his heart was turning into. In the end, he was forced to a stop. It was as though physical bonds were holding him back.

Juaan growled and turned around, striking out on another path through the darkness. But the results were the same. He could not leave. The bright spirits of the night passed slowly overhead, watching as Juaan wandered along one path, then the next, but the invisible tether would not release him. The only path that did not cause him pain was the one he would not take: the one that led back to her.

Exhausted, he sank down at the end of his latest route. Maybe if he waited here long enough, Nyri herself would leave, either into the Mountains to find this Last Kamaali, or back to the Thal camp with Bahari.

Dawn was approaching over the eastern rises, throwing sharp shadows from the surrounding crags and boulders. Juaan's path had brought him to the top of a rise; a vantage point, he saw with a sinking heart, that gave him a full view of the Mountains of the Nine Gods looming in the near distance. The throb and pull of the silent sentinels tugged at the beast inside him, calling him to them. Juaan glared at the distant peaks.

"You not go far, then?"

Juaan stiffened at the sound of soft footsteps on the rocks behind him. He had been so wrapped up in his misery, he had not been as alert as he should have been. "Leave, Bahari," he said, without turning. "I do not wish for company."

Bahari ignored him. "I did not think you could abandon her so easily." There was a note of disgust in the other man's voice.

"You think it is easy for me to leave her?" Juaan burst out, nettled. Why would Bahari care if he left? Surely his absence would please the Cro man. He knew as well as Juaan that he was not worthy of Nyriaana. "Why do you think I only made it this far?"

"Nyriaana has sacred path to follow. But has no strength. No will. She cannot find these things she needs... because you abandon her." The admission sounded strained to Juaan's ears.

"She has you to help her now." Juaan kept his eyes on the

Mountains ahead. "You are an able warrior."

"She no want me. You are a blind man."

"She doesn't want me, either! She wants the boy she remembers. But I am not him. Not anymore. She refuses to see the truth."

"Who are you?"

Juaan tensed as the memories of two lives, two beings, swirled together, warring with each other. "I do not know."

The loud clatter of wood on stone made Juaan start. He turned to see the spear his mother had gifted him rolling to a stop behind him. He lifted his eyes to Bahari, startled to see the other man levelling another spear at him, shifting into a battle stance.

Juaan rose warily to his feet. "What are you doing, Bahari?"

"Pick up the spear."

"No."

Bahari lunged. Caught by surprise, Juaan barely made it clear of the spear tip seeking to pierce his heart. He side-stepped just in time, but the flint scored a mark, grazing through the furs at the top of his arm.

"The stories of the Jade Killer's skill must be blind," Bahari said, jabbing another blow, this time aimed at Juaan's legs. Juaan dodged again, but Bahari twisted his wrist and caught his foot, sending him crashing to the ground. Juaan winced as the hard rock drove the air from his lungs and the loose shale cut at his skin. But he had no time to regain his breath as Bahari came for him again. Juaan rolled, struggling to stay ahead of Bahari's strikes as the spear jabbed repeatedly into the ground beside him, seeking to taste his flesh. He twisted and threw himself to his feet, putting distance between

257

them.

"I won't fight you, Bahari!" he gasped, a hand going to his side. His old injuries were telling.

"Then you die." Bahari twirled his spear. "If won't fight, then death is your wish." Another swipe, this one grazing the side of Juaan's cheek.

"Yes."

"Why?"

"I don't deserve to breathe after what I have done." Juaan hissed as he narrowly avoided another blow.

Bahari grunted. "I agree." Reaching into his furs, he swept out a long hunting knife and Juaan had no more time to think as Bahari brought the full force of his skill and fury to bear. Juaan twisted between the two slashing blades, seeking to escape. It took all that he had just to keep from being impaled.

"Strange. If Jade Killer wants to die, then he is trying so very hard to stay alive," Bahari growled through his efforts to bring Juaan down.

Juaan flinched. Indeed, why was he making such an effort to avoid the blades? It would be so easy just to let Bahari put him out of his misery. But for some reason, he could not allow the killing blow to fall. He ducked and weaved, his body remembering every skill Rannac had ever taught him. All he could see was the despair on Nyri's face if he fell.

"She going into the Mountains this day," Bahari grunted as though he could read Juaan's thoughts.

A jolt of panic caused Juaan to miss a beat. Bahari's knife slashed his ribs. He winced. Anger was the next emotion.

Bahari's words were as relentless as his strikes. "She needs

258

you and you break her. You are a coward."

"You have no idea what I am trying to protect her from!" Juaan snarled. "You cannot comprehend."

Confusion pinched the dark face. "What you need to protect her from if not the Watchers?"

"Me!"

Surprise made Bahari freeze for the fraction of a moment. "You?"

"Yes. You say it yourself. I am a killer, Bahari. I pick up a weapon and I become *him* again. I won't be a monster."

"I have a spear. I fight. I kill. Am I a monster?"

"That's different!"

Bahari hissed through his teeth. "You more a coward than I thought. To fear self enough to let the woman you love die."

"No!"

"She will face the Watchers and she will die."

"No!" Horror tore through Juaan's chest.

"They tear her to pieces!"

The beast inside roared to life, clawing to be free. Juaan ducked and rolled away from Bahari's onslaught and, before he knew it, the spear was in his hand. He met Bahari's next blow with a cry on his lips.

A gleam of triumph flickered over Bahari's dark face. He pressed his taunt home. "And you let her walk that fate. You abandon her! Her blood with stain your hands along with the rest."

"No!" All sense of restraint fled. Numbed to his physical pain, Juaan attacked, lashing out at Bahari and the images the other man had shoved into his head.

Now it was Bahari's turn to be hard pressed as Juaan's

spear returned all the marks Bahari had given him. Sweat began to drip from Juaan's face. Twice, the opportunity for the killing blow arose. Furious as he was, some small part of him held back, letting Bahari narrowly escape each time.

Juaan thought he saw a faint smile flash over the other man's face. Bahari was enjoying this. Juaan's fury found new depths. The other man must have had a death wish himself. Fire burned in Juaan's veins. He would play this game no longer. In three savage moves, he separated Bahari from his spear and knocked the other man to the ground with a hard kick to the midsection.

Bahari landed heavily, gasping into the dirt as Juaan stood poised above him, battling the red haze threatening to overcome his vision as the other man laughed.

"She is right. You not Jade Killer now."

"No?" Juaan's hands were shaking on the haft of his spear with the effort it took to hold back, the tip a mere hand's breadth from Bahari's face.

"No. Jade Killer would not hesitate. You not him." The Cro man tilted his head. "The evil of the Red Bear commands you no longer. She does."

"She always has," Juaan rasped.

"Then why you not defend her?"

"I would protect her from anything, everything! With everything that I am!"

"Then do it! Use skill to defend as *magiri*. To defend is not evil! If you not kill me, then you not harm her."

A shudder passed through Juaan, the red haze receded. *I would protect her from anything.* Could he protect her from the monster within? The thought of entering the Mountains with Nyri stole the breath from his lungs. But Bahari was right. To run from that fear of himself and let Nyri face the darkness alone made him the worst of cowards. Shame burned him, cutting through the mire of doubt. He could not abandon her. He would not let the monster win.

"Who are you?" Bahari asked again.

Juaan floundered. Who was he? *Not evil to defend,* Bahari's truth sang through his veins. He wasn't either of the men that he had been, he was no one, but he would always defend Nyri to the bitter end. And if that was his sole purpose for living, then it left only one answer. All else became meaningless. "I am her *magiri*. And I will not leave her side until my death."

The Cro man grinned up at him. "Very well, *brother*." He swung his arm up and Juaan caught it, pulling the other man from the ground.

* * *

14

First Step

The ground was shaking. Nyriaana felt cold. Chills ran like lightning along her spine. Juaan was close by. She could feel it. He was fighting, trying to get to her, but to no avail. He would be too late.

My brother was a fool to create you, *a voice rumbled, coming from all around, throbbing through Nyri's bones.* Goodbye, Daughter of Ninmah.

Pain such as she had never known crackled through Nyri's body, searing through her veins. Her vision exploded in a flash of burning light and then... nothingness.

"Nyriaana?"

His voice shattered the vision like rock striking water.

"Juaan?" Nyri dashed the tears from her cheeks, hardly daring to hope as the reality of the present moment folded back around her.

He was there, standing uncertainly in the entrance to the shelter she resided in. "Oh, Juaan." She threw herself to her feet and ran for him, wrapping her arms around his waist and burying her face in the furs at his chest, hiding the vestiges of her vision she knew still clung to her features. His arms fell around her, familiar as her own skin, as his lips pressed gently into her hair. Nyri tightened her arms, letting the thrum of his life force ground her until she was ready to draw back.

She looked up into his face. The green eyes met hers, still haunted, still wary, but his mouth was set into a familiar line of determination.

"You came back."

"Yes."

She reached up to touch his cheek, and he leaned into her palm. "Are you alright?"

A sad smile touched his lips. "No," he said. "But as Bahari reminded me, it doesn't matter who I am or what I have become. All that matters is that my place is at your side. You are my Nyriaana, and I will protect you to the end."

Nyri buried her face in his furs again, unable to speak.

A soft clearing of a throat drew Nyri's attention to the space behind Juaan. Bahari stood there, a satisfied expression on his face. Nyri mustered a watery smile for him. "Thank you," she whispered, before noticing the cuts and blossoming bruises littering both men's skin. "What happened to you both?"

Juaan ducked his head. "Bahari had an interesting way of reminding me where my place was."

Nyri frowned, glaring at the long fresh cut on Juaan's cheek, and then at a slash mark along Bahari's brow. "You can deal with those yourselves," she said. "I have no energy to waste on male foolishness."

Bahari laughed, even Juaan chuckled softly, his eyes warming.

But the moment of levity could only exist for a moment. Bahari had brought Juaan back to her and, with him, Nyri's centre, but it did not change what awaited. The old, familiar sense of time running out grated across the back of Nyriaana's skull like fleshless fingers, causing her to shudder, the call of the Mountains squeezing her heart. She closed her eyes, seeing again the vision of her death. She had always known this path would lead to that, but it was the first time she had seen it happen, in a blinding flash of pain and light. There was no avoiding it now. She only hoped she could find Ariyaana before it happened.

She had to hide this from Juaan. If he knew that there was no hope of her leaving the Mountains alive, he would never let her go.

Banishing all doubt from her face, she opened her eyes. Both men were regarding her solemnly, waiting upon her direction. She drew comfort from their presence. "I need to see Yatal." Straightening her shoulders, she strode from the shelter, Juaan and Bahari falling in on either side.

Ninmah had risen above the craggy peaks that surrounded the Eagle camp. Many of the clan were already outside their shelters, hands occupied with daily chores, curing hides, repairing tools and hunting equipment, striking fires to cook meals. Wooden racks of fish stood between the shelters, the latest catches drying in the morning rays.

Nyri paid no mind to the stares that followed them, the black whispers about the witch who had enchanted their leader. She kept her eyes fixed on the Chieftess' shelter ahead. Sakal was guarding the entrance. The Eagle warrior dipped her chin cooly at Nyri and let her pass, before following on her heels, spear at the ready. Nyri could not help but notice that the tip remained trained on Juaan the entire time.

Although she was now expecting it, Nyri fought the urge to cover her nose and mouth to protect herself against the smell that permeated the space. Yatal lay in her custom position at the centre, propped up on furs gathered at her back. Even from the entrance, Nyri could hear the rattle of her chest. The Eagle leader was deteriorating rapidly now.

Nyri approached her with caution, still wary of the woman who, until yesterday, wanted nothing more than her head spiked outside her dwelling.

"Nyriaana." A withered hand lifted to beckon her close. "You have decided?"

"Yes."

Yatal peered into her face, reading from Nyri's grave expression the truth of her answer. She dipped her chin in approval. "Good. May the gods, or whatever power that sent us our vision, watch over and protect you on your journey."

Nyriaana did not respond, the vision of her impending death still fresh in her mind. No power would watch over her on this journey. Only those seeking to destroy her. To destroy them all.

"Sakal will join you," Yatal gestured at the battle-hardened half-Thal waiting in the shadows.

Nyri glanced up into the unwelcoming face, alarmed. "No, that will not be necessary," she blurted. The thought of this woman at her back was not a comforting one. What lay ahead was enough of a concern.

"Sakal will go with you," Yatal repeated, and Nyri knew from the bite of her voice that there would be no argument.

"She is my most skilled warrior hunter and will help guard you against any threats."

Nyri could not help but notice the old leader's eyes flicker towards Juaan as she spoke and guessed why Sakal was being added to her guard. No matter what she had seen in Nyri's memories, Yatal still could not bring herself to trust Eldrax's former raknari leader.

"Sakal, see that the provisions are prepared."

"And who will protect you, Yatal?" Resentment dripped from the Eagle warrior's words. It was clear this had not been her choice. If possible, Nyri's heart sank further.

Yatal chuckled, the motion of which turned into a wracking cough. "I do not think I will need protection for many more passings of Utu, my dear Sakal. Now, do as I ask."

Sakal stalked from the shelter, glaring at Juaan in warning as she went.

Nyri swallowed. Yatal was at her end. She could not fathom how this frail, diminishing soul could be expected to bring the Peoples together against the threat of Nunamnir. She put the concern angrily from her mind. The *genii* speakers who had laid this doom upon them could worry over such things. All she could do was concentrate on surviving long enough to find a ghost.

"Alok's honour-son." Yatal's attention shifted to Bahari. "You have sent your speaker to carry my story to your father?"

Bahari shifted his feet. Nyri could see he was still unhappy at Yatal's declaration that they must fight the gods. The Thals, like her own People, were still deeply loyal to those whom the stories claimed created them and Nyri knew the Thals would never join the Cro in this fight. The People they believed had roused the gods' anger in the first place. "I sent speakers, Yatal," Bahari said, "under the protection of Nisaru. Spitter cat happier away from here."

Before Yatal could respond, the hide curtains of the shelter were wrenched aside. A figure barrelled through them, heading straight for the Eagle leader. Juaan's hunting knife flashed out. It was at the intruder's throat before he made it two strides.

"Yatal!"

"Drop your weapon, Khalvir!" Yatal snapped. Her gaze went to the man Juaan had halted mid-stride. "Speak, Benir."

The Eagle totem hung about the man's neck, carved in the green stone the Thals traded. He was one of Yatal's clan. Nyri recoiled internally from the panicked horror that radiated from him. The man moistened his dry lips. "I travelled to observe the Hunting Bear clan as you asked, Chieftess."

"And?"

The Eagle scout opened and closed his mouth several times, but no sound emerged. The icy hand of dread curled around Nyri's heart and squeezed.

"Speak!" Yatal commanded.

"I-It's gone," Benir's voice rasped out at last. "Destroyed. Bodies everywhere, t-torn to pieces. Spiked, dangling from totems. A-and footprints... the footprints." The man's throat closed, cutting off his words once more. He was shaking.

The horrors in his memory hazed against Nyri's mind's eye. "Kyaati." Her tribe-sister's name slipped from her lips.

Yatal's sallow face drained of what little colour was left in it. "It has already begun," she said. "The Red Bear?"

267

The scout raised his hands. "Unknown. We did not see his body, but... the remains were so badly mangled, it would have been hard to recognise our enemy had he lain among the fallen. Many were without heads."

Bile rose in Nyri's mouth. The names of the clan members she had come to know and grow fond of flew through her mind. Halima, Kikima, Akito, Galahir... Kyaati. Surely she would know if her tribe-sister was dead. Surely she would know it.

Her eyes went to Juaan. His knuckles were white on the knife still in his hand, and Nyri knew the same names and more were in his thoughts. She could feel the questions he wanted to throw at the scout burn in her own throat, but she knew the man would never be able to answer.

Kyaati. The sobs were clawing their way up her throat as the shock gave way and the knowledge that her tribe-sister and her precious new baby were likely dead sank in. She hadn't even known the little one's name.

"Now is not the time to grieve!" Yatal's feeble voice cracked over them with all the callousness of a hardened survivor. "Many more will die if we do not keep to our paths. Worry not about the fallen, they are already gone. Go, Nyriaana. Do not look back."

Nyri could not have stayed in that shelter a moment longer, drowning in the horror rolling from the scout, seeing the half-formed images of slaughter in his distant thoughts. She turned and bolted from Yatal's home. She stopped when she reached open ground, gulping in clean lungfuls of air, balling her fists to try to stop the shaking. A hand gripped her shoulder, and she reached up to take it.

"We do not know what happened, Nyriaana," Juaan spoke

softly, though she could hear the weight of grief in his voice. "There may have been survivors."

Nyri sniffed and nodded. She had to cling to that hope. If she was to continue to move forward, she had to believe Kyaati and her baby had made it out. As Yatal had declared, it had begun. The Watchers had wiped out the most powerful clan on the Plains. No longer a bodiless vision, reality settled on Nyri's shoulders like a shroud. "We need to leave," she whispered.

As though in answer to her declaration, Sakal appeared, shouldering slings filled with rations, extra furs and weapons. She paused before them, reading Nyri and Juaan's desolate expressions, and raised a querying eyebrow.

"Hunting Bear clan has been wiped out," Bahari answered before Nyri could find her voice. She watched numbly as a range of emotions crossed over the Eagle warrior's face. Shock and elation battled for dominance. Her most hated enemy was gone, and yet she was imagining the force it would have taken to accomplish such a feat. Her lips pressed together as she acknowledged Bahari's explanation.

She handed Bahari and Juaan a share of her load. She eyed Nyri critically for a moment before thrusting a sling full of dried fish at her.

Nyri's chin came up as she accepted the load, refusing to show weakness in front of Sakal, and settled the weight upon her shoulders. Sakal snorted, unimpressed, then jabbed a thick finger towards a path leading towards the north. "Fastest route to the Mountains," she explained gruffly.

"Lead the way, then," Nyri responded.

The Eagle warrior hefted her long spear and turned her

back, setting off with ground-covering strides towards the trail she had indicated, making it clear that she would not be waiting for anyone.

Nyri froze. Her feet had turned to immovable rocks. Her breath shortened in her throat. The path through the hills ahead appeared to her like jaws, ready to snap shut behind her as soon as she entered the maw. No escape, no turning back. Her breath came faster.

The hand on her shoulder squeezed.

Will you protect me, Juaan, the voice of her old child self rose in her mind.

To the end, came the boy's voice in return.

Nyri steadied her breathing and concentrated on her body, forcing her foot to lift and take that first step forward. Somewhere in the back of her mind, unseen energies exalted.

* * *

15

Unexpected

The light of a new day stung Kyaati's eyes as she stumbled on in Galahir's wake, and she lifted a hand to dash away the moisture that started there. They were the tears of dry, sleepless eyes. Kyaati had cried herself out long before dawn began. All through the long night, she had struggled to come to terms with what had happened. A part of her still could not accept that she would never see Halima again. Never to hear her strong, unwavering voice, never to be on the receiving end of her uncompromising judgement. Kyaati had come to respect and love her as a leader. And now she was gone and Kyaati felt oddly off balance. Halima had been part of her new life almost from its beginning.

Kyaati could not imagine what Kikima was going through. When she looked to her friend, her amber eyes were dry, staring, her emotions... frozen. Kikima was still in shock.

Kyaati stumbled over a stone, a shot of adrenaline jolting through her as she almost fell. Her arms instinctively went around Elhaari in his sling to protect him. Kikima's hand shot out, steadying her.

"Thank you," she whispered, her voice rasping through her sore throat.

Kikima jerked her chin in acknowledgement, but did not meet Kyaati's gaze. She kept staring straight ahead, her eyes fixed on a point Kyaati could not determine.

Kyaati forced her legs to continue bearing her weight. She and the small band of survivors that surrounded her had walked throughout the night following their headlong flight from the fire and the screams, putting as much distance between them and the vengeful Watchers as they could. Even after the cacophony of destruction had faded behind them, they could not rest, and so they had just carried on trudging, driven on by fear and grief.

The youngest members of the party had been the first to succumb to the trek. Galahir now carried Akito in his burly arms, the blind boy's lashes, sticky from tears, brushing his scarred cheeks as he slept against Galahir's shoulder. Kyaati was glad the youngster had escaped reality, however briefly. Lorhir's son, Zinir, was similarly slung across his father's shoulders.

Kyaati's eyelids drooped, and she stumbled again before she managed to wrench them back, feeling them scrape painfully against the surface of her eyes. Jostled for the second time in his sling, Elhaari awoke and wailed.

"Shh, shhh!" Kyaati hissed, glancing around, still terrified that a Watcher might yet lurch out at them from a hidden dell in the rolling Plains.

Galahir turned, Kyaati lifted her face to his, attempting to feign strength, but could not keep the strain from her face. Galahir brushed her cheek and tucked a strand of hair that had fallen across her face behind an ear. "We should rest," he said. "I think it's safe enough now."

Lorhir shook his head. "We should find more cover." Elhaari wailed louder when his cries for food continued to go unheeded. Lorhir snarled in his direction. "Shut him up!"

Galahir stepped in front of Kyaati, squaring up to the smaller man. "We rest," he rumbled. "You can take first watch, Lorhir."

Lorhir's eyes sparked, but to Kyaati's amazement, he gave way to her mate. Lorhir placed his sleeping son on the ground and moved back in the direction they had come to watch for signs of pursuit.

Galahir stooped to set Akito next to Zinir. Even from where she stood, Kyaati could hear his stomach growl. Ordinarily, she would have teased him for his appetite, but he was not alone in his need. The pang of hunger gnawed at her own belly. They carried no rations and Galahir would not leave them to find game. They no longer had the luxury of a clan to guard the vulnerable, while the strongest left to provide. Kyaati swallowed. It was a risk they would soon have to take. The others might last a couple more days without food, but as a nursing mother, Kyaati needed nourishment. She could see her worry reflected in Galahir's eyes as he watched her settle to feed their infant.

A whistle of alert shattered the stillness. Kyaati's head snapped around towards the point where Lorhir had disappeared. Her heart leapt to her throat, adrenaline pumping to her legs in preparation for flight. They had not been fast enough. Their enemies had come for them.

"Stay with the children!" Galahir commanded. Gripping

his arshu, he ran in Lorhir's direction. But Kyaati could not be still. She could not bear for Galahir to be out of her sight, and she followed on his heels.

They did not have to go far before they came upon Lorhir, crouching in a hollow. He turned his head upon hearing their approach and signalled for silence, before pointing with a finger towards whatever had alerted him.

"What is it?" Galahir breathed in his raknari brother's ear.

"Not a Watcher. Smaller. I caught a glimpse of fur. Perhaps an animal." He shifted his spear into a ready position. "We need meat."

On the other side of the rise, the sound of stones skittering over a bare patch of ground had them all tensing. Their quarry was close enough for a strike.

Lorhir was out of hiding in a flash, his spear poised to launch just as Kyaati cried, "No!" Her senses alerting her to a human presence.

A shrill scream drowned out her denial, and Lorhir cursed. "Selima!"

Selima? A heartbeat later, Lorhir reappeared, dragging the red-haired daughter of Eldrax into view, his face a mask of fury.

"You!" A snarl came from behind Kyaati. Before she could move, Kikima had barrelled past her and launched herself at Selima. "It was you! You betrayed her! You murdered her!" She knocked the red-haired girl to the ground, punching, kicking, and gouging at any part of her she could reach, shrieking with inhuman fury as Selima squealed and tried to break her grip.

"Kikima!" Galahir yanked the tall woman away from her victim as Lorhir hauled Selima out of reach. Selima's pale skin was torn with scratch marks, her lips split, as blood spilled from her nose.

"You spawn of a swine!" Kikima continued to scream. "It's all your fault! She would still be here if it weren't for you!" She fought against Galahir like a wild beast. Kyaati recoiled as she was buffeted by Kikima's release of emotion, all of her grief, shock, and anger finally boiling to the fore, triggered by Selima's appearance.

"Quiet!" Lorhir hissed at the crazed half-Deni girl. "Do you want to bring our enemies straight to us?"

"Too late for that." A new voice silenced Kikima's crazed tirade.

Kyaati and the rest of her group spun around. The lilt of the words told them this was not another Hunting Bear straggler. Kyaati had been so caught up in Kikima's outburst, she had not been alert to another approach.

Galahir and Lorhir shouldered together in front of the women as six men broke cover and arrayed themselves before them, their totems clear to see. Kyaati shrank behind Galahir as her heart pounded in her ears. Eagles. The last time she had been in their company, she had murdered one of their clan members, allowing herself and Nyri to escape their barbaric death sentence. Kyaati knew her appearance was distinctive enough for them to recognise her on sight. Acting quickly, she pulled a fur up over her head, trying to conceal her silvery hair.

Lorhir cursed, and Kyaati risked peering around Galahir's elbow to see that two of the Eagles had Akito and Zinir in their grip. Lorhir made to rush the enemy who held his whimpering son.

"I wouldn't if I were you," sneered the man in the centre

of the enemy ranks. "One wrong move and we will cut their throats."

Kyaati sank further down as both Galahir and Lorhir took exactly two heartbeats to decide that they were beaten. She tasted their shame and frustration as they dropped their weapons to the ground and knelt before the superior enemy force.

"What shall we do with them?" the man nearest the Eagle scout leader asked.

"They're Hunting Bear," the leader grunted. "I'd know their stench anywhere." His face darkened dangerously as he regarded the two men kneeling in submission before him.

A knife rasped. "I've always wanted to taste the blood of Hunting Bear." Another of the men started forward. Kyaati's mouth went dry.

"No," the leader gave a sharp command, halting his vengeful follower in his tracks. "We take them back alive."

"But…"

"Yatal wants an alliance with the Red Bear against the great threat she foresees," the leader responded.

Kyaati was aware that it was not just her own shock she was experiencing at the Eagle warrior's words. Surprise vibed around her whole group.

"Yatal has lost her senses!"

"That may be, but she is still our Chieftess," the leader growled.

"Not for much longer," the other man responded churlishly.

"Does that give you the right to turn traitor in her last days of life? Patience, Matal, soon we will have a new leader, and then we will do as we wish with these Hunting Bear hogs."

Matal grumbled, glaring at Galahir and Lorhir. "Very well, Narak." He sheathed his knife. Kyaati breathed again.

"Bind them," the leader, Narak, ordered. "We will take them to Yatal."

Clutching Elhaari close to her breast, Kyaati was helpless as four of the Eagle men came forward. As they rounded Galahir, intending to tie his hands behind his back, Kyaati had nowhere to hide. The fur covering her head could not conceal the differences between her and the surrounding men and women. The Eagles' eyes fell upon her and widened.

"By Ea!" the first exclaimed, grabbing the fur and ripping it back. "The other one!"

"The witch that killed Honad! I know that hair."

Kyaati backed away from the vengeful fury that swept over the Eagle group. Kikima was faster to react, drawing her knife and pulling Kyaati and Elhaari behind her. "Stay back," she snarled.

The Eagle warriors chuckled in dark amusement.

"Well, this is interesting," Narak, the leader, said.

Kikima clutched her knife until her knuckles turned white. "If you want her, you'll have to go through me!"

A gleam that Kyaati did not like entered the Eagle men's eyes as they took in her friend.

"I call to be the first to tame that one," the warrior holding Akito hostage leered.

Narak laughed. "We will see. Bring them all."

The command startled the rest of the men. "We should at least kill the witch! She took the life of one of our own.

277

And the other has already done enough damage to Yatal."

"The whole clan deserves the chance to decide what this witch's fate should be," Narak responded. "Don't worry, we will not make the mistake of letting this one near Yatal."

Through her panic, Kyaati felt a shiver of confusion. Nyri had damaged Yatal in failing to heal her granddaughter, prompting the Eagle chieftess to sentence them to death. But the way these men spoke hinted at a more recent trespass. Had Nyriaana run afoul of Yatal again? It was the first hint of her tribe-sister's existence that she had heard spoken since Nyri had fled the Hunting Bear camp with Khalvir. She did not dare open her mouth to question their enemies, however. For the moment, they were letting her live. With Elhaari's safety to consider, Kyaati kept her head down.

Two of the Eagles yanked Galahir and Lorhir back to their feet at spearpoint. The other four circled Kikima, Kyaati, and Selima, thrusting Akito and Zinir at them. Kyaati quickly took Akito's hand as the enemy scouts pressed them forward.

They travelled in silence, the Eagles alert both to their surroundings and any sign of rebellion from the prisoners in their midst. Kyaati felt they were monitoring her especially. One wrong move and she knew they would kill her.

At Kikima's side, she stumbled on, numb to anything except placing one exhausted foot in front of the other, continuing in a daze. She did not notice they had arrived at the foothills of the Mountains of the Nine Gods until she tripped over the first rock and looked up to find the maze of craggy hills looming above her. The scent of damp, cold rock sent her hurtling back to the terrible days following her capture from her home, travelling with the Cro, and the terror that she had experienced at the hands of the Eagles. Kyaati balked.

Kikima caught her by the elbow. "Keep moving, Kyaati," she said, her voice once again devoid of emotion.

Although her every instinct screamed at her to resist, Kyaati forced herself to step forward, climbing into the foothills of the Mountains for the second time in her life. Selima came behind her and Kyaati could sense that she was every bit as terrified as she was. Not that Kyaati gave a rock for what Selima felt.

Ninmah was hot on Kyaati's back as she climbed the steep trails. The sweat trickled under her furs, irritating her skin. Her throat was parched. She eyed the water skin at the hip of the closest Eagle, but she dared not ask for a drink. She knew what the answer would be. The man would as soon pour it over her head as favour her with a drink. Though, Kyaati mused, that might be welcome, too.

The trail the Eagles had taken climbed on and on, seemingly without end. Kyaati was beginning to wonder how she would force her aching feet to carry her one more step when something horrifyingly familiar brushed against her senses, the energy ahead shifting. She scrambled backward until she came up against the immovable body of the Eagle man behind her. He shoved her forward with a growl.

"No. Stop! We need to go back. Right now!"

"I will not play games, witch," Narak growled. "Get moving!"

Then the wind shifted, bringing with it the stench of blood and rotting flesh. Kyaati felt her Hunting Bear companions stiffen around her. They all recognised that awful smell for what it was.

"She speaks the truth!" Galahir hissed to the Eagle leader. "We have to turn around, now, or we will all die."

A loud skitter of stones sounded and Narak's head snapped around. Settling into a hunting crouch, he started forward, his spear ready in hand.

"No!" Using his strength to tear away from the man that held him, Galahir threw himself on top of the Eagle leader, driving him to the ground not a moment too soon. The tread of heavy feet crunching over shale echoed down the passageway ahead.

"Behind those rocks if you value your skins!" Lorhir snarled at their captors. The smell of death and decay grew stronger. Shaking from head to foot, Kyaati watched as instinct took hold of the Eagle warriors and they chose to heed Lorhir's warning, rushing behind the cluster of rocks he had indicated. Galahir and Narak, scrambling back to their feet, were the last to take cover.

The heavy footfalls drew nearer, accompanied by the sound of a slow, rasping breath; air passing through a throat like the growl of a predator. Kyaati reached out and took one of Galahir's bound hands, clutching it in her own, trying to still her trembling and hold herself fast.

"Ea protect us!" Narak whispered. The Eagle scout leader had dared to peer out from their scant cover. Unable to stop herself, Kyaati leaned far enough out to follow his gaze, though she already knew what she would see.

A Watcher had lumbered into sight. Most of the creature's flesh was concealed under a coating of blood, but what bare skin she could see had a sickly bluish cast under the revealing light of Ninmah. Bile rose in Kyaati's throat as she beheld the human skins dangling from the creature's coverings. From one hand dangled the upper half of a Cro man, one arm was missing. An Eagle totem dangled from the dead man's neck. Kyaati closed her eyes as the Watcher lifted the torso towards its face, opening its mouth wide. She could not block out the nightmarish crunching sound, however. Ducking her head, Kyaati buried her face in Elhaari's sling to block out the scent of fresh blood.

The sound of the beast's tread paused and Narak drew back quickly, pressing his back against the rock that lay between him and the monster standing all but ten strides away. Hunting Bear and Eagle alike held their breath. Kyaati's skin crawled as she felt the Watcher's regard swing in their direction, its nose sniffing at the air.

A whimper escaped Selima's lips and Kikima clamped her hand tightly over the other girl's mouth and nose. The sound of sniffing grew louder, and rocks skittered as the beast shifted its weight. Around her, Kyaati watched shaking hands clutch spears. Without a sound, Narak severed Lorhir's and Galahir's bonds, thrusting their weapons back at them. Galahir pointed at his eyes and Kyaati read his meaning. *Go for the eyes.* Narak nodded.

Preparing to fight for their lives, they waited for the best moment to strike. Kyaati closed her eyes.

But whatever power held sway in these lands must have been watching over them. A spine-chilling cry sounded in the distance. The sound of sniffing ceased, replaced by the sound of retreating feet as the Watcher loped off in the direction of the call. Something heavy thudded to the ground in its wake.

Silence reigned for a handful of moments before Kyaati

and her companions dared to breathe once more. Galahir and Narak let a few more heartbeats pass before raising their heads above the rocks.

"It's gone," Galahir whispered. "Kyaati?"

Kyaati knew what he was asking of her, but it took her a moment to centre herself enough to stretch out with her senses, afraid of what she might feel. "N-nothing," she breathed when her search came back empty.

The Eagle warrior named Matal promptly vomited into the rocks.

Kyaati crawled out of cover on Galahir's heels as the rest followed. The hills were disturbingly still. Not even the vibration of a rodent quivering in its hole could be felt. Kyaati shuddered. The Eagle men gathered around the object that the Watcher had dropped in its wake. Kyaati did not look, knowing what she would see. Her empty stomach turned over.

"Grefel." Narak named the half-eaten remains of the fallen warrior. Kyaati watched as the Eagle leader turned away and approached Galahir, his face grim. "How did you know that creature was out here?"

"The gods have released them upon us," Galahir spoke. "After the lights over the Mountains disappeared, they came. We were the only ones to survive."

"The Hunting Bear are gone?" one of the Eagle scouts demanded.

"Yes," Galahir said. The grief in his voice and the weary defeated set of his shoulders gave the Eagles no reason to doubt. Sharp intakes of breath betrayed their disbelief. "They came for us in the night," Galahir continued. "The Red Bear prepared, but it was no use. You need to warn

Yatal of the danger before the same fate befalls your own clan."

"I think she already knows," Narak murmured, sharing loaded glances with his clan brothers. "She was right," he whispered just loud enough for Kyaati to hear.

"What if they've already destroyed us? What if Grefel wasn't out on a hunting foray?" The sudden spike of anxiety from the nearest Eagle scout flared across Kyaati's senses and was immediately picked up by his brothers.

Narak lifted his spear and set off at a dead run.

The encounter with the Watcher had lent Kyaati the extra strength she needed to keep up with the renewed pace. She loped along over the rough ground, barely noticing the taxing terrain; her higher senses were thrown out, watching for any sign that the monster might have turned around to hunt them, bringing others with it.

As Ninmah rose to her peak, the Eagle warriors' apprehension grew and Kyaati knew they must be getting close to their home. Were they about to face the ashes of another dead camp filled with piles of dismembered corpses? Kyaati's stride faltered.

When they reached a point where two peaks loomed over the trail, Narak halted and let out a long whistle. There was an edge of desperation to the sound.

Silence.

Panting, Narak repeated his call, louder than before. "Where *are* you?" he muttered.

Then it came, an answering whistle, trilling through the hills and echoing around them. The entire Eagle company let out a collective breath.

"They're alive!" Narak bounded forward, beckoning to

Galahir and the rest of the remnants of the Hunting Bear. In the wake of their brush with the Watcher, any enmity between the two clans appeared to have been forgotten.

More slowly now, Narak led them on. Kyaati could sense others on the ridges above them, watching their progress. Confusion and wariness at the sight of the unbound prisoners walking freely into camp drifted across Kyaati's awareness. She held Elhaari close, hoping none of the silent sentinels above lost nerve, and decided to throw a well-placed spear between the shoulder blades of the evil elf-witch. Her eyes kept flickering to the ridges, but she could not see them, only feel their growing animosity.

Narak let out another rolling whistle as the last of the rocks and ridges parted before them, revealing the sprawl of the Eagle camp. Some wood-and-hide shelters were tucked into the sides of the surrounding hills, others were stretched and pinned down with rocks in the centre of the open space; all revolving around the largest shelter at the very centre. The dwelling of the Chieftess herself. It had not changed since Kyaati's last ill-fated visit. The hairs rose on the back of her neck, and her eyes strayed unwillingly to the stumps of two trees where she and Nyriaana had almost met their bloody end. The rest of her companions were similarly ill at ease, and they bunched closer together in the midst of their enemy's stronghold.

Whispers followed them as the Eagle clan paused in their daily routines to stare. Kyaati soon discovered that she was not the primary target for the glowers of hostility. Selima was. Her bright red hair announced her as a spawn of Eldrax more efficiently than any word of introduction. Selima kept her head lowered and tried to shrug further into the centre of their group, but Kikima vindictively kept her out in plain sight.

Kyaati noticed for the first time that her friend had brought her tawny hair down to cover her forehead, hiding the marks of a Chief's mate that adorned her skin there. Kyaati guessed a Claimed mate of Eldrax would be little more welcome than one of his offspring. One of which Kikima now carried in her belly. Kyaati took hold of Kikima's hand with her free one and squeezed. The other she kept tightly on Akito, guiding him forward through the maze of shelters as Narak led them to the centre of the camp.

Two guards stood on either side of the entrance to Yatal's private domain. Narak spoke to them. "We found these Hunting Bear out on the plains. I bring them to speak with Yatal."

To Kyaati's surprise, the guards did not block the way, demanding an explanation. They nodded in grim understanding and pulled the draping hide curtains apart, admitting them. Narak also appeared slightly nonplussed by the lack of resistance but started forwards. Kyaati and her companions had no choice but to follow him into his Chieftess' domain with the other Eagle scouts pressing at their backs.

Kyaati choked as the smell inside assaulted her senses. Akito clamped his hand over his nose and whimpered softly. Taking shallow breaths, Kyaati spared a few moments to allow her eyes to adjust. The first thing that came to her attention was the shapeless heap in the centre of the shelter, surrounded by anxious elders and guards. A thin, laboured breath rattled in the air.

"Chieftess," Narak spoke. "You sent my hunting group to seek other clans. We came upon these Hunting Bear. They say—"

"The Hunting Bear are no more." The heap in the middle of the shelter shifted. One of the elder women hovering to the side rushed forward, aiding her Chieftess in rising to a half-seated position, gathering furs behind her back upon which she could lean.

Kyaati's breath caught in her throat at the sight of Yatal. She had been ailing upon their last meeting. Now it was like looking into the face of a corpse draped in rotting skin. Against her higher senses, the flame of life occupying the space where Yatal sat stuttered and flared.

"Y-you know of their fate?" Narak stammered.

Yatal grunted. "Benir brought the news but yesterday. The gods have loosed the Watchers from their lair."

"Yes," Narak said, his voice strangled. "We encountered one of the beasts… in the foothills."

Gasps went up around the collected Eagles. "So close?" The woman next to Yatal clutched at her chest.

"Were it not for this Hunting Bear warrior, and this witch, we would be dead." Narak indicated Galahir and Kyaati behind him. "Grefel… was not so lucky."

A wail shattered by grief went up from the corner of Yatal's shelter. An older woman leaped up and ran from the dwelling, crying her denial as she went. Kyaati's heart sank in her chest. Another mother who would never see her son again. She released Akito's hand to put her arm about Elhaari.

Yatal's yellowing eyes roamed over the group before her. To Kyaati's horror, they settled upon her first.

"Ah, the second witch returns. Fate has a strange sense of humour indeed. There is no need to tremble, girl. You no longer have anything to fear from me. Your kin stood before me upon Utu's last rising. We made our peace."

"Nyriaana is here?" Kyaati blurted before she could stop herself. Her heavy heart lifted, swelling until she thought it would burst. The thought of seeing Nyriaana stole her cares from her shoulders and banished all the horrors to the recesses of her mind. "Where is she?" Kyaati cast around with her senses, searching.

"She has departed on the path the spirits laid out for her," Yatal rasped.

Kyaati's elation drained away. "What are you saying?"

Yatal pointed with one shaking finger. "Into the Mountains. I take it, as a witch, you have heard your People's tales of the Last Kamaali, and all that she promises."

"The Mountains?" Kyaati shrieked.

Unperturbed by her outburst, Yatal blinked slowly. "To find the Last Kamaali, as she was bidden."

"But the Last Kamaali is just a story! The same as all the rest," Kyaati raged. "She doesn't exist! The last Kamaali of my People died to save my life. Nyri has gone into the Mountains to find…"

"Your only hope," Yatal cut across her.

Kyaati glared at the Chieftess, all fear forgotten. "You seem very sure, Cro," she spat. "What do you know of Ninkuraaja fables?"

"More than you, it seems," Yatal wheezed. "When the god lights appeared in the sky, your tribe-sister and I shared a vision. We were both given a fate. Nyriaana has gone to meet hers."

287

"She is going to her death!" Kyaati spun on her heel, not knowing what she was going to do, but needing to do something. She could not be still knowing Nyriaana was, at that very moment, heading into the worst danger imaginable.

"You're too late," Yatal said. "She already has a day's start on you and is being led by my best tracker. She is out of your reach now."

Angry tears started in the corners of Kyaati's eyes. Galahir reached for her, but Kyaati pushed his hand away. There was no comfort for this. It had been one thing awaiting word of Nyri's capture by Eldrax's hunters. At least then there had still been a sliver of hope. Now there was none. She had lost her tribe-sister after all, even after everything she had tried to do to save her. Eldrax had never been the one who would take her away. So soon after losing Halima, this news was almost enough to send Kyaati to her knees. She stared hard at the hide wall of the shelter, fighting to maintain her composure, wanting nothing more than to be alone in her grief.

"I never thought to have a daughter of Eldrax in my presence." Kyaati heard the cold bite in Yatal's voice as her attention turned to Selima.

"I-I am n-no daughter of his," Selima's terrified whisper came, almost inaudible. Where was her smug bravado now? In Yatal's presence, she was no more than a cringing child.

Kyaati bared her teeth, savouring every bit of Selima's terror. This spawn of Ninsiku had set Nyriaana on this path. She had never hated Eldrax's daughter more than she did in that present moment. She wished Kikima had gouged her black eyes out.

"Hmmm," Yatal's deliberation was almost a growl. "And it seems we also have a Claimed of the Red Bear among us."

Now Kyaati did turn. Kikima's hair had shifted, revealing the tattoos across her forehead. Her friend's rich skin burned.

"Tell me, do you bear his child?"

Kikima lifted her chin. "No," she lied. "The Red Bear only Claimed me just before the attack. He had no time to put his seed in my belly."

Kyaati was aware of Lorhir and Galahir's eyes going to Kikima, but they kept their silence.

Yatal nodded, satisfied. She gestured to one of the waiting men. "The evil of the Red Bear should not be permitted to spread through the lands. Take that one and keep her under watch until I decide her fate."

The Eagle man dipped his chin and caught Selima by the arm. Kyaati watched, detached, as Selima struggled, begging for deliverance, but none of the Hunting Bear stepped forward to defend her as she was led from the shelter and out of sight. Kyaati did not care if Yatal decided to feed her to the jackals.

"But she is not the only spawn of my enemy. I see Eldrax got his wish and sired a witch child."

Kyaati blanched, knowing that the Eagle chieftess' attention was now back on her, on Elhaari. She tightened her arms around her son. It was clear what the Chieftess had meant by not allowing Eldrax's evil to spread; why Kikima had concealed her condition.

"No, respected Yatal," Galahir, who had remained unobtrusive until this moment, thrust himself forward before the Eagle Chieftess. "The child is mine. He is mine!"

"And who are—" Yatal's ancient gaze shifted unsteadily to the man now standing before her. When she found her focus, Kyaati watched the sallow skin pale. "No. It can't be!" she gasped, her wasted hand going to her breast.

Kyaati's eyes went to Galahir, but her mate appeared just as confused by Yatal's reaction as she was.

"Jharan?"

Kyaati stepped to Galahir's side, taking his hand as her mate stiffened in shock, an array of half-formed emotions rushing through him. "I am Galahir," he said, though his voice wavered as he took a half step back.

"No," Yatal whispered. "I would know Elahi's son anywhere. Your beloved mother..."

Galahir's grip was becoming painful upon Kyaati's hand. "My mother?"

Tears leaked down the old Chieftess' face. "Oh yes. Elahi. Our noble matriarch. I was there when the Red Bear cut her down and stole you away. I could not stop him." Yatal closed her eyes as though to shield herself from a distant horror, then reached out a trembling hand. "Now you return in my time of need. I have been waiting for you, Jharan, and I didn't even know it until this moment. *This* is what my vision foretold." And then Yatal's voice boomed with a forgotten strength as she lifted her arms, encompassing all of those present. "Chief Rikal's son has come home to his rightful family!"

All faces turned to Galahir even as Kyaati stared up at her mate in shock. But none appeared more stunned than Galahir himself as Yatal beckoned him towards her.

"Here, boy," she rasped. Galahir hesitated for a moment, then stepped slowly towards the pile of furs upon which the Eagle Chieftess reclined. She stretched both her hands towards him and Galahir bowed his head, allowing her to place her shaking palms on his shaggy hair. "Witness, all of you, I, Yatal, with my last breaths, name this man the new Chief of the Eagle Clan!"

* * *

16

Gathering Storm

150,000 BCE

Enki stared down at the disaster below. The giant Nephilim tore through Eridu, destroying and killing everything in their wake, hulking abominations born of the Igigi and the daughters of the Adamu who had been gifted to them by Enlil. Enlil, ignorant of the reproductive enhancement Enki had bestowed upon them.

Enki's skin rippled. All his plans were now laid to waste at his feet. Enlil knew what he had done.

"What are we going to do now?" Ninmah was by his side, her glowing lavender eyes fixed on the chaos unfolding below.

"We must prepare to fight and protect what remains," Enki said, watching as his creations were chased from the sanctuary of Eridu. "He is coming."

* * *

Eldrax limped on into the landscape. The gash to his leg

dripped with blood, but he had no time to tend to it, no witch, not even the useless Johaquin to sew his flesh back together. Perhaps he shouldn't have thrown his daughter into the path of a Watcher in order to escape. Even she might have been of use to him now.

Injured as he was, Eldrax refused to lean on his battle club for support. He kept his back and shoulders straight, showing nothing but strength to the ten who had followed him from the destruction of his clan. Fury fuelled his body and burned like fire through his veins.

He had suffered a humiliating defeat, lost his clan, his camp, his only witch and her offspring. The last rankled most of all.

"How far until we are safe from those things?" a whimpering voice grated across Eldrax's ear and he turned his head to glare at the woman clutching her babe to her breast.

"You think I am running?" Eldrax asked her in his softest, most deadly voice. The same voice that had had the toughest warriors trembling where they stood. The woman quailed. "You think I am fleeing to some bolt hole to cower?"

"B…but," the woman stammered, looking to the others for help.

"This changes nothing!" Eldrax spat, rounding fully on the woman, towering above her. "Nowhere is safe, do you not understand that, you pathetic wastes?" He punched his chest, the fury burning ever hotter. "I vowed to you. I will not lie under a god's rule. I will have my vengeance for this and save us all!"

His followers stared at him, agape. They thought him mad. Eldrax jabbed at the way behind them with his club. "Go back if you wish. Beg for the gods' forgiveness. But when the Watchers squeeze your babe's head into pulp before your eyes, know it will be me who will avenge his blood. I will avenge every drop of blood ever spilled in the name of the gods!"

He did not wait to see if any of them followed or crawled back towards the Mountains on their bellies. When they were free of the gods' tyranny, Eldrax would want only the strongest under his rule. They would see. They would soon see. He was no fool. Not much farther now. If he had judged it right, he would make it before nightfall. He had planned for this ever since he had left boyhood behind.

Rannac had helped him do it. The Old Wolf might not have agreed with him, but he had known the importance of obeying his Chief. The Plains had run with the blood of felled Chiefs and all those that would not bend to his vision. Many fine warriors had been lost. But what were the lives of a few foolish men when he would save so many more? When he could be rid of the very last force that could hurt him?

The scent of campfires in the distance blew across Eldrax's face as Utu began her descent towards the west. Eldrax inhaled deeply and bared his teeth in a grin. His men had not let him down. The wound on his leg plagued him, the blood slipping down his calf to leave a trail of red for the survivors of the Hunting Bear clan to follow, but the fresh scent renewed his determination. Ignoring the moans of despair behind him, Eldrax increased the pace. The scent grew stronger on the breeze with every step.

At last, he mounted a low rise and paused. "Ahhh," he sighed, savouring the vision before him. Behind him, he heard the awed intakes of breath. *Yes,* he thought, *now you see.*

Filling his lungs with air, he let loose a signalling howl, announcing his presence. A man leapt to his feet from the side of the nearest campfire below and bounded up the hill to greet his leader, prostrating himself before the mightier man.

"Revered Red Bear," he said, alarm in his tone. "We were expecting to meet you at the camp of the Hunting Bear."

"That will no longer be necessary," Eldrax said, still taking in the sight below. The man would find out soon enough from others what had become of the clan. He would waste no time reliving what was past.

"Do you approve, my Chief?" The warrior swung his arm out to encompass the vast camp below. Never had such a sight been witnessed. Shelters and campfires stretched away as far as the eye could see. A force like no other. And he, Eldrax, was its master.

"You have done well," he growled at the man who nervously awaited his approval.

"What are your wishes?"

"Find me an *ashipu* skilled in mending wounds," he barked. "I will rest only long enough for my injury to heal."

"And then, my Chief?"

"Then we will move on the Forests of the Nine Gods and make the gods rue the day they dared to rule us."

* * *

17

Decisions

Kyaati watched Galahir as the last of the rocks were placed over Yatal's grave, the final rays of Ninmah flickering over the broken hills. The death of their leader sent ripples of grief and despair through the Eagle Clan. The elder woman had been their Chieftess for many of the younger members' whole lives. And now she was gone and a new leader stood above her body. A stranger. An enemy warrior.

Kyaati's mate.

Kyaati could feel Galahir's discomfort, his confusion. He was hiding it well from the wary stares of his new clan, but beneath the stalwart expression that was fixed upon his face, Kyaati knew Galahir was more frightened now than she had ever known him to be. There was a tremble in his hand as he raised it to speak the traditional words of farewell to the Chieftess.

When the rite of death had been completed, an elder woman came to Galahir's side. Kyaati could not name her. Everything had happened too fast since their arrival at the

Eagle camp.

"Yatal named this man, Jharan, son of the great Eagle Chief Rikal, to be your Chief after her!" the elder declared to those gathered in a voice stronger than her frail figure hinted at. "May his strength lead us true and shelter us from our enemies. Pledge yourselves to his protection from now until the day he can protect us no more!"

Galahir's panic flared. His eyes darted as though seeking escape, but none presented itself as the Eagle clan gathered around him, drawing knives. No matter his or their feelings, their last leader had chosen Galahir to be the Chief. By their own traditions, Yatal's choice was to be honoured. Galahir bowed to his knees.

Kyaati planted herself against her mate's back, letting him feel her presence as, one by one, the men and women of the Eagle clan bloodied their fingers and pressed them to Galahir's forehead, marking him with their life essences, lives that he now held in his hands as their anointed Chief.

Lorhir was the last to approach with his son. Kyaati tensed as Lorhir stared at her mate for a drawn out moment, before glancing around at the Eagles surrounding him. He let out a defeated breath. Whatever he thought of Galahir, Lorhir, too, was bound by tradition. If he wanted a haven for his son, then he would have to bow to the man he had always ridiculed as his new leader. Kyaati watched these thoughts pass through Lorhir's mind with fierce satisfaction as Lorhir sliced his finger and that of his son, before pressing them to Galahir's forehead.

It was done.

Galahir rose to his feet, his forehead stained red with the weight of his new responsibility. Pulling his great shoulders back, he looked out over the faces watching him. Kyaati felt his hand slip around hers and grip it tight as he spoke. "I pledge to honour Chieftess Yatal's last wishes. I pledge to protect you all from now until my dying breath."

Upon that announcement, Galahir turned away from his followers and drew Kyaati after him into the Dwelling of the Chief. Once they were inside, Galahir spun, caught her up in his arms and buried his face in her shoulder.

"Kyaati, Kyaati, I cannot do this." He was trembling faintly. "I am not a leader. I never was."

Kyaati drew him down onto the furs at the centre of the dwelling, blessedly refreshed after their last occupant. She stroked his sandy hair. "Shhh," she murmured, letting the fear pass through him in the safety of her embrace. "I am here."

"How am I supposed to lead them?"

"By being who you are," Kyaati said, now thrusting him back to look him in the face. "You are a strong, good and gentle man, Galahir. This clan is blessed to have you as their leader."

"Gentleness does not protect a clan from threats." His face twisted. "It is a weakness. Eldrax…"

"You are ten times the man Eldrax was!" Kyaati snapped, giving him a shake.

Galahir blinked in the face of her sudden fury and gave a rueful smile. "I wish I had your fire," he said, touching her cheeks. "You could scorch forests with those eyes."

She caught his hands. "Listen to me. I would follow you to the edge of the known lands, Galahir. What more do these people need from their Chief? You are a skilled hunter, a formidable fighter. You can protect and provide for the weak. You are more than what you think."

Kyaati found herself crushed to his chest as he buried his face in her shoulder again. Moisture gathered against her neck. "Thank you, my love."

"I am here," she said again. "I will always be by your side. You are not alone."

"My Chieftess." Kyaati felt his mouth pull into a grin against her neck.

It was Kyaati's turn to freeze. In the swift turn of events, she had not had time to consider this. As Galahir's chief mate, she was now the top-ranking female of a Cro clan, occupying the role Halima had filled within the Hunting Bear. *Halima,* her heart cried. How could she ever replace such an indomitable figure? She wasn't even Cro. But Halima would not want her to flinch before responsibility, and so Kyaati straightened her shoulders. For Galahir, for Halima, she lifted the burden.

As she mastered her trepidation, a sense of relief rushed in to take its place. She and Galahir were the leaders now. There was no Eldrax threatening to tear their lives apart. Elhaari would live in peace as the son of the Chief himself within the stronghold of the foothills. Kyaati's heart swelled.

"He killed them, Kyaati." Galahir's pain broke through her glowing thoughts. "All my life, I have served the man who murdered my parents and almost wiped out my birth clan." Anger and shame mixed with his pain and uncertainty.

"You could not have known, Galahir," Kyaati said. "You were an infant when Eldrax took you. You are home now. I have not heard many stories, but I can sense how the Eagles feel when Rikal's name is mentioned. He was a beloved Chief. You can now uphold his legacy and teach Elhaari to do the same."

At the sound of their son's name, Galahir pulled back from Kyaati, blue fire burning in his eyes.

"There it is," she smiled. "Now you look like you could scorch a forest with a glance, my Chief."

Galahir chuckled and pressed her hand to his cheek.

"My Chief." A soft voice called them from the entrance of the shelter. Kikima stood there, cradling Elhaari in her arms. Akito stood behind her, clutching her furs.

Kyaati rose and went to her, holding her arms out for Elhaari.

"My matriarch," Kikima dipped her proud head to Kyaati, keeping her eyes down.

"Please don't, Kikima," Kyaati said, shifting Elhaari in her arms so she could reach up to lift Kikima's chin with her fingers. "This is the place Halima prepared you for. I am a Ninkuraaja. I still know so little of the Cro ways. I am going to need your guidance as my friend... and sister."

For the briefest of moments, Kikima's dull eyes sparked with their old spirit, filled with love and gratitude, before giving way once more to blank despair. It would take her a long time to recover from the grief of losing Halima. The pain of her loss still weighed upon Kyaati's own heart, catching her by surprise and stealing her breath at the slightest thought, but she had Galahir and Elhaari to keep her spirit whole. What did Kikima have? Only the distant idea of the unborn child of the man who had abused her. The sworn enemy of the clan she had now been adopted into. Kyaati bit her lip and reached out to squeeze Kikima's hand.

Galahir blew out a breath. "We should get some rest," he

said.

"C-can I stay here with you?" Akito asked.

Galahir's blue eyes softened. "Of course."

"I'll go," Kikima said.

"Kikima," Kyaati kept hold of her hand. With so much changed, her heart ached with the need to keep everything dear and familiar as close as possible. "You can stay, too."

"I won't be far. I need to be alone for a while," Kikima offered a sad smile. "I need to think." And with that, she extracted her hand gently from Kyaati's and was gone.

Kyaati watched after her, her brow creased. "Do you think she's safe?" she asked.

"No one will harm her," Galahir assured. "I am now Chief and Kikima is a woman of the Eagles. Every man here is sworn to protect her."

"Even if she was their enemy's mate?"

"Yes. Kikima is not Eldrax's blood. Clans need strong women. She will be safe."

Akito had curled up in the furs next to Galahir and Kyaati went to her mate's side, sinking down beside him as exhaustion swept through her. Galahir lay down and pulled her against his chest. Kyaati kept Elhaari in her own arms, not yet settled enough in this new place to suffer any space between them now darkness had fallen. With her loved ones near, the hard days of travel, all the anguish, and all the confusing and sudden events of the past days caught up with Kyaati. Before she knew it, oblivion overcame her.

Kyaati woke before dawn. At first, the sounds and smells foreign to her senses disorientated her. Now that she had had a full night's sleep, Kyaati was sure the strangeness had awoken her. She tried to close her eyes again, but knew that it would be no use. Thoughts of what the new day might bring were already intruding on her mind.

Sighing, Kyaati untangled herself from Galahir. Elhaari was still sound asleep and so Kyaati tucked him next to his father before rising. She was thirsty. Stretching her stiff limbs, Kyaati made her way to the entrance of the shelter, hesitated for a moment, then lifted her chin and strode out into her new domain.

The black sky above was just fading to a faint blue and the cool air blew gently across Kyaati's face, instantly making her more alert. A few of the women were already about, lighting fires and preparing tools for the day. They looked up as she passed by, eyes uncertain, resentful, as they dipped their heads to her. These emotions were to be expected, but it was the faint taste of fear that surprised Kyaati. It did not take her long to figure out the cause of it. The last time she had been among the Eagles, she had been an enemy; many of these women had been prepared to stone her to death. Now here she walked, the Claimed partner of their new Chief. Their matriarch. A witch. She had the power to make their lives as miserable as she wished.

Kyaati was more than a little unnerved by this situation, too. She would need to prove to them sooner rather than later that she would not hold a grudge.

A stirring and a growl of desire in the dwelling next to her drew Kyaati to a halt as the curtains to the shelter parted. With an unpleasant jolt, she saw Kikima emerging with a partially clad Narak.

The Eagle man chuckled against Kikima's neck. "I could die a satisfied man to know I have taken what the Red Bear had. I'll say this for him. He knew a woman when he saw one."

Kikima forced a laugh and pushed him playfully away, wrapping her furs around her as she strode away from his tent. She had not noticed Kyaati standing in the shadows.

"Kikima!" Kyaati hissed, going after her. Kikima flinched and turned. Her face closed when she saw the censure in Kyaati's eyes. "What are you doing?" Kyaati demanded.

"What needs to be done." Kikima lifted her chin.

"Laying with every Eagle man within the first day of your arrival?" Kyaati could not keep the harsh judgement from her voice.

In a flash, Kikima caught hold of Kyaati's furs and pulled her close. "No!" she hissed. "Think, Kyaati, I am carrying the spawn of Eldrax. What do you think will happen when I give birth at a damning time? If I waited to be Claimed properly, the Eagles would know my offspring could not be that of my mate. Fortunately, I am a new and exciting conquest to these men. It was not hard getting what I needed. Now they will never be certain that the babe belongs to Eldrax. I have ensured its safety. So please," Kikima let Kyaati go and walked away, "do not judge me, Kyaati."

Kyaati was left standing in her wake, feeling wretched. She hated that Kikima had let herself be used and humiliated. But if it protected her innocent child...

Kyaati wrapped her arms around herself and made her way back to the Chief's Dwelling. Galahir was awake and cradling Elhaari, who was cooing in his father's huge hands. Akito was sitting close by, toying with a carving, a heavy frown between his scarred brows.

"What's wrong?" Galahir asked, seeing her drawn expression.

Kyaati shook her head. "Just worrying about Kikima."

"Oh." Galahir looked down at their son. He obviously did not know what to say in response.

"My Chief?" The elder that had proclaimed Galahir the new leader of the Eagle Clan pushed her way into the dwelling.

Galahir appeared to forget she was addressing him for a moment, before hesitantly waving her forward. Kyaati could see his new position lying ill at ease upon his shoulders. This would take some getting used to.

"My Chief, now you have had time to rest from your journey, the elders seek your guidance. More Watchers have been sighted on our borders, and the clan is getting skittish."

Ice slipped through Kyaati's gut. It had been ridiculous to think the threat had died with the Hunting Bear clan. The words she had heard spoken by the beasts on the night of the attack still seared through her mind. No matter how much she tried to bury them deep down and believe they were safe here, the threat still loomed.

She found Galahir's hand and gripped it hard. He squeezed back as he dipped his chin at the old woman. Upon his agreement, the old woman pulled the curtain of the dwelling aside to admit five other men with grizzled heads, the last and youngest of which was Narak.

They all looked at Galahir with cool eyes as they squatted down in a loose circle before him. Although they had accepted the son of their previous Chief, they were, as yet, untrusting of this untried leader. Only Narak watched Galahir with any hint of confidence.

"My Chief," the most venerable of the men began, "Since the night the lights of the Sky Gods were seen over the Mountains, the clan has been divided between the paths to be walked. You must choose a way and bring us together."

"And what," Galahir cut his words off as he cleared his throat. Kyaati shifted closer to him, letting him feel her presence and remind him he wasn't alone in facing this challenge. "What paths are these?"

"There are those," at this point, the elder glowered at his closest neighbour, "who wish to appease the gods, as we did of old. To gift women and children to the Watchers to prove our loyalty."

"That," Galahir growled, all uncertainty fleeing his voice in this one decision, "is not going to happen. No women or children will be sacrificed to those monsters, not while I am your Chief."

The second elder glowered. "Then what do you propose we do? Wait until they come to kill us all?"

Kyaati scowled at the man. It was clear that this one had never Claimed a woman or sired children.

Galahir ignored him. He just gestured for the first elder to continue. Kyaati could sense that his mind was working hard, and he was stalling for time on making a ruling.

"I say we should flee," the first elder went on. "Eldrax is no longer guarding the borders waiting to slaughter us should we venture from the hills. We are free to leave. We should travel far south, out of the Watchers' reach."

Kyaati got the uncomfortable sense of time repeating itself as the Eagles put forth the same options the Hunting Bear clan had faced. But this time, they didn't have Eldrax recklessly trying to prove his might against insurmountable forces. This time, they would be led by a man who cared for his People. She flexed her fingers in Galahir's hand, letting him know that this was the decision she favoured.

"But that is not what Yatal wanted," the elder woman snapped at the first man. "She told us we needed to fight. She told us the only hope was to stand with the other clans against the might of the gods. It was the only way she saw us being free. I trusted Yatal. She kept this clan alive, and I am not about to start going against her final wishes now. We cannot run from the gods."

"And neither can we fight them!" Kyaati was on her feet before she was aware of it. "I have seen what those monsters can do! I have witnessed their power. I will lose no more to them. Eldrax stood against them, and he lost. I say we flee. Yatal did not know what she was facing. She was a proud fool to suggest fighting."

The old woman's nostrils flared. "Yatal did not decide to fight upon a prideful whim, girl," she said. "She was given a vision. Your own witch sister saw it too and believed it. She believed it so much, she has gone off to face the gods alone in the Mountains. Yatal confided in me. All the Peoples must stand together, Cro, Thal, all the clans. Only then do we stand a chance."

Nyri had seen a vision of them fighting the Watchers and agreed with Yatal? Kyaati ground her teeth together, looking down into her son's face. Nyri had not seen what had happened to the Hunting Bear camp. "If we fight, we will lose," she said.

"You cannot know that," Akito interjected. His young voice was soft but surprised Kyaati with its strength. "Dugnamtar taught me the stories." The boy's slight shoulders shuddered. "I do not want to live under a god's rule. I do not want to spend my life running and living in fear. I will stand and defend the women and children, just like Eldrax did."

"Akito," Kyaati whispered.

"What?" Akito challenged her. "You heard that voice when the Watchers attacked. They will not stop, Kyaati. The gods only want us dead. No matter where we go, we will not be safe."

Kyaati closed her mouth. Where was the boy who had been terrified at the mere thought of the Eagles' return? His fear had vanished, and all Kyaati could feel was a cold, hard determination.

"You heard them, didn't you?" Akito pressed. "They promised to wipe us out. We cannot run, Kyaati."

Kyaati shook her head, her fear choking her. If they fought, who would she lose next? She could not bear it.

"Kyaati," Akito said. "It is what Halima would have wanted."

"Halima is dead!" Kyaati all but shouted, as the pain shivered through her. "She died to save our lives. Would she want us to throw them away now?"

"Fighting for the right to exist is not a waste of our lives!" Akito silenced her. "Running away and being slaughtered for nothing is. I know which death I would rather face." The boy lifted his chin.

No, not a boy. Kyaati blinked as she beheld his face. In this, Akito had found a purpose, a cause for which he was willing to sacrifice his young life. To be free. "When did you become a man?" she asked.

Akito shrugged, suddenly bashful. Kyaati bowed her head,

seeking the same courage within herself, but the icy claws of dread squeezed it far from her heart. *We can't, we can't face them...*

"What is your decision, Chief?" Kyaati heard the first elder ask. She looked to Galahir, but he avoided her gaze. His pale face was carved with grim determination, and she knew his decision before he even spoke. The claws sank deeper, stealing her breath. "I promised to uphold Yatal's final wishes upon being made Chief," he said gravely. "Yatal believed standing together was the only way to face this threat, and I believe the same. Akito is right. Now that the gods' fury has been unleashed, we no longer have a choice. I would rather die facing my enemy than have my throat cut from behind.

"Gendi." He gestured to the elder woman. "Find Lorhir and bring him to me." Galahir then faced the elder men and Narak as she scrambled to obey. "The Eagles will not run or bow. This clan defied the Red Bear himself, and now it will stand and defy the gods. Prepare all the men able to hold a weapon. I want them ready by nightfall."

"B-but," the elder who had wanted to sacrifice women and children stammered. "You're going to kill us all!"

Galahir shot to his feet. "I am your Chief now and I say we are to fight and defend our children's existence. You are welcome to Challenge me if that is your wish?"

Kyaati blinked at Galahir, trying to recognise her mate through this sudden force of nature. Out of the corner of her eye, she saw Narak smirk as the elder quailed before the tower of muscle and bone looming over him.

"A-as my Chief wishes," he said as he scurried after his peers to obey Galahir's orders.

Gendi returned with Lorhir following on her heels. Kikima was not far behind. Her smooth brow pinched as her eyes went to Kyaati. Lorhir was scowling, making his displeasure at being summoned clear.

"You sent for me, my *Chief.*"

Galahir ignored his tone. "Lorhir, the Eagle warriors will join the other clans in a fight against the Watchers. I am naming you my leader of the raknari."

Lorhir reared back, his eyes widening in shock, but before he could respond to this honour that had been bestowed upon him, Galahir had swept past him, leading him out of the shelter. "Come, there is much to do. We leave when Utu rises into the sky. We must gather as many clans as we can find before Nanna is full in the sky."

Silence reigned in the Chief Dwelling as Kyaati, Akito and Kikima were left alone.

"Is it true?" Kikima whispered. "We are going to fight the Watchers?"

Kyaati could not speak. She railed against Galahir's decision. Cursed him for it. Each time she started to feel safe, the illusion was snatched away from her. *Courage, Kyaati. It is what Halima would have wanted.* Kyaati breathed once, twice. Elhaari cooed against her chest. She looked into his innocent face and choked. *My baby.* She had to protect him. The claws around her heart retracted enough for her to breathe. *We are to fight and defend our children's existence.* Galahir's declaration echoed through her head.

Kyaati did not know how they could overcome the might of the Watchers, but if it was to be so, she could not lie down and accept death for Elhaari without doing all she could to give him the best chance.

Nyri had seen a vision, Gendi had said? A vision of the Peoples standing together and believed they had a hope. Kyaati gripped on to that one spark with all her might. She had to have faith that Nyri knew what she was doing. "Yes," she responded to Kikima at last, not recognising her own voice. "We are going to fight."

"Then we had better help the men prepare." Kikima stood, waiting for Kyaati to lead the way out of the shelter.

"No." Kyaati did not move. "I know what I have to do."

"And what is that?" Kikima asked.

Kyaati smiled without humour. Eldrax had wanted witches to use in his fight against the gods. The Peoples had to stand together. There were more People in this world besides the Cro and the Thals. She raised her gaze to Kikima's.

"I am going home," she declared.

* * *

18

Ghosts of the Past

Nyriaana had not been mistaken in her suspicion that Sakal would set a brutal pace. Sure-footed as a mountain goat, Yatal's warrior led them deeper into the foothills, never hesitating, never questioning a path. These trails were as familiar to her as her own skin. Nyri grudgingly admitted they would never have found their way without her, but she remained ill at ease with the presence of their guide and their reliance upon her.

Yatal's spirit had reverberated with sincerity in Nyri's mind, convinced that what Nyri needed to do was vital. Nevertheless, now that she was away from the old Chieftess, doubt gnawed at Nyri's gut. She had lived in fear of Yatal's hatred and lust for vengeance far longer than she had lived with her as an ally. Might all this be an elaborate trap, and Sakal was in fact leading them to the grisly end Yatal had always imagined for her?

And if Yatal had been sincere, just how loyal was Sakal to her leader? Their release and Yatal's declaration that they should make peace with the Red Bear had turned half of the Eagle clan against their long-time leader. None of them had seen what Nyri and Yatal had, only the lights in the sky. While the sight had terrified them, it was not enough to convince them of the need to join forces with their most hated rival.

Nyri drew comfort from the two men at her back. Sakal would not be so foolish as to take them both on in a fight. But she was keenly aware the Eagle woman's unerring knowledge of the territory could be turned against them in an instant. All Sakal had to do was disappear and she would ensure their doom without ever having to raise a spear.

Nyri was careful to keep her full attention on their guide, alert to any shift in her mood or thought pattern that would indicate an imminent betrayal. If nothing else, worrying about Sakal helped distract her from what lay ahead.

The Eagle warrior never spoke. She led them on in stolid silence, making it clear she resented every moment. But, thus far, Nyri had not detected any wavering in her intent and so she followed on. The first day of their journey towards the Mountains was a quiet one.

As Ninmah sank behind the craggy rises, Sakal came to an abrupt halt. "We will find a place to sleep for the night," she informed them in a clipped tone. "It is too treacherous to travel these paths at night." Without sparing them a glance, she began to climb what looked like the bed of a long dried-up stream. Nyri shared a glance with Juaan, but he just lifted his shoulders slightly and indicated that she should follow the Eagle woman.

Nyri scrambled over the loose earth and pebbles, trying not to swallow the dust Sakal had already kicked into the air. She slipped and slid and by the time Sakal led them onto a wide flat ledge overlooking the trail below, Nyri was bruised, cut and sweating, covered in an uncomfortable layer of grime.

"No fire," Sakal ordered. "This place will give us a good view of anything that approaches. I will take first watch."

"I will take it with you," Juaan said as he came up behind Nyri.

Sakal scowled. "That will not be necessary."

"Even so," Juaan said. "I will watch, too."

The Eagle warrior grimaced, but argued no further. She took herself to the farthest point of the ledge and squatted down with her spear in hand.

"Here," Bahari had unslung his load containing their supplies and was now holding out a portion of dried fish meat to Nyri. "Eat."

Nyri's lips pulled down as she accepted the offering and Bahari thrust the sling at Juaan, making it clear Juaan could get his own food out. Nyri's empty stomach grumbled as she toyed with the morsel of food she had been given.

"What is it?" Bahari tilted his head. "Kua good. Sustain you."

"She doesn't like eating meat," Juaan interjected. "It is not the Ninkuraaja way."

"Oh," Bahari's eyebrows shot towards his hairline, then he tipped a hand apologetically. "I not know. Never heard such a thing." He cast around uncomfortably, as though he would like to offer something else, but unable to do so.

Nyri reached out and touched his hand, strangely aware of Juaan watching the movement. "It's alright, Bahari. There isn't a choice. I've been growing accustomed to it." She took a bite of the foul flesh, trying not to make a face as she chewed.

"It has to be better than gora root." A smile played around the corners of Juaan's mouth as he took his own ration.

Despite herself, Nyri chuckled, then choked on her mouthful. "No, this is definitely worse. I would sacrifice that whole bag for one gora root right now."

"Hush!" Sakal hissed from her corner.

Nyri glared at her but held her tongue, forcing down the fish in two swallows. Despite the awful flavour, she felt stronger for it. The others completed their meal in silence. After exacting a promise from Juaan to wake him so he could take second watch, Bahari rolled himself up in his furs and drifted off to sleep with the ease of someone used to travelling beyond the protection of his home. Juaan shifted to take up position on the ledge opposite Sakal, his gaze missing nothing on the trail below, but Nyri had no doubt a part of his mind was also on their unwilling guide.

The captured spirits of Ninsiku were twinkling overhead when Nyri lay down upon the unforgiving rock and tried to fall asleep as Bahari had. But she was no seasoned hunter. The rocks bit at her skin and, now that there was nothing to distract her, her mind refused to quiet. One fear after another chased its tail through Nyri's consciousness. Flashes of light and pain. Endless nothingness. The beckoning of the Mountains ahead made her restless, and then there was the ever present knowledge that the Hunting Bear clan had been extinguished.

Kyaati, Kyaati, Kyaati, her heart cried. The fish turned over in her stomach. Not knowing the fate of her tribe-sister was almost more than she could bear.

It was no use. Nyri got up, pulling her furs more tightly

around her to protect against the chill of the night, and moved to where Juaan was keeping watch. He said nothing as she settled beside him. He did not draw away when she leaned into his side. The relief she felt at his acceptance was a balm to her soul. He wrapped his arm around her and let her be, seeming to find as much comfort in her closeness as she found in his.

"Do you think any of them survived?" she asked after a moment.

His chest lifted under her cheek as he drew a deep breath. "I don't know," he said. "But I have to have faith. Galahir is a formidable warrior with good sense, despite what he may believe about himself. If there was any way they could have escaped the attack, Galahir would have got Kyaati out. He would have fought to the death to give his family a chance."

Tears leaked from Nyri's eyes. Kyaati had finally got everything she ever wanted. A loving mate and a living child. What fate could be cruel enough to rip all of that away from her?

She committed the Forbidden. The uninvited thought slithered through her head, strangely taking on the voice of Aardn. *She deserved punishment. Such things cannot be. Watch yourself, Daughter of Ninmah, or the same fate will await you.*

"What is it?" Juaan asked, feeling her sudden tension.

"Nothing," she lied.

"I will not let anything happen to you, Nyriaana," he comforted. "We will find this Ariyaana if she exists, and then we will return. I promise."

Nyriaana closed her eyes, but she was no longer at ease against his body. Flashes of light and nothingness taunted her. Was that her punishment for allowing herself to feel for a Forbidden? How could she tell Juaan her fate was sealed? Whether they found Ariyaana or not. Nyriaana would not follow him back along the paths to home.

* * *

Nyri fell asleep just before Bahari rose to relieve Juaan of the watch. Juaan looked down at the face propped against his chest. Even in sleep, her features were not at peace. A frown creased the purple tattoo between her brows. Her eyes rolled beneath her closed lids and her breath hitched now and then. One hand clutched at the large seed dangling around her neck.

Juaan sighed. Right or wrong, he had come here to protect her, but he could not shield her from the demons within. It was all that he could do to protect her from his own. The power inside him was already tugging against its weakening tethers. The closer they drew to the Mountains, the more closely Juaan would need to keep his emotions in check. If he lost control... He tightened his arm around Nyriaana. He would not let it best him. It had already cost him too much.

What will you do if you come upon a Watcher? Juaan gritted his teeth. Those creatures had wiped out the Hunting Bear clan. Juaan would shed no tears over Eldrax, but that camp had been filled with his friends, brothers in the hunt, innocent children. His fingers flexed upon the spear in his free hand. He forced it to relax.

"I take over now," Bahari murmured behind him. "She

sleeping?"

"Yes," Juaan let the answer out in a breath.

Bahari lowered himself to the ground on the opposite side of Nyriaana, extending his arm as though to take over as her support.

Out of nowhere, resentment flared. He could not have Nyri for himself. He did not deserve her, but the thought of her sleeping in another man's arm while he watched could not be borne. He lifted Nyri as gently as he could so as not to wake her. Bahari had reminded him that no matter the cost to himself, protecting this girl was his purpose. The only one he had, and he was damned sure he was not going to let another take on that duty.

Leaving Bahari's arm hanging awkwardly in midair, Juaan turned on his heel and carried Nyriaana to the back of the ledge, where they would be more sheltered from the cool breeze. With her smaller body, Nyri suffered from the cold more than the rest of them did. Choosing the smoothest spot, Juaan lay down, drawing Nyri's back against his chest. Having her close soothed the beast, he told himself, though it stirred the existence of another.

Stop it, he told himself, resisting the urge to pull her closer still, to relish in the sensation of her body against his. For a distraction, he turned his eyes to where Sakal still crouched, poised like a spear cat on the edge of their viewpoint, her back studiously turned to them. She needed to rest after the hard day's travel, but Juaan knew any words from him would not be welcomed. His thigh ached where she had dealt the spear blow, and any concern he might have felt over the other warrior's wellbeing evaporated.

Sakal could take care of herself.

317

Juaan kept his eyes on her, not comfortable enough to sleep while his former enemy remained alert. *Khalvir's* former enemy, he reminded himself. But, try as he might to see it Nyri's way, having his old identity back did not absolve him of his crimes at Eldrax's right hand. He had been Khalvir far longer than he had ever been Juaan. The thought frightened him. Juaan shifted his grip on Nyriaana. No. Childhood memories didn't change anything. In Sakal's eyes, he would always be the Red Bear's butcher and he was under no illusion that she would dearly love to place a spear between his shoulder blades given the opportunity.

Rest, however, was something he sorely needed. Juaan clenched his teeth in frustration. Ordinarily, he could have lasted days without sleep, but the wound to his leg had taken its toll. The day's journey had not been as effortless for him as he would usually have found it, though he had been careful to hide his weakness from Sakal and, most especially, Nyriaana. He needed sleep if he was to continue to keep up.

Juaan's gaze shifted to Bahari. Despite the undeserved jealously he harboured towards the man, Juaan was grateful for his presence. They were far from friends, tentative allies at best, but he knew the Cro man would thwart any murder attempts that Sakal might be tempted to make while he slept. It would have to be enough. He had to be strong for Nyriaana and to resist the power inside. Keeping half of his mind alert to attack as he had been conditioned to do, Juaan closed his eyes.

It felt like he had only just blinked when he was jabbed unceremoniously in the back. Juaan shot upright, his spear already in his hand.

"Get up," Sakal's nasally voice grated against his ears. "It's time to move on."

Juaan cursed. He had slipped into a deep sleep. He glared at the Eagle warrior, ready to tell her the next time she woke him in such a fashion, he would snap her spear in two, but she had already moved off to gather up their supplies and his ire was wasted on her back.

Juaan let his irritation go on a breath, cooling his temper before he did something he regretted. It wasn't Sakal he was angry with. He was furious with himself.

Stretching, he stifled a groan at the aches and pains that still plagued his body, limiting his mobility. He would never be the warrior that he had been before his fight with Eldrax, he thought ruefully. No matter Nyri's skill, that damage was permanent.

Sighing, Juaan looked out on the waiting world. Dark clouds were gathering on the horizon. There would be a storm this day. He could taste it on his tongue.

"Are you alright?" She was awake and watching him, all too aware of his discomfort.

Juaan mustered a smile for her. "Nothing I can't handle," he said.

Her lips twitched, but she did not smile in return. Her skin was pale and drawn. Nightmares lurked in her eyes.

"Tell me," he offered, deflecting her concern over his physical wellbeing.

She just shook her head.

A stab of hurt. "You can always tell me anything."

"I know," she said and squeezed his hand, but said no more.

Unease snaked through Juaan's gut. She had never hidden

319

anything from him before.

"Here." Sakal was back, thrusting their share of the load at them. "I am leaving now. Follow me or not, I don't care."

Once again, she was gone before Juaan could display his displeasure. For the briefest of moments, he wished he could plant a spear in Sakal's back. Growling under his breath, he pushed himself to his feet and reached down to help Nyri to hers. Bahari was waiting for them at the edge of the old stream bed that would lead to the rocky trail below. Sakal was already halfway down.

"Help?" Bahari offered as Nyri came up beside him, eyeing the steep slope.

"It's alright, Bahari," she said with a bite of impatience in her voice. "I am not quite as delicate as I look. We'd better hope not, anyway." And with that, she stepped off from the stone ledge and plunged down the slope, slipping and sliding until she alighted in a cloud of dust at the bottom.

Bahari looked to Juaan, but he just shrugged and made his own way back down the slope, using his spear to steady himself. Bahari followed.

Juaan kept a close eye on Nyri as they travelled, trying to divine what was plaguing her mind and alert for any sign of ailment. Despite her strong words, she was unaccustomed to such travel. The terrain was challenging and Sakal's pace did not allow for weakness. With her smaller stature, Nyri was having to work twice as hard to keep the pace. Her feet must have been sore, perhaps even blistering by this time, but she strode on with a single-minded purpose, as though what lay ahead was all that was left to her. The coils of unease in Juaan's gut tightened. He did not like what he saw on her face.

Utu was high above the lowering clouds when Sakal led them to the top of a rise and lifted her fist to halt them. "There," she pointed ahead. On the horizon, the Mountains loomed closer than ever. Before them, a line of thick black forest threatened. "We will reach the Forest in two days. We rest." And, without another word, the Eagle warrior sank to her haunches and stuffed a mouthful of fish from her own supplies into her mouth.

The relief on Nyri's face betrayed the depth of her exhaustion. But the relief quickly evaporated, to be replaced by an expression of panic. "Where's Bahari?"

Juaan spun around. He had been so focused on Nyri, he had failed to notice that Bahari was no longer behind him.

"Wait here!" he said, preparing to sprint back down the path to find their absent companion. He had not gone two strides, however, when Bahari appeared.

"Bahari!" Nyri cried, rushing to greet the other man. "What happened?"

The Cro man caught her in his hands, appearing gratified by her obvious concern for him.

Juaan lifted his lip. "Where were you?" he demanded.

Bahari raised his chin at Juaan's tone. "Not far," he said. "Found something."

"Something so important you risked getting separated?"

Bahari raised a hand in a Thal equivalent of a shrug, then reached into his sling of supplies to draw out a bunch of fleshy, edible roots. "Saw familiar plant," he said.

Nyri's face lit up for the first time since they had been forced to flee the Hunting Bear camp. Juaan wanted to be jealous that Bahari had been the one to return such a gleam to her beautiful eyes, but found he could not be angry. Not when she was looking like that.

"Oh, Bahari," she said. "Thank you."

Bahari grinned, relishing the fact that his consideration had brought a smile to Nyri's face. He held the roots playfully out of reach as she leaped for them. Inciting a game.

"Bahari!" Nyri scolded.

He laughed. "No wonder Dryad is so short when they only eat such things."

Juaan spied a very familiar expression cross Nyri's face as he fished in his own sling for a suitable morsel. "I wouldn't, Bahari."

The other man cocked his head, still amused by his game. "Why not?"

"She'll just climb you."

The words were hardly out of Juaan's mouth before Bahari let out a startled cry as Nyri scaled him in two heartbeats and snatched the roots from his unprepared hand, leaping down and landing neatly in front of him with a smug expression of triumph.

Juaan chuckled under his breath. "I told you so."

"When you've finished playing like a bunch of suckling babes," Sakal's scathing voice punctured the moment of levity, "it's time to move." The Eagle woman flicked away some fish skin, glowered at them over her shoulder and stalked on towards the looming line in the distance. The strengthening breeze tugged on her furs. The first peel of thunder rolled on the glowering horizon.

Nyri's face paled. "Already?" It was the first time she had voiced her plight at the brutality of the journey.

"Sakal, we need to slow the pace," Juaan called after the

Eagle woman.

"No," Nyri hissed.

Sakal spun on her heel. "I am not coddling weaklings!" she spat. "Yatal says she has a path to follow and I have to show her the way. If she is not strong enough, then we turn around now. I am not sacrificing my life for her."

"And I will not let your misguided malevolence put her at risk. Slow down."

Sakal's eyes blazed. "My malevolence is anything but misguided." Her face twisted into a sneer. "But perhaps it is not just the witch who needs a child's pace. Leg bothering you, dear Khalvir?" She feigned a jab towards him with her spear. "Please say yes. You cannot imagine the pleasure it gives me to see you suffer."

The power inside flexed its claws as Juaan faced the belligerent Eagle warrior. "Do not provoke me, Sakal," he warned between his teeth.

Sakal curled her lip. "Or what, Khalvir? You'll kill me like you have so many others of my brethren. Without me, you are lost. Remember that, savage!"

Red mist played at the edges of Juaan's vision, the beast inside writhing, only a thin veneer holding it back. "Sakal—"

A warm hand slipped around his wrist, as familiar as his own skin, soothing. Juaan looked down into the pools of deep indigo that waited. He drowned in the calm she offered. His breathing became easier; the red receded. Seeing his centre return, Nyri shouldered her load, lifted her chin defiantly at Sakal and stalked past the Eagle woman, continuing on down the path ahead.

Sakal grumbled in her throat and set off after her, taking back the lead in a couple of strides as the first spots of rain began to fall. Calmed though he was, Juaan waited until Bahari had passed, the other man providing a barrier between himself and Sakal, before following on.

The Forest of the Nine Gods dipped in and out of sight as the trails led Juaan and his companions up steep crags and then plunged into deep gullies where the barren hills loomed over them, frowning down on the travellers that dared to pass.

They were traversing one such pass when Sakal came to a halt and cursed. Juaan looked up. A landslide had blocked their way with an impassable wall of boulders.

"What now?" Nyri asked in a small voice.

"We go back, and lose a day returning to the last division in the trail, or…" Sakal lifted a finger, pointing above. Running along the cliff face above was a crumbling ledge that led over the top of the landslide.

"There is no other way?" Bahari asked. Juaan scanned the ledge. It didn't appear that it would hold more than a rabbit.

"We can't lose a day," Nyri said, her face pinched. "I-I cannot go back."

In that moment, Juaan could almost see the forces tugging on her. Invisible, unassailable. Powers he could not fight away. He gripped her shoulder, drawing her back against him.

"Then do as I do, all of you." Sakal shifted around the boulders, and began scaling the rock face, climbing towards the ledge that would lead them over the impasse. Putting a hand against her back, Juaan indicated that Nyri should go before him. Foot and handholds were few. He was prepared to boost her if needed, but he needn't have concerned himself. Once again displaying her astonishing agility, Nyri leaped up the cliff face like a monyet, overtaking Sakal on her way up. She was sitting crossed legged, munching on the last of her roots when Juaan and the rest caught up to her. In spite of everything, he grinned. "Still the best."

She swallowed her food and smiled in return. It wasn't the smile that Juaan loved. But it was a smile nonetheless.

Even Sakal appeared faintly impressed, and the Eagle guide dipped her chin once in Nyri's direction before facing the ledge they would now have to traverse. "Follow my every step," she growled.

Feeling the way with her spear, Sakal set off, picking her route across the cracked and crumbling rocks. They grated ominously beneath her weight. After waiting a few moments, Juaan sent Nyri ahead of him and then followed as closely as he dared. Bahari brought up the rear.

A flash of lightning. Nyri flinched and covered her face with a small cry. Juaan steadied her as the clouds unleashed their promised load. Rain poured in blinding sheets as the thunder rolled on overhead, echoing through the surrounding rocks and cliff faces. The wind tugged this way and that. Juaan cursed. The timing could not have been worse. The ledge became slick, water sluicing from the cliff top above. "Keep moving, Nyri," he encouraged. She was trembling under his hand.

Step by step, they edged across, squinting into the storm. Juaan could now make out the solid ground on the far side of the ledge, offering safety.

"Almost there."

A second bolt of lightning lanced from the sky, drowning out his words. Juaan's hands flew to his ears to protect them from the deafening crack. Nyri threw herself to the ground with a cry of denial. Stones blasted apart above their heads. The treacherous trail was not about to allow their escape. The cliff face began to shift.

"Run!" Sakal cried. Sacrificing caution for speed, the other warrior bounded forward. Juaan dragged Nyriaana to her feet and threw her after the Eagle woman. She sprinted ahead, leaping over a wide fissure. Nyri's feet were extended to land when a loose rock from above tumbled into view. Juaan could only watch in horror as it smashed into the path ahead of Nyri, destroying the ledge before her. Her feet met air.

"No!" both he and Bahari cried as Nyri tumbled away.

Then Sakal was there. With the reflexes of a honed warrior, her hand shot out, catching Nyri by the ankle before she managed to fall one body length.

Something fell from Nyri as she dangled upside down. Juaan heard her cry of dismay, and she twisted, stretching to catch it. Sakal lost her grip. Cursing loudly as she made a grab with her other hand, reestablishing her grip just as Nyri snagged her lost treasure.

"Pull her up!" Juaan cried over the peals of thunder.

He leaped the gap himself, just as Sakal hauled Nyri to safety.

"You fool! You almost pulled out of my grip!" The Eagle warrior screeched.

"I'm sorry," Nyri panted as she clutched her fist and its contents to her chest.

"What could be so important that it risked plunging both of us to our deaths?"

His heart still in his throat, Juaan felt like screaming

the same question at her as Nyri slowly opened her fist. Inside was the large seed that had dangled around her neck since the night Juaan had ripped her from her home under Eldrax's orders.

"A nut?" Sakal cried and made as though to slap it from Nyriaana's hand.

Quick as a bird, Nyri closed her fist and snatched her hand back. "It is an *enu*," she said. "Entrusted to me by the one who set this path before me. I have to give it to Ariyaana."

"And… who… i-is—" Sakal's voice cut off in a strangled gasp for breath, Juaan's head snapped around. It was as though someone had caught the Eagle woman about the throat, cutting off her airway. The blood had drained from the pale face.

"Sakal?" Nyri was on her feet. She caught the other woman's arm in her hand. Juaan's attention was immediately drawn to her wrist where a large swelling highlighted a deep puncture wound. Nyri cursed. "She's been stung!"

"Leave me alone!" Sakal tried to push Nyri away. "I-I d-do n-not."

"Be still if you want to live!" Nyri snarled at her as she secured Sakal's wrist in both hands. "You will not die in these hills, Sakal, that is not for you. You will go home to those you love."

Sakal was startled into stillness by the force of the other woman's tone as Nyri closed her eyes.

"The gods," Sakal gasped a heartbeat later. Juaan watched fear and wonder battling for dominance on her features. His lips twitched. His own face must have resembled hers the first time he had experienced Nyri's healing skills inside the Pit.

Bahari stood at Juaan's shoulder, watching in fascination as fluid drained from the wound at their guide's wrist and the colour returned to her cheeks before their eyes. The warrior's breathing evened out.

"There." Juaan caught Nyri as she sagged backwards, the healing having drained her already exhausted body.

Sakal blinked, pulling her arm back. "W-we should move on," she croaked. "Before another rock slide comes down on our heads." She staggered to her feet, dusting her hands off on her furs as she retrieved her spear from the ground and started down the path into the pounding rain. "I know somewhere safe where we can shelter."

"Come, Nyri." Juaan helped her to her feet. She would not suffer being carried, but it pleased him when she allowed him to support her as they followed Sakal on along the trail leading back down into the gully on the far side of the avalanche. The water was up to Juaan's ankles by the time Sakal turned off the path and climbed a short way up the nearest slope.

"In here," the Eagle warrior said before disappearing inside a cave.

Juaan guided Nyri through the entrance, swiping his wet hair out of his eyes as the cave enveloped them in its embrace. Bahari peered out at the sky above.

"Should stop soon," he said. "Clear sky following."

Juaan dipped his chin in acknowledgment. "Rest, Nyri," he said, lowering her to the ground. "Eat something."

Sakal was stroking her wrist where the puncture mark had been, her expression quizzical.

"Can you do that?"

Juaan turned to find Bahari eyeing him. "Do what?"

"Heal. You half Dryad. Can you conjure magic?"

Juaan felt Sakal pause in her study to listen in.

"No," Juaan said in a closed tone that he hoped Bahari would heed.

"You have no magic?"

"Bahari," Nyriaana shook her head at the other man in warning.

"He father Dryad?"

"My mother," Juaan answered testily, the pain of her memory twisting through him.

"Then why you have no power?"

"Oh, I have power," Juaan growled, needled by his pain and self-loathing.

"If no heal, then what do?"

"You had better pray to your Eron that you're never close enough to find out," Juaan said with such menace that Bahari took a step back from him.

"Juaan." Now Nyri's warning was for him.

"A monster inside and out, eh?" Sakal muttered.

Juaan's heart thudded in his chest. The hatred on Sakal's face stoked his shame and anger, gouging away at his control. He had to get out. Spinning on his heel, he stalked from the cave, gulping in the cold, wet air. He sat down on a flat rock partway down the slope and let the rain sluice over him, soaking his furs.

He wasn't alone for long.

"You should not listen to Sakal," she said as she settled on the rock beside him, drawing her knees to her chest. "She does not know you."

Neither do you, he wanted to say, but he kept the words behind his teeth, knowing they would only hurt her. "I am trying, Nyri," he said. "But the closer we get to the Mountains, the more afraid I become. It, it is too strong for me."

She took his hand, entwining their fingers. "I won't let it happen, Juaan. I won't let you be hurt."

"You should not be the one protecting me. My whole purpose for being here was to protect you."

"We look after each other now." Her fingers flexed. "We always promised, didn't we?"

A sad smile ghosted across his face as he dipped his head, resting his cheek on her crown, drinking in her presence. "If at any time I tell you to leave me, you must do it, Nyriaana. Please."

"Never."

He groaned. "You're impossible."

She laughed once, shrugging closer to him. "That's why you love me," she said.

Juaan's breath caught in his throat. In an instant, he was hyperaware of the soft feel of her hair beneath his cheek, the tantalising warmth of her hand in his. She had grown very still, as if only just noticing what she had said.

"Juaan…"

Fire licked down his back at the way she said his name. Her face was so close, her lips…

"Time to move on," Bahari's voice made Juaan flinch, shattering the moment. Only now did he realise the rain had dried up and shafts of Utu's light were chasing each other among the rocks as the breeze herded the clouds from the sky above.

Clearing his throat, Juaan got to his feet. He did not miss the breath Nyri let out as he released her hand. He frowned.

Was that relief he heard in her sigh? He studied her face, but she avoided his eyes.

"Nyriaana?"

"I'm alright, Juaan," she said, misunderstanding his concern. "I've rested enough." And she fled to Bahari's side without looking back.

Juaan bowed his head, letting out one rueful laugh. For a moment he had let himself believe… He shook his head. He had already declared himself once before as Khalvir and felt the bitter sting of her rejection. Why should anything have changed?

Oh, she did love him. He would be blind not to see that. She would always care for him and support him. It was her way. But he was a fool to think she could ever fall for the monster that he was. She could never love him the way he loved her.

And she never should. Shuttering away lost hopes, Juaan set off after his companions, bracing himself for another gruelling trek until nightfall.

The trail began to lead them out of the gullies and back into the hill tops as the day wore on. The barren landscape was strange to Juaan, but an odd feeling was taking root in his heart. He paused for a moment, looking around, the hairs on the back of his neck prickling.

"Juaan, what is it?" Ever in tune with his emotions, Nyri had turned.

"I don't know," he answered. "Something about this place. It's like… I've been here before."

"Probably while hunting down innocents for the Red Bear," Sakal sneered.

"No," Juaan shook his head, too distracted to feel the sting of Sakal's words. The sense of familiarity was unnerving him. He shook his head and strode on, hoping to leave it behind.

"There is a small copse ahead," Sakal said, more to Nyri and Bahari than to Juaan. "We can rest there."

Just the day before, Sakal would have refused to stop until nightfall. Now she had allowed for two halts during the day. Perhaps the Eagle warrior was beginning to feel the effects of her own malicious pace, but then Juaan saw Sakal glance at Nyri. While her gaze was not warm, it was no longer hostile. She had softened towards the girl. If only a little.

The copse Sakal had promised loomed into view, the dense growth of the trees offering thick cover. Juaan's sense of inexplicable familiarity grew stronger. He found himself hesitating to approach the trees. Something about the copse filled him with an echo of fear and dread. His insides twisted. But Sakal's critical eyes were on him, and so Juaan pushed his feelings aside and ducked under the first branches.

The scent of the leaves hit him in the face like an axe. He had travelled many woodland terrains, but the smell of the earth and damp bark in this place set off an explosion of half-formed images and sensations behind his eyes.

He was wrapped in fur. Ragged breathing and the sound of a rapid heartbeat pounded against his ear. Everything appeared bigger, fresh, new.

Juaan staggered, shaking his head, trying to dispel the blurry visions. He caught himself against a tree and found himself staring into a deep hollow at its base. He gasped as the hole sucked him down into the blackness, a voice sounding in his head.

"I-I'll be back. I will not leave you." A tear-streaked face was

above him and terror was all he knew as he was separated from her. She was leaving him. "Stay quiet until mama returns."

"Juaan?"

"I love you. More than anything!"

And then his mother's face, and the vision was gone.

Juaan became aware of the moisture rolling down his cheeks. He gripped the tree until the bark cut at his fingers. The echo of panic at being abandoned thudded through his chest and he could feel the power inside him swirling unpredictably.

"Juaan?"

He raised a hand. "Stay away, Nyriaana. Please. Just keep your distance."

"Let me—"

"No," he backed away. "It's not safe. Please, just stay here with Bahari." And Juaan fled, running headlong through the trees and back on to the trail. He did not heed where he was going for a few moments, lost in his confusion and grief. Ahead of him, the path forked, and he dived to the left. The trail led between the hills until Juaan came upon another rockslide. This one, however, was old. Moss had settled on the tumbled rocks and all was in stillness.

Juaan leaned on his spear, fighting to centre himself. He had to regain control before he went back. Now that the haunting scent of that dreadful copse was not filling his senses, it was easier to do so. But something was still tugging on him, teasing, demanding his attention. Out of the corner of his eye, Juaan saw a flash of a familiar red disappear along the trail ahead of him.

Eldrax! His spear leaped into a ready position. If the Red Bear had survived the Watcher attack by escaping into the foothills, then Nyriaana was in grave danger. Sinking into a hunter's crouch, Juaan set off in pursuit, every instinct on alert. The hairs on his neck stood on end. Though he strained his senses, he could detect no sound except that of the wind, no betraying roll of rocks under feet ahead of him, but Juaan knew he had seen something.

And there it was again, the flash of red, teasing him just out of sight, pulling him forward, inviting him, silently calling his name. Juaan gripped his weapon tighter and increased his pace, breaking into a run.

"Ah!" Juaan hit the ground, a low pile of rocks taking his feet out from under him. He stared at the mound until movement drew his gaze up. Juaan scrambled backwards in alarm as he locked eyes with a red-headed Thal woman standing on the escarpment above. Her black gaze took him in for a moment, then she beamed widely. *"Gor cha tarhe, ki juaan."*

"Juaan? What is it?"

Juaan's head snapped around. Nyri was leading the other two towards him, her brow pinched in concern. Bahari was wary. Sakal angry.

"I…" Juaan returned his gaze to the escarpment. The Thal woman had vanished. He blinked. "Where did she go?" he asked Nyri as she drew closer.

"Who?"

"The Thal woman."

Nyri shook her head, her frown deepening. "There was nobody else."

"She was standing right there. She spoke to me."

"Perhaps the *genii* visit you, too," Bahari said quietly.

Juaan stared at the empty escarpment. The betrayal of his

senses frightened him. The woman had seemed so real. Felt so real.

"Juaan!" Nyri had turned her attention to the low mound of rocks his short chase had led him to. She beckoned without taking her eyes off the stones in front of her. "Bring your spear."

Juaan hesitated, then did as she asked, following her direction as she pointed at the highest stone on the mound. He saw now what had taken her attention. The stone was carved with markings. Very familiar markings.

"They match." Nyri pulled the carved end of his spear down next to the stone.

"Eron's markings of protection," Bahari spoke. "This is a Thal resting place."

"Not just Thal markings." Nyri's fingers traced the uppermost symbol, a half circle with two flattened lines, a shape like Utu as she dipped below the horizon. "This is the Ninkuraaja symbol for Ninmah."

"But what Dryad symbol doing here?" Bahari asked.

And then Juaan knew. He understood. His eyes went to where the Thal woman had stood, then down to the grave. He did not speak to his companions. He lifted the tip of his spear to his forehead, whispering a silent prayer before touching it to the headstone. *"Shalanaki, ki tarhe,"* he whispered. Bahari stared, startled by his fluent Thal speak, but he ignored the Cro man. He was not about to explain. Turning, he continued on up the path, leaving his companions confused in his wake, hiding his tears.

* * *

335

19

Return

re they even still alive? The thought crossed Kyaati's mind as it had countless times since she had set out from the Eagle camp.

They were now two days across the Plains, heading south for the forests of her birth. Kikima walked at her side. The dozen men that Galahir had insisted on sending with her moved in a loose circle around them, Narak at their head. Galahir had appointed the Eagle hunter her personal guard while he led the Eagles' main forces in a search to gather others in the fight that was to come. Narak kept his men on alert, watchful for any sign of threat; predator, human or, worst of all, Watcher.

Kyaati was careful to keep her own senses attuned for the slightest quiver in the Great Spirit. Her gifts would give a far earlier warning than the mortal sight of the men. She spoke only when necessary. She could not let herself become distracted. Such a mistake could be fatal. Elhaari rested in his sling against her breast, unaware of the danger and vulnerable. Kyaati had not fully slept since they had departed the Eagle camp, for the nights posed the greatest danger. She only allowed herself to doze during the brief respites in the day to keep herself from succumbing entirely to exhaustion. She fed Elhaari on the move.

On the third day of travel across the Southern Plains, a dark line appeared in the distance.

"Is that the *shin'ar* forest?" Kikima asked, pointing.

Kyaati dipped her chin once, watching the line grow.

"Your home," Kikima murmured. "Are you… happy to be returning at last?" Her friend was no doubt remembering the turbulent time when Kyaati and Nyriaana had first arrived in the Hunting Bear camp. How they had fought to return to their homeland.

"I don't know," Kyaati answered. And it was the truth. She did not know how the looming tree line in the distance made her feel. The River Line beneath the forest called to her like an old friend, softer and more awake with the buzz of the trees. Very different from the mighty but rigid flow of the great River Line that passed beneath the Mountains she had become accustomed to existing beside. The familiar energy soothed her soul, welcoming her back. But Kyaati did not think she was happy.

Her old life had been littered with misery and loss. Her every pain caused by blind, misguided Elders too stubborn to see that their rigid belief in the gods was the very reason their People were being tortuously wiped from existence. And now she was going back to them, with everything they despised cradled in her arms, surrounded by their enemies.

Kyaati pressed her lips together in a cold, determined line. Akito had been right, the gods needed to die. The suffering had to end here. Her People had to be freed. If they hadn't already perished in the name of Ninmah.

Despite her hatred of what they had forced her to suffer, Kyaati did not think she could bear it if her People were no more, if she and Nyriaana, wherever she was, were the last of their kind. And so Kyaati watched the line of the forest loom larger with a cold dread at what she might find growing in the pit of her stomach. But if they were alive, what then? How was she to convince them to join the fight? What danger was she taking Elhaari into? She drew reassurance from the guard of Cro that had sworn oaths to their Chief to protect both her and Elhaari with their lives.

Still, she was not ready when at last they stood at the feet of the first trees. A breeze made the newly sprouting leaves and the branches sing overhead, wafting the scent of rich earth, moss and tree bark across Kyaati's face. She sucked it in as a lifetime of memories rushed through her mind. This was her home. She did not need to be afraid. Resolute, she turned to her men.

"The *eshaara* grove where my People dwell lies deep within the forest. The ground is treacherous and the life within does not take kindly to strangers. Watch everything that I do and follow my lead. Do not stray."

"As you wish, my matriarch," Narak dipped his head in deference. It still amazed Kyaati how easily the Eagle warriors accepted direction from a female. She had learned from Gendi that Eldrax had wiped out all the men from the Eagle Clan on the day the Red Bear had kidnapped her mate from his family, leaving the women to die without hunters or warriors to defend them.

That was when Yatal had emerged as the leader they had needed. Under her guidance, the remaining women of the Eagle Clan had survived with determination and cunning, growing in strength under Eldrax's nose as rogue males gradually joined them, grateful to be accepted into the protection of a clan and not be killed on sight. Even now, women were still a dominant force in the Eagle ranks. Half of the hunters that Galahir had sent with Kyaati were female.

Elhaari's green eyes were wide with wonder as Kyaati wrapped a protective arm around him and took her first step back into the trees, his tender senses awash with new sensations and the sounds of the forest where his mother had spent her childhood. He cooed in response to the ceaseless sound of the birdsong, the croaking of tree frogs, the rustle of insects and the distant rush of the many streams that wove through the trees. Kyaati laughed quietly, shaking her head as the same sounds and sensations assaulted her.

The forest was almost too chaotic for her now, just as the Plains had once been too still. The relentless noise blinded her ears to the sound of approach and she struggled to block out the overwhelming wave of life and focus on her immediate surroundings. She needed to know if any of her People might be watching.

Kyaati continued to tread her way through the familiar pathways of her old life, leading her company deeper into the forest. She could feel their apprehension. The Cro had listened to tales of the dreadful magic of the witch forests since they were children sitting on their mothers' knees. The only one not wary was Kikima.

"I have always wanted to see the *shin'ar* forest," she murmured, staring up into the canopy far above, the dead, haunted expression that had adorned her features since

Halima's death all but gone. "It's beautiful."

Kyaati smiled and concentrated for a moment. Kikima gasped as a large, brightly coloured bird swooped down from overhead to land on her shoulder. He fluffed his bright blue and yellow feathers in an affectionate manner and held out a bunch of berries in his large, red beak.

Kikima's face was a carving of astonishment as she took the gift from the creature on her shoulder. "A…are you doing that?" she asked.

"I might have invited him," Kyaati said, reaching up to stroke the smooth feathers. With shaking fingers, Kikima did the same until the bird took wing and disappeared back into the canopy to rejoin the rest of his flock roosting above.

"Eat," Kyaati reminded Kikima of the berries she now held in her hand. Kikima broke off a sprig and handed it to Kyaati, before taking a tentative taste.

"Hmmm!" Her eyes rolled in pleasure as the juice exploded across her tongue.

"Better than the flesh of an animal," Kyaati grinned as she took her own bite and hummed in satisfaction and relief at the taste of the sweet fruit.

"We should rest," Narak whispered. "We have been travelling since dawn. My men are hungry."

Kyaati glanced up at him, guiltily swallowing the last of her berries. "Follow me," she said. She knew a place close by that would shelter them while the Cro recuperated. The sound of water drew her to a thicket next to a wide, babbling stream. Once they squatted down, they would be out of sight from prying eyes. Not that the attention they needed to avoid required eyes to see them. But Kyaati could sense nothing other than the wildlife of the forest. If her People still existed, they were not in the vicinity.

With practiced efficiency, the Eagles crouched amongst the undergrowth, dividing up rations and passing them around. One young man approached Kikima. He was tall, athletically built, with deep brown eyes. He held out his hand, offering her a large ration of fish. Kyaati felt a jolt of surprise at the nervous hopefulness radiating from the young hunter. His approach reminded Kyaati of Galahir's first hopeful advances on the first terrifying journey to the Hunting Bear Clan. Kyaati smiled secretly to herself as the hunter's heart gave an exalted leap when Kikima accepted his offering with a confused smile of thanks.

Perhaps her friend would not have to wait so long for a permanent mate to find her after all. Kyaati probed deeper. This young hunter had a gentle spirit under his strong exterior. Eldrax he was not. If they survived what was to come, perhaps Kikima's future would be a happy one after all. And that was all Kyaati wanted for her friend.

Caught up in her thoughts, Kyaati almost missed the situation unfolding on the other side of the gathering.

"Don't touch that!"

Narak froze, his fingers halting just shy of the bright blue frog climbing the tree close to where he squatted.

"One touch of the *bizaaza* will cause you agony beyond speech. The poison in its skin burns through flesh and steals the ability to move. Without a Ninkuraaja healer, you'd be dead before Ninmah touches the horizon."

Narak paled as he withdrew his hand from the unassuming amphibian and shifted away.

"Do not touch anything in this forest unless I tell you otherwise," Kyaati snapped. "Understand?"

341

"Perfectly," Narak said between his teeth, clamping his hands beneath his armpits. Kyaati noticed the rest of the Eagles were similarly keeping their hands closer to their bodies.

They were wasting time. Kyaati was anxious to move. In stillness, the fear of what she might find when she reached the *eshaara* grove crawled beneath her skin. She had to know. Was she the only one of her kind left? Was Nyri still out there somewhere? Kyaati's throat closed. She had not felt any presences since entering the forest to reassure her that her People were still here. She stood. "Let's move on."

Kyaati waded through the stream with her companions keeping close behind. A wild boar rooted through the earth on the far bank. It raised its thick head as it saw them approach, ears flicking curiously.

Kyaati heard Narak's intake of breath. The hunter gripped his spear.

"It's not even running away!" a female voice hissed in disbelief. "How long since we hunted anything but fish, Narak?"

"Don't," Kyaati put out a hand. "There is to be no hunting here. If my People are alive and they witness you butchering a Child of KI in their territory, there will be nothing I can say that will convince them to side with us."

"But," Narak protested, his fingers still twitching on his spear as the boar ambled away, lazily swishing its tail.

"No."

Narak snarled under his breath. Such was his frustration and hunger for something other than fish, Kyaati knew that if he had not sworn to Galahir to obey and protect her, Narak would have happily choked the life from her body in that moment.

But as the boar retreated, Kyaati stiffened. Many bright presences were homing swiftly in on their position.

"Don't move," she hissed. "Keep absolutely still if you want to live."

"What now?" Narak demanded, bringing his spear into a ready position, eyes everywhere at once.

The first wolf burst from the undergrowth, answering his question. The alpha was followed by the rest of the pack, each one shouldering into view until Kyaati's small band was completely surrounded. Snarls broke out as the pack circled the fur-clad Cro in their midst.

"Batai!" Kyaati cried, recognising the young wolf mixing with the pack. But the golden gaze remained unfriendly as the grey wolf paced. He did not recognise her yet.

"Get on your knees and lower your heads, all of you," Kyaati ordered.

"I am not exposing my neck to those teeth!" Narak argued.

"If you don't do as I say, right now, those teeth are going to be the last thing you ever feel on your neck," Kyaati said.

"Get down, Narak," Kikima snapped, sinking to her own knees and bowing down to the wolf pack. One by one, the rest of the Eagle group followed her example. The angry lupine snarls subsided.

When she was the only member of her company who remained on her feet, Kyaati stood tall, commanding her space as the alpha male approached.

I am not your enemy; she soothed across his mind, sharing her energy with him. *I am a part of this place. I am a part of you, Son of the Great Spirit.*

The lead wolf's head snapped up. Recognition sparked

in his mind as his ears pricked forward. The raised hackles on his neck relaxed and he strode forward to push his head against her chest, letting a rumble of greeting roll from his throat.

Kyaati grinned and pushed back against him, running her fingers through his thick fur, ignoring the wordless vocalisations of disbelief from the bowed Cro. Her own breath caught as a picture in the alpha's thoughts came to the fore, a flavour of protective energy encircling it: her tribe huddled in fear within the *eshaara* grove.

"They're alive!" Kyaati cried. She turned to her followers. "The wolves picked up our scent and came to guard my People against the intruders. They're alive."

Joy drove out her doubt. Suddenly all Kyaati wanted was to rush through the trees and be home, to look upon her long lost family. But the wolves were still eyeing her companions in suspicion. Any wrong move could end in blood. Kyaati extended a calming energy over the pack, letting them know that the strangers were no threat.

"Get up very slowly," she murmured. "No quick movements, and keep your eyes lowered. Do not give them any reason to believe you are challenging them."

This time, the Cro obeyed without question. Kyaati felt a rush of grim satisfaction in the face of their awe, even fear, of her. For the first time, they had witnessed a witch display what they believed to be complete control over one of the most dangerous predators to walk the land. She doubted they would second guess her orders again. Not in this forest, at least.

Kyaati moved forward, the alpha wolf pacing her as both their packs followed in their wake.

"Can I touch him?" Kikima asked, gazing at the wolf travelling at Kyaati's side.

"Here," Kyaati moved to the side so that Kikima could take her place at the alpha's head. "Let him scent you first. Do not extend your hand. If he wants to, he'll make the first move. Do not show fear."

Kikima walked alongside the lead wolf for a few moments before the great furry head swung in her direction, taking a curious sniff at the half-Deni woman's arm. Just to be on the safe side, Kyaati extended her will and wrapped Kikima's scent in a cocoon of familiarity. The wolf let out a rumble of greeting before turning his head from Kikima, ambling along companionably at her side.

"Now you can touch him," Kyaati murmured. "Put your hand on his shoulder."

Kikima's fingers were hesitant at first, ingrained instinct making her wary of the predator beside her, but as she buried her fingers into the warm fur, a grin broke across her handsome face. "I wish I could feel what you do, Kyaati," she murmured. "What an incredible gift your People were given."

Kyaati squeezed her free hand. "You might not possess Ninmah's Gift, but I can teach you to observe and learn to speak to them in your own way. The Children of the Great Spirit have much to teach us. That is what the Cro and the rest fail to see."

"Yes," Kikima agreed. "I wouldn't have thought this possible until you and Nyriaana walked into my life. To walk beside a wolf as an ally is an honour indeed."

Warmth filled Kyaati. She had opened the eyes of this woman to the possibilities of the world around her; showed her that the Children of KI and the Great Spirit himself were not things simply to be exploited.

The warmth faded when Kyaati noticed the trees changing around her. They were getting close now. Soon, she would be among her People again. For the first time in a long time, she felt conscious of the furs wrapped around her body. What would they think of her now? She knew the answer to that. *Outsider, heretic.* And the babe in her arms… Her thoughts went to the story of Rebaa and her son. This time, there would be no Sefaan to protect Elhaari.

"Stay close to me," she murmured to Narak as the first of the great *eshaara* trees loomed into view, drawing quiet gasps from the Eagles.

Kyaati's outer awareness quivered as she felt the energy of her People. They were muted, hiding. Kyaati had been instinctively keeping her own presence quiet since entering the forest. She radiated it out now, letting them know who it was that approached, and that it was safe.

A rush of leaves was her only warning. A figure dropped from the branches above to land before them, blocking the way. She had not sensed the hidden sentry. This individual was extremely skilled at hiding his life force. The cloud of dry leaves kicked up by his landing settled and the figure straightened, holding a pipe to his lips as his dark eyes glared down the length of it.

"Daajir?" Kyaati fell back a step as the shock rocked through her. "You are… you. H-how?"

"I could ask the same of you," Daajir gritted between his teeth. There was no flicker of warmth or greeting in his eyes. The blow pipe raised to his lips did not waver.

"Daajir," Kyaati swallowed, pushing Elhaari's sling around

behind her where he would be out of harm's way and cloaked his energy with her own. "It's me. I have come home. Drop the pipe."

"Is it you? The Woves took you, Kyaati. Now you stand, dressed as one of them, leading a force against us. You are under the dark magic of Ninsiku and I am here to stop you!"

Kyaati was still too shocked by Daajir's appearance to react. Her erstwhile friend closed his lips around his blow pipe. The Cro sank into fighting stances and levelled their spears, preparing to defend their matriarch.

"Daajir!" Another voice broke the standoff. "Daajir, stop!"

"Father!"

Pelaan rushed forward, thrusting Daajir aside. Kyaati felt the Cro twitch, ready to strike first and think later on this new, sudden intrusion.

"No!" Kyaati cried. "He's my father!"

"Kyaati?" Pelaan halted, wide-eyed and wary, guarded, as though bracing himself for the bright vision to dissolve and leave him in misery.

"Father," Kyaati whispered. "Father it's me. I've come home."

"My daughter." His voice broke upon the word. "My daughter!" He closed the gap between them in a rush, sweeping Kyaati into his arms, his hands running over her hair, convincing himself of the solid reality. "Oh, my Kyaati."

He pulled back to drink in her face, his eyes drowning in tears. His face had changed, Kyaati saw in an instant. Gone was the cool haughtiness that she remembered, the fanatical gleam. Grief and loss had carved it out, stripping away what had once seemed so vital to him. She could feel nothing but relief and the love of a father whose daughter had returned from the dead. He did not see the furs covering her body, or the Cro at her back. Just her. Kyaati sobbed and, this time, it was she who threw her arms around Pelaan, holding him until she was able to stem her tears.

"Come," Pelaan grabbed her hand, pulling her towards the *eshaara* grove.

Kyaati hesitated a moment, turning to Kikima and the rest of the Cro waiting uneasily behind. For the first time, her father appeared to register their presence. His alarm and hatred shot through her.

"Father!" Kyaati protested as he shouldered her behind him. "They are not here to hurt us. They are here to escort me home. They are my friends!"

Pelaan pinned her with a stare. The same suspicion that had glinted in Daajir's eyes flaring to life. Kyaati took a deep breath and opened her soul, letting him feel the truth of her emotions. "I am under no dark spell." She shifted her attention to Kikima and Narak. "Wait here."

"Matriarch," Narak protested. "I cannot protect you if you are out of my sight." He eyed Daajir, who was still glowering at the Cro man behind Pelaan.

"I am safe here," Kyaati said, injecting as much certainty into her voice as possible. "I will signal you if I have need. Come," she said, now tugging on her father's arm, "I will tell you everything."

"But…" Pelaan's eyes were fixed on the Cro.

"The wolves will guard them," Kyaati said.

"Daajir, stay here," Pelaan ordered.

"No!" Kyaati could only imagine what Daajir might try if left alone with the Cro. She would return to a bloodbath. "Daajir also needs to hear my story. The wolves will stay.

My friends are not foolish enough to challenge the pack."
She caught Narak's eye with a stern stare.

Pelaan's gaze went over the Cro and the pack that surrounded them. Then he dipped his chin, reassured by the
wolves' superior numbers. "Come, Daajir," he said.

"Respected Elder!" Daajir protested. But Pelaan levelled
a glare that held a ghost of his old self. Scowling, Daajir at
last lowered his weapon and fell into place on Pelaan's other
side as he led Kyaati towards their home.

Despite the show of confidence she had displayed for
Narak, Kyaati found herself holding her breath. Daajir's
reaction had shaken her. Would the rest of her People react
as he had? If so, she could be walking her baby into a snake
pit.

Kyaati watched her old friend out of the corner of her
eye. She had no idea how he had survived the wounds Nyri
had dealt him on that fateful night before their journey had
begun. She was happy to see him alive, but also frightened
by what she saw on his face and felt in his soul.

Her father had not treated her as a heretic, she told herself.
Growing up, she had always believed that Pelaan held his
faith more dearly than his own daughter. Kyaati forced her
fists to unclench. If he had changed, then there was hope
for the rest.

"My daughter has returned home!" Pelaan exalted as they
broke through the *eshaara* trees. Kyaati was hit by a storm
of conflicting emotions as her childhood home reached out
to envelop her. This was home, the home she had fought
so hard to return to. Everything here was as familiar to
her as her own skin, unchanged, and yet… everything was
changed. She was different. She had grown, and she no

longer fitted within these confines. Kyaati had returned, but she could never truly go back. Her heart ached. Even the scent was strange to her now, too rich and cloying, a far cry from the cold, clean air of the Plains.

Her tribe was waiting for her, huddled together outside the great bulk that was the healer's tree. There was Aardn and Oraan, Umaa and Imaali and…

"Baarias!" Kyaati was broadsided by yet another miracle.

"Kyaati!" The old *akaab* healer broke away from the crowd and ran towards her. Like her father, he did not appear to see her foreign dress. Kyaati's eyes ran over him. The left arm of Nyri's old guardian remained immobile as he moved, tucked against his chest. He caught up her hand with his right and brought their foreheads together. "You have no idea how much it gladdens my old heart to see you alive, dear one."

Kyaati could not speak the words. She had spent so long thinking Baarias dead, felled by a Cro spear. And now here he stood, his presence alive and vital against her own. "I-I wish Nyri was h-here," she choked out.

Kyaati felt Baarias' heart skip a beat as the blood left his face. "Sh…she's not? Is she…?"

Kyaati caught him by his injured shoulder with her free hand. "No! No, Baarias. Nyri is alive. She has done honour to your teaching, dear *akaab*. Or, she was the last time I saw her, I…"

"Enough!" Aardn's voice cracked out through the *eshaara* grove. The lead Elder had recovered her senses. The atmosphere over the settlement dropped, covering everyone and everything in an icy layer of fear and hate. Everything Kyaati had felt from Daajir, only now it was worse, doubled, tripled, by the combined feeling of the entire clan.

Elhaari, disturbed by the dark emotions overwhelming his tender senses, cried out in his sling against Kyaati's back. Kyaati stiffened. No amount of skill would hide the sound of his strident wail.

"Kyaati?" Pelaan took a step back.

"Father." Her eyes went to him, pleading for understand as she drew the sling around to her front and lifted Elhaari out of the fur. Swallowing around her suddenly dry throat, Kyaati held her son up for Pelaan to see. "Father, this is my son. I-I named him Elhaari... for your father."

Kyaati tightened her arms around her baby as a maelstrom of emotions ripped through Pelaan. "H...he's," he stammered.

"A Forbidden heresy!" Aardn shrieked. "Daajir, finish it! The existence of the last abomination earned us Ninmah's displeasure. I shall not suffer another. Snuff it out! Feed it to the wolves! Ninmah forgive us."

"No!" Kyaati cried as Daajir and several others started forward. But before she could raise the alarm to her Cro followers, before she could even move, her father was there. Pelaan blocked Daajir's eager advance, planting a hand against the younger man's chest. There was a wave of energy. Daajir's eyes rolled back into his head and he crashed unconscious to the ground.

"You will not touch my grandson!" Pelaan snarled.

The rest of the advancing tribe halted in their tracks, stunned by the actions of one of their Elders.

Pelaan turned back to Elhaari. He drew one breath, then another, before he reached out with a trembling hand. Kyaati forced herself to remain still as her father placed his fingers on her son's forehead. A shuddering breath went through him, a tear escaping from one eye as their energies met for the first time. For a handful of heartbeats, Pelaan remained motionless. "Elhaari," he whispered. He began to explore his grandson, lifting his hands and his feet, studying each of his fingers and finding no weakness, no deformity. "Kyaati… he's perfect." Kyaati had thought she had no more tears left to cry, but they blinded her again as Pelaan lifted Elhaari out of her arms and cradled him against his chest. "My grandson," he whispered in awe. "A whole and *perfect* child."

Beside them, Baarias was gazing upon the infant in Pelaan's arms, his face contorted with some unnamed emotion.

"Ninsiku's magic!" Aardn hissed, stealing the moment. "That thing has already bewitched you, Pelaan. It can't be allowed to live! Take it," she commanded the rest of the tribe, "before we are further cursed by Ninmah!"

Fury curled through Kyaati's gut as they started forward again. *Enough.* She let out a long, shrill whistle. Before the tribe could take another step, the Eagles burst from the undergrowth. A bristling wall of spears arrayed itself around Kyaati and her family.

"Woves!" The Ninkuraaja shrank back.

"You dare to threaten our Chief's son?" Narak shouted over their cries of terror.

Aardn's eyes bugged in her head as she retreated. The rest of the tribe moved with their leader, on the verge of flight.

Kyaati needed to salvage the situation and quickly. She placed a hand on Narak's arm, urging him to lower his weapon. "Easy," she whispered. "If they run, we have failed."

She stepped around her lead hunter, her gaze locked on Aardn. "They are not here to harm us," she called out, "only to protect me. Leave my child in peace, and no one needs to get hurt. The Cro are our allies. I came home because we are all in mortal danger."

"Yes!" Imaali cried. "Danger that you brought straight to us!"

"For the sake of the Great Spirit himself, be quiet, Imaani," Kyaati snapped, losing patience. "Listen to me, or your willful blindness will be the end of you. You think you know evil?" Kyaati laughed. "You cannot imagine what is coming for us."

"What could be worse than the demons of Ninsiku?" Imaani gripped his mate, Umaa, by the arms, pulling her further away.

"The masters of your imagined demons. The gods themselves!"

"Heretic!" Aardn shrieked into the ensuing silence.

"Hear me!" Kyaati shouted over the Elder. "I would not have believed it myself had I not borne witness to their evil. The gods have awakened. Our teachings are blind. They have never loved us. They mean to wipe us from the land. All of us." Kyaati swept her arms out to encompass the Cro and her People together.

Aardn's laugh was maniacal. "Ninmah protects us!"

"Does she?" Kyaati challenged. "Look around you, Aardn? Where is Ninmah, now? Does this suffering look like the protection of a loving goddess to you?"

"Silence your poison!" Aardn cried, jabbing a finger at the Cro. "It is the evil spawn of Ninsiku that has caused our suffering!"

"Really?" Kikima raised an eyebrow, watching the foam gather at the corners of Aardn's mouth.

"Aardn," Kyaati beseeched. The lead Elder had always been the most zealous of them all, but she too had changed in the intervening blinks of Ninsiku since Kyaati had last seen her. Aardn's transformation, however, was not Pelaan's. Her father had had time to experience the loss of his daughter and know how it felt to lose everything that truly mattered. Now his family had returned from the dead, and nothing, not their hollow beliefs, nor the love of an absent goddess, could mean more to him than having Kyaati home and a grandchild in his arms.

In contrast, Aardn had sunk deeper into depravity. The desperation to preserve a lost cause that continued to fall around her ears had shattered her mind. Kyaati could feel the shards cracking even now, and she pitied her. "Aardn, please," she tried to get through. "The Woves stand here before you, unmasked. Be still and look at their faces. *Feel* them! All of you! They are human, just like us. There is no dark power here."

The tribe around Aardn shifted, confusion curling through the air as their senses confirmed the truth of Kyaati's words, throwing their beliefs into turmoil.

"We have all suffered. We have all slaved to keep to the paths the gods set out for us. And for what? Where is Ninmah?" Kyaati demanded again. "Does she acknowledge us? Where are our children? Deformed, starved, dead!"

At this, Umaa whimpered and fell to her knees. Kyaati was hit by a wave of raw pain. It was only now that she noticed Omaal, Umaa's blind son, was nowhere to be seen. Her heart jolted in her chest.

There was no time to think. Kyaati absorbed her grief and pressed on. This was the brutal truth, and she *had* to make them see before more children were lost. It was their only hope. Even if the Ninkuraaja had already doomed themselves, they had to try to make it right for the rest of the Peoples.

A few accusing glares had turned in Aardn's direction now. Kyaati could see that the harsh Fury, and the tide of loss it had left in its wake, had caused more than just Pelaan to question Aardn's wisdom.

"This is what the gods always wanted," Kyaati pressed her advantage. "We served our purpose, and now they come to cleanse the land of the creations they no longer see fit to breathe!"

"Lies!" Spittle flew from Aardn's mouth.

A groan from the direction of the ground announced Daajir's return to consciousness. He glared up at Pelaan, betrayal burning in his dark eyes. He reached for his blowpipe, but Pelaan stamped on it, crushing it into useless pieces.

"No!" Daajir cried, but then he saw the ring of Cro surrounding him. Without his weapon, he scrambled away, returning to Aardn's side.

Kyaati ignored the pair, giving her full attention to the members of her tribe who appeared to be crumbling before reason. "Please. I opened my eyes to the truth and found my happiness. A life without starvation, a life with a healthy babe in my arms. All I want is to share the same truth with you." She extended her hand. "Let me show you. If you still think I am bewitched and Ninmah will protect you, then you may run and we will leave, but for the sake of your children and all you hold dear, you must judge for yourselves." Kyaati stretched her fingers further.

All of them drew back. All except Umaa. The Ninkuraaja woman's gaze was dead, frighteningly so. A woman with nothing left to lose. "I will see the truth of your words," she said, her voice cracking from disuse as she stepped towards Kyaati.

"Umaa!" Imaani protested.

His mate brushed him aside.

Kyaati pressed her lips together and closed her eyes as Umaa caught hold of her hand with cold, bony fingers. The backlash of pain that came through their connection stole Kyaati's breath, echoing the familiar agony she kept buried deep within her own heart. For a moment, she and Umaa wept bitter tears, sharing in the grief of a mother's loss. Gritting her teeth, Kyaati forced herself to refocus on the task at hand. Gathering her memories, she unleashed them upon her fellow tribeswoman, revealing all that she had experienced, all the good and the bad, the love and the hate. Kyaati held nothing back. If Umaa thought she was concealing even the slightest detail, she would lose her, and so Kyaati suffered the intrusion into her innermost thoughts and memories, culminating in the terrible night when the Watchers had destroyed her new home.

Umaa shuddered at Kyaati's sharp recollection of the Watchers and the unearthly voice promising their extinction. Kyaati experienced her denial followed quickly by the anger and despair. Kyaati let her move through the emotions without interruption, understanding what it was to find that all one's pain and suffering had been meaningless. And Kyaati had had many blinks of Ninsiku to come to terms with the lies. Umaa was experiencing it all in just a matter of moments. Kyaati worried it might break her. But when Umaa opened her eyes, they were clear and determined. She offered Kyaati a grim nod, eyed the Cro around her warily, but then turned her back on them to face the rest of her People at Kyaati's side.

"Kyaati speaks the truth," she said.

"Umaa!" Imaani snapped.

"Imaani! You know better than anyone I am no fool. Look for yourself if you have the courage."

Imaani hung back.

Umaa's gaze softened. "Trust me, my *ankida.*"

A silent exchange passed between the two Joined souls. Kyaati watched Imaani's will crumble. As much as he wanted to cling to his beliefs and his loyalty to his leader, he could not deny his mate. Ignoring Aardn's protest, Imaani was next to seize Kyaati's hand, and the exchange of truth began again.

One by one, Kyaati's tribesmen came forward, taking what she offered. A few attacked her mind, actively probing, questioning, digging for the lies or underlying influence until they had turned out everything they could find. Then Kyaati had to live through each of their reactions. The ones who had raided her mind reacted the most violently to what they saw. Sorrow, anger, pain, disbelief.

When the last of her tribe members retreated, Kyaati sagged against Pelaan, her mind bruised by the assaults and her heart exhausted by the emotional turmoil. But she had achieved her goal. None of them could deny her truth now. Too much of their own experience had proven Kyaati's thoughts and words to be true.

In the end, only Aardn and Daajir stood against the Cro and the newly awakened Ninkuraaja, facing down the anger and disgust of their former followers. Kyaati tasted Aardn's wild desperation. The lead Elder's energy had the flavour of a cornered animal.

"Don't you see what she has done, you fools!" Aardn jabbed a finger at Kyaati. "She has cast the demon magic on you! That's why these Woves have brought her here! What shame Ninmah would feel, to know her beloved People could be so easily swayed against her."

"No, Aardn," Pelaan's voice was gentle but firm. "It is time to let go. Let Kyaati show you. Let go."

"Never!" Aardn snarled. "Heretic! I am loyal to Ninmah! Daajir!"

Without their notice, Daajir had produced another blow-pipe. He levelled it at Kyaati.

"No! Stop her!" The rest of the Ninkuraaja tribe charged forward at Pelaan's command, blocking Daajir's line to Kyaati. Within a heartbeat, they subdued Aardn and Daajir, knocking the pipe and its deadly contents aside.

"Traitors!" Aardn continued to rave as her former followers held her fast.

"Kyaati! Now." Pelaan gestured as Imaani struggled to keep the lead Elder subdued. "Show her."

Kyaati would have done anything not to go near Aardn's mind, but she *had* to cure her of the misguidance that tormented her soul. Bringing her hand down on Aardn's forehead, she unleashed her memories for the final time. Aardn fought back, rebelling against the intrusion, but Kyaati was like a river against stone, eroding, breaking down the defences until her thoughts flooded Aardn's inner mind.

The Elder heard it all, experienced it all.

Aardn did not react as the others had. The absence of emotion was more frightening than those who had reacted violently. There was no grief or fury; the more Kyaati revealed, the more calm Aardn became. The turbulent river became smooth, tranquil, before turning to ice when Kyaati finished her story. Now only one emotion ran through the Elder. A cold determination that unnerved Kyaati with its strength.

She withdrew her hand. "Now you see?" Kyaati asked cautiously.

"Yes," Aardn's voice was soft. "Yes, I see." The Elder's thoughts were oddly still, giving nothing away.

"Will you stand with us, revered Elder?"

Aardn tugged herself loose of Imaani's grip and rose to her feet, facing the Cro. "The Children of Ninmah will stand with the Children of Ninsiku," she declared.

"Aardn!" Daajir stared at his leader in disbelief.

"Silence, Daajir!" Aardn rounded on him. "You will do as your Elder commands." The two locked eyes as the Elder conveyed her will to Daajir. After a handful of tense heartbeats, Daajir's eyes widened slightly before he bowed his head.

"As you wish, respected Elder," he said.

"Gather your toxins," Aardn ordered him. "The Ninku-raaja will join with the Cro."

* * *

20

Forests of the Nine Gods

J uaan had not spoken a word since they had left the
graveside of the unknown Thal. He kept himself apart
from the rest of the group, brooding into the ground.
Nyri had been unable to approach him. She clutched the
enu seed around her neck miserably. She had thought that
their relationship was beginning to mend, and that, while
Juaan might be a long way from healing, he was no longer
pushing her away. Until now, Nyri had not realised how
much that small step was helping her, too. She no longer
felt so alone.

Now she was lost again.

Something about these hills they travelled had affected
Juaan deeply, and he was not ready to let her in. With
his renewed aloofness, the full weight of loss and her fear
of what lay ahead settled over Nyri's shoulders. She was
exhausted. The dreams of a great flash of lightning, followed
by endless nothingness, were becoming more vivid. Worst
of all, now that she was on this path, Aryiaana was getting
harder to see. The voices that had drawn her here were

becoming blurred. A stronger energy was drowning them out, warning Nyri away, threatening nothing but pain and destruction if she did not turn back.

This sense of inevitable doom only increased as they drew nearer to the Forest of the Nine Gods. The stronghold of the Watchers. Nyri shuddered. They would reach the trees before nightfall.

Sakal called a halt. Though she would never admit it, Nyri was grateful for the gentler pace their Eagle guide was setting, along with the respites she was now permitting at the height of the day. Her fears about Sakal's motives had waned. Not once in the days they had travelled together had Nyri detected any lessening of her single-minded drive to take them where they needed to go and return to her beloved leader's side.

"I will find us some game to supplement our rations," Juaan announced as soon as Sakal sank to her haunches and Nyri had collapsed upon a rock. "I doubt we will have time to hunt once we enter the forest." He jerked his head towards the looming treeline.

"I'll go with you," Bahari said, lifting his spear.

"There is no need," Juaan said, turning his back. It was clear he had hoped to go alone.

Bahari made a twisting gesture with one hand. "Wish to learn Cro tricks of hunting small game."

"Why?"

"Thal still cling to traditions of hunting big ice beasts. Shun other learning." Bahari shifted his feet as though the admittance of his People's shortcoming cost him. "I believe this is mistake. Not many big game left."

Nyri watched the exchange with mild interest. Bahari

had been raised by Thals, but he was still Cro. His mind was enquiring and flexible, open to new learning in ways that the other Peoples' weren't, Nyri surmised with a hint of chagrin. If she had learned one thing since being taken from her old life, it was that the Cro's rise to dominance and the waning of the others was thanks, in part, to their own inability to change. The Thals, the Deni and, yes, the Ninkuraaja, had wrought their own destruction. Nyri flicked at a pebble.

Juaan hesitated in the face of Bahari's reasoning, resisting company for a moment longer, then blew out a breath and beckoned to the other man, who followed eagerly.

Nyri's heart jolted, realising a beat too late the situation she was about to be left in. She scrambled to her feet. "You might need me, too."

"Nyriaana, you need to rest," Juaan cut across her. "I can handle a hunt. We will return before Utu sets."

Nyri clenched her teeth, pleading with her eyes, but Juaan had already turned away and she could not think of a valid argument for accompanying the two capable hunters, not without making it obvious that her only wish was to escape being left alone with Sakal.

Helpless, she watched as her two companions disappeared into the rock scape. The wind whistled through the awkward silence that swept in to fill their absence. Nyri moved back to her rock, keeping her eyes lowered. She could feel Sakal watching her and knew the Eagle woman had not been fooled by her attempt to escape.

Although the forbidding energy Sakal had worn around herself like a defensive cloak had loosened since Nyri had saved her from the deadly scorpion sting, Nyri still did not dare speak to the unapproachable warrior woman. And so she sat, trying to appear engrossed with the seed bound around her neck. Her mouth went dry at the thought of how she had almost lost it.

Ninmah passed slowly overhead. It wasn't long before Nyri's eyelids began to droop. She wrenched them back stubbornly, stretching her arms out to chase the encroaching weariness away.

"You did not sleep again last night." Sakal's voice made Nyri flinch. She turned, surprised, to the Eagle woman.

"Wh...what?" she stammered.

"The men might not notice, but I do." Nyri tensed as Sakal moved to her side and perched upon the rock next to her. "You can sleep. I will keep watch."

"I can't," Nyri whispered.

"I will not harm you."

"It's not that. I fear..." Nyri trailed off, not knowing how or wanting to explain.

She felt Sakal weighing her for a few moments. "Ah, I see. I know what that's like," the other woman said, staring into the distance.

"You have visions, too?"

Sakal barked a harsh laugh. "No. I am no witch. But memory can be as strong as any vision."

Nyriaana did not know how to respond to that and so she lapsed back into silence, willing Juaan and Bahari to reappear.

"Are you sure you need to enter that place?" Sakal spoke again after a few moments. Her dark gaze was fixed on the looming tree line ahead.

No! I am certain of nothing! Nyri wanted to cry, but she couldn't, not to Sakal. "I have something important that I need to do," was all she said.

Sakal didn't appear impressed by that.

"Are you sure you can trust the Red Bear's Spear Cat?"

This question caught Nyri off guard. Immediately defensive, she snapped: "More than anyone! Certainly more than I trust you."

Yatal's battle-hardened warrior did not flinch. "Perhaps you shouldn't."

"I don't really care what you think, Sakal," Nyri growled, ire overcoming her caution. "When we reach the Forest of the Nine Gods, you are bound by Yatal no more. You can go home."

"No."

Nyri blinked. "No?"

"I think I will continue."

"Why?"

"Going in there," Sakal pointed to the Forest, "you're going to need all the fighters you can get at your side. And what is the point of returning? The only leader I have ever thought worth following will be gone, replaced by another."

"But Sakal," Nyri floundered, her anger forgotten. "You have others who care about you. Children? A mate?"

Sakal did not appear to move, but Nyri thought she perceived a hardening in her posture as she stared out at the forest before them, her skin turning to ice. "Such attachments were torn from me long ago."

"I," Nyri paused, unease curling through her gut. "What, what happened?" As soon as the words were loose, she wished she could call them back. Something told her she was better off not knowing.

Sakal chuckled coldly, as though the answer should be

obvious. "My mate and children were murdered, witch, killed without mercy in a raid sent by the Red Bear."

The warrior's icy composure cracked and Nyri experienced a backlash of the pain, hate and resentment that consumed this Eagle woman's entire soul. Flickering against her consciousness were a few blurred images; two infants, laughing under Ninmah's rays as they ran through an unfamiliar camp into their mother's arms.

"He led them," Sakal's attention shifted. Nyriaana followed her gaze. Juaan was climbing back up the trail towards them, two dead rabbits dangling from his grasp. Blood dripped from his hands.

An invisible grip closed around Nyriaana's throat. "I am sorry," she forced the words from between her lips. "Believe me, Sakal, he is not the same man, he is different." Even to her own ears, the assurance sounded hollow.

"That will never bring my children back," Sakal said as she thrust herself away from the rock, returning to her distant post as Juaan neared, leaving Nyri alone again.

"Nyriaana," Juaan's voice was soft as he came before her. He shot a look at Sakal's departing back. "Are you alright?"

She could not remove her gaze from his bloody hands.

"Nyriaana?"

Nyri forced her eyes away and looked up into his face. Her stomach turned over as he read everything he needed to know in her stricken expression. She had not had time to absorb or accept this new learning of the savage life he had led as Khalvir, and not nearly enough time to remove the naked reaction from her face.

Juaan's attention shifted to Sakal again and then he dropped his gaze, giving one somber nod of understanding before moving away to give her some space.

"Jade Killer very skilled hunter," Bahari said to Nyri as he approached, holding another three rabbits. "Maybe get Alok to accept these new ways when I return to *etuti.*"

"Alok would be a fool not to listen, Bahari," she said, struggling to keep her voice even. *He may not even have been the one to kill her children.* The thought spiralled through Nyri's mind. *He only led the raid. It would have been impossible to control all his men in such a situation.* Even as Khalvir, Nyri did not believe he would have killed innocent babes with his own hands. He had told her himself, very few men would murder women and children. She had to believe that.

"Here," Bahari handed her a rabbit and a knife. "You look like you need to be busy."

"Bahari," Juaan's growl rolled out in warning.

"No, Juaan," she said. "He's right. Being busy will help." And she took the rabbit from Bahari's hand, waving the knife away. She already carried her own.

"Need fire," Bahari said as he cleaned his rabbit. "To cure meat. We can light no fire in there." He tilted his head towards the Forest.

Sakal got up without a word and disappeared. She returned not long later with an armful of wood and dried grass. Choosing a spot surrounded by rocks to protect it from the wind and any prying eyes, she began to strike a fire.

Ninmah was dipping low over the hills by the time their supplementary meat had cooked over the spitting flames. Sakal doused the hot tongues with gravel and rocks before the glow could betray their position in the gathering gloom.

"Utu is too low now for us to continue on," she announced.

366

"I will not enter the Forest of the Nine Gods at night. Rest as much as you can. Tomorrow we travel fast. If we do not stop, perhaps we will make it through the forest to the Mountains themselves before darkness falls again."

"We?" Juaan arched an eyebrow.

"Sakal is coming with us," Nyri interjected quietly.

Sakal lifted her chin at Juaan, challenging him to argue. "We eat hot food tonight. We don't know when we might taste another. Bahari, ration out some of the coney."

Nyri felt Juaan's flash of irritation at Sakal's continued assumption of leadership. They had reached the edge of her known range. They no longer needed her guidance, but Bahari accepted the orders with grace, dividing up a meal from the still-hot rabbit flesh and passing it around.

Nyri devoured her portion, habitually blocking what was entering her mouth from her mind. The flavour might still be repulsive but, she had to admit, the warmth in her belly was a comfort.

Ninsiku stared lazily from under a hooded lid as Sakal rolled up in her furs. Bathed in the silver light, Nyri wrung her hands together, fresh panic shooting through her chest. The day was over. Tomorrow would take them into the Forest of the Nine Gods and the long-avoided fate that awaited her.

Her time was up. She could feel the malevolence of the energy running through the ground. They were so close now to the powerful River Line that flowed under the Mountains of the Nine Gods. Closer than they had ever been in the Hunting Bear camp. Nyri's skin prickled. She was aware that in the shadows to her side, Juaan was also staring towards the Forest and the Mountains, his face grim.

367

"The *genii* speaking to you now?" Bahari murmured in the dark.

Nyri shook her head. "No." What was she even doing here? Now that she was so close, she had never been more uncertain.

She felt Bahari's hand reach out and take her own, folding it in warmth. He squeezed once. "In Thal tradition, nothing happens for nothing. The *genii* drew you here, Nyriaana. I have faith in you."

In spite of everything, Nyri's heart swelled. A trickle of courage returned.

"Thank you, Bahari," she whispered. "I never expected when I set out on my path that I would find a friend such as you. Ninmah indeed smiled upon me the day you came to our rescue."

Doubt and guilt clouded the Cro man's thoughts. "Friend? I almost send you to death."

Nyri released a breath, and with it any lingering resentment she still harboured towards Bahari for bringing her before Yatal.

"But you didn't send me to my death, and you did not put me at risk knowingly. You could not disobey your father, Bahari," she said. "You just said it yourself. Everything happens as it is meant to. From the very moment Sefaan shared her vision with me, I was fated to be here. It is not your fault, and without Sakal, I doubt I would have found my way. Perhaps that is the true reason the *genii* guided your father to send me to Yatal."

Bahari processed her words and let out a soft laugh. "Perhaps. The spirits do not often make meaning clear." The weight of the air around them eased. Nyri realised then just how much guilt her companion had been carrying. Bahari hesitated for a moment, then he leaned in and pressed his lips to her forehead. A scattering of rocks told her that Juaan had almost leaped to his feet.

Bahari was awkward in his show of affection. Nyri guessed that he had never been permitted within arm's reach of the Thal women he lived with, much less kissed a female, and he was unsure he should do so now, afraid of breaching the sacred law. The thought that Bahari had never been permitted to love made Nyri sad.

"Thank you for your forgiveness, Nyriaana," Bahari murmured. "I rest easier tonight."

At least that makes one of us, she thought. Nyri squeezed Bahari's hand, glad she had been able to grant him this one gift, before the Cro man moved away to find a space to sleep.

Juaan made no move to rest. Nyri guessed he had appointed himself first watch. She hesitated for a moment, unsure of her welcome. She hated that it had come to this again and decided she wasn't going to allow the new distance between them to continue. She got up and resettled at his side. She did not presume to lean into him this time, however.

He tensed at her proximity, as though expecting a tirade. Guilt swept through Nyri for her earlier unguarded reaction. "Don't," she said. "I am not here to judge you. I am sorry, Juaan."

"What for, Nyri? You had every right to look at me as you did. Sakal has no doubt been regaling you with tales of my past deeds and why you should not trust me. And she would be right."

Nyri sighed, rubbing her forehead tiredly. "She lost her

mate and children in a raid led by you."

Juaan's breath hitched, and Nyri felt him curl deeper into himself.

"Juaan." Nyri reached out to touch his arm, ignoring him when he tried to pull away. "I know you would never have killed those babies yourself. Even as Khalvir, you were above committing such horrors."

"Still, I was there leading them. If I hadn't…"

"Eldrax would just have sent someone else," Nyri cut him off. "Someone who might have allowed more bloodshed under their leadership."

Juaan let out a humourless chuckle. "I do not deserve the faith you place in me, Nyriaana."

"Yes, you do, and I will remind you of it every day until—" she cut herself off. How many days did she have left?

This time, he was the one to pull her into his side, gripping her shoulder. "Nyriaana, what are you not telling me?"

The vision of lights, pain and darkness flew through her mind, and Nyri tensed. "I-I don't know. Nothing is clear." She swiftly changed the subject. "What happened back at the copse? Whose was that grave?" She had wanted to distract him, but instantly regretted the question. Perhaps Juaan had been the one to kill that Thal. Another torment.

"My mother travelled through these hills," he said. "This is where she fled with me after the destruction of my father's clan."

Shock rippled through Nyriaana. "How do you know that?"

He shrugged against her. "Snatches of memory, half-forgotten feelings of fear. Something happened in that copse. I was there and my mother was in agony." He stopped and stared hard in the opposite direction, his jaw working.

"Juaan," Nyri wrapped her arms around his waist as far as they would go.

"What she must have gone through to protect me," he said. "What they both suffered."

"Both?"

Juaan rolled the spear laid across his lap. "Upon her death, mother spoke to me of a Thal who had helped her. She said this Thal vowed to be my *tarhe*. Protector mother. That is a scared vow in Thal tradition. The grave was hers. This spear was hers."

Nyri stared at the weapon with fresh eyes in the darkness. "And so those markings on the stone…?" The answer fell into place faster than Juaan could answer, the reason a Ninkuraaja mark had been present among the Thal runes.

"Were made by my mother," he finished for her.

Nyri could not speak, her thoughts getting lost in another time. She imagined Rebaa fleeing through these hills alone. Juaan's mother had been a braver woman than she.

"Eldrax murdered her." Juaan's sudden growl made Nyri flinch. "If I kill one more person in what life is left to me, it will be him," he vowed. "I will exact my vengeance for everything he has taken from me. From all those that I loved."

The hairs on the back of Nyri's neck rose as she felt the power inside Juaan build, his anger and hatred thinning the bindings that kept it trapped.

"Shhh." She took his hand, radiating soothing energy through their contact. "Juaan, don't. Eldrax is most likely dead. The Watchers would have ripped him to pieces."

The prowling monster within quieted at her touch, tamed

371

for the moment. Nyri's brow pinched together, wondering how easy it would be to control once the River Line of the Mountains was directly beneath their feet. She shunned the fear. She did not wish for him to question the wisdom of his presence on this journey any more than he already did if he detected her apprehension. She could not lose him.

"He escaped them once before," Juaan reminded her.

"Then he would have to be extremely fortunate to escape a second time," she said. "Juaan, don't think about him." *I need you.* She had no idea whether he caught the last thought in her head.

"I'll try," he said. "If you try to sleep. Sakal is right. After tonight, who knows when we will rest again."

Nyri swallowed. Giving comfort to Bahari and Juaan had distracted her from her own fear of what was to come once Ninmah climbed back into the sky. "I…I don't think I can," she said.

"You must," a whispered voice said. Both Nyri and Juaan turned to find Sakal standing behind them. "Once we enter the Forests, we will be relying on you to know the way."

Nyri's breath hitched. She had not thought it was possible, but Sakal's words doubled the terror she was experiencing. Once they entered the forest, she would be the leader. Juaan tightened his arm.

"Sakal," he warned.

"Here," Sakal jabbed a small leather pouch at Nyri.

"What's in this?" Nyri asked uncertainly.

"Herbs," Sakal said. "Swallow them with your water. Believe me, they work." And with that, she walked back to her resting place.

Nyri opened the pouch and sniffed. The scent was heady

and powerful. She recognised the distinctive scent of some of the herbs as those Baarias used to use.

"You don't have to take them," Juaan said. But the promise of an escape, of a dreamless sleep, was too much for Nyriaana to resist. She pinched some herbs from the bag and placed them on her tongue before snatching Juaan's water skin and swallowing them down. Replacing the plug, she dropped the water skin and leaned back into Juaan's side, staring up into Ninsiku's eye. She didn't even remember closing her eyes.

It was in the pre-light of dawn when Sakal came to shake Nyri awake. Blinking, she sat up, feeling the chill of the night settling over her bones as the fur that had been laid over her fell away. Bahari and Juaan were already dividing the supplies between them: food, weapons, and the extra furs for travelling in the snowy heights of the Mountains themselves.

Nobody spoke as their breath curled in the pre-dawn air. Nyri was glad of the silence. Her throat was so thick with dread, she wasn't sure she could have answered had her companions asked something of her. This time, Juaan took point as they set off on the last stretch of the journey that would lead them into the trees. In the centre of the group, Nyri kept her eyes down, hiding from the sight of the ever-looming treeline. Memories of what she had seen and felt the last time she had ventured inside mired her thoughts in inescapable horror.

No! she wanted to cry out. *Turn back. I was mistaken. Please, let's go back.* But she could not. The words lodged in her throat, a force greater than herself keeping them trapped within. Invisible tethers dragged her forward.

It seemed like forever and yet no time at all when she heard Juaan mutter the words: "We are here."

Now Nyri did look up. The black trees hung above her head, their branches reaching for her like ensnaring claws. The energy radiating from the Forest threatened to crush her soul beneath its tangled roots.

"Keep close," Juaan whispered to the group. "Make as little sound as you can. Disturb nothing. If I say run, obey me without question."

Nyri glanced at Sakal. But, though she scowled, the Eagle woman held her silence. Nothing was to be gained by arguing.

Nyri watched as Juaan drew a breath, hesitated as he tested his control, and then stole forward, the gloom of the trees swallowing him whole like a vast carnivorous creature. If it hadn't been for the sight of Juaan disappearing inside, Nyri wasn't sure she could have moved forward, but her fear of letting Juaan out of sight was stronger than her fear for herself.

And so, Nyri entered the Forest of the Nine Gods.

The stench hit her like a fist, just as it had before. The stale smell of death and decay seeped from the black mud itself, cloying. And the sound, or the lack thereof, pressed down on her ears. Not even the rustle of a bird could be detected. The sound of her own breathing felt like it could be heard all the way to the unseen mountain tops above, and for a moment she cut off her air flow.

Bahari came next. He blinked as his eyes adjusted to the gloom. Nyri could not help but notice that his rich dark skin had paled considerably. This place made the bravest of men tremble.

Juaan was already several strides ahead of them, his spear held in a ready position at his side. Nyri hurried to catch up, drawing comfort from Bahari and Sakal at her back. She had never expected to feel so when it came to the Eagle woman.

The stillness was unnatural as they travelled. Nyri's mind was quick to supply the movement it imagined should be there. She started and flinched at nothing more than once.

"Will you stop!" Sakal snapped at her.

"Shhh!" Juaan hissed from up ahead.

Time soon lost all meaning. Ninmah travelled unseen above the thick, twisting branches. They could have been walking for days and they would not have known it.

"How long until we're free?" Bahari asked. There was a note of desperation that Nyri had never heard in his voice before. "Should be through by now. We going in circles!"

"Steady, Bahari," Juaan breathed. "We are going straight. Feel the incline under your feet. We are travelling up."

"Where do you think the Watchers are?" Sakal asked.

"Well, if there is any kind of benevolent power in this world, pray to it that they are not in this part of the Forest," Juaan responded.

Nyri tripped on a rock jutting from the earth. She gasped as she steadied herself. The stone was angular and flat, with straight sides and corners. She had never before seen such a rock. This was the first stone they had encountered since entering the Forest, she realised. Until now, only gnarled roots had broken the monotony of the ground.

"Keep moving, Nyri," Bahari murmured, placing a hand on her back.

The strange stone was the first, but not the last. Footing became treacherous as the way became clogged with more and more of the strange sand-coloured rocks, jutting from the black earth that was in the process of swallowing them. Nyri had to keep all of her attention on her feet to avoid turning an ankle as she scrambled over the rough terrain. Then, quite abruptly, the ground evened out. The sucking mud disappeared and Nyri stumbled onto a hard surface.

"By Eron!" Bahari breathed.

Juaan had stopped. From behind him, Nyri stared at the clearing opening out before them. Under her sodden, fur-covered feet, the ground was now made up entirely of rock, but not as she had ever seen it. The stones were not random, scattered, differing in size, nor were they the solid unbroken bedrock of the earth. These rocks were flat, interlocked, fitting together perfectly in a pattern that stretched away from her until they ended against a pile of stone. It was not natural. Nor was the pile of stone. Same as the strange ground, these stones were flat with angular sides, fitting together so perfectly as they rose from the ground that Nyri doubted she'd be able to pass a leaf through them. The formation ran the body length of three men before crumbling away into the encroaching forest on either side.

"What is this place?" Sakal breathed, stooping to run her hands over the perfectly flat, patterned ground, then on to study the vertical stones on the far side.

"It is a place for the gods," Bahari hissed. "We should not be here. It is not for us. We anger them further. Jade Killer, we must go."

Juaan appeared inclined to agree with him. "Sakal," he called softly. But the warrior woman was not listening. She was transfixed by the stones on the far side of this strange clearing. "Sakal." Juaan strode over to where she stood. Nyri and Bahari stayed close on his heels. Bahari kept his spear cocked as he watched their backs. "Sakal, what…" Juaan's voice cut off, and Nyri moved to see what had caught his attention.

Into the flat stones, pictures had been carved. Nyri caught her breath. She had seen Thal drawings inside the caves they called home, but these images had been hewn into the stones with precise and lifelike detail.

Nyri struggled to make sense of them.

"It is the story of the gods," Sakal said. Her voice was not reverent, nor awed. It was grim and filled with bitterness.

The gods. Nyri studied the pictures again as understanding dawned. In the highest image, there were beings. Nine of them. They appeared like humans, but their bodies were stretched, elongated. The rays of Ninmah shone above their heads. Their cold faces were cruel, sharp and long like the rest of them.

Nyri's eyes travelled down to the next row of carvings. Three of the beings appeared to be working around a symbol made up of a straight, vertical line. Two other lines twisted around it. Nyri became uncomfortably aware that her three companions were now staring openly at her forehead. Her hand went to rub at the mark of the Ninkuraaja between her brows. It was a perfect match. She flicked her eyes to the next image where two of the strange creatures stood, their long arms cradled around their bellies. Inside their protective embrace, two infants were curled.

"It is the gods giving birth to us. Look." Sakal pointed and, on yet another level of pictures, the three beings were now surrounded by others whose hands were raised towards them. The limbs and bodies of these new beings were in natural proportion, dwarfed by the tall, stretched-out creatures that they appeared to worship.

"Their faith was misplaced." Sakal ran her hands along a stone further down the rock formation. Humans, on their knees, toiled in the earth with tools Nyri could not name in their hands, as the beings looked down on them coldly, watching from ledges above with pitiless eyes.

A sick feeling took hold in the pit of Nyri's stomach, the images bringing to mind the Dugnamtar's tales of the gods and human beginnings at the Hunting Bear campfire. The tales she had denied as Wove lies now stood carved in stone before her. All this time, she had desperately clung to the belief that, while Ninmah's teachings may have become twisted over the generations, there had still been a grain of truth in what she had been taught, that her People's suffering had not been entirely in vain. These stones snuffed out that final hope. Nothing she had ever believed in was the truth. Silent tears of anger and despair slipped down her cheeks to splash on the smooth stones below.

When her eyes reached the lowest carvings of the Peoples being massacred and devoured, running for their lives while cradling babies in their arms, Nyri could take no more. She turned her back on the images, burying her face in her hands.

"What lies are these?" Bahari jabbed at the stones with his spear in a sudden rage. His fear and confusion raged against Nyri's senses, echoing against her own more muted emotions. Living with the Cro, Nyri's childhood teachings of Ninmah had already been challenged time and again over many cycles of Ninsiku. She had become somewhat numbed to this final breaking of faith. For Bahari, bound by the Thal tradition of unwavering loyalty to Eron, this was all fresh. "It's not true!" he cried.

"Bahari!" Sakal hissed. "You are only seeing what the Cro have known since the Great Winter of Sorrow. The gods are evil. They made us to serve and to suffer."

"Stop!" Bahari was now pointed at the Eagle woman. "It was the Cro with their *ikkibu* young that angered them!" He glared at Juaan and Sakal, both the issue of two Peoples. "Your fault!"

"THE LORD OF THE SKY JUST WANTS PEACE FROM YOUR UNREST."

Nyri's heart stopped beating. The voice rumbled from all around, shaking the air, vibrating her bones. Only now, too late, did she realise the stench that had smothered her senses since entering the forest had grown stronger.

"HE JUST WANTS PEACE."

Glowing blue eyes opened. Towering over the strange stones, the Watcher glared down at them.

"Run." Nyri heard Juaan whisper, then louder he cried: "Run!"

The warning came too late. A great hand shot out of the trees, snatching Sakal from the ground.

"No!" Nyriaana screamed, as her companion was yanked into the darkness. She tried chasing after the Eagle woman, Sakal's cries of defiance ringing in her ears, but Juaan caught her by the arm.

"Nyri, run, run!"

"No! Sakal!"

The sound of crunching bone and rending flesh assaulted

them as the clearing was sprayed with blood. The droplets peppered Nyri's horrified face as Sakal's howls cut off. Another loud crunch and Sakal's headless body smashed back to earth upon the smooth rocks.

"THE LORD ENLIL ONLY WANTS YOU GONE." The Watcher pushed its way from the trees, its mouth dripping red. In its hand, it wielded an axe that shone and gleamed with a strange light. "WE WILL WIPE TIAMAT CLEAN OF YOUR INFESTATION."

Juaan pushed Nyri aside. "Nyri, run!" he screamed at her. "Go! Now!" Nyri could feel the wild power inside him building, clawing its way loose as the Watcher lumbered closer. "Nyri, please!"

"Bahari!" Nyri could not see the Cro man. "Bahari!"

And then he was there, flying through the air towards the Watcher from the tree he had scaled. His spear was extended as he landed upon the creature's shoulders, and he plunged it down through the Watcher's throat.

The Watcher roared as Bahari twisted his weapon with one hand while plunging his stone hunting knife repeatedly into the Watcher's exposed jugular with the other, severing the pathways of life. Blood spewed from the wounds as the Watcher staggered, swiping wildly over its shoulders with its gleaming weapon, cutting at its own flesh in its need to rid itself of its bane.

Nyri thought she heard Bahari scream. Then he was flung loose, disappearing into the trees amid a snapping of branches as the Watcher crashed to its knees, Bahari's spear still protruding from its throat.

Juaan snarled, darting in as it bowed forward to drive his own spear up through one glowing eye and into its head, killing it outright. He yanked his weapon free and danced back before the monster dropped to the ground at his feet.

Silence reigned.

Nyri stood, immobile. She could not have moved had she wanted to. Her mind could not catch up as she stared at the droplets of blood caught on her furs.

"Bahari," Juaan called. "Bahari?"

The name returned some feeling to Nyriaana's limbs, and she awoke, stumbling in the direction the Cro man had been hurled, following the path of broken branches. Juaan ghosted her heels. "Bahari!"

At first, there was no answer and then: "Nyriaana." The voice was so weak, at first she did not recognise it as Bahari's. Then she saw him, lying against the base of a tree.

"Bahari." Nyri rushed forward, but slewed to a halt at the sight that met her eyes. In his one hand, Bahari still held his hunting knife. His other was not to be seen. Only a bleeding stump remained, cradled against his blood soaked furs. His eyes fluttered as he struggled to remain conscious.

"No, Bahari." Nyri moaned as she fell to her knees at his side. "You should have run! Why didn't you just run?"

"I-I'm *magiri*," he strained out. "The unsubmissive…" Tremors ran all over his body as Nyri watched. His teeth began to chatter.

"Juaan," Nyri reached back, snatching the bundle of extra furs from his shoulder and piling them around Bahari. "Stay with me," she demanded, feeling the same desperate determination that had filled her when Juaan had lain dying from the wounds inflicted by Eldrax: the day she had rediscovered her healing powers. She would not lose Bahari, too. Wrapping her hand around the remains of his left arm,

Nyri plunged all of her concentration into saving the Cro man.

Nyri felt a rush as she summoned the energy of the Great Spirit. With the River Line of the Mountains almost directly beneath them, the power that flowed to her fingertips was intoxicating. She became connected to this abominable forest, with all its malevolent energy.

And it was just as keenly aware of her.

Nyri's concentration faltered as the attention of many unseen eyes all turned in her direction at once. By healing Bahari, she had alerted the rest of the Watchers to their position. Their murderous intent smothered her senses.

Nyri gritted her teeth. In using her power, she was drawing them in, but she could not stop. Not yet. Pouring the raw energy of the Mountain into Bahari, she pinched and knitted together his life pathways, skin and sinew, closing off the stump of his severed hand.

"Nyri…" Juaan growled. He could feel them, too.

"Almost," she hissed. And then it was done. She released the energy quickly, concealing her presence once more. She only hoped she had been fast enough.

Nyri opened her eyes and looked down at her work. Bahari's arm was healed, but she could never replace his hand. No one had the power to do that. Her tears fell on his furs.

"We must go," she hitched out. "The other Watchers know we are here now. They are coming."

"Th-then you must go." Bahari pushed her away with his remaining hand.

Nyri caught and grasped at it. "You are coming with us!"

Bahari shared a loaded glance with Juaan, who took hold

of Nyri's shoulders.

"I will only be hindrance now." Bahari lifted the stump of his arm with a grimace. "Go with Juaan. Find magic being to save your People."

"I will not leave you here to die!" Nyri pulled on Bahari's furs.

Bahari's lips lifted in a ghost of his old smile. "No, you gifted me life. Not intend to waste it. I go back to my People now. Tell them the truth. You go."

"He is right, Nyriaana," Juaan spoke in her ear. "This is the best way. Let him return to his People. The Thals deserve to know what is coming."

Nyri choked on tears as Juaan leaned down, catching Bahari by his good wrist and pulling him to his feet, steadying him as Bahari swayed for a moment before finding his balance. "Good luck, brother," he said, handing him a weapon. Only now did Nyri notice that Juaan had retrieved Bahari's spear from the creature who had claimed his hand. "Thank you. For everything."

Bahari dipped his chin once. "I hope we meet again, Jade… Wolf."

Nyri could not speak. She threw her arms around Bahari, only able to let go when he himself broke the hold. "Go, Nyriaana," he said.

Juaan caught her by the wrist and pulled her along in his wake, giving her no choice but to follow. She kept her eyes upon Bahari to the last. The Cro man raised his hand in farewell, just as the trees stole him from her sight.

Somewhere in the far distance, the Watchers howled.

21

Surrender

70,000 BCE (The onset of the Great Winter of Sorrow)

The earth shook beneath Ninmah's feet as another volcanic eruption ripped through the crust, spewing burning mantle and choking dust into the already polluted air.

This small island in the stars that she had come to love lay in ruins, the warmth of its sun blocked out by the destruction their war with Enlil had wrought.

And for what? She and Enki had lost. She had failed in her mission to destroy the energy source planted deep beneath the mountains, the energy that powered all of their technology; tools, weapons. Ninmah had failed and Enlil had almost fulfilled his promise. The Lullu Amelu, in all their forms, had been reduced to all but nothing. Only four of the nine strains of man that Ninmah and Ningishizidda had created were still clinging to life. The other five had already succumbed, culled by Enlil or choked to death on the changes his weapons had wrought on this world. If they did not stop fighting, her beloved Ninkuraaja would also cease to exist.

Numb, Ninmah flicked her fingers over the device on her wrist. She did not have to wait long. Enlil's face appeared over her hand.

"Ninmah," he greeted coolly.

"I surrender, Lord Enlil. This destruction can stop."

A triumphant smile curled over his face before his image flickered out. Ninmah sank to her knees. Reaching out, she took a handful of the now barren earth, then let it slide through her fingers, watching it billow away in the rising wind. She closed her eyes. There was a flash of light. When she opened them again, Enlil stood before her, several of his Nephilim at his back.

"Your surrender tastes almost as sweet as Enki's will. The Snake is about to fall."

Ninmah gazed up at him from where she knelt. Ignoring his gloating, she said, "I give myself to you willingly, Lord of the Sky, and will stand for judgement as you wish. I just beg you, let the remaining Lullu Amelu live. They did not ask for their creation."

Enlil sneered. "Take her." He waved the Nephilim forward.

Ninmah made no fight as the Igigi's monstrous offspring bound her hands behind her back and pulled her to her feet. "Enlil, please."

"Beg for them all you will. It is already too late." Enlil gestured to the polluted skies and ruined landscape. "You shortened their life spans and made them vulnerable to sickness. I will not even have to lift a finger. Safely stripped of our knowledge and technologies, they are no more than the animals you created them from. They will not survive the global cooling that is to come. They are weak."

At this, Ninmah's chest filled with a fierce, motherly pride.

"They are more than you believe. Naanshi will come and show them the way. The Lullu Amelu will become strong once again without you, without us."

Enlil's glowing blue eyes bored into hers as he laughed. "No. I have weighed and measured their worth. While you rot in confinement, awaiting judgement from An, I will be watching them, and I will enjoy seeing them fail."

* * *

38,000 BCE

Juaan kept a tight hold of Nyriaana's wrist as he ran through the tangle of trees, ducking and weaving around the hanging branches. He had to put as much distance between them and the encroaching Watchers as he could.

He only hoped Bahari was doing the same.

They were there in the distance, holes of nothingness moving through the Great Spirit enraging the monster inside him. If it hadn't been for Bahari killing that beast when he did, Juaan knew he would have lost control there in the clearing. He could have killed Nyriaana. Juaan would not risk facing another Watcher. His legs burned, his old wounds ached and tugged, but he continued to run.

Through his awakening senses, he knew Nyri was in shock. She had not witnessed many battles and the sudden, irreversible loss of brothers in arms was not something she was accustomed to. He grieved for her, wishing he had been more alert and saved her from the horror. Fighting against the monster inside was dulling his senses to other threats.

Juaan did not know how long their flight through the murk and mud lasted until the pressure of the Watchers' presence receded from the edges of his awareness. The monster quieted and Juaan let out a breath of relief.

Nyri was at the end of her endurance. A deep hollow under the roots of a tree caught Juaan's attention, and he pulled them down into it. Nyri collapsed against him as he sank to the earth and out of sight. She was trembling, her breath hitching in her chest as she battled to steady herself. Juaan put his arms around her, holding her in a ball to keep her warm and the shock at bay. "Shhh, shhh, it's alright," he whispered. "It's alright."

"S-Sakal," she forced out between chattering teeth. "I-it ripped her apart. She shouldn't have come! This is all my fault!"

"No, Nyri. Sakal was a warrior who made her own choice. Her death is not on your hands."

"I brought us here, a-and I don't even know wh-what I am doing, Juaan. Following visions and the promise to a dead Kamaali. I-I'm losing my mind. If I lose you, too," her voice broke off. "Take me back, Juaan. I want to go back. I-I can't do this."

"Nyri, no. You would not have made it this far if some part of you did not believe it to be right. You are meant to be here. I know it." And, in that moment, Juaan knew his words were more than just an empty comfort. He had not been privy to the visions that so plagued her, but as Nyri herself doubted, something whispered inside his heart that this place was where she was meant to be.

And not just Nyri. Him as well. The monster inside calmed further.

"I do not deserve y-your faith in me."

Juaan twitched a smile into her hair. "Yes, you do. You have had it since the day I met you, and I will remind you of it every day until the Great Spirit takes me, or until you believe it. Whichever comes first."

Another wave of tears as she wrapped her arms around his waist and just clung there.

"D-do you think Bahari escaped?"

"Bahari is a cunning and skilled warrior. He is a survivor. I am certain we will see him again."

A wave of grief passed through the girl in his arms, but this time, the tenor of it was different. It was separate from her sadness and shock over losing Sakal. He frowned, filled once more with the certainty that there was something Nyri was not telling him. He would not press, however. She was already near the breaking point. She would confide in him when she was ready. Ninmah knew he did not like being forced to speak before he was ready. Juaan rested his chin on her head and let her move through her shock as she needed.

Somewhere in the world outside, it began to rain. Juaan could hear the faint rush of the water on the forest canopy, and the drips of moisture that made it through splashed on the damp mud below.

Lulled by the sound, Nyri soon fell asleep. Juaan saw no reason to prevent her. He could detect no immediate threat in the area. Her mind needed the escape to recover from the ordeal she had just experienced.

Juaan closed his eyes, amazed that even in the midst of this hell, with Nyri cradled against him, he felt nothing but complete.

Warm lips pressing hard against his woke Juaan with a start.

"Nyri," he gasped, startled. He had no idea how much time had passed. The darkness outside their hollow was unchanging. But at some point, Nyri had woken and was now lying full length against him. The numb shock had disappeared and a storm of emotions had swept in to fill the void. Juaan felt them burn through her. Confusion, desperation, pain, need. "Nyri. What are you doing?"

"I don't know," she whispered against his chin. "I don't know what I am doing. All I am certain of is that I love you, Juaan. And if we are to die today, I want you to know that. I want you to know I have always loved you more than anything else under Ninmah."

Her arms went about his neck as she kissed him again; clumsy, uncertain, the first intimate act of an UnClaimed girl.

And Juaan was lost, all of his barriers breaking down. As a child, he had loved Nyriaana more than his own life. Since meeting her again, those feelings had only grown, morphing into those a man felt for a woman. He had given up on any hope that she could ever want him the same way, beyond the love of friendship, beyond the bond of family. But she did.

His heart soared, galloping in response to her advance, but still, he hesitated. Juaan pulled his mouth away from hers. He had to know this was truly what she wanted, and not a survivor's reaction to the trauma she had just suffered. "Are you sure?" he breathed. "I am not Ninkuraaja, Nyriaana. I am Forbidden."

She laughed as tears spilled down her face. "Juaan! What does that matter? After all we have witnessed, why should we care what the gods deem a heresy? I do not care. Not anymore. You are all that matters." The last words were bitten out with a fierce vehemence and she pulled herself as close as she could while they were still dressed in furs, wrapping her legs around his waist. "I do not want Eldrax's touch to be the last I remember. Drown him out."

Juaan let out a low moan as she captured his lips again, the heat from her body seeping through his coverings. A part of his mind screamed that this was not the moment or the place to finally express his love for her, but he ruthlessly quashed it. He had been with women before, but this was different. This was not a command by a ruthless Chief. His senses were not distorted by vision water. This was like breathing air. This was home.

He slipped a hand through a gap in her furs, sliding his palm along the smooth skin at her flank. "Nyriaana," he murmured, and he felt her quiver, a throaty sound escaping her lips at the feel of his hand upon her bare flesh. He nuzzled her throat, kissing his way up to her chin...

And then he was looking straight into her eyes, wide open and burning.

Indigo eyes.

It all happened very fast. It was no longer Nyriaana sitting before him. The eyes he stared into were those of the unnamed Ninkuraaja woman Eldrax had forced him upon; scared, in pain, and flaming with untold hatred. And ultimately dead. Killing herself and the half-breed child inside her, just like his seed had killed all the others Eldrax had brought before him.

"No!" Juaan threw her off and leapt to his feet. Leaning against the inside of the tree, he buried his face in his hands as the vision slowly dissipated, leaving behind cold hard reality. He groaned. How could he be expected to drown out her ghosts when he could not even escape his own?

"Juaan?" Nyri's voice was thick with hurt and shame. "I…I am sorry. I thought… I'm sorry."

Juaan's heart contracted, knowing how she would have interpreted his rejection. Pushing his memories down as deep as they would go, he mastered the tremors shivering through his body and knelt at her side. "No," he said, taking her hands. She tried to pull away, but he held on to her. "Nyriaana, listen to me. Before we travel another step, I want you to know you are the most important part of my life. You always have been. It is a gift beyond anything I deserve to know I have somehow Claimed your heart. It's just—" He broke off, losing courage.

"You do not love me the same way?" The agony pinching across her face was more than he could bear. "You wanted me as Khalvir. But not as Juaan?"

More so. He swallowed, the words that would take that pain away lodging in his throat. "I can't." His voice cracked. He could not lie to her. She had to know how broken he was. Reaching up, he touched his fingers to the skin beneath her eyes. "Nyri. These eyes. The last time I looked into eyes like yours in such a moment…" He choked again, bowing his head.

There was a long pause. Juaan could almost hear her mind turning, the stories he had once told her of what he had done under Eldrax's orders clicking into place. His cheeks burned, but he should have known she would never push him away. Her hand tightened around his, the other found his cheek before she ducked down and curled herself against him again. "What have they done to us?" she murmured brokenly as the rain continued to drip around them.

Juaan returned her embrace in silence. All he could do was exist with her in this moment shattered by past horror. But it could not last for long. He pressed his lips to her forehead. "We need to move."

She said nothing, but he felt her head dip in agreement before she pushed herself away from him and stood straight. Her face, thinned and carved out by grief and hardship, cut at his heart. He hoped there was some meaning to all of this, a reason for her suffering.

Juaan raised himself to his own feet. Shouldering his *tarhe*'s spear, he took Nyri by the hand and ducked out of the hollow, feeling the incline as the Forest climbed slowly into the Mountains.

The River Line of the Great Spirit pulsed beneath his feet, stronger than Juaan had ever felt. His Ninkuraaja senses, always dulled and tethered when not in proximity to these crisscrossing veins of energy, were now fully awake, unfettered. He could *feel* everything; the shifts in the atmosphere, the whispers of communication through the roots of the trees beneath his feet. He had experienced similar sensations under Nyri's guidance when he dwelt in the Pit within the *shin'ar* forest, but the River Line that ran beneath the territory of the Ninkuraaja paled in comparison to the power of the vein that ran beneath the Mountains of the Nine Gods.

Juaan struggled to keep his mind focused, but the growing influx of sensation was overwhelming. He wondered if this was what a Ninkuraa lived with every day. The fear of the beast inside him was a constant companion. Should he lose control of his emotions now, he knew there would be nothing to prevent the monster inside from destroying everything around him. The last thread of its tether had dissolved.

Juaan kept his breathing even, his thoughts on his feet, the feel of Nyri's hand in his. He had to get them free of this Forest and its nightmarish guardians. But once they were in the Mountains, what then? Had Nyri's visions shown her where they needed to go to find this Last Kamaali of hers? Juaan's faith in Nyriaana was absolute, but he couldn't help but wonder how a Ninkuraaja had come to dwell in the Mountains of the Nine Gods. The Mountain range was vast, and finding a single being amongst the peaks would be impossible without knowing where to start.

He hesitated, debating whether to ask Nyri to share more of what she had seen, anything that might give them a direction. He knew her visions frightened her, but if they were to find this Last Kamaali, he needed to know more.

Juaan had just opened his mouth to broach the subject when a chill crawled up his spine, causing the hairs on the back of his neck to stand on end. Nyri's fingers stiffened in his. She felt it too.

They were being watched.

"Juaan," her whisper was barely a breath. "They're here."

Juaan jerked his chin, letting her know he was aware.

"H-how?"

He could not answer. He only knew one thing. They were surrounded. He had witnessed Nyri hide her presence when she had most needed to, blending her energy into the surrounding landscape. It appeared the Watchers had the same ability, camouflaging themselves into this Forest they guarded. They had walked right into a trap.

No matter in which direction Juaan stepped, the blank presence of a Watcher pressed down on his senses. He hissed between his teeth, his hand tightening on Nyri's as his own monster flexed in response inside him.

The Watchers were still, keeping unseen, waiting to see what their prey would do next. Juaan gripped his *tarhe's* spear. There was only one way this could end. Nyri was the one who needed to reach the Mountains, not him. If she could hide her presence, if he could keep the beasts distracted long enough for her to get away, then he would achieve what he had come here to do. *This* was why she had needed him. This was as far as he went. Despair pulsed through Juaan's heart. He hadn't told her. He had had his chance, and he hadn't told her. Now all his chances were passed. She would go on never knowing. He just hoped she could make it on her own. She had to. She was strong.

"Follow the incline into the Mountains," he told her, keeping the grief from his voice. "I will keep them occupied for as long as I can."

With his heightened awareness, he felt the violence of her denial. "Juaan, no!"

He turned and pulled her against him, kissing her fiercely. "Nyri, Nyri, Nyriaana," he murmured against her lips. He hoped it was enough for her to understand. Their time was up. He was shaking with the effort to keep the beast within restrained. "You have to go, now."

"No!"

"Nyri!" He threw her back away from him as far as he could get her. "Go! Get away from here. Please!" The intent of the Watchers shifted. He spun to face them, letting loose a threatening snarl as he took hold of his spear in both hands. The carvings below the tip filled his vision. Thal marks of protection. If they held any secret magic, he needed it now.

Juaan.

Juaan's head snapped around. The voice had not been Nyri's.

Juaan

A familiar flash of red flickered through the trees to his right. She was here. Juaan did not question. Releasing one hand from the spear, he ran to where Nyri still hesitated, snatching her hand into his own as he bolted, chasing the ghost of red hair flickering through the trees ahead of him.

His flight triggered the unseen Watchers. Blood-curdling bellows tore through the trees as they charged, ripping the trunks from their path. How many, Juaan could not guess, too many. The energy inside lashed against his will, his flight-or-fight instincts battling to take over conscious thought as the monsters closed in.

Where, where? Then he saw her. His *tarhe* was waiting for him between two trees, as insubstantial as the wind, but as vital as the ground beneath his feet. Her black eyes locked on his for a brief instant before she vanished.

Juaan raced to the point where she had disappeared. A hole yawned in the ground. It was exactly like the one he and Rannac had escaped into the night he had killed the beast that had threatened Nyriaana and Kyaati. The pounding of giant feet shook the ground. Juaan did not hesitate as the black maw opened out before him. He leapt into oblivion, bringing Nyri behind him, just as the first hand snatched out to grab them.

* * *

22

Alliance

Coiled upon a fallen log, Daajir watched as the rest of the tribe gathered supplies, their Wove enemies at their sides, bundling together food and *haala* nuts filled with his precious invention. The poison for which he had worked so hard and sacrificed so much, now being handed over to the demons it had been created to destroy.

The betrayal was more than he could bear.

Kyaati. Daajir's lips peeled back off his teeth as he caught a flash of her silver hair. The Woves had put her under the influence of their dark magic, violated a sacred Daughter of Ninmah, and kept her alive in order to subvert the rest of the Divine Mother's loyal followers. To destroy them at last, as per Ninsiku's plan.

He had not allowed her to touch him. He had pretended to go along with this heresy to keep himself free of her polluting influence. He was disgusted by the rest of his People, a long Fury and the loss of a few of their number had been all it had taken to shake their faith in Ninmah.

Yes, none of the children had survived the cold and the deprivation, but more could be born. It was no excuse to fall into heresy.

The back of his head throbbed where the other traitor had attempted to kill him. *Nyriaana.* A weakened Baarias had possessed just enough energy to save his life, but, contending with his own wounds, the *akaab* had not had the power to heal Daajir fully. His skull still ached whenever he was agitated.

One of the Woves was now inspecting a blowpipe. A giant female with tawny hair and angled golden eyes. She peered down the length of it, assessing. Daajir snarled low in his throat. *Get your filthy hands off it!*

Unable to stomach the sight of the Woves any longer, he thrust himself to his feet and prowled off into the trees.

"Daajir." A voice called just loud enough for him to hear.

Aardn. Daajir turned in the direction of her voice. He found the Elder was waiting for him a short distance into the trees. He came to a halt a short distance from her, the person he respected more than anyone in existence. He would have followed Aardn into the jaws of Ninsiku's damnation. Her betrayal hurt most of all.

"So, are you ready to bring down the Cold One's demons once and for all?" The Elder spoke.

Daajir's brows leapt towards his hairline. A smile curled Aardn's mouth in the face of his surprise. "You," Daajir fumbled as the truth dawned, "you did not succumb to the lies, respected Elder?"

Aardn snorted. "Of course not, my dear Daajir. You know me to be stronger than that."

Daajir let his head fall back in praise to Ninmah. He had

hoped, but to hear it confirmed was like a beam of light cutting through the doubt in his heart. He wasn't alone. Aardn had resisted. "Then why did you make me give up my weapon?" he accused. "We should have fought, as Ninmah would have wanted."

"And wasted our lives in a futile battle? Daajir, if you are to be a leader to our People, you need to learn the art of patience and cunning. We now have the opportunity to finish this once and for all."

"How?"

Aardn shoved a blowpipe into Daajir's hands. "Go with Kyaati and her pet Woves. She will take you straight into the heart of their territory. Once there, you will be perfectly positioned."

"For what?"

Aardn gave him a pitying stare. "To cut off the head of Ninsiku's forces at last. Slaughter their leaders. Once they are dead, Ninsiku's hold will be broken. The golden days of old will be restored and Ninmah will return her favour to us."

Daajir's chest swelled. He was too overcome to respond. Aardn was entrusting this task to him. To be the one who ended Ninsiku's reign. He sank to his knees, finding his voice at last. "I will not fail you, Aardn," he said. Perhaps he would even cross paths with the Forbidden filth who had stolen Nyriaana away. A smile curled over Daajir's face at the thought of it. He had promised, after all.

"Go." Aardn waved him away. "May Ninmah shine upon you."

Daajir rose to his feet and went back to where the preparations were taking place, gripping the blowpipe

Aardn had given him tightly in his fist.

* * *

Three days later.

Galahir stood watching over his forces as Utu rose high overhead. In the days since he had left the Eagle camp, he had managed to double the strength of his numbers, collecting together the stray elements of clans already destroyed by the Watchers unleashed from the Forest. These were desperate men with nothing to lose, ready to lay down their lives in a fight to the death, for blood and vengeance against the ones who had taken their families from them.

Their fear and hatred of the Watchers and the looming threat of the gods had been enough for them to put aside old feuds and band together with their fellow men behind a new leader. Galahir.

Galahir shifted. The thought that the lives of these warriors were now in his hands was terrifying. Yatal's impulsive decision to name him Chief of the Eagle Clan still rocked him to his core. He did not know the first thing when it came to leadership. His first and only experience in leading a band of men, when Khalvir had been held prisoner within the *shin'ar* forest, had ended in humiliation. Doubt gnawed at Galahir's gut. He longed for Kyaati's fierce presence to give him strength.

Not for the first time, his eyes turned to the south, searching. With every day that passed, his fear for his mate and son increased.

"Will you stop staring at the horizon like a lost wolf-pup, *revered* Chief," Lorhir's voice came from beside him. "She has not been gone long enough for such old woman fears."

Rather than be rankled by Lorhir's prickly words, Galahir drew comfort from them. The whole world might have changed, but Lorhir had not. Galahir didn't suppose he ever would. But there had been a softening to Lorhir's insults. Galahir fancied they now sprang from the affection of familiarity, of, not friendship, but at least the long-standing bond of brotherhood. They had saved each other's lives on too many occasions now to remain true enemies and rivals. And Galahir had been the one to gift Lorhir the honour he had always desired. The leadership of the raknari.

"She promised to join you at this landmark whether she was successful in mustering the witches or not."

Galahir glanced at the distinctive outcrop of stones his forces had gathered around to rest and recuperate. Narak had claimed it to be a common meeting place for the Eagles on the hunt and he would lead Kyaati back to it after finding her People. Galahir hoped that Narak was right. He could not risk lighting a signal fire to draw the Eagle hunter in, for he may instead attract the attention of the horrors they hoped to avoid.

He and Lorhir had already discussed their plans with the other battle-bitten men of their company. When Kyaati and Narak caught up with them, they would return to the destroyed Hunting Bear camp. Galahir was not sure he had the stomach to face the remains of his previous life, but the defences that Eldrax had already put in place around the old camp would give them an advantage. Galahir just hoped that they had time to build on what Eldrax had begun. Nanna was almost at the full.

"I just need her back, Lorhir," he admitted. "Those beasts are loose and the witches are stubborn. They will look upon her as an outsider now. What if they decide to kill her for siding with us? What if—?"

"It would take a lot more than that to kill off that vicious vulture of yours," Lorhir cut him off. Galahir glared at him, but, to his surprise, Lorhir clapped him on the shoulder to soften the blow of his words. "She will return, Galahir."

Galahir nodded his appreciation of the other man's efforts to set him at ease, but he knew, until he looked into the face of his mate and his son once more, he would not know peace.

"Come, revered Chief," Lorhir turned from the southern horizon. "The scouts returned with the news that a herd of ox has been sighted. Now, do you want to lead a hunt and feed all these mouths, or continue to stand here wallowing?"

Despite himself, Galahir grinned. He hadn't tasted ox for many turns of Nanna. "Let's hunt!" Returning to the rest of his men, Galahir quickly chose ten of the strongest. It was more than he would usually take on a hunt, but an ox was a formidable foe and he could not risk any more of his men getting injured, nor losing the prize itself.

Many of the new joiners to the Eagle forces already bore crippling wounds, wounds inflicted when the Watchers wiped out their own clans. Despite Lorhir's insistence that they should not waste their already stretched supplies on unnecessary burdens, Galahir had been unable to leave them behind.

As Galahir led his chosen hunters out of the temporary camp, he passed by one such burden. The man wrapped in grey furs lay on the ground, the skin on his leg torn open from his groin to his knee. His breath came in tortured gasps as fevered sweat rolled from his brow. In his hand, he gripped an Elk totem.

"Will he make it?" Galahir murmured to the red-haired girl leaning over the wounded man.

Selima looked up. Galahir experienced an unpleasant thrill as he met those black eyes, eyes that so resembled her father's. There were many who had desired her death, the custom fate for the offspring of a feared enemy, but Galahir had not wanted to begin his life as Chief stained with this girl's blood. Instead, he had decided to keep her close, much to Kyaati and Kikima's displeasure. Now he was glad about that decision.

Selima might be a treacherous snake, but she was an intelligent female with an inventive and enquiring mind, showing great promise in the art of healing. It would have been a waste to put her to death. In Galahir's eyes, she far surpassed her stubborn old mentor, Johaquin. He might never trust her, but she was an asset to him now.

"I-I don't know," she answered his question. "I am applying the herbs and sap that will help keep curses at bay, but I have no gut with which to sew the flesh."

Galahir pressed his lips together in a grim line. "Do your best."

"Yes, my Chief." She lowered her eyes in a show of humility, all of her old swagger gone. Giving a nod to her ever watchful guard, Galahir continued to lead his hunters out onto the open Plains.

"The scouts saw the herd to the west," Lorhir said, pointing in a general direction. "Half a day's travel."

"Then let us begin."

Utu beat down upon the hunters from above, her rays of light the strongest Galahir had experienced in recent memory. Sweat soon began to slide down his back as they trekked over the rolling plains. He stripped off his upper furs, leaving his torso bare to the cooling breeze. Many of the other hunters did the same.

Utu was at her zenith when Galahir caught sight of the first warning and raised his fist, bringing the men to an abrupt halt. *Get down,* he signalled. He wasn't sure if they all understood Hunting Bear hand speak, but those that did not soon picked up on the meaning from the others.

"What is it?" Lorhir whispered, crouching at his side.

Galahir pointed, indicating the crushed grasses and scuffed rock before them. The tread that marred the ground had carried far too much weight to have been made by an ordinary man. A thin spattering of blood accompanied the tracks. He judged the trail to be half a day old.

"Watchers," Galahir said. The sight of blood unnerved him. He gestured to his hunters to stay low as he crept forward, bracing his heart for the sight of another massacred clan that was surely waiting.

"Ea above!" One of the men swore.

The herd of oxen lay before them. Or what was left of it. Great dark corpses littered the blood-soaked plain. Many of the dismembered body parts had large human-like bites ripped from them, the rest had been left to rot.

"They wiped out the whole herd," Lorhir said. "A whole

herd!"

"If they are slaughtering the herds as they migrate north, they mean to starve us," another voice spoke. "We are lucky to have beaten the worst of the scavengers! We need to take all we can before the flesh begins to fester."

Galahir hesitated, looking out at the killing field and the waiting piles of meat, there for the taking. A couple of vultures were already busy. Flashes of movement in the grass betrayed the jackals that were closing in, drawn by the scent of blood. Worse would soon follow. Only the scent of the Watchers had kept the scavengers at bay this long. Still, Galahir did not give the word as he weighed their need for meat against the risk that they could be walking into a trap.

"Split up," he said. "Search the perimeter. Make sure none of those beasts are lying in wait for an ambush." In wordless agreement, they divided their forces, Lorhir leading half the hunters in the opposite direction to Galahir's group.

"Nothing," Lorhir said when they met back in the middle.

Galahir made his decision. If he knew one thing about leadership, it was the importance of food. Hungry men lost faith in their leaders very quickly. He had to take the risk. And they needed to move fast. A howl sounded in the distance. Vultures and jackals they could chase away. A pack of wolves would not be so easy. "Gather as much as each man can carry. Be quick. Wolves might not be the worst returning for a feed."

Grim-faced, Galahir's hunters drew their cutting flints and began to butcher portions of meat from the slaughtered oxen, favouring haunches that could easily be slung over a shoulder.

Soon each of Galahir's men was laden with the dripping

portions, enough to feed their number for two turns of Nanna. Shouldering two haunches on his own, Galahir led them at a swift pace back towards the outcropping where he had left the bulk of his followers.

Utu was tilting towards the west behind them when at last Galahir spied the tall rocks marking the location of the camp. As they drew closer, a distinctive flash of silver caught his eye.

"Kyaati!" he cried. Forgetting the growing ache in his shoulders under his heavy load, Galahir sprinted the remaining distance to camp. "Kyaati!"

She had been occupied with a man seated on the ground before her, but turned at the sound of his voice, her glorious lavender eyes alight with the same joy he felt at their reunion.

Then she stiffened, her hand going to her face as she got her first real look at him. He got the impression she was covering a low oath. Galahir ground to a halt, frowning at her reaction, before his eyes lighted on the seven leaf-clan figures behind her. All witches, each with the same horror-struck expression frozen upon their fine, red-gold features.

Kyaati shifted, clearly wishing Galahir had appeared in any other state than the one he was currently in.

The man Kyaati had been stooping over when Galahir first appeared rose to his feet, standing at his mate's side. Elhaari was cradled in his arms.

"Galahir," Kyaati spoke, her voice uncharacteristically tremulous. "This is my father, Pelaan. Father, this is my *ankida* and Elhaari's father. Chief of the Eagle Clan."

The two haunches that had been perched on Galahir's

shoulders dropped to the ground with a loud thud. Galahir flushed, uncomfortably aware of the blood sliding down his bare chest and into the furs at his waist. One of the female witches passed out and was caught at the last moment by her nearest fellow. Pelaan's mouth dropped open.

Not knowing what else to do, Galahir hid his bloody hands behind his back and bowed his head in respect to his mate's father as the uncomfortable silence lengthened. "P-Pelaan," he said. "You and your People are very welcome here."

One of Pelaan's wide eyes twitched, but he managed to dip his chin once in acknowledgement.

"I, er, I'll just take these out of sight," Galahir mumbled, unable to escape fast enough as he grabbed the two oxen haunches and dragged them behind the nearest heap of rocks, where they would no longer cause offence. As the rest of the hunters caught up to him, he hastily directed them to do the same.

"The witches came." Lorhir's voice betrayed his surprise.

"Yes," Galahir hissed, "so don't go swallowing down anything once belonging to an animal directly in front of them if you can help it."

Lorhir snorted, eyeing the small group. "I will do as I please. They're in our territory now. They'll have to get used to our ways, same as your mate did. They look like they could do with a decent meal. I fail to see how such bags of skin and bone will be effective against a Watcher. More useless mouths to feed." He rolled his eyes. "Where are the rest of them?"

"I don't know," Galahir replied, watching Kyaati pass among them. He could see the unconscious tension in her shoulders as she tried to set her People at ease. An impossible task when all eyes were turned upon the witches, and the witches' eyes were in turn trained upon their former enemies.

"We will cook this meat in the morning," Galahir said to Lorhir, studying the fading light. "Fires only in the day. Once the supplies are cured, we will move on. We must reach the Hunting Bear camp before Utu sets again."

"As you wish, revered Chief." Lorhir stretched a mock bow.

Galahir ground his teeth together. "I'm going to bathe." He did not want to meet Kyaati's father again appearing as a blood-soaked savage. He made his way to the stream running not far from the camp and stripped the rest of the furs from around his waist before wading into the cold water. Galahir sighed as he lay down in the refreshing flow, letting the current wash the sticky sweat and blood from his body. Somewhere close by, a bird was singing. Focusing on the sweet music and nothing else, Galahir closed his eyes.

"Well, that could have gone better," a wry voice said.

Galahir sat up in a rush of water to see Kyaati standing upon the bank, a smile playing about her lips as her silver hair, the exact colour of Nanna, flowed across her shoulders in the breeze. As was usual when he looked at her, Galahir forgot to breathe for a moment. Forgot his own name. How had this unworldly creature become his?

It didn't matter. All that mattered was that she was.

He rose to his feet and stalked towards her.

Kyaati was quick to read his intention. "No! No, you don't!" But before she could escape, Galahir grabbed her around the waist and yanked her back down into the stream with him. Kyaati let out a shriek as the cold water sluiced over her in a tide.

Spitting and gasping, she swiped her dripping hair away from her face and glared at Galahir as he grinned. "You—!" And she swiped her arms, cascading another spray of water into Galahir's face.

Two could play at that game. Galahir flexed his arms, ready to cause a wave that would be a lot more impressive than hers. "No!" Kyaati cried again. Laughing, she splashed away from him as fast as the thigh-deep water would allow. Laughter bubbled from Galahir's own chest as he gave chase. In the midst of all this fear and uncertainty, he hadn't realised how much they had needed this.

Utu had sunk below the western horizon when he finally caught Kyaati around the waist and brought their game to a halt, breathless as he buried his face in her shoulder. "I've missed you," he murmured.

She wrapped her arms around him as far as they would go, letting him know without words that she felt the same way.

"I am sorry not all of your People would listen to you," he said.

He felt her tense. "These *are* all of my People," she murmured and, as clearly as if he were a witch, too, Galahir felt her light mood fade away.

"Oh, oh," he said. "I am sorry, Kyaati."

She tilted her head. "It is nobody's fault but the gods," she said, flint entering her voice. "The sooner we are free of them, the better."

Reality settled back over him and Galahir nodded against her head, stroking her wet hair.

"Kyaati?" She pulled away at the sound of her name. Pelaan stood upon the bank watching them. Elhaari was wailing lustily in his arms, making it clear what the problem was. Another younger, dark-haired male stood beside Kyaati's father. This one's eyes were fixed upon Galahir and Galahir felt a chill run up his spine, like he was caught in the gaze of a viper.

Kyaati disentangled herself from Galahir's embrace and waded back to shore. She lifted Elhaari from her father's arms and carried him away to a sheltered spot where she could feed him out of the cooling breeze. Galahir was relieved when the younger male released him from his piercing glare and followed her away.

Pelaan was still waiting upon the bank, however, when Galahir waded to the shore. He eyed the older witch male warily, trying to read his face and failing. He sighed. This impassive wall was something he had first encountered upon meeting Kyaati, and it had put him on the back foot then, too. After a time, he had come to recognise it for what it was. His mate wasn't without feeling. Elf-witches were simply so accustomed to sensing each other's meaning with their magic, they neglected to display their emotions for the eye to see.

In her time with the Hunting Bear, Kyaati had adjusted to showing her emotions in a more physical manner. The change had been so gradual that Galahir had not consciously been aware of it until he was now faced with her impassive father, left without a clue as to what the man was thinking or feeling. It was unnerving.

"I haven't seen my daughter laugh like that since she was a child," Pelaan spoke. His voice was light for a male, but still

410

full of gravitas. Galahir opened his mouth, but could not think of any words to speak. What should he say to that? Hadn't Pelaan been able to make his daughter happy? And so he stood, dripping and feeling more foolish with each passing moment before Pelaan took pity on him, dipped his head and walked away in the wake of his daughter and the younger male.

Galahir blew out a breath, letting his head fall back in supplication to the sky. He already had Lorhir. Did he really need witches making him feel like even more of an inadequate oaf?

The next morning, Galahir ordered fires to be lit. Another risk, but the ox meat needed to be cooked before it spoiled. If the Watchers were slaughtering the herds as they returned to the northern territories, then every scrap was precious.

The witches had brought supplies from their own forest, but Galahir did not suggest that they share their woven baskets full of large nuts, roots and fruits. If Kyaati and Nyriaana were anything to judge by, it would take at least two turns of Nanna before they even dared to sniff a piece of meat, much less eat it.

Galahir hadn't failed to notice that while the cooking of the oxen went on, Kyaati had led her fellow witches off on a forage just outside of camp to boost their plant-based supplies.

Waiting for her return, Galahir moved through his people, checking on the well-being of his followers as they prepared to break camp. He halted in his tracks when a man clad in grey furs and bearing an elk totem walked past him. Galahir blinked, wondering why the man had given him such pause.

Then the reason struck. This man had lain before him not a day before, wounded and in agony, while Selima did her best to keep curses away from his open injury.

Galahir caught the man by the arm, wide-eyed as he stared down at his leg. He did not even have a limp. "H-how?"

The man grinned, his dark eyes alive with joy, and gestured towards a point at the centre of the camp where a hushed crowd had gathered. It appeared not all of the witches had deserted camp with Kyaati. A silver-haired male with a scar marring his jaw was crouched over a woman in the midst of the avid audience. Selima stood to one side, appearing mortified but resigned.

Galahir pushed his way through the crowd to investigate. The male witch did not react as he encroached on his space. His eyes closed, a frown of the utmost concentration on his face as he cradled the woman's hand in his. She had lost three of her fingers. Awestruck, Galahir watched as the open and bleeding stubs healed over before his eyes. The onlookers gasped as the miracle unfolded before them, an excited murmuring broke out.

Galahir was aware of Selima watching him, gnawing on her wide lower lip. Galahir did not have to stretch his thoughts to divine the cause of her unease. Her presence here was precarious. Healing was the one tribute she could offer to keep from being cast out to the wolves. With such a miraculous skill now among them, what further need did he have of her? Galahir sighed, wishing once again Yatal had not placed the burden of leadership upon his flinching shoulders.

Releasing the woman's healed hand, the male witch opened his eyes and rose to his feet. He appeared a little uncomfortable with the crowd of large bodies pressing around his delicate frame, but he held his ground as his pale lilac gaze came to rest upon Galahir. He had the same unreadable expression as Pelaan, but his face had a softer appearance. There was more compassion around the eyes. He bowed his head to Galahir.

"You have my thanks," Galahir said, gesturing at the healed woman, who was now staring mesmerised at her mended hand.

Galahir got the impression the man had shrugged, though he had not twitched. "It is my calling."

The expressionless stare was becoming unnerving. "I, um, welcome you on behalf of my clan…"

"Baarias," the male witch supplied.

"Baarias."

Dropping his gaze away from Baarias' face, he noticed that the other man's left arm was held immobile against his chest. He frowned. "You're injured?" The *how* hung in the air between them. If the witch could heal others, why hadn't he mended his own trauma?

Baarias hissed softly between his teeth. "I wasn't really fully conscious the night I healed this injury," he said.

"What happened?"

Baarias' eyes, if possible, became even more piercing. Galahir stepped back. "A spear to the shoulder the night your People took Nyriaana and Kyaati from us."

Galahir flushed. Did this healer recognise him as one of the raiders who had been present that fateful night? He had been wearing his ox skull over his face at the time. He thought it best not to speak on that. "I-I am sorry," he said.

Baarias gave that strange non-existent shrug. "We were

413

enemies."

"Were?"

Baarias dipped his chin. "I spent a long time distrusting your kind for the suffering you caused my family." Baarias ran a finger along the long scar on his jaw and lifted his maimed shoulder. "But how can I continue to hate when I, myself, am not innocent. Blinded by my fear and prejudice, I, too, am guilty of contributing to that agony." The weight of memory appeared to shrink him before he straightened. "No more misery," he declared. "As Kyaati showed me, we have all been misguided. There is good and bad in all our Peoples. It is time to stand together, all as Children of KI, against the ones who truly inflicted this suffering upon us."

Galahir raised his chin, his heart lifting in the wake of the other man's words. In an impulsive move, he stepped forward to grip Baarias' good arm. For a moment, he thought he had made a mistake when Baarias stiffened, worried that he had insulted him in some unknown way. But then the other man relaxed and gripped Galahir's elbow in return. His thin lips lifted into a first tentative smile. Then, without warning, his head whipped around to Selima. "What is it that you are so frightened of, child?"

"Oh, I er," Selima appeared startled by the sudden attention.

"Selima was our *ashipu*, our healer."

Selima flinched at Galahir's use of the past tense.

"Ah," Baarias said, his sharp mind wrapping around the problem in an instant. "So you were the one who treated the wounds with the poultices before I arrived?"

Selima nodded mutely, her eyes tightening in defence.

But the healer was pleased. "You must be very skilled in

414

herb lore," Baarias praised. "Who taught you these ways?"

"No one," Selima whispered, her gaze on her feet. "I taught myself by watching what plants the animals ate when they were sick and what bark they rubbed themselves against when injured."

Baarias' eyebrows actually rose in visible surprise. "You're a very smart girl," he said. "I'll need your help. If what Kyaati told me of is to come to pass, there are going to be many more injuries that will need to be cleansed and tended. Without my Nyriaana, I am only one man and I am still becoming familiar with the energy of KI in this land. You know this territory, you know where to find your herbs and bark. It is vital you treat and keep wounds clean until I can heal them fully."

"Y-your Nyriaana," Selima stammered.

"Yes," Baarias said, sadness settling over his shoulders again. "She was like a daughter to me. I raised her from a child and taught her the art of healing. I hope wherever she is now, she is safe."

Selima's pale skin turned a shade of green. "Excuse me," she said, before scurrying away into the crowd.

"Did I say something wrong?" Baarias asked Galahir.

Galahir sighed. "No. It is a long story to tell," he said. He had no doubt Kyaati would fill Baarias in sooner rather than later. He did not have the will in that moment to do so himself. Galahir wondered if the aging healer would still want Selima's help once he learned the truth.

"Chief," a young Cro man called Galahir's attention. "The ox meat is cooked and supplies are gathered. We are ready to move on as soon as it pleases you."

"Th-thank you," Galahir stammered and waved the boy

away.

"You have not been their leader for very long," Baarias said.

"Is it that obvious?" Galahir said, mortified.

"Forgive me," Baarias said. "You're very easy to read. Your discomfort rolls around you in a cloud. Rest assured that most of your followers have faith in you and believe you to be a good man who will strive to do his best for the wellbeing of his clan."

"Most?" Galahir's shoulders dropped.

"No leader can win the love and confidence of all his followers," Baarias said. "There will always be those with their own idea of what should be done."

Lorhir caught Galahir's attention. The lean man prowled the ranks of hunters and warriors as clan began to form up around them. "Yes," Galahir agreed.

"I will let you continue," Baarias said, and with no more words, the witch-healer walked away into the crowd. Galahir could see Kyaati and the rest of her People had returned to the edge of the camp. She met his eyes and dipped her chin. They were ready.

"Move out!" Galahir cried over the noise of the mustered clan. Moving to their head, he led them east across the Plains. It was time to go home. Kyaati was quick to catch up, taking hold of his hand, letting him know they would face returning to the ruins of their old life together.

"How is Kikima?" he asked. The trauma of losing the only mother figure she had ever known had barely begun to heal, and now Kikima would be returning to the place where Halima's scavenged bones lay rotting.

"Learning the finer points of how to employ a poison

dart," Kyaati said, a grim twist to her lips.

Galahir shuddered at the thought of a cold hard, determined Kikima in possession of such a weapon. "Selima had better sleep with one eye open from now on," he said.

Kyaati snorted, making it clear it would be no loss if Kikima did decide to test a poison dart on Eldrax's daughter in the middle of the night. Galahir sighed.

"Chief!" A scout hurried up to Galahir's side, panting. "A large wolf pack has started to trail us. I believe it is…"

"Nekelmu," Kyaati finished his sentence with a smile that clearly confused and unnerved the scout. His restless eyes darted to Galahir, but Kyaati continued. "Do not fear. He and his pack are not here to hunt us. They are merely curious." Her expression grew distant. "Nekelmu is currently wondering if he risks an approach for the warmth of a campfire."

"He's what?" The scout blinked.

"Never mind," Galahir said. "If your matriarch says the wolf isn't a threat, then he is not. Do not make any move against the pack. If all they are doing is following, leave them be."

"Y-yes my Chief," the young man stammered and faded back into the ranks behind.

"You knew the wolf was there the whole time?"

"Of course," Kyaati said.

Galahir sighed.

"He has never forgotten the partnership he shared in the hunt that night with Nyriaana, nor the rewards it brought him afterwards. He is still wary of man, but is hopeful of another successful joint hunt… and a campfire."

Galahir shook his head, "Kyaati." There were times he

thought he would never become accustomed to his mate's strange ways, but he could not deny the leap of his heart at the thought of hunting alongside a wolf pack. What a formidable hunting force they would make! He would gladly share scraps and the warmth of a campfire for such a privilege.

His thoughts sobered as Utu rose higher in the sky and more and more familiar land marks began to stand out to him. They were getting close to the remains of the Hunting Bear camp. The stream that had rushed alongside their temporary camp joined with the river that ran south through the Plains. Galahir followed its course, letting it draw him in to where he needed to be.

He had expected silence. Perhaps an empty, mournful whistle as the wind caressed the remains to the fallen. What Galahir had not expected was the distant sound of many voices carried down to him in fits and starts on the fractious breeze. He raised a fist, drawing his company to a halt. He looked to Kyaati, who was staring ahead, frowning.

"Watchers?" Galahir asked. He prepared to order his clan to turn around, but Kyaati shook her head.

"No," she said. "Cro. Lots of them."

"Our clan survived?" Galahir's heart leaped in hope.

"There are lots more there than the Hunting Bear Clan," she said. "Lots more."

Galahir frowned then whistled a short blast. A young scout appeared at his side. "See what lies ahead," Galahir directed. "Keep your distance, do not risk yourself. Go."

The boy rushed away. Galahir waited, pulling Kyaati into his side. Long moments passed in silence before Kyaati let out a sharp gasp. Before Galahir could ask the cause of her distress, a cry of terror split the air.

The scout.

Without a second thought, Galahir released Kyaati. "Wait there!" he shouted back at his mate, already running towards the sound of the boy's distress.

Flying around the bend in the river, Galahir slewed to a halt at the sight that met his eyes. In the place where the Hunting Bear camp had once stood was a new camp, one larger than Galahir had ever seen, arranged in tight defensive rings. The clan that moved around it was easily twice the size of the one he had managed to amass in the days since assuming control of the Eagle Clan.

Directly ahead of him, his scout struggled in the grip of a thick-set warrior while another held a knife to the adolescent's throat. The man holding the boy was a stranger. The warrior holding the blade, however, was not.

Galahir's knuckles cracked, gripping his spear as the red-headed tower of muscle and bone caught sight of him and turned, lips peeling back off his teeth.

"Galahir," Eldrax snarled.

Frozen, Galahir stared into the vicious black eyes of his former Chief. Eldrax had survived. Eldrax had succeeded in bringing together the clans he had subjugated and brought them to the destroyed Hunting Bear camp. Now Galahir had led the Eagle Clan right into his grasp.

"Deserter," the Red Bear snarled as he lowered his knife from the throat of Galahir's scout.

Galahir lifted his spear as Eldrax stalked towards him. He knew he stood little chance against the Red Bear. He had bested even Khalvir. But Galahir would not go down without a fight. The dark gaze fell upon the totem of the

419

Eagle Chief that now dangled around Galahir's neck, and Galahir knew his moments among the living were few as a crazed black fire flared to life.

"Traitor!" Eldrax roared. "Eagle filth!"

"Eldrax!" A female voice cracked across the air, and then Kyaati was at Galahir's side.

The Red Bear reared back, his eyebrows shooting towards his mane of red hair as he beheld Galahir's mate. "You survived," he breathed.

Galahir tried to shoulder Kyaati behind him, wishing she had not revealed herself.

Eldrax's lips twisted into a smile. "It is a sign that Utu shines upon me. When the threat of the so-called gods is defeated, I will Claim you as mine as I should have done from the first moment. A spoil of the victory to come."

Fury curled through Galahir's gut. "Over my dead body!" he snarled.

"That was the idea," Eldrax said, flexing his hand around his knife and shifting fluidly into a battle stance.

"Eldrax." This time the voice was Lorhir's. There was a rush of feet and the rest of Galahir's forces appeared at his back, spears bristling. "Back down or die where you stand."

Without rising from his crouch, Eldrax's eyes flicked over the fighters at Galahir's back and laughed in the face of Lorhir's threat. "I think not. My warriors will wipe you out before Utu sleeps. Your corpses will make fine bait for the Watchers." He raised his fingers to his lips. Galahir tensed.

Lorhir's thoughts as usual worked faster than his. Galahir was grateful for his clan brother's presence as Lorhir faced Eldrax with an unruffled air. "Yes, you could destroy us," he said. "But what would it accomplish? We lose, then you lose.

420

Consider, old Red Bear, whose heads would you rather see mounted upon spikes. Ours… or the gods'?"

Eldrax glared at Lorhir. "I always knew your insolence would overreach you one day, my dear Jackal. Your treacherous head on a spike would be a welcome sight indeed." But Galahir could see his better sense warring with the berserker fury twitching in his muscles.

As their fates hung on the fragile sanity of a madman, it was Kyaati who let out a thrilling whistle.

Upon her command, her People broke cover from the centre of Galahir's forces and revealed themselves in plain sight.

Eldrax's knife dropped to his side. "Witches!"

Kyaati lifted her chin. "Yes. Witches willing to fight with the Cro. Just as you have always wanted, Eldrax," she said.

Eldrax's shrewd gaze swept over the handful of leaf-clad tree-dwellers, his face twitching furiously. Galahir held his breath, fearing his mate's gamble would tip the Red Bear towards attack in a fit of jealousy. Galahir had achieved what he had strived for over a lifetime.

Kyaati saw the danger, too. "We will serve only Galahir," she said. "Attempt to overthrow him and you will not have us. We will fight by your side, Red Bear, only if we remain free."

Galahir held his breath as Eldrax's great gnarled hand trembled upon the knife he held. Then he sucked in a breath through his nose, and a wide grin spread across his face. "Agreed," he rumbled. Sheathing his knife, he stepped forward and seized Galahir's arm, gripping it at the elbow. "A truce will exist between the Eagles and the Hunting Bear as we face our common enemy."

Galahir, caught off balance at the sudden turn, hesitated for one moment before returning Eldrax's grip. But as he did so, Eldrax pulled him closer, his hand tightening painfully on Galahir's elbow. "After that, I make no promises, there is only room for one Chief of the Plains," he hissed in Galahir's ear before releasing him, the grin still fixed upon his face.

"Come," the Red Bear beckoned. "Your men must be weary from travel and they must be strong if they are to be any use to me. We will share in our bounties." He eyed the cooked haunches borne on the shoulders of Galahir's strongest men.

"You honour us," Galahir said, inclining his head. He would have done anything but ally himself to this man, but fate, it seemed, was not offering another choice. When the Watchers came for them, all the clans, all the Peoples, needed to stand together. It was a promise Yatal had exacted from him upon her death, and he was bound to keep it. The only hope for man. The only hope for his family. If that meant a truce with Eldrax, then so be it.

As Galahir followed Eldrax down towards the vast new camp by the river, Nanna rose on the horizon, her belly almost full. Galahir winced. There wasn't much time left.

* * *

23

Lord of the Skies

Nyri landed on the hard stone of the underground tunnel and ducked down as the massive hand, almost as long as she was tall, reached through the hole after them, gnarled fingers grasping and straining as the creature struggled to catch them. Juaan yanked her back, his face a mask of grim concentration in the faint light from above as he jabbed his spear into the palm of the beast. A pained yowl sounded from above as the hand was snatched back.

Loud thuds and the sound of scraping began to echo through the space.

"They're trying to dig us out," Juaan said through clenched teeth. He was holding on to the strange, untamed power inside him with everything he had. Through sheer force of will, Nyri mastered her frozen body and dragged Juaan away from the hole above their heads, away from the monsters determined to reach them.

Impenetrable darkness pressed upon her eyes. Icy air that had never known the warmth of Ninmah brushed past her face, carrying the scent of damp stone. Their footsteps echoed faintly off the unseen walls. Nyri did not need her eyes to know they were inside a tunnel identical to the one Rannac had once led them through so many blinks of Ninsiku ago. Disorientated by the blackness, she reached out her hand, needing something to ground her. Sure enough, her fingers found a hard stone wall. But it was not the usual rough, uneven touch that her skin instinctively expected. The surface was as smooth as water, curving gently upwards and over their heads. Nyri shuddered.

With one hand on the wall and the other gripping Juaan's, Nyriaana fled the sound of the ground being torn apart above their heads; sprinting into the unknown blackness until all that remained was the echo of their own footsteps and the rush of blood in her ears.

"Nyri," Juaan whispered, pulling her to a halt. "I think we're safe now."

Nyri gasped and threw herself at him. Unable to see his face, she needed to feel his solid warmth against her body and be reassured of his continued existence. "I thought I was going to lose you," she hitched into his furs.

"So did I," he said as his arms went around her.

Nyri remained silent for a few moments, absorbing their new situation. "How did you know where to find this place?" she asked, trying not to shiver as the bone-cold air began to seep through her coverings.

Juaan hesitated, his hands flexing in the furs at her back. "The Thal woman, my *tarhe,* appeared to me again. She led me to the entrance."

Nyri sniffed and lifted a hand to stroke his cheek reassuringly. "It appears I am not the only one being visited by the *genii."*

Juaan's chest lifted under her ear as he blew out a breath. "She's still watching over me, it seems. Now we just need to find a way out of these tunnels and into the Mountains." Nyri felt him shift as he tried to peer into the impenetrable gloom. "I would give a whole haunch of ox for a flame right now."

"We need to go this way," Nyri said, taking his hand and pulling him with her down the tunnel, placing her hand on the wall once more to keep her equilibrium.

"How do you know?"

"I don't," Nyri told him. "But this is the first time I have felt certain of my direction since we left the Eagle camp." And she was, Nyri could feel it. The energy running under her feet and through the tunnel walls was drawing her forward, tugging at her. She had the strangest sense of being called home.

The further they went, the deeper the feeling rooted inside her heart, sinking in until it sucked all other awareness from her. Nyri broke into a run, dropping Juaan's hand in her need to reach her destination.

"Nyri!" Juaan called after her. But she didn't heed him. She only ran faster, blind in the dark, but all-seeing inside her mind. The tunnel branched several times, but Nyri's instinct did not falter. She wove through them, heedless of the growing ache in her legs.

A waft of fresh air passed over her face, carrying with it the scent of earth and growth and the light of Ninmah. Nyri drank it in, letting it fuel her tiring body. Another turn. Light appeared ahead, a circle of promise in the blackness. Nyri hurled herself towards it without a thought. Full tilt, she exploded from the tunnel and into the light. Ninmah seared across her dark-adjusted eyes, making her gasp and shield her face, breaking her from the trance she had fallen into.

"Nyri!" A hand grabbed her furs, yanking her to a halt just in time. Loose stones scattered from under her feet and tumbled away, bouncing down the cliff-face as Nyri hung, braced on her toes, staring down at the ground far, far below. Had he not caught her, she would have run straight off the smooth narrow ledge upon which she now stood, and into empty air.

"Juaan," she gasped as he pulled her away from the edge and back against his chest. She took a moment to recover her stolen senses, her eyes adjusting to the sudden brightness.

"What in Ea's name?" Juaan breathed above her head.

Nyri blinked and her breath caught in her throat. Instead of a maze of barren, snow-capped peaks, a vast green forest stretched away below them, protected and encircled by the Mountains on all sides. The sense of life radiating from this lush garden overwhelmed Nyri's awareness. It poured from the very earth, from the trees, from the creatures within, so strong it was almost visible, like the steam curling over the green canopy, moisture from below meeting the cool dry air of the Mountains above.

Nyri breathed in the heady scent of flowing sap. So long had she lived in the grip of the Fury, she had almost forgotten what it was to experience the height of the Blessing.

"This should not be here," Juaan muttered uneasily. "The trees should not be in full leaf."

426

Caught up in the sensations that assailed her, it took Nyri a moment to register the structure rising from the very centre of the forest below. It was as big as a mountain, but it was unlike any mountain Nyri had ever seen. The stone that formed it was flat and smooth on all four sides, sloping and tapering up to a perfect point at the peak.

"What is that?"

"I don't know," Juaan whispered. "But can't you feel it?"

And Nyri could. The structure blazed against her senses like a torch. The power of the great River Line concentrated on this one point at the centre of the Mountains of the Nine Gods. But interwoven with KI was another power. A strange invasion weaving through the earth like a spider's web that Nyri did not understand. It sucked on the Great Spirit like a parasite. She shuddered away from the unnaturalness of it.

"As the Thals say: *Ekur.* The dwelling of the gods."

The hairs rose on the back of Nyri's neck. This was the presence that had drawn her through the tunnels. As she looked out over the strange forest in the middle of the mountains, she experienced once more the most peculiar feeling of *home* and yet, opposing that, was the sense that the oasis before her was not for her eyes, it was forbidden, only to be looked upon by those of a greater power.

"Was this in your vision?" Juaan asked. "Is this where we are to find the Last Kamaali?"

"No," Nyri shook her head without taking her eyes from the Ekur. "Not this place."

"Then we should move on. Nyri, we have to get away from here." The pitch of his voice brought Nyri's eyes up. Juaan was quivering against her back. Whatever she felt, he was experiencing the same, but many times worse. His green eyes blazed as they gazed down at her, almost glowing in the shadow of the dark tunnel behind him. "Which way?" he asked.

Nyri panicked, casting around. She did not know. Her mind was silent again. She looked at the peaks beyond the forest. How was she to find the steaming lake of her vision and the Forbidden girl that awaited?

Sefaan, Sefaan, help, she pleaded. But the voice of the old Kamaali did not come to her, just a rising buzz sounded in her ears. The energy of this place was confusing her senses, blocking everything out. "We need to get across," she said. "Get out on the other side of this forest and up into the peaks beyond." Perhaps if they got away from its influence, she would somehow find the path she was supposed to take.

She saw Juaan visibly clench his teeth, but he dipped his chin. "We do not stop until we reach the other side," he said tightly.

He was fighting with himself, with the influence this place was having on the beast within. Nyri took him by the hand, lending him her strength and soothing his electrified nerves. To her right, a narrow path clinging to the cliff side led down from the smooth ledge the tunnel had issued them onto. The path did not simply slope downwards. Odd descending levels had been cut into the stone, evenly spaced, causing her to step down a short way onto each smooth, horizontal surface, each one the width of a grown man's foot, with every step she took.

Nyri pulled Juaan along with her, slow at first, watching her feet carefully to make sure she planted them squarely on the next level down, until her body got used to the pattern and the strange way of moving. The path was solid. At no point had the stone into which these stepping levels been hewn crumbled as the trail zigzagged its way ever downward towards the forest beneath.

When the path lowered them beneath the forest canopy, the humidity hit Nyriaana in the face like a wave. She coughed as the moisture filled her throat. Water droplets gathered on her furs as her ears were assaulted by the din. Birds, insects, frogs, creatures of all kinds, sang, croaked, howled, and rustled around her. Nyri felt like clamping her hands to her ears, but that would mean letting go of Juaan's hand, and she did not think that would be wise. He needed her.

When at last the long descent was over, Nyri stepped off the last stone ledge and onto the forest floor. Her nerves prickled again when the expected rustle of old dead leaves beneath her feet did not meet her ears. The faint whiff of leaf mould did not fill her nostrils. The ground was clear, untouched, as though the leaves had never fallen, the trees had never aged. The Fury had no place. It was life everlasting. A paradise.

It was wrong.

Harsh as it was, the Fury was a natural cycle of life. A time for the trees to rest, to shed the old and ready themselves to bloom again with new vigour in the Blessing. A time for the weak to be weeded out, making way for a stronger generation to be born as the seasons warmed.

This absence of death spooked Nyri more than she could put into words. It went against the balance of the Great Spirit of KI.

The stone trail that they had descended upon now morphed beneath their feet into a straight pathway cutting through the mossy ground of the forest. It was formed of the same smooth, interlocking stones they had stumbled upon in the clearing of the black forest, just before…

Nyri closed her eyes, willing away the image of Sakal's headless body smashing to the ground before her. She did not want to travel the stone path before her, but this was the most direct trail. If they continued straight, they would bypass the massive stone structure at the centre and reach the other side of this unnerving forest before Ninmah reached her zenith.

She did not ask Juaan for direction and he did not protest as she set out at a dead run along the hard path. Instinctively, Nyri formed a cocoon around them both, drawing on the heady energy the forest produced, blending them with their surroundings. With their footfalls muffled by the furs wrapped around their feet, she and Juaan passed like ghosts through the trees.

The deeper they travelled, the greater the sense of familiarity and foreboding grew, swirling and battling together. This place was like a memory from a forgotten dream. Or a nightmare. Nyri kept her eyes ahead. They had to get across, they had to get free. There was movement all around. The creatures of the forest were watching their passage. For the first time in her life, Nyri had no desire to call out to them. She did not even turn her head as the flickers in the trees taunted her periphery.

"The Ekur," Juaan rasped behind her. "We're half way."

Nyri could see it, one angular corner stone abutting the path. Her heart turned over, realising they would have to pass right by its feet. But she could not stop. She drew harder on the Great Spirit, thickening her cloak.

Her efforts were in vain. The Ekur was looming above when the sensation of a cruel, bodiless regard crawled over her skin. It pierced through all her defences, laying her bare.

Nyri's stride faltered as the whispers found her again, breaking through the cloying energy of the forest. *Nyri, Nyri, Nyri,* her own name echoed through her head, all the voices blending together in desperation. *He sees. Stop, stop, stop.*

They cut off just as Juaan yanked her to a halt.

"Nyriaana," he gasped, "We—"

Too late. Juaan's words were lost in a rush of wind as the ground fell out from beneath their feet and they tumbled into nothingness.

The rush of cold air was the only sensation. All other senses had been deprived. Nyri could not see, hear, smell, nor *feel* anything around her. She was blind, falling away in the dark, not even knowing which way was up. If it wasn't for the wind buffeting her this way and that, she would not even have known she was moving and not just floating, forgotten in the void.

And then it was over. With a loud ringing sound, Nyri crashed down onto a hard, smooth surface. A heavy thud told her that Juaan had landed beside her. She wrenched open her eyes, then screwed them shut again as the brightest of lights pierced her vision, jabbing into the back of her skull like a thousand spears. Robbed of her sight, she instinctively reached out with her higher senses, but the void that met her questing touch was like a brutal slap to the face. Her breath came in panicked gasps as she reached again and again for the Great Spirit, but he was not there. She was alone. Completely alone. Nyri opened her eyes. Without her higher senses, her sight was all she had.

The light tortured her, but she stubbornly ignored the pain. Her hands were resting on a smooth cold surface, but it was not stone. Nyri recoiled at the sight of her own face reflected back at her. It was as if she had fallen on solid water. There was no break, no imperfection as she ran her hands over the hard, silky silver surface.

She flinched as something caught her around the arms, drawing a startled cry from her lips.

"It's me." Juaan's voice.

She had not known it was him. She had not felt anything.

"Juaan, I'm blind. Ninmah's Gift. It is gone. It's gone!" She put her hands around her head, tugging at her hair.

"Shh, shh." Juaan caught her hands, clasping them in his. "Stop, you'll hurt yourself. Breathe. Focus on me."

"I can't!" Nyri burst out. "You're not there. Nothing is real! How can I know anything is real if I can't feel it?"

"I don't know. But I am here, Nyri, Nyri, Nyriaana. You have other senses. Listen to my voice. That is real. And this." He placed her hands on his chest and held them there, letting her feel his solid weight, the rise and fall of his chest and the vital pulse within. But was that truly him? Gone was the unique signature of his life under her touch. Nyri had never felt more crippled. Her breathing refused to calm.

"Nyriaana. Look at me." One hand released hers and caught her by the chin, drawing her gaze to his face. Warm green, the colour of fresh leaves, filled her vision. Her thudding heart slowed as she centred on this one thing that was Juaan alone.

"That's better," he whispered, seeing her calm. "Stay with me, Nyriaana."

This was easier for him. Juaan had lived a life with an unpredictable connection to his Gift. He was not so reliant upon it. And Nyriaana imagined, though she could no longer be certain, that she spied a hint of relief in his face; an easing. Cut off from the Great Spirit, he was no longer battling to control the fearsome energy that raged inside him. A battle he had been fighting since they had come back to the Mountains. The tension that she was so used to seeing in his shoulders that she hardly ever noticed anymore was gone.

"Where are we?" Nyri gripped Juaan's furs as another wave of disorientation crashed over her. She breathed through it.

"Nippur. Or what remains of it," a disembodied voice answered.

Juaan was on his feet in an instant, moving so fast Nyri felt dizzy at the motion as he thrust her behind him and lifted the spear in his right hand.

An unpleasant sound filled the unnaturally still air. It sounded like a laugh. It was the closest noise Nyri could liken it to. "And now the creatures have the audacity to threaten me within my own domain as well as on my borders," the voice sighed. "My brother and his spouse can continue to rot in Irkalla for giving primitives their own will. Put that twig down, *enkidu*," the voice turned into a hiss.

Juaan gasped as his arm began to twist under an unseen force. Nyri thought she heard his bones creak before his fingers flew open and the spear clattered to the smooth floor.

Nyri whipped her head around, searching for their invisible attacker as best she could. The loss of her higher senses tormented her. The cruel light glared, hampering her vision, making her flinch and squint.

"Who are you?" Juaan demanded of the air, gripping his abused wrist.

"My, what short memories you have. To go with your brief lives, I suppose," the voice mused lazily.

Nyri forced her eyes fully open. She had no words to describe the place she and Juaan were in. The light stabbed at her, unnatural, white and overly bright, reflecting off the smooth solid water surfaces that enclosed them; above, below and to the sides. There was no sky, no trees, no mountains. Nothing lived. Nyri's breathing began to accelerate again as she felt the space closing in about her, entrapping her.

Across the gleaming floor, a soft rustling broke the stillness. A tall barrier began to turn, accompanied by the sound of whirring. Nyri and Juaan stepped back as a seated figure revealed itself, its arms resting on two protrusions emitting from the vertical back of the rotating raised platform upon which it sat. Nyri recoiled from the sight of it.

Even seated, the being towered over them. The thin, elongated body was draped in a material that glimmered under the bright light, throwing rainbows from its folds. A headdress fashioned from the same shining material as the surfaces that enclosed them, partly concealed the long face and skull.

The face itself could only be described as beautiful.

Symmetrical, with high cheekbones, and golden skin that appeared to ripple subtly in the light. But it was a cold, inhuman beauty. There was no compassion in the large, glowing blue eyes.

Nyri's blood turn to ice in her veins. She had seen such a likeness before, in the stone carvings within the Forest of the Nine Gods. But the carvings had not been enough to prepare her for facing a Sky God in the flesh.

"Nunamnir." The name slipped from Juaan's lips, and Nyri felt him tighten his hold upon her. Nyri's mind was still struggling to come to terms with what they were facing, but the name triggered a memory: the warmth of a campfire flickering over her skin as a blind old man told of Nunamnir, the Sky God who had become irritated by the voices of his fellow gods' creations. The one who had ordered their destruction.

The creature's full lips curled into a mirthless smile. "Ah, so you haven't quite forgotten, though your memories are diluted." The being rose to his full commanding height. "I am Enlil, Lord of the Skies, leader of the Anunnaki on TiAmat."

Juaan backed them away as the Sky God began to walk around the room, leisurely and without hurry. Nyri's skin prickled. He was a predator circling prey that had no hope of escape.

"Why have you brought us here?" Juaan asked.

"Curiosity." The voice was soft in the still, odorless air. "Ninmah promised me she had stunted your DNA, and yet despite my many efforts to cull you, you continue to plague me with your incessant clamour, waking me from my sleep, and daring to defy your masters by killing my

Nephilim. I cannot understand it." Enlil continued to circle, his enigmatic eyes raking over them. "It has been millennia since any *enkidu* dared to descend the Great Staircase into the Garden of Eridu. Since you took it upon yourselves to trespass, I thought I would look upon the creatures that have so stubbornly refused to fade away."

And then Nyri found herself immobilised. An inescapable force had closed itself about her. She could not so much as flex a finger against it. Deprived of Ninmah's Gift, she could not detect the source of the power that held her, only feel the terrifying physical effects.

"Ninmah always said there was more to you than met the eye, that you were worthy of existence. What did she mean? What secret was she holding back? What have I missed?"

Ninmah?

"Oh, you remember that traitor, too?" The Lord of the Skies answered as though Nyri had spoken the name aloud. A peculiar pressure pressed against her mind, like fingers stroking under her skin. It was her only warning before invisible claws lanced down through her skull, piercing and raking through her consciousness. Every image and thought of Ninmah that had ever existed in her mind was ripped to the forefront, to be turned over and studied as she screamed, writhing internally. A warm wetness slid over her mouth, and Nyri knew her nose was bleeding.

Juaan was shouting. She could feel his hands pulling on her, helpless against the invisible force that held her. Tears streamed from her eyes, but Enlil was indifferent to her pain. The noise that resembled laugh emitted from the Sky God's throat again. "What interesting beliefs you have woven for yourselves. Enki would be wounded if he learned

436

you thought him a demon in the form of a moon."

And then Nyri was in the air, torn from Juaan's insubstantial grip. Before she could blink, she was suspended before the face of Enlil himself. Her heart pounded as his long fingers took hold of her chin, cold and reptilian. Glowing eyes slid over her, pitiless, like Nyri was of no more consequence than a curious rock he might pick up for study.

"You must be one of the failed projects. Small, useless for the work desired of you. Why did Ninmah keep you when the Adamu line proved superior?" The cool, long-fingered hand went over Nyri's head and the probing began again. This time, she could not detect what he was searching for. She closed her eyes as dizziness swamped her. There was a soft gasp, then a threatening sound, not quite a growl or a hiss, but an odd combination of them both. "Great An above! What did she *do*?" The invisible fingers sank deeper. "Telepathy and empathic abilities, skills of the Anunnaki themselves! Were you not so physically *weak*..." One long hand lifted and flexed. Nyri screamed as the bones down the right side of her body snapped, her arm and leg shattering.

"Stop!" Nyri barely recognised the voice as Juaan's. "Stop it! Leave her alone!"

The elongated head whipped around, faster than Nyriaana could track. She was gasping, fighting against the agony that wanted to suck her under. Then she was falling, released from the paralysing effect of the Lord Enlil's attention.

Dark spots danced before her vision as her broken bones contacted the ground. Struggling against the blackness, she watched Juaan charge the Sky God, barrelling into him full force and sending the towering being toppling. The space rang with a strange sound as they hit the ground, Juaan fighting to get a hold their enemy's long throat.

It was a desperate effort, doomed to fail.

Enlil flicked his wrist, and in the next instant, Juaan was suspended in the air. His eyes blazed as, like Nyri, he found himself unable to move, watching as the Sky God leaped to his feet with the lithe grace of a serpent.

"Savage!" Lord Enlil stalked the helpless man before him. "You, *enkidu,* you—Wait. What are *you?*"

Nyri saw Juaan's pupils dilate, his skin paling, and knew he was suffering the same brutal study she had just endured. The growling hiss ripped and echoed through the space, louder than before. "A hybrid!" The blue eyes flicked between Nyri and Juaan. "Half Adamu form, half Ninmah's pet experiment."

And then Nyri knew true agony as Enlil placed his long fingers on Juaan's temples. Juaan could not move, but somehow Nyri perceived him writhe. He did not make a sound, but Nyri knew his silence was for her benefit. "No."

Enlil's fingers twitched. Blood began to gush from Juaan's nose and seep from the corners of his eyes. And then Juaan keened, panting between his locked teeth. Enlil's eyes widened with a flash of fear so quick Nyri couldn't be sure it existed before it vanished. The fingers sank deeper into the sides of Juaan's head.

"Stop!" Nyri struggled to rise on her shattered leg. "Stop, you're killing him!"

But the Lord of the Skies paid her no more mind than he would a bothersome gnat. Juaan's tortured breaths went on and on.

438

"The power Ninmah dared to bestow on a weakling species, locked in the body of the stronger Adamu! *This* is the power that killed my Nephilim and woke me from my sleep. Gah!" Enlil flicked his hand and Juaan was hurled with tremendous force away from the Sky God. His body smashed against one of the smooth walls and tumbled boneless to the ground. He did not move again.

Nyri sobbed, dragging herself across the ground.

"Great An, forgive me! It is fortunate that the creature did not have the force of will to wield the power it possessed. I was a fool to let Enki play with such science." Enlil paced up and down, muttering to himself. "To give sacred sentience and the ability to reproduce to such creatures. How could he hope to control it? Madness! And my fault. My own curiosity and pride blinded me. I should have corrected the mistake when I had them on their knees instead of bating Ninmah. I have let their defiance grow with their numbers." Enlil paused in his pacing, and Nyri found herself under his inescapable regard once more. She snarled at him, hatred burning through her broken body.

Her airway cut off, and she choked on nothing. Her one good hand went to her throat, but there was nothing there to grasp. Panic flooded through her.

"*Why* were you trespassing in my Garden?" Enlil demanded as spots began to dance before Nyri's eyes. She choked again, battling for the air that was being denied to her. "You thought yourselves mighty enough to kill me within my own domain? Is that why you brought *him*?" Claws inside her skull again. Images swept through her mind as Enlil raked through them. Sefaan's vision, the voices that had beckoned her here to search for the Last

439

Kamaali. One image stood out above all others, the burning purple eyes that had tormented Nyri's dreams since her departure from the Hunting Bear Clan.

"So. Ninmah has found a way to meddle even from her confines in Irkalla." Enlil's strange laugh echoed hollowly through the chamber. "She still thinks to save you from me. She believes this Naanshi will save you." Ariyaana's face floated to the forefront of Nyri's mind. "Another hybrid."

Nyri was barely conscious when she was released and dropped to the ground once more. Her bones shifted, wrenching her back to full awareness as the pressure around her throat released. She dragged the air back into her starved lungs as best she could. Even without Enlil's choke hold, she was having difficulty breathing. A spear went through her broken side every time she tried to draw breath.

"Ninmah could not save you all those eons ago, and she will not save you now. The Nephilim are prepared."

"Wh-why?" Nyri croaked from the cold, smooth ground. "Y-you created us. My People have given their lives, s-suffered to follow your teachings. Why d-do you hate us so?"

"My brother created you, not I," Enlil sniffed. "He and his beloved Ninmah. We created you as slaves and my need for you ran out long ago. Enki and Ninmah might have developed some sentimental attachment to you out of curiosity, but I do not share such weakness. It is time to cleanse this world of their mistake and set it back on its natural course."

"B-but," Nyri pleaded. "We are no threat to you! Can't you just leave us in peace?"

"No threat?" Enlil challenged. His eyes flickered to the

prone Juaan before returning to Nyri. "You war against each other, steal, destroy and kill, the base parts of your DNA plain to see. It is an insult and a terror to know such creatures wield the blood of the sacred. Already my Nephilim have died at the hands of a power that should never be placed in the hands of a savage. My calls for a display of fealty in return for mercy have gone ignored. The Lullu Amelu are no longer in line. If allowed to advance, the Anunnaki are at risk. I will protect my race from my brother's mistake. The scourge of humanity ends here."

"No!" Nyri dragged herself forward until she could clutch at the strange material that draped over Enlil's body, uttering anything she thought might sway him. "I beg of you, great Lord of the Skies. Let us live. Love us, teach us how to be better. We will not challenge you. We owe our existence to you. Please, we just want to live in peace."

The depths of the cold blue eyes flickered as the Sky God stared down into her face, and for a moment, just for a moment, Nyri thought she had touched something within. She saw pride there, a vulnerability, a need to be loved and worshiped, to dominate and rule. But then the eyes shuttered and Enlil's face became blank, as if he were concentrating on something far away.

Nyri did not have time to figure out what had drawn his attention before the long face twisted in fury. His hand flicked again. Nyri flew back, striking the wall next to Juaan and landing in a heap beside him. Numb, she saw her own blood spatter the shining floor beneath her.

"Liar!" Enlil roared out.

"N-no."

"Already humanity moves against me!" The Lord of the

Skies jabbed at a thick, shining bracelet on his wrist. A transparent image appeared, floating in the air above his arm. Nyri could make out a vast camp on the edges of the distinctive black tree line of the Forests of the Nine Gods. Weapons flashed and men laboured as pits were dug. And at the centre of it all stood a figure she knew all too well, the promise of bloodshed on his face. Eldrax.

Nyri closed her eyes in despair. They were lost.

"Peace!" Enlil mocked. "Peace! I will give them eternal peace!"

"Nyri," Juaan groaned, shifting on the ground.

Enlil snarled as he caught the movement. "Starting with this one!"

Nyri's heart flew into her throat as the enraged Sky God turned the bracelet on his arm against Juaan. Time slowed down, revealing everything in stark and haunting detail; she had seen this before, and she knew what she had to do. It was time.

Oddly, she felt no fear as she faced the death she had run from for so long.

With the last of her strength, Nyri threw herself between Juaan and the one who would do him harm. A bolt of lightning erupted from Enlil's wrist. Nyri's vision exploded as it struck her full in the chest, burning through her body, searing away her skin, her senses, her very being.

Then everything went black. She was floating again. Floating away. And Nyri let herself go, welcoming the nothingness that enveloped her. Curiously, she was aware of the moment when her heart beat its last.

* * *

24

Pledge

The campfires roared as the clear blue sky above gave way to a golden hue. The defences were in place. Galahir had been surprised at how well Eldrax had cooperated with him and his men, preparing this place where they would make their stand. Pits had been dug, traps laid, weapons stockpiled. There was nothing left to do now but wait.

Just as in Yatal's vision, tonight, Nanna would reach her zenith and their fate would come to find them in the form of an army of hulking giants. What other creatures the gods might summon, Galahir could not guess, and he did not want to dwell on such things.

He sat next to Kyaati, laying an arm around her shoulders as he drew her against him. Now was the time to live in the moment, for who knew what tomorrow would bring? And so Galahir watched and laughed, gasped and commiserated as stories were shared between the joined clans.

Although they kept away from the fires, the witches tentatively joined the exchange of tales. The Cro listened with rapt attention to these stories that had never before been heard on the Plains. Eyes bugged with amazement as some of the witches grew comfortable enough to demonstrate their prowess in the control of the wild beasts, and others caused seeds to sprout forth to the accompaniment of startled cries.

The only witch that did not make any effort to join with the mingling of Peoples was the young, dark-haired male. He kept to the edges of the crowd, his large dark eyes watchful as a jackal as he studied them all. It made Galahir's skin crawl.

"Is he alright?" he murmured in Kyaati's ear as she nursed Elhaari, nodding to where the young man now lurked on the fringes of the camp, his lips twisting in contempt as one of his tribesmen caused an owl to swoop down low over their heads and perch upon an adolescent boy's knee, much to the child's delight.

Kyaati followed his gaze. "Ah," she said. "Don't worry about Daajir. He's always been a proud, frustratingly stubborn boar. He might not like this, but he is loyal to Aardn. She ordered him to help us, and so he will."

"Hmmm," Galahir acknowledged her words, but he remained uneasy. He would not be turning his back on this Daajir any time soon if he could help it.

The heat from the fires washed over him, and Galahir found his eyelids drooping. The past days had been hard.

"Come back to the shelter with me?" Kyaati murmured in his ear. Elhaari was now sound asleep in her other arm. And just like that, all his weariness evaporated as he beheld the smouldering promise in her eyes. If this was to be their last night on earth, then he wasn't about to waste a minute of it on sleep. He got up willingly as she tugged on his hand, almost but not quite oblivious to the furious glare of Daajir in the shadows.

All pleasant thoughts shattered at the sound of a strange horn blasting in the near distance. Raw and throaty, it froze everyone in place as it rolled through the camp like thunder. Then came the frantic drumbeats of the sentries signalling an approach. Galahir cursed. From somewhere unseen, Eldrax roared orders. The stillness broke. Everyone was moving at once. Food was thrown down as men leapt to their feet, grabbing weapons from the stockpiles littered around the camp.

Recovering his wits, Galahir swept an *arshu* into his hand. "With me!" he bellowed to his own men, trying not to let his hand tremble upon the haft of his weapon at the thought of the horror that approached. With his men at his back, he rushed to the edge of camp where Eldrax already waited, his battle club in hand.

Galahir stared out into the gathering gloom, straining to see while at the same time flinching from the sight that was surely to come: inhuman eyes glowing out of the dark.

But that terrifying vision never materialised. Instead, a call in the darkness: "Thals! Thals arriving in peace!"

Relief stole the strength from Galahir's limbs, his hand trembled as he lowered his weapon and gestured to his followers to stand down. Eldrax, however, snarled and spat on the ground. "Thals. I ought to run them back to whatever cave they crept from."

"But we need them," Galahir spoke, startled.

Eldrax grunted. "Then you deal with the cowards if you wish." He jabbed his spear at Galahir. "I will not have them among my ranks." And he stalked back into camp, leaving Galahir to watch as one Thal, then another ghosted out of the darkness, swelling in number until a vast array of the Northern People came to a halt a respectful distance from the Cro camp.

At their centre stood an ageing man, his bold features now beginning to sag under the weight of experience and the passing of the seasons, but his body still spoke of a raw power set with the arrogant confidence of an undefeated warrior. From his dress, Galahir judged him to be the leader; handsome black feathers were arrayed over his head, fanning from his fur-lined shoulders; a far more flamboyant display than any of his followers boasted. The only one that came close to matching him was the young man standing on his right side.

Galahir blinked and looked again. The young man was Cro. Even in the shadows of the night, his tall, lithe figure and dark face stood out from the rest of his pale, heavy-featured company. From behind his Thal chief, the Cro man studied Galahir with keen grey eyes.

"Who speaks for Cro?" the ageing leader barked.

Galahir shifted, resisting the habitual urge to glance to the side for a man other than himself. He squared his shoulders and called back. "I do."

The Thal measured Galahir with a slow, impassive regard and Galahir grew conscious of his half-blood appearance. The Thals, like the witches, still had unfavourable views on the Forbidden mixing of blood between Peoples. Would the proud man before him refuse to speak to such an abomination as himself? But Galahir must have passed some unspoken test, for the Thal leader beckoned him forward. "We meet in middle," he said. "One man each."

Galahir dipped his chin in agreement. He already knew Lorhir was at his shoulder as he stepped away from the ranks of Cro to meet the Thal leader on open ground.

At an equal distance between the two companies, they came together.

Galahir opened his mouth to speak, but then checked himself, some long-forgotten memory flickering to the fore. In Thal tradition, the more senior leader in a meeting spoke first, and so he held his tongue, waiting for the grizzled warrior before him to break the silence.

The Thal leader raised a closed fist to his mouth before flicking his fingers open and lowering it. "I Alok, Sag Du of Spitter *imrua*," he said. "I chosen by *nabu* seers to lead *puhrum*." He gestured at the ranks of Thals arrayed behind him. It was hard to tell in the dark, but Galahir perceived that not all the Thals' coverings were the same. Feathers were arranged in differing patterns. This was not just one Thal group. Alok had assembled many Thal tribes together. "This my honour son, Bahari, and *magiri* leader of fighters." He introduced the Cro man who had accompanied him.

"I am Galahir, Chief of the Eagle Clan," he said, trying to match Alok's grave tone. "This is Lorhir, raknari leader."

"Eagle Clan?" Alok's features stiffened. "Where Chieftess Yatal?"

Galahir and Lorhir exchanged a startled glance. "Chieftess Yatal?"

Alok brought his hands up, hooking the fingers of each hand together before his face. "Yatal and I *kataru.* Allies. Share in bounty for survival. Agree *trade*."

Galahir's eyes flickered to Lorhir's again. The other man

shrugged, as confused as he was. "I am sorry, Sag Du Alok,"
Galahir said. "Yatal has passed over to the Great Hunting
Plains. Before she departed on the last journey, she named
me the new Chief of the clan."

Alok cast his proud face towards the sky above. *"Eron,
Yatal, La'Atzu,"* he whispered.

"Have you come to stand with us, great Sag Du?" Galahir
asked, eyeing the wall of Thals.

Alok returned his attention to Galahir, his face betraying
nothing. "Yatal sent speakers. Claim *genii* bid us to stand
against gods with other Peoples. Bahari return to *etuti*
attacked by *shargaz*. Tell me gods are evil and threaten to
bring death."

"He speaks the truth," Galahir said. He could not help but
notice Alok had not answered his question. "Will you stand
with us against them?" he pressed.

Alok's face hardened. "Thals loyal to gods, always loyal.
It is the Cro the gods come to punish. People no believe in
fighting ones who gave them life."

Galahir's heart sank.

"Then why have you come?" Lorhir asked, his voice sharp.
"To stand and gloat over our demise?"

"Ngathe," Alok spat, eyes flaring at Lorhir's tone. "Hate
Cro, yes, but I not so dishonour. I come to honour Yatal,
persuade other *imrua* to follow. Thals agree to observe, bear
witness. We will seek truth, then decide."

It was the best Galahir could hope for. He bowed his head.
"As you wish, great Sag Du of the Thal."

Alok's gaze speared him. "And I ask you, Galahir of Eagle
Clan, I trust you still honour Yatal's *kataru* with us."

"I will," Galahir vowed without really understanding what

449

Yatal's alliance with the Thals entailed. He was willing to promise the proud Sag Du anything in that moment if it would cause the Thal leader to look more favourably on them when it came to the fight.

"You and your People are welcome to join our fireside and share in our hunt, Sag Du Alok," Galahir invited.

Alok eyed the vast Cro camp. "A kindness, Galahir of Eagle Clan," he said, stiffly, "but Thals not rest with Cro, we make our own camp at safe distance." And with that, Alok brought his open hand up to his mouth before curling his fist closed. Galahir guessed that meant their talk was over. The Thal leader began to walk away.

"Oh, last thing," Alok said, and let out a soft, low whistle. Two shadows broke away from the ranks of the Thals.

"Great Ea!" Galahir exclaimed, backpedaling with Lorhir as the shadows morphed into two great spear cats. Their long fangs gleamed in the flickering firelight from the camp. Galahir risked taking his eyes off the approaching predators to glance at Alok, seeking his intent. He thought he saw a smile flicker across the solemn face of the Thal leader. The Sag Du was enjoying their unease. Galahir growled, betrayed, but at the last moment Alok made a throaty sound and the two stalking cats broke off, circling Galahir and Lorhir at a safe distance, yellow eyes fixed upon the two men in their midst.

"If we be *kataru*," Alok said. "Best Nisaru and Dullu know your scent. No like strangers. Hold still if you value limbs."

The cats circled closer. Galahir gritted his teeth, tightening his grip on his arshu as the larger of the two beasts stalked up to him. The cat sniffed around his legs and his feet, lifting its lips occasionally and opening its mouth to take in the scent. Galahir felt his skin recoil from the curving fangs merely a hot breath away.

And then it was over. The cat bumped itself up against Galahir, rubbing its rough fur along him with a vibration in its throat, before returning to Alok. The slightly smaller cat had also finished with Lorhir and followed in the wake of the other. Galahir breathed again.

"Nisaru like you," Alok stroked the head of the larger cat, eliciting more rumbles from the beast's throat as Galahir watched, now in fascination rather than fear. "Good. I think *kataru* between us will be well. Eron watch over you this night, Galahir of the Eagle Clan."

Alok returned to his People, his cats shadowing his steps.

"That was not necessary," Lorhir growled, swiping cat hair from his furs.

"Spear cats," Galahir breathed. "He tamed spear cats. They," Galahir cut himself off, lost for words. He had never been so close to such a majestic creature.

"Don't start getting any babe's ideas into your head, respected Chief," Lorhir said. "If you want to capture one and try to be its friend, you can risk your own limbs." With that, Lorhir stalked back to camp, muttering the entire way.

It was only then that Galahir noticed that the Sag Du's honour son had not moved to follow his leader back to the Thal ranks. The Cro man was staring towards the edge of the Cro camp, his grey eyes wide. Galahir turned to follow his gaze and saw Kyaati standing in a pool of torchlight, watchful and awaiting his return.

"Kyaati?" the Cro man breathed.

Shock shivered through Galahir at the sound of his mate's name on a stranger's lips. He shifted his stance to block the man's view of Kyaati, bringing the Cro man's attention back to him.

"May I speak with her?" the Cro man flicked his fingers in front of his mouth and then pointed towards Kyaati. "I promise no harm," he added when Galahir remained a solid wall in front of him. "Have news she might want to hear."

Galahir weighed Alok's honour son for a moment longer and then relented. This was only one man and the entire Eagle clan would be ready to defend their matriarch at the first sign of a threat. He beckoned the Cro man, leading him back to where Kyaati stood.

His mate eyed the newcomer as they approached, then stepped back in surprise when he lowered himself to his knees in front of her, laying the spear he carried at her feet.

"Beautiful Dryad," he said, his face earnest. "I am Bahari, honour son of Sag Du Alok." He raised his arms towards Kyaati, the furs that had hitherto concealed the left falling back. Another pulse of shock went through Galahir. The arm ended just above the wrist. His hand was missing. "I bring story of…"

"Nyriaana," Kyaati breathed, staring down at Bahari's stump. Galahir studied the skin at the end. There wasn't even a scar to betray the violence of the injury.

"Yes," Bahari whispered.

"Where is she?"

Bahari gestured towards the Mountains behind them. "Seeking Last Kamaali as *genii* bid her," he said. "I travelled with her a short time to protect. Wanted to stay with her, but *shargaz* attacked us. Did best. I killed *shargaz*, but," he broke off and looked mournfully at the space where his left hand should be. "Could not go further. Nyriaana saved life, sent me home to muster Thal."

There were tears in Kyaati's eyes as she lowered herself to her own knees before the Cro man, taking his good hand in hers and placing the other on his severed wrist. "Is she alone now?" she whispered.

Bahari tilted his head back and forth. "No. In company of Jade Kill—Wolf. Juaan."

Kyaati let out an audible breath and bowed her head. Galahir thought he heard her whisper something that sounded like a prayer.

"Forgive me, could not stay with her, Kyaati."

"There is nothing to forgive," Kyaati said, squeezing his arm. "You suffered greatly for her."

"Not enough to honour my mistakes and my life that she returned," he said, lifting his face to look Kyaati straight in the eye. "I failed to stay by Nyriaana's side, and so I will protect her *imrua.* For Nyriaana, I pledge my life to you now, Kyaati of Dryad People."

* * *

25

Life

The crackle of lightning burst against Juaan's ears. He screwed his eyes shut to protect them from the flash of blinding white light. Heat flared across his skin, singing his furs.

"Nyri." He struggled to focus and regain control of his body. The back of his head throbbed, pounding against his skull. He could feel the bruises forming down his back where he had struck the solid barrier.

Then the hot light staining his eyelids red vanished. Juaan blinked his eyes open, forcing down the sick feeling of disorientation. He gasped as his fingers sank into soft moss. The strange, shining room had vanished. He was once more in the midst of the forest outside the *ekur,* his senses assaulted by the power of life buzzing all around. The beast was back, prowling around inside him. Juaan gritted his teeth. Ignoring the pain, he whipped his head around, seeking his enemy, but there was no sign of Enlil. He was alone.

"Nyri," he gasped. "Nyriaana!"

And then he saw her. A small heap of furs lying sprawled on the forest floor several strides away. The only movement was a faint curl of smoke rising from her body. Juaan reached out with his awakened senses and felt… nothing.

"No." He scrambled to her side. "Nyriaana!" He reached out, rolling her over so that he could see her face. Juaan stopped breathing. Angry red burns scoured her skin. The smell of singed hair and melted flesh turned his stomach as he sought her eyes.

They stared back at him, half-lidded and lifeless.

"Nyri!" Juaan grabbed her up into his arms, feeling broken bones shift. "Nyri, Nyri, Nyriaana." He willed her to look at him, for her to wake and speak his name, but her head tumbled back, lolling on her shoulders. Juaan caught it and bundled her against his chest, burying his face in her hair.

"No, no, no. Nyri, no." This was not how it was supposed to end. "Nyri, wake up. You have to find Ariyaana. Y-you have to stay. There is still so much you have to do. Nyri!" His fingers trembled as he touched her face. There was no breath, no pulse of life against his own. Just a lifeless husk. All other reasoning fled as he begged. "Nyri, please. You have to stay… for me. I can't exist without you. I can't. You don't know. I never told you. I was always too frightened. But I need you to know and come back. You are my light in the darkness. My solace. My home. And I love you. Nyri, please. Do not leave me to the night."

Silence.

A shudder ran through his body, his words falling dead in the air. Too late. This was the secret she had kept from him. The realisation tore through Juaan's gut. She had known she was going to die. She had known she was going to leave him. And he had failed to see it, failed to save her. He had led her to the slaughter. A cry keened through his teeth as his skin crawled over his body. This was not real. It was just another nightmare.

But this was a nightmare from which he would never wake.

Nyri lay dead in his lap. The very centre of his world, his only reason for existence, was gone.

Juaan shattered. Searing pain crackled through his body as if he too had been struck by the lightning. Throwing back his head, he screamed to the sky, letting go of everything. His confusion, his fury, it didn't matter anymore. The monster inside flew free, the Mountains themselves echoing with the sound of his agony until his flayed throat burned dry and he bowed over the empty shell in his arms.

The surrounding forest was now a reflection of his soul, withered and stripped of life by the force of the power that had broken loose from within. He did not care.

What was he to do now? Go on alone and finish what Nyriaana had started?

Juaan closed his eyes. He was not going anywhere. Alive or dead, he would not leave her side. The whole world could burn for all he cared. There was nothing in it for him now. His heart, his hope, and his love had all gone with her.

Juaan collapsed onto his side with the broken body of his only love in his arms. *She's dead. She's gone*. It was too much. Too much to bear. Unable to contain the enormity of his loss, Juaan's mind closed down, fleeing towards the escape it needed as he surrendered to the relief of oblivion.

Juaan.

Someone was calling his name. But it was not the voice Juaan needed to hear. He curled more tightly upon himself. He just wanted to die.

Juaan. The ghost of a hand brushed across his damp cheek. *Juaan.*

This time, Juaan twitched, the sound of the call cutting through the distortion of memory. He knew that voice, though he had not heard it since he was a child and had never thought to hear it again. *Mother?*

The voice smiled. *My Juaan.*

Juaan blinked open his eyes. He was still lying amid the ruined trees, but now everything around him was diffused in a hazy aura. And he was no longer alone. Three figures stood before him. Unlike the forest, they were solid and clearly defined. The first and farthest back was a tall Cro man. Striking grey eyes stood out against his dark skin. An ornamental spearhead hung about his neck, the carving of a black wolf upon it. Juaan kept the same totem tucked in a fold within his furs. He was looking at the face of his father for the very first time. The grey eyes were filled with pride.

The second figure was the red-haired Thal woman he had seen in the foothills. His *tarhe*. Her face was so alike to her brutal son's and yet not alike at all. Where Eldrax's face was carved by madness and hate, hers was gentled by tenderness and warmth.

Then Juaan's eyes came to rest upon the closest figure. Fresh tears spilled loose. *Mother.* She was just how he remembered her, but her face was no longer ravaged by sickness and starvation. Her dark indigo eyes were bright.

My precious son.

Have you come to take me away? Hope swelled in Juaan's

heart. He could be with Nyriaana again.

Rebaa's smile faded as she shook her head. *No, Juaan. You still have a destiny to face before you can be at peace.*

Resentment flickered through his chest. *I want no part of a destiny that does not include her.*

No, His mother took a step forward. *Your fates are entwined. You must save her, Juaan.*

Shock reverberated through his body, forcing his dead heart to beat again. *How?*

You are stronger than any Ninkuraaja alive. The power lies within. Call upon it.

Juaan balked, knowing of what she spoke. *No! You know as well as I do it is nothing but a curse. Death and destruction are all it is capable of. Look around you. It is a monster. I am a monster, mother. I was never meant to be! I am everything the gods hoped to avoid.*

There was no doubt in Juaan's mind his mother knew of all the terrible things he had done in the course of his lifetime. Bent to Eldrax's will. The splinters of his shattered soul tore against his heart more sharply than ever. He bowed his head over Nyri in shame, unable to meet his mother's eyes. How could she look upon him in anything other than disgust?

The lightest of touches fluttered across his cheek, feeling more akin to the warm caress of a breath than a physical touch. It lifted his face. His mother's loving gaze filled his vision. A lump formed in Juaan's throat, rendering him speechless. He leaned his cheek against the insubstantial touch.

You are not a monster, Juaan. You simply forgot. You lost your way. Now you must remember your last promise to me and live.

Remember *all the People who have loved you and given their lives for you, knowing you were worth such a sacrifice.* Rebaa's eyes went to Nyri, her hand ghosting over her ruined face. *She knew. Now you must believe it yourself.* Her hand moved to his heart. *Save her.*

I don't know how.

You do.

Juaan could feel her presence fading. Panic shot through his body, just as it had when he was a child. *Mama, don't go.*

Ghostly lips brushed across his cheek. *Never, my Juaan. I carry you always. Now go, be everything I know you to be. She needs you. The world needs you both.*

Mother!

Water sluiced across his face. Juaan gasped and opened his eyes. Rain pounded through the canopy above, splashing onto the rocks and earth below. The haze had lifted and the space the three figures had occupied stood empty. Tears slipped down Juaan's cheeks as he felt the sting of loss for his mother a second time.

She needs you.

Nyriaana. Juaan forced himself to look upon her lifeless face, placing a hand over her ruined heart. So much damage. His breathing hitched, more sobs threatening to break free. Surely no power under the heavens could fix this. But he could not bear to be without her. He would do anything. Even face the monster inside.

Drawing in a deep breath, Juaan closed his eyes and reached down to the place where his power, his connection to the Great Spirit, resided, untamed and unpredictable. He shied away instinctively, the memories of the times it had been unleashed without control rushing through his mind.

459

He was no pure Ninkuraaja; he did not have the skill.

But it was more than that.

Juaan frowned. The connection between this innermost part of himself and his conscious mind was clamped, strangled, like the cord of a newborn infant. Juaan had never looked close enough before to notice this oddity. He pushed against the block, to no avail. He gritted his teeth. The hold was powerful, but he knew well that it was not insurmountable. The overwhelming strength of the River Line flowing beneath these Mountains could break it. Whenever his life was in danger and primal instinct took over, the beast would break loose, like water cascading around a dam, wreaking havoc.

But his life was not in danger now. He was ice cold. The dam kept the sleeping tide back. Nyri had been able to help him. Using her power as a bridge, he had bypassed the hindrance and tamed the beast for the first time in his life, tempered the mighty flow to do his bidding. Without her, he was helpless.

"I can't do it, Nyri," he moaned. "I can't do it. Without you, I'm lost." Despair washed through him. He *needed* her.

Juaan pushed again in desperation, struggling to remember all she had taught him, but the power slipped through his fingers, as insubstantial as the wind.

You do not possess the force of will to wield it. The Lord Enlil's sneering voice echoed through his head. The cold, golden face glared down at him.

The beast inside blinked, anger flaring in Juaan's gut at the memory of the creature responsible for taking Nyri from him. Enlil had burned her alive like she was no more than a piece of meat. The most precious being in the world. Fury burned away his despair, stirring the tide, and the invisible dam inside trembled, the first leaks springing loose. *Yes.* He did not attempt to hold it back. Without her, his power was just a blunt tool, incapable of anything but destruction. His mother was wrong. He could not use it to bring her back. But the release would feel good.

Keeping Enlil's face in his mind's eye, Juaan let his pain fan the flames, gripping Nyri's furs as the red mist descended. If he destroyed this entire forest and everything in it, so be it. He would make the very roots of the Ekur tremble. Because of that so-called Sky God, he would never look into her glorious eyes again, never feel *home* again. He was far from cold now. He snarled as the monster inside raged in response. The power of it was taking his breath away, fuelled by hatred, anger and his insurmountable grief. It splintered the dam.

No, not that way! His mother's command ripped through his mind, staying the beast. *Remember, Juaan.*

And he did. Images flooded his mind, dousing his anger.

Hello, Juaan. Don' cry. I be your friend. Make it better? Nyri's child-like voice upon their first meeting. He remembered her tiny arms around him, giving him a light to cling to in a sea of darkness. The first time he realised he loved her.

Look, for you. Pretty rock, pretty, like your eyes.

A shuddering laugh went through Juaan as fresh tears fell upon the ruined face beneath his. The tenor of the power inside him shifted.

Laughter through the trees. Sweet red berries.

I promise I look after you, too, Juaan. We got to look after each other now.

Another memory, her hands on his, guiding him, showing him the way, proving to him what a gift his power could be.

The memory of her touch was like a balm, bearing away his hatred with the force of his love for her. Juaan shivered. He wasn't angry any more, but his power did not diminish.

It grew.

Swelling, rising on a tide, too great to be contained. No longer a destructive wildfire, it flared like the light of Ninmah in his mind's eye.

Now, Juaan.

He laid his hand flat against her breast.

"You are mine, Nyri, Nyri, Nyriaana," he whispered against her lips. "Come back to me." And he let go the power inside him.

This time, it did not burst around the dam. The dam exploded, loosing the full might of the river. It rushed through his veins in an unstoppable tide. Nyri's body jolted under his hands. Juaan kept his eyes closed as the healing flow filled them both. He could not see, but he could feel. Pathways were being sealed, burned skin returning to health, what had been broken becoming whole once again.

"I love you," he whispered, as the first heartbeat thudded to life under his waiting palm.

* * *

"Juaan?" Nyri sucked a breath into her lungs, tasting the relief like it was the first she had ever taken. Greedily, she pulled in another, the darkness relinquishing its grip with every life-giving expansion of her chest.

Confusion swamped her mind, remembering the flash of light, excruciating pain and then… nothing. Nothing until this moment.

Panic shot through her as she remembered Lord Enlil. She tried to sit up, but a gentle grip held her in place. Instead of feeling panicked by the unseen restriction, she felt… at peace. Perhaps this was what it was like to be dead. Her face was wet. Wet? She could hear what sounded like the soft tinkling of rain on leaves and earth. Nyri frowned. Locating her eyes, she blinked them open.

His face was the first thing she saw. He was staring down at her as she lay cradled in his lap, the rain dripping from his wet hair mingling with his tears.

"Juaan?"

"Hello, Nyri, Nyri, Nyriaana."

A sound tore from Nyri's throat. She wasn't sure if it was a sob or a laugh. "Juaan!" She threw herself at him, knocking them both to the ground. Burying her face in his neck, she let her own tears flow. Not dead. Alive! "You did this," she whispered as the rain fell and the forest sang around them. "You brought me back."

"Yes." His voice cracked, raw.

"How?"

"Can't you tell?"

And she could. "Oh," she breathed, placing a hand against his chest. The power inside him was different. Always before, it had felt like an angry, frightening force, hungry to rip the life from all it touched. Now it was beautiful; a warm, life giving, radiant light.

He caught her hand, holding it where it rested. "You were

463

the secret all along, Nyriaana."

Her brow pinched. "I don't underst—"

Before she could finish, he answered. His hands went around her face as his lips captured hers, moving with a fierce and possessive edge. His whole heart was in this one action. He held nothing back. Nyri could feel it all as his soul wrapped around her. "Juaan," she gasped. Her doubt and pain burned away. He wasn't too damaged. She wasn't too changed. He loved her, and he wanted her, with every fiber of his being.

A muffled cry of joy broke loose and Nyri locked her arms around his neck as his hands slid around her waist, crushing her against him. It was hard to tell where he ended and she began. Nyri basked in the glow of his love as she matched his every action, conveying her own feelings back to him. She never wanted this moment to end.

At last, with a ragged breath, Juaan broke away and sat up, Nyri straddling his lap. He rested forehead against hers. "I love you, Nyriaana," he spoke the words. "I love you. I could not let you go. Y-You are all I have."

Nyriaana placed her hands against the sides of his face, smoothing her thumbs against his cheekbones, wiping away the tears. "I am here." She pressed her lips against his once. "Thank you for not letting go. I would have walked through death to hear you say it."

He let out a small nervous laugh. "You just did."

They were silent for a long while, each wrapped up in the other, touching, caressing, speaking no words, simply marvelling at the new truth between them, until at last Nyri found it in herself to lift her head and face the world beyond. "What happened?" she asked, looking at the trees. The immediate area was shrivelled, withered and blackened. Juaan had not controlled his powers immediately, it seemed. "How did we get back here? Where is Enlil?" The memory of the Sky God was enough to puncture the moment they had existed in. Nyri leapt to her feet, half expecting the golden being to materialise out of the trees at any moment.

"I don't know," Juaan said, rising to his own feet, but he caught her around the tops of the arms again, as though loath to lose contact. "All I remember is a flash of bright light, then we were back here and you..."

His hands tightened and Nyri gasped as the echo of the agony he had suffered spasmed across her senses. She caught his hand where it clutched the top of her arm and drew it to her mouth to kiss his palm.

The renewed sense of peril did not leave her chest, however. Memories were coming back to her. The image floating impossibly over the Sky God's arm stood out above the rest.

"Eldrax," she said. "He's gathered the clans together. He means to challenge the gods themselves. Rannac once told me that Eldrax wanted to look the gods in the eye and demand they answer for their treatment of man. He drew Enlil's attention away."

Juaan cursed under his breath. "He will get them all killed!"

Nyri swallowed. Even with the gathered clans, Eldrax was provoking a force he could not imagine.

"What are we going to do?" Juaan asked.

Nyri closed her eyes, feeling the flow of the Great Spirit around her, relishing in her ability to feel him once more. The call, the tug that had drawn her here, was back and clearer than ever. She knew which way she had to go.

"I have to do what I came here to do," she said quietly. "I have to find Ariyaana, Naanshi, whoever she is."

"Still?"

"Yes," Nyri said. "Enlil said Ninmah hoped to save us. She is the one who wants me to find the Last Kamaali. I have to believe it, believe that at least one of these so-called gods cared about us enough to want to save us."

Juaan's doubt was palpable, but his hands flexed against her arms as he sighed. "You know I will follow you anywhere," he said. "And if you believe this Last Kamaali exists, then we will find her together."

Smiling, Nyri turned and stood on her tiptoes. She still would not have been able to reach had he not leaned down to meet her waiting kiss. Pleasure shot down Nyri's spine at the ease of this newfound contact between them. She caught his furs, dragging herself up against him, wanting him closer still. Their first kiss had been a desperate affirmation of reunion and their long denied love for one another. Now there was something else. Nyri's lips burned fire where Juaan's touched hers.

Juaan moaned and then laughed as he pulled away, softening the separation by cradling his hand around the back of her head. "Which way?" he said.

Nyri shook herself, flushing. "Oh, um, this way," she pointed into the trees, disentangled herself from him, and set off. Something caught her eye in the undergrowth. *Impossible.* She swooped down to pick it up and thrust it at Juaan. "Here."

Juaan blinked and took his spear from her.

"It does not seem to want to be parted from you," she said.

"Apparently not." He held the weapon in his right hand and caught Nyri's in his left as she set off at a rapid pace through the trees. She could not help but notice there was something different about the way Juaan moved. There was no longer the almost imperceptible limp when he walked, the stiffness with which he had held himself since Eldrax had impaled him upon the spikes of his battle club. She wasn't the only one who had been healed, it seemed. He was moving with his old cat-like grace.

Together, they left Enlil's strange mountain behind them, losing sight of the flat stone walls in the trees. But Nyri could still feel its oppressive weight looming somewhere above the thick green canopy. She increased her pace. This undying forest was almost as unnerving as the black forest on the outside of the mountains.

Fast as they travelled, the light above was dimming when the trees thinned at last and the stones of the Mountains reached out to envelop them once more.

Nyri did not stop. "There!" A thin trail leading up into the rocks caught her attention, beckoning. She was exhausted, but a familiar urgency had stolen over her limbs again. The call to keep moving and reach her destination pounded in her blood. She was so close now. After all this time, after all her doubt and fear, she knew this was where she needed to be. Ignoring her protesting body, Nyri clambered up the stony trail as it rose out of the tree line and into the lofty peaks.

The great light in the sky, Ninmah, Utu, or whatever it was, waned in the west as they broke free of the canopy, and the cold dry air of the Mountains hit Nyri like a fist. She shuddered in her damp furs, wrapping her arms around herself, tasting snow on the air.

"We should find a sheltered place to rest for the night," Juaan said.

Nyri shook her head vehemently, her eyes locked on the path ahead. She would not be able to rest. The call of the Great Spirit prickled over her skin almost painfully now. "We need to keep moving," she said. "Please, Juaan. We're close, I can feel it."

She could sense how tired he was. She knew well the toll healing another could have on one's energy, but she could not stop. She was grateful when he squeezed her hand and acquiesced.

The temperature continued to plummet as the night closed in about them. Nyri sorely missed the extra furs they had left back in the Forest of the Nine Gods when the Watcher attacked. The wind coming from ahead was light but cruel as it sought her shrinking flesh. The darkness was almost absolute. Ninsiku was not in the sky to light the way with his silvery light. Nyri wished for him now as her eyes strained into the shadows, guided only by the Great Spirit, and hoped that, in her tiredness, she did not make a misstep and plunge to her death in the empty space she could feel beckoning to her right. They climbed on.

Dawn was at hand when the ground mercifully flattened out. Nyri stumbled, her exhausted limbs thrown off balance by the sudden change in the kilter under her feet. Eyes blurring with tiredness, she barely caught herself. Only Juaan's continued hold on her saved her from pitching face forward into the rocks. Straightening with difficulty, Nyri peered into the growing light. A white haze appeared to be hanging over the surrounding grey rocks. Nyri blinked rapidly, but the visual impediment did not dispel. The white haze remained.

"Steam," Juaan said, his voice hoarse with fatigue.

Steam? Nyri looked again. The hazy white clouds were rising from the rocks, condensation settling on the grey stone as the moisture dripped to the ground.

The memory of Sefaan's vision blazed through her mind; the steaming lake in the mountains, the green-eyed girl that waited for her upon the shore, an *enu* seed dangling about her throat.

This was the place. She had made it! Ariyaana was waiting just around the rocks ahead. *I did it, Sefaan!* Nyri exalted in her mind. *I have kept my promise.*

Renewed strength shot through Nyri's limbs. She released Juaan's hand as she stumbled forwards in a rush, rounding the damp rocks, knowing in her heart what she would find. And there it was. The great mountain lake opened out before her, steam curling lazily from its surface into the cold air. The rocks, the sky above, everything was as it had appeared in her visions.

Nyri turned to where she knew the girl would be standing, green eyes alight with welcome... and froze.

An empty space was all that met her expectant gaze.

"Ariyaana?" Nyri called. But only the wind answered, whistling through the void where the Last Kamaali should have stood. "Ariyaana!"

The steam curled over the dead rocks, unperturbed by her summons. The lakeside was deserted.

"Nyri," Juaan said gently, placing his hands on her shoulders.

Nyri could feel his pity for her and she could not bear

it. She pushed away from him, rushing from outcropping to outcropping, peering into the shadows. "Ariyaana! Naanshi!"

"Nyri, stop," Juaan said.

"No!" Nyri cried. It hadn't been for nothing. It could not all have been for nothing. Sakal, Bahari, the suffering they had faced at the hands of Enlil. Death itself. "It can't have been for nothing!" she cried. "The Great Spirit brought me here. She has to be here! She has to save us! Ariyaana!"

"Nyri," Juaan said again, his voice calm in the face of her anguish. "You know as well as I do that there is no one here. It is just us."

He was right. They were utterly alone. Despair crashed over Nyri, robbing her of her remaining strength as she fell to her knees. Ariyaana, the Last Kamaali, did not exist. "Then what did it all mean, Juaan?" she choked. "What was it all for?"

He sank to the ground next to her, pulling her against his chest. "I don't know," he whispered. "I don't know."

A sob shuddered from Nyri's chest. Enlil had said Ninmah had wanted to save them. He had read her thoughts, seen her visions. He knew why she had come here. To find Ninmah's hope. Nyri hissed. She should have known better to have any faith in a Sky God.

Her eyes went again to the space where Ariyaana should have stood. Empty, empty. All for nothing. Another trick of the gods.

Nyri buried her face in the furs at Juaan's chest and cried out her despair in the safety of his embrace. He said nothing, just let her anger and hopelessness bleed out.

"What are we going to do now?" he asked when at last she

grew quiet.

"Nothing," she croaked, staring into emptiness. "There is nothing left. There is no hope for us now."

26

In the Moment

A loud splash jolted Nyri from the fitful sleep she had fallen into. She tried to cling to the sanctuary of her unconsciousness, but it fled from her grasp, denying any further escape. Groaning, she shifted, feeling warm but oddly off balance. Juaan's arms were no longer around her. A jolt of alarm shot through her chest before his nearby presence allayed her panic.

His mind was turned inwards, deep in thought. A strange aura of nervousness and determination flickered around him, but Nyriaana did not have the will to devine the focus of his ruminations. She lifted a hand to rub the prickling sleep from her eyelids as moist air blew across her face, bringing with it the scent of damp rocks. The sky above was a clear blue, framed by cold grey peaks.

Nyri lay there for a moment, trying to find the will to raise herself into a sitting position. She had cried out all of her bewilderment and crushing despair at the terrible dawn. Now she just felt numb, weary and resigned. The Last Kamaali did not exist. Sefaan had been tricked. They both had. Given visions for the amusement of a goddess who still enjoyed playing with their lives at a safe distance.

Growling low in her throat, Nyri threw an arm over her face to block out the surroundings that mocked her gullibility. All that remained now was to escape these accursed Mountains and survive for as long as Enlil allowed. She wondered where he was now, when the first strike would come.

Another splash of water, accompanied by the sound of ripples lapping gently against the shore, pulled Nyri from her spiralling despair. She lifted her arm away from her face. Realising she felt far too comfortable for a woman lying on bare rock, Nyri rolled slightly to look down. A pile of grey furs were gathered beneath her. Juaan's furs. She flushed as her eyes went to the lake. Sure enough, he was there, standing waist deep in the calm waters.

He was leaner than the last time she had beheld him so, the ravages of pain and hardship throwing every ridge and hollow into sharp definition. But none of that could take away from the raw perfection of him.

Nyri swallowed, her troubles fleeing for a moment. The numerous scars that marred his rich skin only seemed to enhance his masculine beauty. His torso glistened with water droplets in the daylight. A deep ache coiled in the pit of her stomach and Nyri averted her eyes out of habit.

"What's wrong?" Juaan asked, his voice carrying over the water.

"Nothing," Nyri said, curling her fingers into her palms.

There was a pause, and the edge of nervous energy receded from his aura, leaving behind a single-minded sense of purpose. Whatever it was he had considered so seriously, he had come to his decision.

"Come here to me, Nyriaana," he beckoned.

Her breath caught, shivering at the thought of stripping the furs from her body and joining him in the water. She recalled the night in the black forest when she had first confessed her true feelings for him, so much more than the love of friendship. She remembered the brief feel of his hand under her furs, calloused fingers grazing down her flank...

The sound of the water breaking made Nyri flinch as Juaan waded out of the lake towards her. She kept her eyes down, embarrassed and self-conscious.

"Nyriaana," he said. And before she could raise a protest at how cold it must be, she was in his arms. He bore her to the lake, cradling her against his chest as he submerged them both in the calm waters.

Nyri gasped in surprise as warm water soaked through her furs and enveloped her body. She had been braced for the bite of icy liquid, but instead the lake soothed across her sore muscles like the warm breath of a fire.

Juaan watched her facial expressions with a quiet smile playing about his eyes. He brushed a hand over her hair, tucking a strand behind her ear. "If we are to be tricked, I thought we might as well enjoy the rewards," he said.

"We should be getting out of these Mountains," she murmured.

His chest rose in a sigh. "Nyriaana." He put a hand against her cheek, bringing her face around to him. "Please. Stop. We have done everything asked of us and nothing that has happened can be undone. We are here now. Here, alive and alone, just us, no prying eyes, no one to judge us. I almost lost you, and no one can say what will happen now. Can I just steal this moment? Just this moment to give you everything of me before the world finds us again? No more regrets."

Nyriaana forgot to breathe, forgot everything, her heart breaking into a sprint as her mind caught up with the direction of his thoughts.

"I did not win the right to Claim you," he rushed into the silence. "Your Elders did not choose me for you, but... will you have me, Nyriaana?"

She felt the pound of his heart vibrating through them as he awaited her acceptance. Even after everything they had been through, he was still unsure of himself in this most vulnerable of moments. She swallowed, helpless before him. Bringing her hand up to his cheek, she gave the only answer she could, the only answer she had ever wanted to give. "Yes. Juaan of the Black Wolf. I will take you as mine. You are all I have ever wanted."

The smile that broke across his face shamed the Light Bringer itself. Gone was the hard, world-weary warrior. His pure, boyish elation was enough to make her heart ache. She had never loved him more.

His lips were on hers before she could catch another breath, one hand tangling in her hair as her body arched in response. If this moment was all they had before death found them, then this was the one Nyriaana wanted to live in. Her visions, Enlil, the discovery of the lie, past and future, all crumbled around her. Nothing mattered now but being here, alone, with Juaan. The world be damned.

Her hands caught his hard-muscled shoulders. His wet skin was silky under her fingertips as she pulled herself closer, deepening the kiss as she turned, wrapping her legs around his waist to steady herself in the water.

He released her for a moment and Nyri let out a soft protest. But his hands soon returned, sliding under her furs and slipping them from her body before slinging them towards the shallows where they would cause no further trouble.

Laid bare as she had been before Eldrax, a small part of Nyri's mind braced for the panic that was sure to set in. But it never came. She could not fear in this man's arms. Juaan's touch scorched away the nightmare as her naked flesh contacted his for the first time. She felt him tremble.

"Nyriaana," he breathed, pressing his lips into the curve between her shoulder and her neck as he pulled her tight to his body. Her heart bucked, a jolt of electricity shooting to her fingertips as his desire pressed hard against her thigh and belly, but the motion of his hands against her back quickly soothed away her sudden nerves, licking heat down her spine. Every touch and caress stoked a fire within until all that remained was an exquisite burn in the face of his want.

Moaning softly, Nyri tightened the embrace, relishing in the feel of his warm body against every part of hers. Suddenly, it wasn't enough. The ache at her centre grew until it was unbearable. He was quivering, his own tension reflecting hers, feeding, doubling her need.

"Juaan, please," she gasped, not really knowing what she was asking for but pleading all the same.

His groan was throaty against her ear as he moved them to the shallows, cradling her head as he laid her back in the water, gathering the cast-off furs beneath so the pebbles would not bite her skin as he laid his weight on top of her. Their fevered panting was all that could be heard as his heart skittered against her leaping pulse.

"Y-you're nervous." Nyri rubbed a hand across his rough cheek.

He turned his head slightly to kiss her palm. "Yes."

"You've done this before." Nyri tried not to feel the pain of imagining another in her place.

"Never while in my right senses." He was staring into her eyes as he spoke. His chest hitched and he turned his face away from her, features twisting into tortured lines. The determination she felt inside him wavered. Nyri experienced an unpleasant jolt, but she forced away the instant, childish sense of rejection as the full meaning of his words settled around her. He needed her now. He needed her to drown out his ghosts as he had so effortlessly banished hers. Eldrax was not going to take this moment from them.

"Juaan," she brought his head back around. "Juaan, look at me." He opened his eyes slowly, and Nyri could see the pain and the fear warring with his love and desire for her. "Look at *me*," she said again. "I am with you, and I love you, Juaan. You would never hurt me. I want this. Please." She leaned up to kiss his throat.

A breath shuddered through him as he placed his hands on either side of her face. The doubt still haunted the green depths as he hesitated, questioning.

With a soft growl, Nyri lifted aside all barriers, letting her innermost soul flood his senses, leaving him with no doubt who it was he shared this moment with, how much she loved him, how much she wanted him, freely, and with all her heart.

"Nyri," he gasped, the fear and pain melting from his eyes as she removed his hands from her face and placed them on her body. His mouth swooped down to claim her lips, moving now with a slow and purposeful edge. When she at last began to gasp for air, Juaan pulled his lips away from hers, only to replace them against her neck, proceeding to kiss his way down her body. Invisible flames trailed over Nyri's skin as he explored every part of her with both hands and mouth, teasing, learning, delighting in every shudder and moan he elicited from her.

She wanted to do the same for him. Unsure at first but with growing confidence, Nyri ran her hands over his shoulders, following the smooth plains of his chest and down to his stomach. She grinned in pleasure and triumph whenever he moaned her name against her ear. Emboldened, she let her hands slide down his long flanks to his hips, hesitating for the slightest moment before gripping his straining manhood in her palm. Nervous energy jolted through her gut once again, mingling with her pleasure.

"Nyri!" he yelped as his hips jerked forward. He grabbed her hand, pulling it away from him, and pinned it to the lake bed.

Nyri felt the blood flush to her ears. "Did I do something wrong?" she panted.

"N-no," he grinned, nuzzling her face to soften his hasty action, "but you keep that up, and this will never happen."

"Wha…?"

Before she could ask, his mouth descended, capturing a hard nipple between his teeth, flicking his tongue as his fingers dipped between her legs. "Juaan!" she cried, bucking violently beneath him. She could take no more. "Juaan, please."

Nyri didn't think he could have waited any longer either. Positioning himself, he entwined their fingers, keeping his eyes locked upon hers as he pressed forward. Nyri ceased breathing as she felt him enter her. Clenching her hands around his, Nyri kept her breathing even as he claimed her as slowly and as gently as his desire allowed. She had expected discomfort, this was her first coupling, and Juaan was hardly a Ninkuraaja male, but even so, she could not hold back a whimper when something inside resisted for a moment, then gave way.

Alarmed by the sound of her distress, he made to pull back.

"No!" she protested, winding her legs around his and locking him in place. "Just… give me a moment."

He held still as she breathed through the pain, stroking and placing feather-light kisses on her face while her body slowly relaxed, adjusting to accept him. At last, her grip on his fingers eased and his attentions shifted, moving lower, and when his mouth rediscovered her breasts, Nyri's desire flared back to life in full force. "Juaan!" She arched her chest into his mouth, muffling the moan that her motion pulled from his throat.

Unable to hold back any longer, Juaan withdrew before re-sheathing himself again. This time, there was no pain, only the most intense pleasure as she accepted the entire length of him. Nyri threw her head back, gasping at the sensation of his body filling hers.

"Nyri." Juaan reared himself up on his arms, looking down at her. His eyes were wide, pupils dilating, his lips slightly parted. He was drunk, but not on vision water. Not this time. Nyri laughed softly at his almost startled expression, happy beyond reasoning that she was the one who had brought him such rapture. Reaching up, she tangled her fingers in his hair, pulling him back down as she flexed her hips beneath him. An invite.

"Oh, Nyri," he whispered against her forehead. "Yes." And he began. Every motion sent shock waves cascading through Nyri's mind and body. His confidence only grew as she sighed and panted his name, falling into a steady rhythm. The lines blurred between them. They were one, body and soul, their spirits mingling together, the energy inside Juaan rushing forward to envelop hers, enhancing every sensation, encompassing the land around them with the throb and ebb of the Great Spirit.

Nyri wrapped her legs tighter around his waist, only wanting him closer now, deeper. The feel of him inside her was the most sacred experience she had ever known. There was nothing she could feel that wasn't Juaan.

The delicious tension in her centre continued to tighten as he led her in the dance, losing herself completely as the tempo increased, moving faster, ever closer, building to a crescendo until with a shout she thought must have been heard even by the eagles wheeling distantly overhead, Nyri's release exploded through her. She clung to Juaan, muffling the rest of her cries into his shoulder as the shock waves continued to roll, setting off a chain reaction. Her name keened across her ear as Juaan snatched her up in his arms, burying himself as deep as he could go as he convulsed, releasing himself inside her.

The beauty of the moment seemed to go on forever, and

somewhere, in a part of her brain that still functioned, Nyri thought she felt the Great Spirit exalting in the mighty River Line flowing directly beneath them.

"Nyri, Nyri, Nyriaana," Juaan whispered as they slowly returned to earth, his damp forehead falling against hers. "Mine."

"Yours." And she knew it in her bones. She was truly his now and he hers. They had not needed the power of a Kamaali. She and Juaan were bound, mind and soul. A bond that could only be broken by death. Perhaps not even that. "My *ankida*," she murmured tenderly, planting feather-light kisses along his cheek. "My Joined One."

The joy she felt radiating from Juaan in that moment banished every shadow from her soul. Lifting her from the ground, he drew them back into a sitting position, her legs still wrapped around his waist as he rested his chin on her hair. Utterly content, Nyri curled into his chest, blinking sleepily, her muscles strangely like liquid, until she heard Juaan's sharp intake of breath. *Ea above!* was the main thought in his head

"What is it?" she asked, trying to look up.

"Um, is that normal?" he asked, pointing.

Now it was Nyri's turn to draw breath. "N-no, she stammered, as she gazed wide-eyed at their rocky surroundings.

But the rocks weren't there anymore. At least, not as they had been. The grey landscape had been transformed. A thick green coating of moss now covered every surface, thrumming with vitality as flowers burst into life where once there had only been a barren void.

A smile spread across Nyriaana's face as she basked in this new oasis she and Juaan had brought into being. "No.

Not normal at all." And she tilted her head back to kiss his mouth.

* * *

27

The Fight for Existence

"Where your People?" Bahari's voice carried to Kyaati, muffled through the hide wall of a nearby shelter. The Cro man had taken upon himself to keep Kikima company within her protective confines. The Sag Du's adoptive son had seemed quite… taken with Kyaati's friend from the moment they had been introduced. To Kyaati's surprise, his favourable first impression had not been one sided. Kikima had accepted his companionship with a quiet grace.

"I cannot answer." There was a note of mourning in the half-Deni woman's voice as she answered Bahari's question. "My mother was the only Deni I knew, and she died when I was still young. They may not even exist anymore. Not in their true form, only in half-breeds like me."

Silence fell. Kyaati couldn't help but graze against her friend's thoughts and caught a hazy glimpse of Bahari lifting his hand to her cheek to brush away a single tear. Kikima sighed, leaning into the touch. Bahari's shock pulsed against Kyaati's own. Kyaati knew well that Kikima was not above using her strong physical appeal to bend a man's desire to her advantage. This was different. Kikima's heart fluttered at the contact. Bahari was an easy man to like, but it wasn't usually in Kikima's nature to warm to a stranger so fast.

The Cro man's own pulse picked up, a nervous delight shooting through him at Kikima's acceptance of his over-ture, though he appeared at a loss as to what he should do next.

Kyaati tore her mind away from them and cast her eyes to the sky above. Whatever was happening there would have to wait. Ninmah had disappeared below the horizon. The day had been unusually clear, the blue sky filled with a brightness she had never before witnessed. She had spent much of it with her father as Galahir busied himself showing Bahari the defences that had been put in place for the attack Yatal had claimed to have seen in a vision.

Kyaati shuddered. Self-preservation screamed at her to run, run with Elhaari and never look back. Doubt and guilt were her constant companions. She had brought the last of her People to the slaughter. Kyaati buried her face in her hands. "What have I done, Elhaari?" she whispered to her sleeping son. But, somewhere in her heart, a voice whispered it could not be any other way. If they did not fight, then Elhaari would never be safe. One such as him was in the most danger from the retribution of the gods. Kyaati had to protect this most precious bundle in her life. Even if it meant sacrificing Galahir's life, her People's lives, and her own.

"Kyaati, what are you doing out here?" Daajir's voice came from behind her. "I thought you were with Pelaan."

Kyaati half-turned to face him as he approached. She

surmised one of the things she had missed the least about her previous life was the reproving look in Daajir's dark eyes. She shrugged in response to his question. "I don't know," she said. "Didn't you feel it? Just before Ninmah sank. The Great Spirit swelled, all the birds started singing, it was…" Kyaati trailed off. She couldn't rightly describe what she had felt, but the sensation had drawn her outside. For a fleeting moment, she had felt the closest she had to Nyri since their separation. Kyaati had almost hoped to see her tribe-sister emerging from the Forest of the Nine Gods, safe at last. Of course, that had been a foolish imagining.

Nevertheless, Kyaati had not wished to return to the confines of the shelter her People huddled beneath as they adjusted to the openness of the Plains, so she had remained outside, watching as Ninmah gave way to Ninsiku's staring eye. It was fully open now, watching and waiting.

"You should come inside," Daajir said, keeping to the shadows, eyeing the silver light in the sky.

Kyaati laughed. "Oh Daajir," she said. "Who is Ninsiku going to send to catch us? We're already surrounded by his *dark spirits.*" She sobered. "Wake up."

His indignation at her mockery rolled across her awareness. "Did you ever stop to consider that your actions invited the gods' wrath? Committing the Forbidden, bringing our People into the company of the *Woves* to defend your filthy mistake. Did you consider that they send these *monsters* you speak of to cleanse the land of heresy and abominations?"

"Heresy?" Kyaati leaped to her feet, her tenuous hold on her composure flying apart. "Is it heresy to want to survive, Daajir?" she demanded. "Is it a heresy to want to be happy?"

She held Elhaari out. "Look, a living and breathing baby. Tell me, Daajir, how many healthy infants have you ever seen born as you cower behind the lies?"

"Ninsiku's curses…"

Kyaati laughed again, her fury giving way to pity. He would never see it. "Go away, Daajir," she said, sitting back down. She spied Galahir patrolling the edges of the camp. Her mate caught sight of her and a grin broke over his face as he swung a quick salute with his weapon. Kyaati smiled back, her spirit lifting at the sight of his loving, good-natured face.

Daajir made a disgusted sound in the back of his throat. "What is it like? To sully yourself with a creature like that?"

Fury rose in Kyaati's throat once more, but this time she didn't rise to fight. She took a deep breath. There were better ways to hurt Daajir. "It is the most blessed experience," she said sweetly, eyeing Daajir's much smaller physique. "A pleasure you will never give."

"You vile—!" Daajir started towards Kyaati.

"Kyaati?" Kikima emerged from the shadows of her dwelling, Bahari at her side. Outnumbered and facing the Cro man's spear, Daajir drew up.

"Goodnight, Daajir," Kyaati bit out.

He scowled, glaring murderously at Kikima and Bahari, and backed away before fleeing into the shadows. Kyaati blew out a breath.

"What a hog's backside," Kikima said, watching after him with distaste. Bahari chuckled.

"Thank you. A few more moments and I might have put a knife between his ribs," Kyaati said.

"Ah, then I should have waited," Kikima lamented. "Nobody would be sorry to see the back of his scrawny hide."

"Kikima," Kyaati sighed. "He is my kinsman."

"He's making everyone extremely nervous. Someone *will* put a knife between his ribs soon if he does not stop slinking around."

Kyaati changed the subject. "You should not be out, Kikima."

"Narak is keeping watch," Kikima said. "The Red Bear is inside his shelter. Occupied."

"It is too risky." Kyaati shook her head. "If he sees you, Kikima, you will never escape him again."

"I know," Kikima's mouth down-turned. "But I could not stay in that shelter another moment. I needed to see the sky."

"You should have returned to the Eagle camp the moment we discovered he still lived," Kyaati said.

"Red Bear not touch her."

Kyaati blinked at the proprietary edge in Bahari's voice as he stood at Kikima's side.

"We cannot spare men to escort me back and I wasn't going to leave you alone," Kikima went on. "Don't worry about me, Kyaati. Besides my impressive *magiri* companion here," she bumped Bahari with her shoulder. "I have been getting skilled with this blowpipe. I will not sit by with the babes and hide from this fight."

Kyaati lifted a sad smile. "I know you won't. But one word from Selima to her father is all it will take. I can't see you back in his clutches, Kikima. You must stay hidden."

Kikima scowled.

"Perhaps I offer a solution," Bahari said. "Take Kikima with me to Thal *etuti*. Not far away, still within sight of camp, but Red Bear no see her."

"Will she be welcome there?"

"Thals will shelter her," Bahari promised. "I take her as my guest."

Kyaati turned to Kikima. "Go," she commanded.

Kikima chewed her lip. She was clearly weighing up the need to stay near Kyaati versus being trapped inside a tiny shelter day and night and the risk of being recaptured by Eldrax. Her golden eyes came to rest on Bahari's earnest face and Kyaati saw her make up her mind. "All right," she blew out a breath. "Take me to your camp, Bahari. I will stay there until…" her voice trailed off and her gaze shifted towards the dark outline of the forest in the distance. "I will come straight back, Kyaati, at the first hint of trouble."

"I know." Kyaati got up and kissed her friend's hand. "Now leave, Kikima, while you still can."

Kikima pressed Kyaati's hand and then followed Bahari from the camp. The Cro man tentatively put his wounded arm against the small of her back.

"I wouldn't have betrayed her," a voice broke the silence as Kyaati watched the two figures disappear into the dark. She stiffened. *Selima*. The red-haired girl stood in the shadows between two shelters, weighed down with herbs and strips of hide.

"Forgive me if I take that as a blind story," Kyaati growled. She regarded the armfuls of material in Selima's arms. "You're helping Baarias with the wounded. Perhaps when I tell him of what you did to his Nyriaana, he will not be so willing to have you stand where she once did."

The girl's milky face paled. "Please, Kyaati! Please, don't. I'm sorry. I am so sorry for what I did. I see now it was a mistake."

Kyaati snorted, turning away.

"Try to understand! All I wanted was my father's love. Nobody has ever loved me in my whole life! My mother died when I was a baby. Johaquin took me in, but she only ever treated me as a means to an end. I just wanted—" She broke off, shaking her head. "I thought if I gave him his ultimate wish, he would see me as someone worthy of his regard. But he didn't," her voice turned hard. "He tried to sacrifice me to save his own life. He threw me in front of a Watcher. He does not deserve the love of his daughter. He deserves to die!"

Selima spoke the last with such vehemence, the scornful response playing behind Kyaati's teeth died on her lips.

The red-haired girl dropped her eyes, flushing. "I must go. Baarias needs these herbs." And with that, she scurried away.

Kyaati remained where she was for a long moment. She looked down into Elhaari's sleeping face. She would make sure he never grew up without knowing how much he was loved. Weariness stole over Kyaati's limbs and she started back towards the makeshift shelter she shared with Galahir.

She had gone but one step when the hairs on the back of her neck bristled. The Great Spirit heaved. Kyaati gasped, her hands going to her head as the pain ripped through it. Against her chest, Elhaari began to wail.

"Kyaati?" Galahir appeared beside her, catching her by the shoulders. "What is it?"

The warning drums of the sentries broke out with a frantic edge, answering her mate's question, before cutting off, leaving an ominous silence in their wake. "Ea above,"

Galahir whispered.

"I-it's happening," Kyaati choked. A voice ripped through her head. Cold, pitiless, promising destruction. It was just like before, when the lights had appeared over the Mountains. "It's happening. Galahir."

A flash of light shot across the dark sky. The colour of fire, it blocked out Ninsiku's spirits, dazzling in its brightness. Then the earth itself began to shake. Kyaati stumbled. Somewhere in the distance, the wolves were howling.

"Kyaati!" Galahir caught her around the shoulders, launching them both away. Something crunched into the ground behind them a heartbeat later. Kyaati blinked at the massive spear quivering in the earth where she had stood only a moment before.

"Go, Kyaati," Galahir gasped as he pushed her away. "Go!"

The rest of his words were drowned out by the keening howls rising to fill the night. The cry of the Watchers.

"They're coming! Go, Kyaati!" Galahir roared as the ground bucked and shuddered again, the Great Spirit convulsing under the torture.

Eyes watering from the pain in her head, Kyaati pressed her lips once to Galahir's and then tore herself away. "Father!" she called out as she ran to where her People sheltered. "Father, now!" Her People were already outside, small in their terror. Their stricken faces told her they were experiencing the same agony she felt. Daajir was vomiting into a clump of grass.

"Run!" Kyaati shouted. She could feel them now, black holes in the fabric of reality, closing on the camp, answering the summoning of their masters. She had to get her kin to their arranged positions. Her People would not be of any use in a physical fight. That would have to be left to the Cro. They needed to reach their places of concealment, ready to strike with their poison darts and whatever other skills they could bring to bear against their enemies.

Kyaati's breath caught, her legs turning to water as the dreaded blue eyes appeared in the dark distance, issuing from the Forest of the Nine Gods, lumbering in from the Plains. How many, Kyaati could not count.

Calls to arms went up as the Cro surged into action. Gulping down her panic, Kyaati led her People in a race for the boundaries of the camp. She could taste their fear, but also their grim determination. Kyaati let her family's courage seep through her, to give her the strength she needed.

Galahir had ordered smaller pits dug around the outside of the camp, each one just large enough to conceal an individual inside, covered by interlacing sticks with enough gaps through which to use a blowpipe. Stores of Daajir's poison and tree frog toxin had already been placed within. Kyaati wondered if the thorns of the *vaash* plant would be sharp enough to pierce the hides of the Watchers.

It was too late to worry about such things now. The ground lurched again, just as Kyaati helped lower her father into a pit. She placed her forehead against his for a brief moment and then pulled herself away. She had to reach her own place of concealment.

Somewhere within the camp, Galahir was crying out his orders as torches flared to life, setting alight the sharpened stakes bristling out around the perimeter of the camp. Kyaati's strength faltered once more. She may never see her mate again. There was every chance Galahir would not survive this battle. *Don't think. Don't think!* If she did, she would not be able to function. It was unlikely any of them would survive the night. If Galahir fell, at least she would have to live with his loss beyond the dawn.

KILL THEM ALL. The voice invading Kyaati's mind morphed into coherent words. *WIPE MY BROTHER'S MISTAKE CLEAN.*

Kyaati snarled in answer, the collective fury of her People echoing hers. This was the first time they had felt the wrath of the gods first hand, felt the malice and disregard, knowing all their sacrifice and loss had been for nothing. In the gods' eyes, they were no more than the Children of KI in the eyes of the Cro, prey to be slaughtered and wiped out when convenient.

The ground rolled, groaning under the strain. Small fissures appeared, and light akin to the beams of Ninmah burst forth.

Disoriented by the Great Spirit's cry, Kyaati could not define the angry rumbling of the land from the pounding of massive feet.

"Kyaati!" Suddenly Bahari was there, rolling, yanking her out from under the feet of a Watcher that had sprinted out of the darkness. She gasped, holding Elhaari close. She could feel the great power inside her son flexing, the same as she had on the day the Watchers had chased his father from the Forests of the Nine Gods. The day Eldrax had laid down his challenge. Kyaati's senses quivered at the strength of it.

"Come! Come with me!" Bahari tugged on her arm.

"No!" Kyaati cried. "I have to get to the pit. It's where Galahir needed me to be!"

"Too late now!" Bahari cried, dragging her back.

And he was right. Watchers were swarming over the land, charging the flaming ring of stakes protecting the Cro within. She would not make it. It was too late. Bahari dragged her away through the shadows. Kyaati relied on him to keep her upright, for she could not take her eyes off the camp as the Watchers fanned out to surround all that she held dear.

Loud snaps ricocheted through the air as the huge pits that the Cro had dug in defence swallowed the leading beasts whole. Gurgling shrieks leaped for the indifferent sky as the fallen Watchers were impaled upon the waiting stakes below. Several others, blind in their need to carry out their masters' bidding, charged straight into the gaping holes, landing directly on top of their already fallen leaders. Kyaati felt a savage satisfaction rush through her veins at the sounds of their dying cries.

One, two, three Watchers flinched, their gnarled hands swatting at their exposed flesh. Kyaati watched, elated, as the creatures crashed to their knees, the toxins of her People burning through their veins as they convulsed on the ground, eyes rolling, mouths foaming, their unnatural life energies draining away. The *vaash* barbs were more than enough to inflict the needed damage.

A barrage of spears flew from the centre of the camp. Most glanced off the bone armour of the giants, but a few struck true. One lucky spear found the eye of an attacker. It staggered back, bellowing furiously as it blundered into its neighbours, bearing several to the ground.

But it wasn't enough. Like a tide around an island, their enemies continued to advance. More than half of the creatures had made it through the traps, stepping over their fallen and weaving through the pits, until they stood before the flaming stakes ringing the camp and the many souls within. Kyaati could feel the insidious will driving the Watchers on, sending them mad with the need for human blood. Spears as tall as two men and as thick as an arm were launched into the air, arcing over the defensive flames. Kyaati caught the flash of what appeared to be a strange blue rock at the tips of their weapons before they disappeared on the other side of the burning stakes.

BOOM. A bright flash seared across Kyaati's eyes and blue flames burst to life in the centre of the camp, accompanied by screams of agony.

"Magic of the gods," Bahari breathed, his grey eyes wide as he beheld the unnatural flames, the intense heat carrying on the wind to kiss at their faces.

His hand was like the grip of a bear on her arm as Kyaati struggled to free herself. "Galahir!" With the Great Spirit in turmoil and the confusion of the battle, she could not pick out his presence, could not know if her love was one of the many burning to death in a cloak of icy flames as she was forced to watch. "Galahir."

Bahari had now drawn her back as far as the river. Their feet splashed as they forded across it, back where his own People crouched behind a large outcropping of rocks fronting a thick copse.

"Kyaati!" Kikima materialised out of the darkness. "We must go!" Another flare of terrible blue reflected in her friend's wide eyes. Two heartbeats later, the sound of the blast vibrated their bones. "We must do something!"

"Ngathe!" a rough voice ordered. Kyaati recognised

494

the grizzled leader of the Thals. "No go. Only be killed. Sacrifice for nothing."

Kikima snarled in his direction and started towards the river, her jaw set.

"No," Bahari denied. A Thal caught Kikima about the arms, holding her fast. Kikima threw a betrayed look in Bahari's direction. Together with her clan sister, Kyaati could only watch in horror as two Watchers moved from the back of their brethren's ranks. Between them, they bore a boulder made of the same bright blue rock that had tipped their spears. It flashed as they hurdled it through the air. Over and over it tumbled until it crashed against the circle of burning stakes.

The light that exploded forth forced Kyaati to throw her arms up in front of her face to protect her eyes. She thought she felt the air itself quiver, listening to the gasps from the Thals lying concealed around her.

"Ea above!" Kikima wailed. Kyaati pulled her hands away from her face, blinking rapidly against the aftereffects of the bright light. Blue flames were now consuming the defensive ring around the camp, melting away the wood of the stakes, opening a hole.

"Help them!" Kikima rounded on the Thal leader. "How can you stand here and watch? Help them!"

The venerable Thal waved her away. "Gods punish Cro only. Not Thal. Thal never challenge might of gods. I not put People at risk."

"Coward!"

Kyaati ceased listening to the futile debate. The Cro's defences had been obliterated. Nothing now stood between them and the might of the Watchers. The giants swarmed towards the gap their magic had made, intent on cornering and slaughtering their targets within.

But the Cro would not be extinguished so easily. Before the Watchers could enter the camp, the joined Cro clans issued forth, meeting their enemy in the open. Kyaati could just discern Eldrax's flaming red hair at their head as they swept around their attackers, lancing at their legs as they passed, battle cries ringing through the air.

The earth spasmed, groaning, more fissures cracked open, and the golden light flared from the rocks. Watchers and Cro alike were borne to their knees. Those that fell into the light emitting from the earth screamed as their flesh burned from their bodies, disintegrating to ash before Kyaati's eyes.

Consumed by the horror, Kyaati did not detect the danger to herself until it was almost too late. Her senses screamed as the jaws of death reached for her throat.

"Look out!" she cried as the lone Watcher barrelled from the gloom, crashing through the copse where much of the Thal force lay hidden.

Bahari had faster reactions than either Kyaati or Kikima. Hooking his maimed arm around Kyaati, with his remaining hand, he snatched Kikima from the startled grasp of the Thal who had been keeping her in place, whirling them away as the guardian of the gods fell among them. The Thals stumbled back with cries of dismay.

Only the Watcher's own shock at stumbling upon this hidden company of humans saved the Thals in that moment. But it was not to last.

A grin broke out over the hideous face as the creature gazed down on the upturned faces of the Thals as they dropped to their knees, clearly believing the fury of the gods would roll harmlessly over them and move on to the destruction of the treacherous Cro.

"Don't, you fools!" Kyaati cried at them. "Run!"

"SLAVES!" The word slipped past the double rows of teeth, and Kyaati heard the double timbre of it echoing with the bodiless voice in her head. *Eron! Enki's first insult. Stamp them out! Stamp them out.*

A few of the Thals rose back to their feet, confusion flickering across their thick features as instinct warred with their staunch beliefs. A massive hand flashed out, and all faith was torn away as it snatched the nearest man from the ground, lifting the thrashing figure to the waiting mouth. Kyaati closed her eyes, but she could do nothing to block the sound of crunching bone.

"Ngathe!" Kyaati heard the voice of Thal leader and opened her eyes in time to see him rush forward, hands raised in supplication, his two *grishnaa* cats on his heels. "*Shalanaki!*" Kyaati could not understand the words he shouted, but she could easily translate the pictures in his head. *Peace! Thals loyal!*

"Ngathe, *adda*!" Bahari cried. But the Cro man was too late to save his father as the Watcher caught the Thal leader up in its gory hand to the angry snarls of his cats. "KILL SLAVES!"

Bahari's grief and despair triggered something within Kyaati, drowning out her terror. Elhaari's tiny heart pounded against hers, the wild power inside his body swirling. The baby could not control it. But Kyaati could. She had done it before.

Throwing off her fear of such raw power, she merged her mind with Elhaari's, joining his energy to her own and, snarling, ripped the Great Spirit from the earth. Kyaati unleashed it upon the beast as it lifted its hand, intent on biting the head from the Thal leader. "No," she spoke. And the giant convulsed, Kyaati squeezing its heart to a pulp inside its chest. Dark blood spurted from the glowing blue eyes, from the nose, and poured from the mouth as the arms fell slack.

Released, the Thal Sag Du fell to the ground as the Watcher toppled, dead eyes rolling back into the long head. The invading voice inside Kyaati's mind howled in fury. She groaned as the unnatural power scraped against her skull and the earth shook with renewed force, throwing them all to their knees.

"Now you see," Kyaati gasped at the Thal leader as he staggered back to his feet, pale face ashen. "The gods come for us all. Loyal or not, you have outlived your use. We have to stand together, or we will all be wiped out, one by one." She jabbed a finger towards the fires and the battle raging on the other side of the river, hearing cries and the screams of the dying. "The Cro fight for their freedom to live. This earth is where we were created. It belongs to us. We are part of it! All of us. The gods are not. It is they who do not belong." Kyaati could feel the truth of that as the power ripping through the ground tore the Great Spirit apart, destroying all that was natural. "Are the Thals going to lie down and let them take what is ours?"

The Thal leader gazed at her for a long moment, dark eyes burning, before he spat upon the dead face of his would-be murderer. He raised his spear high and bellowed a command.

"Children of the Earth," Bahari translated in her ear. "To

our brothers under *Gisnu!*"

The Thals roared in response. Behind their leader, they charged, splashing across the river with the two *grishnaa* cats bounding ahead.

Bahari hesitated to follow.

"We must go, Bahari!" Kikima hauled on his arm. "They need us."

"But I can't protect you there." His eyes went to Kyaati. "I vowed to protect you."

"Who do you think just did that?" Kyaati jabbed a finger at the felled Watcher. Bahari's eyes widened as he snatched his arm from her as though burned.

"Oh, stop," Kyaati said. She faced the battle. The beleaguered Cro were struggling to keep the Watchers at bay. A few of the beasts crashed to the ground, felled by a lucky spear or from an unseen dart shooting up from the ground, but their losses paled in comparison to those of the Cro. Ten men at a time could fall from one swipe of a massive club. Kyaati could feel their hope dwindling, terror threatening to break their courage. A few of the men had already bolted, fleeing across the Plains and away from the lost cause, hoping to preserve their skins for a few more days before the Watchers caught up to them. Perhaps hoping their enemies' blood lust would be slaked by the fall of their brothers.

Somehow, Kyaati heard Galahir's voice, carrying to her on the wind. Ragged, exhausted as he tried to bolster the last of his men. *Hold on, my love.*

Then the Thals came like a waterfall crashing upon the rocks. Spears and rock-ended clubs flashed out as they joined their forces to the failing Cro, catching the

Watchers between them. The monsters roared in surprise and fury, swinging around to protect their back from the new unexpected onslaught.

"By Eron!" Bahari exclaimed. Kyaati tore her gaze away from the fight long enough to see what had drawn his low oath. The Thals were not the only ones joining the fray. The glimmer of countless twin points of white light shifted in the darkness, closing in. Howls lifted, harmonising with the battle cries of the men.

"Nekelmu!" Kyaati gasped as the great black wolf bounded into the firelight, teeth gleaming as he led his vast pack out of the shadows.

"Did you summon him?" Kikima shouted as they began to run towards the fight.

"No!" Kyaati answered. "The Children of KI belong to this earth. They are defending their home."

For the first time since the start of the attack, hope took root in Kyaati's heart. With the addition of the Thals and the wolves, the Watchers found themselves vastly outnumbered, surrounded on all sides by flint, rock, fang and claw as the first rays of Ninmah broke over the far horizon.

You're going to lose, Kyaati promised the bodiless presence in her head, and stretched out with Elhaari's combined power once more. If the wolves would defend their land, then the rest of the Children of KI should do no less.

The sky blackened as though storm clouds had gathered. A few of the fighters looked up in fear and confusion, but instead of thunder, harsh caws, shrieks and whistles filled the air. Birds scythed from above, adding to the confusion as they flew into the Watchers' faces, striking at their eyes, blinding them to the attacks from below.

The joyous whoops from the Cro and the Thals fueled Kyaati's renewed sense of hope. The tattered Cro forces rallied behind their leaders. Kyaati spied Galahir's bright hair flying in the melee. He was alive and still fighting, his blackened face set with grim determination.

But a fleeting glimpse was all she got before another flash of light, brighter and more intense than anything she had yet witnessed, seared across her eyes. Kyaati shrieked in pain, her influence over the birds flying apart. The earth groaned and bucked anew. When the assault on her vision and mind receded, Kyaati cast about, struggling to see with her dazzled sight.

The energy was the first thing she was aware of. She knew instantly it belonged to the same invisible presence that had vibrated in the air and through her very being since the Watchers had descended. If she had thought it overpowering before, it was nothing to what she was experiencing now. Her mind was on fire, burning with the proximity of the being that had come among them. She fell to her knees, crying out as her hands went to her head.

"Kyaati!" Kikima caught her shoulders as the blood began to drip from Kyaati's nose. "What's wrong?"

Kyaati could only point at the lone figure emerging from the ruins of the Cro camp. He was tall, as tall as the Watchers who fell back in supplication before his advance, but he was not of the same creed. His body was impossibly thin and elongated, his skin the colour of Ninmah's rays under coverings that shone and flowed like water under daylight. A spear was in his hand, but it was not made from wood. It glinted and flashed in the firelight.

And the face, long and chiselled beneath a gleaming

headdress, was terrible to behold. Luminous blue eyes burned out of shallow sockets as he glared down upon the struggling Peoples. A full lip lifted in contempt. The spear levelled and white lightning crackled from the end, burning through an entire swathe of Thals. The battlefield fell silent, all lowering their weapons to stare upon this one being.

This god of the skies.

Kyaati had no doubt that this was what had come among them, even before the mouth opened to speak.

"Silence!" the voice rumbled, rolling over them, irresistible in its force. "On your knees and bow before your Lord Enlil!"

* * *

28

Weak Point

Nyriaana rolled from Juaan's body as the light faded. With a satiated sigh, she curled into his side, savouring the aftershocks of their latest lovemaking pulsing through her centre as she rested her head on his shoulder. They lay upon their furs beside the lake, the warm vapours coiling around them.

"That was a quite a view." A devilish smile curled across his face as his breathing returned to normal. Nyri stretched, recalling the play of his muscles as his body writhed and arched deliciously beneath her, his heated green eyes ablaze with passion as he stared up into her face.

"Yes it was," she grinned into his skin, feeling the responding shudder of his own mirth.

The Light Bringer dipped below the Mountains, bringing an end to this most devastating and yet most glorious of days. Humming in his throat, Juaan gathered Nyri into his arms. Peace reigned as he pressed his lips into her hair.

"I love you, Nyriaana," he whispered, and Nyri felt the sentiment echo through their bond, wrapping her in a cloak warmer than the surrounding furs. She nuzzled her face into his skin, inhaling his scent, knowing he would feel everything his words meant to her without having to speak a sound. They were one now.

"Did you know I always dreamed of this?" she murmured.

Juaan chuckled. "Stranded in the Mountains looking for a girl who doesn't exist while fleeing the wrath of a Sky God?"

Nyri slapped him lightly on the chest. "No. I mean this." She tilted her face and pressed her lips to his jaw. "Even when I was a little girl, not knowing truly what it meant, I always imagined you as my *ankida.*"

"You did?"

"Yes." She touched her fingertips to his mouth. "For then I knew they could never separate us and we would always be together."

His face contracted with emotion. "Oh, Nyri," he said, as he drew her head back down to his chest, and for a while Nyri listened to nothing but the sound of their soft breathing and the vital pulse of life under her ear as Ninsiku's captured spirits blinked to life one by one in the darkening sky overhead. Idly, she began to trace her fingertips across his chest until a stray thought intruded upon her mind.

"I'm curious," she asked, suddenly hesitant. "If you've never loved a woman without the influence of vision water, how did you know...?" She trailed off helplessly, indicating his hand where it grazed up and down her flank, a hand that had so expertly teased and driven her mad with want.

His eyes came around, askance. "I lived in a camp with Kikima."

"Oh."

"And… some Claimings were, um, quite informative."

"Ah." A giggle pulled from Nyri's throat. She returned to her own ministrations. He thrummed, enjoying the sensation of her fingers on his skin.

It took a few moments for Nyri to realise she was tracing the outlines of the many scars that littered his light red-brown skin, highlighted as they were by Ninsiku's fully open eye. Quite suddenly, she was overcome by the need to know them all, know the stories that lay behind the marks he had received during the life he had led without her.

"Where did you get this?" she asked, tracing a crescent-shaped scar on his lightly haired abdomen.

"Hunting," he said without looking down. "A large boar. He didn't want to go down without a fight."

Nyri pressed her lips together and hastened on, finding a jagged scar on his shoulder. "This?" She was surprised by a sudden sweep of embarrassment. "What?" she asked as he smiled into her hair.

"I fell out of a tree."

A peel of laughter broke loose from Nyri's throat. "You fell out of a tree?"

"I, um, was a young and a bit foolish at the time. My first taste of vision water."

Nyri chuckled and continued her journey down his body. She sobered as she skirted around the scars left by Eldrax. She already knew the story behind those. It was a moment that still haunted her dreams, waking her in a cold sweat. Nyri shivered and moved on until she came to three parallel scars slashing across the front of his right thigh, tracing them lightly. "And these?"

He shuddered beneath her, groaning throatily as her fingers moved over his leg. "My first fight with Lorhir," he said. "He tried to take my mother's pouch from me. He regretted it. Very much."

"Hmmm, good," Nyriaana said, her eyes growing heavy.

"Are you finished?" he asked.

She hummed, wrapping herself more firmly around him, relishing in the warmth of his skin next to hers.

He chuckled once. "Sleep, Nyriaana," he said, running his fingers lazily up and down her bare back. "We have our whole lives ahead of us for telling stories."

Nyri flexed her arms around him. "I hope so," she whispered.

His lips pressed into her hair again and stayed there. "I'm not going anywhere," he said as she slipped towards sleep. "It'll take more than a vengeful god to take me from your side."

That was the last peace Nyri knew.

The horizon exploded, a blinding white light splitting the night in two. It blotted out the sky, flaring over the land. Nyri's hands flew to her face, protecting herself against the assault on her eyes. The ground sheared beneath them and the water of the lake cascaded over the bank, bubbling, steam billowing from the surface in great clouds.

Nyriaana cried out as the water contacted her skin, hot as fire. Juaan rolled them away from the shore, and they scrabbled backwards as the cruel light shimmered away. The earth shook again, sending another cascade of boiling water from the lake. It burned through the new life that had sprung up around it. Then came the voice, echoing through Nyri's skull. She was barely aware of Juaan's body folding protectively around her.

KILL THEM ALL! WIPE MY BROTHER'S MISTAKE CLEAN.

Images flashed. A Cro camp burning as the Watchers converged upon it, the promise of death in their glowing blue eyes. A flicker of silver running through the dark. "Kyaati," Nyri moaned.

The vision broke off as the ground bucked and rolled again. She heard Juaan let out a hiss of pain as the Great Spirit recoiled in response to another, unknown power ripping through the land, plundering the energy of the River Line below.

"Enlil," Nyri gasped. "It has begun. He is wiping everybody out! Juaan!" She gripped his hand. The lake broiled again. Spouts of scalding water shot into the air and rained over the ground, killing everything it touched. Juaan launched them to their feet, snatching up their furs and his spear, before grabbing Nyri's hand and retreating from the turbulent lake.

"We have to go!"

Nyri glanced back just once as they fled back down the trail, in time to see the now-deadly water consume the place where she had spent the scant moments of her life that had been the happiest she had ever known.

But there was no time to grieve. Rocks cascaded from above, pounding around down them as they dodged, often missing being crushed by a mere heartbeat.

Nyri clutched Juaan's hand as they sprinted through the darkness, the path they followed lit only by Ninsiku's silver glow. She stayed as close as possible. If Juaan's journey was to end in an avalanche, then she would share the same fate.

The trail tipped them back into the immortal forest. Nyri thought the intensity of the energy quivering through the ground would break her mind. The trees were shivering, groaning. Under the thick canopy, the darkness should have been total, but an unnatural light filled the glade. The dwelling of the gods at the centre of the forest was glowing, pulsing. Nyri could feel its presence like a living being, thrumming through the air, sucking energy from the River Line it was built upon to fuel its own insidious power.

Hitting the smooth rock path that led through the centre of the forest, Juaan snatched Nyri up in his arms and sprinted. Nyri did not protest as he vaulted along. He was faster carrying her than he was towing her in his wake. All Nyri wanted was to get as far away from the torturous presence of the Ekur.

Juaan set her on her feet again when he reached Enlil's Great Staircase that would lead them back to the tunnel in the cliff that had brought them here. Nyri balked at the thought of re-entering the underground passage, but there was no other choice. If there was another way out of the Mountains, they did not have time to find it. And so, Nyri climbed the even levels on Juaan's heels as the Mountains quaked, hugging the rock wall and keeping far away from the beckoning void on her other side as the stepped path switched back and forth.

On they climbed until they were free of the canopy and bathed in the natural light of Ninsiku once more. The forest glowed beneath them, the pointed peak of the Ekur erupting above, blazing like the Light Bringer brought to earth from the heavens. The air around them vibrated, singing, screaming in Nyri's ears as Enlil's presence continued to thrum wordlessly through her mind, commanding his Watchers out on the Plain.

"Inside, Nyri," Juaan panted as they reached the ledge and he thrust her into the round mouth of the tunnel. Nyri gasped. She had been expecting pitch blackness to press down upon her eyes as it had before. Instead, the tunnel was now faintly luminescent, the smooth, round walls glowing with the same light that emitted from the dwelling of the gods, as though they had been coated in *girru* moss.

"It's connected, all connected," Juaan said, his voice hoarse with the strain of fighting the energy that was attacking them both. "These tunnels were carved by the gods."

Though the world outside continued to shake, inside was oddly still, allowing the terrible knowledge to catch up. Enlil had wakened and against his power, there was no hope. Juaan snatched Nyri up into his arms. She could feel his anguish in every motion as he kissed her. Tears spilled down Nyri's cheeks as she tangled her fingers in his hair, locking them in place. But their stolen moment had passed. They could not go back.

"I don't want to die, Juaan," she moaned against his lips. "W-we haven't had enough time. N-not enough."

Juaan buried his face in her shoulder. "No." His answer had a fierce edge, the determination of a warrior banishing his despair. "This is not the end for you, Nyriaana. I promise."

"But what can we do? We cannot escape a god."

"One challenge at a time," he murmured, setting her back down and untangling her arms from his neck. "We need to get out of these cursed tunnels and return to the Plains." He slung his furs back around his body. Nyri shivered, quick to do the same. The light issuing from the walls had done nothing to warm the underground passages. They remained cold as death. Juaan took her hand again, winding his fingers around hers. "Whatever lies ahead, we will face it together, my Nyri, Nyri, Nyriaana."

"Yes," Nyri whispered, closing her eyes. And, with a force of will she didn't know she had, she turned to the tunnel ahead. The *genii* had guided her here. She barely recalled the blind run through the total darkness that had brought her to this place. She had been possessed so utterly. Since finding the Mountain lake and all its empty promises, the voices had fallen silent. She was lost now. Alone.

Not so alone, Juaan's thoughts mingled with hers.

Smiling grimly, Nyri flexed her fingers around his and started forward, her eyes adjusting to the dim glow the walls were emitting. There was no sound; even the tortured rumbles from the outside world were cut off. Only the rush of their breathing remained.

They hadn't travelled far before they came upon the first fork in the path. One tunnel branched to their right, the other led straight on. Nyri's brow pinched together as she struggled to remember making a turn or whether her crazed flight had been straight.

"They feel different," Juaan whispered into the stillness. Nyri's eyes widened as she picked up on the detail she had missed. He was right. The power running through the tunnel leading straight ahead was weaker than the one on the right.

"Perhaps that means we should go straight," Nyri thought aloud, out of habit. The stronger tunnel could lead directly back to the Ekur. Tentatively, Nyri placed a hand against the wall of the tunnel, seeking a clearer picture.

It happened very quickly. As soon as Nyri's fingers contacted the stone, a loud crackle split the air and her hand was engulfed in the golden light. She tried to pull back, but her arm was bound in place. She could not escape.

Daughter... another presence invaded her mind, breaking through Enlil's ever-present humming, fighting to be heard. *Daughter, heed me.*

Nyri was dimly aware of Juaan rushing forward to try to separate her from the wall. The light crackled, and he was sent flying backwards, but Nyri had no time to register alarm before her vision blurred, hazing to black. For a moment, she was weightless, lifting away from the world.

When she blinked her eyes open again, everything was white. Nyri could not tell if she was standing or floating this infinite space.

Nyriaana.

Nyri could never say where the figure came from. She may have been there all along, but one moment Nyri was staring at emptiness, and the next she found herself looking straight into the face of a being she felt she had known all of her life.

That this being was of Lord Enlil's kin was unmistakable. The body and features were elongated and covered in a golden skin that rippled with emotion. A tall, gleaming headdress adorned the skull. But, unlike Enlil, the face of this being was softer; cool and removed, but untouched by the harsh lines of cruelty. Violet eyes blazed as she gazed down at Nyri.

"Ninmah," Nyri spoke.

It shouldn't have mattered, but appearing before the Sky

Goddess in this stark, untouched space, Nyri grew self-conscious of the tattered, dirt-encrusted furs draping from her body, her skin layered in the dust and grime that clung to her drying sweat.

Heed me, most beloved daughter. Ninmah's voice echoed through her mind. *Heed me well, for I do not have long before I am silenced. Enlil* must *be defeated. You have already suffered much, daughter, but there is one last task you must complete before you leave these Mountains. You and you alone are positioned to cripple him.*

Nyri's heart sank. She was sick of being used, tired of this hardship she had never asked for. All she wanted was to be left in peace. To live out her life with Juaan.

An infinite sadness settled over the face of the Goddess. *Courage, my daughter.*

"Why?" Nyriaana flared, her anger making her bold. "Why should I serve you? All I have ever done, all my People have ever done, is serve you and suffer in your name. I followed the path you set and for what? I want no more. You abandoned us. Your *slaves*. Why should I believe anything you say? You do not care."

The otherworldly face darkened as the violet eyes flashed. *The accusations of a petulant child.* Pain flickered through Nyri's mind in response to the goddess' anger. *A child who has no idea of what was sacrificed for her.*

Ninmah's hand flicked out and the white space morphed into a fiery red. Nyri's feet contacted rock. The ground she had fallen upon was scorched, tortured, twisted, blistered from the heat of the black mountains in the near distance, spewing liquid fire. Nyri choked upon the hot, acrid air. Ash rained from the black clouds that blotting out the warmth of the Light Bringer.

Some of your rememberings are true, Ninmah's voice echoed through her mind. *I had to leave to save this little island in the stars, the cradle of my children, in order to save it. Enlil was winning against my Joined One, Enki, Ninsiku, as you name him, Ea by the Adamu. The Order of the Snake was beaten. Had we not surrendered, what little of humanity we had managed to preserve would have been lost. The damage to TiAmat that Enlil caused with his weapons set into motion a glacial winter that would last for many of your generations.*

I sacrificed myself to Enlil's torture and judgement for you and your People. The tenets I set were to protect you from Enlil's notice. Pain? You do not know what pain is, child.

And for a moment, just a split moment, Ninmah offered Nyri a glimpse, a sensation of the prison Ninmah now resided in, had resided in for time beyond Nyri's mortal imagining, unable to move, unable to speak. Agony lanced through Nyri from points in her head, through her finger-tips, staccato, unpredictable, shattering her concentration, allowing her to do nothing but witness what unfolded on the earth below.

Ninmah released her and Nyri let out a gasp. The scorched Plain and burning mountains faded back to the blank, endless white. Trying to regain her equilibrium, Nyri looked up into the golden face regarding her. Only now she could see the flashes of pain, the pupils in the violet irises spasming with the frequency of the shocks. Nyri could only imagine the amount of effort it was taking Ninmah to overcome the torture and reach out to Nyri now.

It has taken me millennia to learn how to break through Lord Enlil's control, Ninmah answered her unspoken thoughts.

"I-I'm sorry," Nyri murmured.

Ninmah's eyes softened with the forgiveness of a parent. *Already, he is attempting to block me out. Heed me, daughter, follow the lines of Enlil's power. You will know you are on the right path as it gets stronger. It will lead you to the source. Destroy what you find, or Enlil will rip this world apart as he threatened to do thirty thousand years ago. I could not reach it when I tried. He had it too heavily guarded. But now, your way is free. I pray to An that you are strong enough. It is time for our reign to end. Mankind must follow its own path, wherever that may lead.*

"But-?" Nyri struggled to comprehend the goddess' words.

Do as I... ask, daughter. The strength of Ninmah's voice was fading, Enlil's calls for destruction getting louder.

"I will try!" Nyri shouted as the white began to recede, Ninmah's presence flickering, becoming faint. "I am sorry I failed you! I am sorry I did not find Ariyaana."

Ninmah smiled before fading into non-existence. *But you did,* she said. *Kill Enlil, or she will not survive.* And then she was gone.

Nyri sucked in a breath as the dim tunnel re-materialised around her, the weight of her body returning.

"Nyri!" Juaan was shaking her shoulders, his thoughts running wordless in his panic. She could see herself in his mind's eye, lying motionless upon the ground, eyes blank and unseeing. Just like...

"Juaan." She pulled herself up and grasped onto him, letting him feel the reassurance of her presence. "It's alright. I'm alright."

"What happened?" His green eyes were wide with alarm

in the glow of the tunnel walls.

"Ninmah!" Nyri breathed. "We have to hurry." She struggled to her feet. It took her a couple of moments to find her balance. Juaan steadied her.

"Nyriaana?"

"I don't have time to explain." She wasn't even sure she could. She had to follow the pull of the energy running through the ground. Nyri just hoped the rest would make sense when she got there. "This way." She took off at a run down the right branching tunnel without waiting for a response.

Juaan was on her heels in a heartbeat, pulling her back; his fear and concern for her overlaying all else. "Ninmah?"

"Yes." Without wasting breath, Nyri shared her mind with him, letting him see all she had experienced. "I have to do as she asks."

"And you trust her? The word of a Sky Goddess?"

"Yes," Nyri whispered. She could not say why, but she did. With all her heart.

Juaan frowned, shaking his head, the memory of the empty lakeside forefront in his mind.

Nyri squeezed his hand. "This is different."

Juaan sighed and released her arm, disagreeing but knowing it was no good to try to dissuade her. Where she went, he followed.

Nyri kissed his knuckles. "Trust me."

The tunnels were a tangled warren of passages. Each time they came to a split in the path, Nyri's only guide was the pulse of strange energy running through the walls, always following the strongest call. She tried to ignore the fear that they were becoming hopelessly lost as the smooth floor sloped away, the frigid air impossibly getting cooler as they wound deeper into the bowels of the Mountain.

Nyri did not know how long they travelled through the maze. The power that ran through the walls grew stronger with each turn until it seemed to vibrate through the air, ringing against Nyri's nerve endings, raw and unceasing. Her head felt like it would split in two when Juaan drew her to a halt. "We have to turn back, Nyri," he rasped. "We are not Sky Gods. If this energy gets any stronger…" his voice trailed off.

Nyri swallowed, unable to deny the blackness that was already playing around the edges of her vision. If they continued, they may never walk out of this cold, forgotten darkness. *I pray to An that you are strong enough*, Ninmah's words echoed around her head.

"Just one more turn." Nyri heaved the words from her chest. She had to be strong enough. They were close now. She could feel it. She forced her leaden feet to move forwards. One step. Two steps, groaning against the vibrations that now pulsed through her entire frame, making her heart leap and stutter. Nyri threw healing energy inwards, guiding Juaan to do the same, feeding off his stronger connection to the Great Spirit in order to keep their bodies from failing.

The light changed. Like the energy they followed, it grew stronger.

"Almost there."

Footfall by footfall, Nyri and Juaan staggered on until they stumbled into a vast cavern.

"By Ea," Juaan choked.

Nyri had no words. The cavern before them was simply

too huge to comprehend. The smooth walls glistened, sparkling like rippling water as they caught the rays of the giant sphere, shining like the Light Bringer brought to earth, at the very centre of everything. Nyri blinked as her stinging eyes, struggling to focus, to even stand in the face of the onslaught of power. The glowing sphere appeared to be contained inside a transparent shell. Beams of light cascaded from it, shooting in all directions into the walls of the cavern, burrowing through the rock and disappearing like veins into the earth.

There could be no doubt that this was what Ninmah had sent them to destroy. The source of Enlil's power.

"What do we do?" Juaan asked. Nyri was alarmed by the blood streaming from his nose.

"I don't know!" Nyri said, her nerves screaming. "Ninmah didn't tell me." She pressed the heels of her hands to her temples. Ninmah had said she had failed in her mission to destroy this thing, humming with killing energy before them. How could they expect to succeed where a goddess had failed?

Juaan stooped, finding a loose pebble on the ground. With a shaking hand, he took aim and flicked it towards the sphere. A thin bolt of lightning crackled out, and the pebble fell to the smooth ground, reduced to a splash of liquid rock.

Nyri's throat closed.

Spear, spear, spear. The word echoed around the cavern, throbbing through Nyri's mind. *Spear, spear, spear.*

Spear? Barely able to focus her wavering vision, Nyri looked to the Thal spear in Juaan's hand. A simple creation of wood and flint. A twig.

Use it. The voice echoed again.

"Th-the spear," Nyri gasped, too befuddled to question. "W-we have to use the s-spear."

Juaan lifted the weapon in his hand as the sweat poured from his skin, the veins in his temples pulsing. His doubt was plain to see as his eyes went from the stick of wood to the sphere before them, but his trust in her was absolute. Then came the realisation. One of them would have to attempt to drive the spear into the ball of light. An attack that would end in a fiery death. But if they did nothing, neither would survive for much longer. Juaan set his jaw. *I love you, my ankida. More than life itself.* And before Nyri could speak, he lurched towards the sphere.

"No! You are not going without me." Nyri caught the back of his furs and staggered along in his wake. Juaan stumbled, but Nyri caught him around the waist and held him up, supporting his weight until he found the strength to rise. She threw all she could into her healing skills, resisting the lethal effects of the sphere's energy by one heartbeat, then the next.

Together they edged forward, fighting against the tide, until they stood before the power source of the gods themselves.

Nyri watched as Juaan's arms shook. Using the last of his strength, he lifted the spear, preparing to plunge it down into the ball of energy. Whatever the outcome, Nyri knew this was the end. She wound her arms around Juaan's waist. "I love you," she whispered.

A soft blue glow flared to life. Nyri's eyes lifted to the spearhead and her breath caught. "J-Juaan, l-look."

The markings in the smooth haft were now ablaze against the fierce yellow light of the sphere.

"E-Eron's marks of protection," Juaan whispered. "My *tarhe*'s marks of p-protection." Joined to him as she was, Nyri experienced all of Juaan's grief and wonder before everything inside burned down into a fierce, single-minded determination.

Taking hold of the haft in both hands, Juaan let loose a cry of challenge before plunging the spear tip down into the glowing sphere with all his strength.

The roar that followed shook the cavern. The transparent shell around the deadly energy shattered, splintering into infinite pieces. Lightning flashed out and Nyri recoiled, but not one bright, burning finger reached her skin. Blue light was all around them, cocooning them from the onslaught as Enlil's power source exploded in a final electrifying death throe. The resulting shock wave hurled Nyri and Juaan across the cavern, crashing them into the smooth rock wall behind.

Breath driven from her body, Nyri remained conscious just long enough to see the terrible yellow light wink out of existence, leaving behind only a shattered shell and the charred, smoking remains of a spear.

* * *

29

Downfall

"N o!" Kyaati's scream sliced across Galahir's ears as the Sky God fell among them. The bright spear in his hand conjured lighting from its tip, cutting swathes through the ranks of Cro, Thals and wolves alike.

Sweat and blood dripped from Galahir's brow. He had thought with the joining of the Thals and the wolves that their battle had been won. Now that hope was crushed into dust before his eyes.

Galahir looked to Kyaati and their son and shifted his grip on his blood-slicked *arshu.* Hope was lost, but that did not mean he would cease fighting for them. He would resist until his very last breath.

The scattered Watchers, bolstered by the appearance of their master, reformed against the men and creatures struggling for their existence.

"Brothers!" Galahir cried out to his quailing men. "Stand! Stand with me!" If this was the end, then they would die with their backs straight, looking their doom in the eye.

"Don't stand here! Charge him!" A guttural voice snarled

in his ear. Eldrax's black eyes were bright, no hint of defeat gutting the light that blazed there; the Red Bear quivered with fierce, triumphant joy. "This is what we have waited for! The true enemy has shown his face at last. If he is here, we can kill him. Take your men, distract him. He is mine!" With that, the Red Bear gave a shrill whistle, calling his surviving men to his back as he disappeared towards the east.

Galahir's mind whirled. Eldrax was insane, but what did they have to lose? Shrilling his own signal, he summoned the Eagle Clan to his back. The Thals followed.

"What need?" Alok was at his shoulder.

"Bring him down!" Galahir whipped his *arshu* towards the terrible golden being standing in their midst. "Kill the god. He falls, or we do."

"We will stand with you, Galahir of Eagle Clan," the Thal leader swore.

Galahir gripped his arm before sounding the attack. As one, Cro and Thal charged the golden destroyer. The god's eyes blazed in the face of their defiance. The shining spear lifted.

"Down!" Galahir cried as the lightning shot forth, singeing the air as he ducked and rolled. His men scattered. Those not fast enough burned to ash where they stood.

Gasping, Galahir rolled to his knees. "Again!" he bellowed, leaping to his feet to continue the charge. Surely even the god could not finish them all before they closed the distance. It only took one man to plunge a knife into a heart.

"Galahir!" Lorhir's cry of warning came almost too late. Galahir ducked the Watcher's club, feeling the wind of its passing ruffle through his hair. Some men who followed him were not so lucky as the Watchers came charging into the fray in defence of their master, scattering Galahir's desperate last stand.

Galahir threw himself away, only just managing to keep from being bludgeoned into the ground by the god's guardians. Sweat and dirt dripped into his eyes and he ducked and rolled, dodged and dived. He lost sight of Kyaati, the Sky God, of everyone. There was no plan, no target. All he could do was keep moving, to keep himself alive for a few moments longer.

He could hear the sizzle of the god's lightning as it slaughtered his People. The charged air raised the hairs on his body. How many lost? "Kyaati!" he panted, not knowing in the confusion if she and his son lay among the fallen.

A Watcher's spear came down on one side of him, blocking an escape. Galahir tried to scramble back the other way, but a giant foot slammed down, cutting him off. He lifted his arshu with battle-weary arms, but there was no defence against the giant club that came for him. It shattered the fighting staff and struck Galahir square in the chest with bone crushing force. The world spun as he flew backwards, tasting blood and dirt as he hit the ground hard, hearing his bones crack.

A warrior without his weapon is a dead warrior. Rannac's voice sounded distantly in Galahir's darkening mind.

Weapon, weapon, his thoughts repeated uselessly as he struggled to see, to locate his feet. *Kyaati, Kyaati, I am sorry I could not protect you.*

It would be his last thought. The ground beside him vibrated as a great foot stamped down beside him. The scent of rotting flesh filled his nostrils and Galahir knew a Watcher was leering over him, preparing to deliver the killing blow. He could not lift an arm in his defence. He was broken. Darkness flickered at the edges of his awareness.

A snarl yanked him from the brink of oblivion. Galahir wrenched his eyelids back as a huge black form leapt between him and his would-be murderer. Nekelmu faced the Watcher down, bloody fangs gleaming as he came to Galahir's defence. Two other wolves flanked their leader.

The Watcher bellowed and swung its club, intent on swiping the wolves away, but the small pack lunged below the strike and closed on the creature. The sound of their growls and snarls ripped through the air as they savaged every part of the Watcher they could reach, trying to hamstring the giant as they would an ox. They twisted and leapt away, avoiding the blows the Watcher aimed at them, only to move in again, working as a team, darting in and tearing chunks out of the sickly pale flesh.

But they could not stop it. With single-minded determination, the creature staggered forward, lifting its club for the killing blow despite the wolves' best efforts to hinder it. Galahir could not close his eyes, could not look away. He had been taught to from a boy to look death in the face when it came. He would travel to the Great Hunting Grounds with his eyes wide open.

But the blow never landed. Leaping through the air, Nekelmu locked his jaws around the Watcher's wrist, sinking his fangs home.

The Watcher's roar of pain tore through the air. It swung its arm with such force it flung the alpha wolf loose, its flesh still locked in his jaws. Nekelmu tumbled through the air, disappearing from Galahir's sight into the darkness. There was a sickening crack, a yelp, and then silence.

The two other wolves snarled and attacked the giant with renewed ferocity, but Galahir did not get to witness their fate. A pair of hands caught him under the armpits and dragged him back. Galahir gasped as his broken bones shifted, the blackness pulling at the edges of his vision. It was pain beyond endurance, but only in his upper body. Panic swept through him when he realised he could not feel his legs. Claustrophobia clawed up his throat.

"Come, come, boy," Alok's voice was in his ear, heavy in defeat. "The fight is lost."

Crushed bodies, blood, smoke. That was all that met Galahir's hazing vision as Alok dragged him from the battle. The air was filled with the cries of the dying, and the heavy scent of charred flesh.

"Galahir!" Kyaati was at his side, her glorious eyes wide, face smeared with blood and her hair darkened with ash. He was vaguely aware that Bahari and Kikima were by her side.

"I-I'm s-s-s-" Galahir could not get the words past his lips.

"Shhh, shhh." Kyaati's hands soothed over his face as her tears fell upon it. "I—"

An inhuman scream of fury cut off Kyaati's words, shocking all who heard it into silence. Galahir tilted his head enough to see the god standing in the midst of the destruction and shock rippled through his broken chest. Eldrax clung to the creature's shoulders, one arm clamped around the being's long neck while his other swung back, a long knife clutched in his fist. The Red Bear's pale face twisted into an expression of fierce triumph as he snarled. "I free mankind from your grip! We are slaves no longer. I, Eldrax, will rule these lands now." And he plunged his knife down.

It never even came close.

"Filthy animal!" Faster than the eye could see, the golden being caught Eldrax by the wrist and flicked his shoulder, slamming the Red Bear to the ground as though the huge man weighed no more than a bird. "Rule?" the god snarled down at the now prone form at his feet. He made a sound like laughter. "You were created to follow, to bow to a leader. It was bred into your filthy, lesser hides! Rule? Never!" The Sky God swept his gleaming spear up into the air. "Witness, brother, the end of your heresy!" Enlil's voice boomed out so loud Galahir thought it would reach the sky above. It vibrated through his shattered bones, the malicious joy and determination of the god penetrating his mind, akin to the relief of swatting an irritating insect from existence at last. The hairs on Galahir's arms lifted as the air charged. The final blow was about to fall. Kyaati gasped in pain and Elhaari wailed in the sling bound to her body as the tension increased, building, building; the strange spear crackled, glowing with the fierce fire of destruction within, ready to be released and burn all in its path.

Galahir managed to lift one arm and pull Kyaati to him, holding her and his child close. At least they would die together.

But the all-consuming fire and lightning never came.

The earth heaved as an enormous ball of light exploded over the Mountains. For a few moments, everything burned with the brightness of day. The rumbling in the ground fell silent, the tremors stilled, and the light of the devastating spear winked out.

The last thing Galahir heard before the pain in his body sucked him under was the howl of the Sky God's denial shattering the light of dawn.

* * *

30

Promise Fulfilled

Nyri staggered to her feet, temples throbbing. Her nostrils were filled with an acrid scent, but the killing power that had vibrated through the air was no more. The cavern was now pitch dark and eerily silent. She heard the scrape of rock as Juaan rose to stand beside her, his fingers reaching out for the physical reassurance of her continued presence.

"We did it," Nyri breathed.

Juaan's fingers pressed once. "Yes."

A nervous laugh found its way from Nyri's throat. "We did it." Her triumph echoed from the unseen walls. They had destroyed the source of Enlil's power. The Great Spirit of KI was at peace, no longer tortured, plundered, and torn asunder by the gods' unnatural invasion.

A heady relief overcame her, and she threw herself at Juaan, leaping up until she could wrap her arms around his neck and capture his lips with hers. He laughed softly into the kiss and caught her around the waist, holding her against him. The joy of surviving and knowing they were still together thrummed through their bond.

It was in that moment Nyri felt another tiny presence blink into being. A small flame flickering to life in the darkness.

"Nyri!" Juaan gasped into her mouth, almost dropping her in his shock as he felt it, too. He placed her on the ground as Nyri's hands flew to her belly. "W-we—Y-you're—"

Nyri could not speak, too stunned to locate her voice as she concentrated, searching. The tiny presence flared again. There was no mistaking it, an essence of her and Juaan binding together. "Oh." A maelstrom of emotions whirled through her. Panic, confusion, disbelief, panic and finally... joy.

She sniffed as tears spilled down her cheeks, her happiness radiating out to fill the vast, dark space around them. So much was uncertain, so much was still to happen, but in this moment, she refused to let anything darken the beginnings of a new life cradled within her.

Juaan was still struggling. The horrific memories of a string of dead women, all killed by his unborn babies, seared across his mind. She could hear his shallow breathing in the darkness, the rapid thud of his heart, feel the panic as it clawed up his throat.

"Juaan." She caught his hand before his fear could seize her own heart. "Be here. Be here with me. I am not them." She radiated calm reassurance, pouring her happiness and contentment across their bond, fighting back the blackness, and was rewarded by hearing his breath slow. The fear was still there, but no longer spiralling out of control. "You said you wanted to give me everything of you." She pressed his hand against her abdomen. "This *is* everything. You could not have given me more."

His fingers flexed as he steadied himself, and she felt his presence extend, searching for and finding the new bright light within her. "Nyriaana. You're…" he swallowed.

"Carrying our baby." A strange thrill went through her as she spoke the words aloud.

Juaan's breath became uneven again, but this time Nyri knew his reaction was not driven by panic, and in the next moment she was back in his arms as he wept into her shoulder. Nyri closed her eyes, forgetting everything, as he wrapped both her and the tiny presence inside within the protection of his life force, binding them all as one.

But the world outside could not wait forever.

"Enlil," Juaan murmured.

The name was ice water over Nyriaana's body. "No." She buried her face into his furs and tightened her arms.

"We have to go, Nyri," he said, stroking his hands up and down her back. "His power might be gone, but Enlil still lives. We will never be safe as long as he continues to exist and all of this would have been for nothing."

"Haven't we done enough?" she sobbed. "Eldrax started this. Let him finish it. We deserve our happiness. Just run with me now, Juaan. Let us find a place where we can live and watch our baby grow. Eldrax might already have got his wish." The pale hope lifted her heart.

She felt his sad smile, sensing the powerful temptation to give in to her plea as her imagining of their lives together ran through his mind, before he denied it. "No, Nyri. You know as well as I that Enlil is still out there. Still beyond the abilities of the Cro. Nyri… I may be the only one able to stop him."

"No. No, I won't let you go."

"You must. We fight with our People, or we abandon them to die, only to be hunted down and slaughtered like rabbits when Enlil rebuilds his power."

Nyri flinched in his arms, remembering the pain of being burned by Enlil's weapon; lightning searing through her veins before the nothingness. She was staring into the same abyss again, but now she had so much more to lose. Juaan was warm in her arms, the vibration of his life force humming in harmony with hers. With their baby's. She tightened her grip.

"The life you image can only exist if he dies now." His hand flexed against her back. "We have a Forbidden child, Nyri. If we allow him to regain what he has lost, he will hunt our baby more keenly than any other, seeking to destroy him."

Nyri shuddered. Her arms loosening.

Sensing weakness, he broke her hold and placed her on the ground once more, cupping his hand around the back of her neck and pressing their foreheads together as he placed his free hand on her belly. "I love you, Nyri, Nyri, Nyriaana," he whispered. "Never forget that."

Something had lodged in her throat. She just nodded silently.

Juaan released her and caught her hand, keeping them together in the darkness.

"How do we even get out to even find Enlil?" she asked, finding her voice as another pale and selfish hope flickered through her. There was no guiding force now. The energy that had drawn them here was dead. They were lost in a maze of tunnels, deep inside the Mountains. If they could not get back to the Plains, they would not have to face a cornered Enlil and, perhaps, despite Juaan's words, Eldrax or some other might have laid down their life to defeat the Sky God and spared her family. "Even if we get out of here, it'll take us days to escape the foothills." She recalled the arduous, days' long journey it had taken to reach the black forest, tracking Sakal's footsteps as the Eagle woman guided them through the craggy trails.

Juaan's thumb brushed her cheek. She knew he could see her hopes. "We might not have to go back the way we came," He said, dashing them. "Remember the tunnel Rannac led us through that night? It led us straight out onto the Plains, near to the Hunting Bear camp. All of these passageways are connected. If we can find that tunnel, we could cut days from the journey."

Nyri's teeth chattered in the cold dark. "How would we ever find it?" she asked. "We can't even see a hand in front of our faces."

"Have you forgotten, Nyriaana?" There was a wry twist to his voice. "We are Ninkuraaja. We have other ways."

Nyri experienced a small thrill of shock at hearing Juaan refer to himself as Ninkuraaja. She had never heard him do so before. It was like a final affirmation that he had truly accepted every piece of himself: Cro, Ninkuraaja, Juaan, Khalvir. They all existed together in harmony; whole at last. A lump formed in her throat again as she squeezed his hand.

The scrape of a hand brushing across stone reached her ears and Nyri felt Juaan's energy extend as he called effortlessly upon the Great Spirit. It flowed through him, through them both, and Nyri drew breath at the power of it.

531

Through Juaan, Nyri could feel the currents of the earth, so much more detailed than she had ever experienced them before. Every ebb, every swell of life, like veins, the spirit of KI radiated out from them. Juaan honed in, seeking the presence of the dead, dank forest, the swish of the river.

"This way," he said and set off at a run, fast enough to cover the ground, but not exceeding Nyri's capabilities.

Left, right, straight, Juaan followed the directions of the Great Spirit unerringly through the blackness. Nyri counted the passing of time by the echoing of their footsteps off the smooth walls, rhythmic, comforting in the eerie silence of the tunnels.

The route they followed sloped sharply down. Nyri's legs burned with the effort of holding her momentum back. Straight, right, left. Down.

"The forest is above us now," Juaan said without slackening the pace.

Already? Nyri quailed, but she could feel the truth. The slow, malicious energy of the trees crawled over their heads. The sound of dripping water now accompanied their footfalls, leaking through the rock from the damp soil above. Nyri flinched as an icy drop landed on her unprepared cheek. The scent of the tunnel shifted, the pure scent of cold stone mixing with that of stale damp.

"Ahead." As usual, Juaan's vision was stronger than hers in the dark, discerning the faint lightening of the darkness a handful of moments before she did. Juaan went from being invisible to her eyes, to becoming a faint shadow, then more and more defined until she could almost pick out the features on his face above her. A bright circle of light appeared ahead. An escape.

A doom.

Juaan slowed, his hand tightening on Nyri's as the happenings of the world beyond the tunnel flared across their combined senses. Fear, pain, loss, fury, hatred, all mixing together to choke the air. Nyri detected a faint scent of burning on the breeze that rushed in to greet them, accompanied by the bitter tang of ash and blood.

"We were too late," she spoke in a hoarse whisper.

"Enlil!" Juaan growled. He turned to her, catching her shoulders in both hands. "When we get onto the Plains, I want you to run, Nyri. I want you to get somewhere safe and hide."

"No!" Nyri protested, panic at the thought of being separated from him sliding through her gut. "We will face him together."

"Nyriaana!" Juaan's hands tightened on her shoulders, his expression hardening in the light of the dawn pouring through the tunnel mouth. "Please. If I am to do this, I *have* to know you are safe. You have to protect our child, no matter what. Promise me."

Nyri's breath shuddered through her lungs as she reached up to touch his face, feeling the wetness of the tears on his cheeks. "Why does it always have to come to this? You leaving me behind?"

"I know." He dropped a kiss onto her brow. "But this time, I promise you, I will come back, Nyri. If it is at all in my power, I will return to you." A smile crinkled his eyes. "That life is all I want, too."

"Juaan…" But she never got to finish. He had already pulled away from her and was sprinting out of the tunnel, his head turned towards his fate.

The empty space beside her was more than Nyri could bear. Gathering her strength, she raced after him. She would honour her promise to him, but she would not go far. She would not let him leave her sight. If she did, she knew she would never see him again. It was foolish to believe her mere proximity would protect him from a Sky God, but she could not help herself.

Even though the Light Bringer was not fully risen, the soft light of the dawn still blinded Nyri for a few moments as she emerged from the dark tunnel behind the last rocks of the foothills. Darting from around them, she saw the sweep of the Plains, the familiar rise and fall of the open land and the curve of the river running alongside the Hunting Bear camp in the distance.

Juaan was sprinting towards his old home. But the camp was no longer there. A black smudge on the landscape was all Nyri could see. Tiny figures were running from the tall serpent-like figure standing in the centre of all.

Enlil.

Nyri growled low in her throat and took off after Juaan, ignoring the exhaustion already sucking at her limbs from the flight through the tunnels. The site of the destruction became more defined. She could make out the bodies now. Countless souls lost. Crushed and broken in the black mud. Some had been completely dismembered by a force she knew only the Watchers to be capable of. A new panic shot through her. The Watchers.

A few of their hulking bodies littered the landscape, but she could see no sign of living giants. The only figure towering above the fighting men was Enlil himself, his shining garments gleaming in the rising light. When Nyri had come face to face with the Sky God in his own dwelling, she had been cut off from the Great Spirit. She had not been able to sense the overwhelming presence as she was experiencing it now. It exploded across her mind like the rays of the Light Bringer. Blinding.

Pressing her hands to her temples in a futile attempt to block it out, she stumbled on in Juaan's wake. The crushed bodies of several Thals littered the ground as Nyri reached the river. She averted her eyes as she plunged into the icy current, wading through the stream until she stumbled out on the other side. More bodies; Cro, Thal, wolf. It was getting harder and harder to avoid seeing their mangled faces as she drew nearer to the camp. At last, she tripped and fell, landing on top of a cooling corpse.

Nyri's heart stopped in her chest as she looked down into the face below hers. "Imaani?" she gasped. The world tilted. Her People were here. Her People had died. Nyri choked. How were they here? A blowpipe lay at Imaani's cold fingertips, purple staining the tip. Daajir's terrible poison. Close by, a Watcher lay twitching and yowling on the earth. Nyri could feel its agony as the poison crawled slowly, relentlessly, through its veins.

Her People had come here to fight.

She reached out for them. They were there, almost blotted out by the sheer presence of the Sky God. Nyri could not make out individual presences under Enlil's influence, but she could detect enough to know only a handful of souls remained, cowering together somewhere on the edge of the camp.

Her eyes went to the golden being who was responsible for this sorrow and bared her teeth, wishing for the power to end him herself. With the slick, bloody leaf leather of Imaani's coverings sliding under her hands, Nyri forgot her promise to Juaan. Wrenching herself back upright, she charged on her mate's heels, driven by a cold, hard fury.

The Sky God stood among the fresh corpses of those who had attempted to bring him down. One man was pinned under Enlil's gleaming spear. The golden being's lips were peeled back from his teeth in hatred. He appeared to be enjoying making the one under his weapon suffer before landing the killing blow. His cruel amusement washed over her.

The figure on the ground was fighting hard. It had its hands up, attempting to keep the weapon at bay. Nyri's gut tightened at the flash of red. She knew those pale hands, knew the feel of them on her shrinking flesh, stealing what should only have ever belonged to Juaan. For a moment, her own savage enjoyment of Eldrax's prolonged demise matched that of Enlil's.

Juaan's cry of defiance tore her gaze away from the execution unfolding before her. She saw her *ankida* sweep a fallen *arshu* from the ground and charge the Sky God.

"No, Juaan!" she cried, trying to run faster. She had thought she would be brave enough to let him face this fight, but she was not.

Distracted by Juaan's challenge, Enlil swung around, releasing Eldrax to face this new threat.

"No!" But before Nyri could reach the figures, she was caught from behind, thrown to the ground and pinned.

"No, Nyriaana," a breathless voice said in her ear.

Selima? Nyri twisted to face the pinched features of the one who had betrayed her. "Let me go!" she snarled, fighting against the red-haired girl's grip, to no avail.

"No," Selima hissed back. "I didn't protect you before, but I am going to now. Be still!"

Blind with fury, Nyri took a swipe at the pale face above her, gathering her energy in preparation to shock Selima, to get Eldrax's daughter to release her. But then another hand was there, dark, calloused and firm.

"Listen to her, Nyriaana," Bahari's voice was low and urgent. "I no let you die! You can do nothing for him now."

Nyri sobbed low in her throat. Pinned below the combined strength of Selima and Bahari, all she could do was watch as the confrontation unfolded.

Juaan was circling Enlil, a *grishnaa* assessing a dangerous prey animal outweighing it many times over. Enlil swung his shining spear in an arc and Nyri heard it ring faintly in the air, but no destructive lightning emerged from the tip. That power was gone.

The cold hissing laugh that Nyri remembered from the Mountains slid across her ears. "Fool. Even without my weapons, I can snuff you out with a single thought, *enkidu*."

Juaan said nothing. His green gaze was cool, focused, as his hands shifted on his weapon. Out of the corner of her eye, Nyri saw Eldrax staggering back to his feet, his furs ripped and his flesh torn. Rivers of red ran down his pale skin. But she could not focus on her erstwhile enemy. Enlil's lips curled into a cruel smile as he raised his hand. The long fingers twisted.

Pain exploded behind Nyri's eyes as the force of his will lashed out, searing through her mind. Tears sprang to her eyes as the blood spurted from her nose. If she had been the focus of such power, she knew she would no longer be breathing. But she had not been the focus.

"Juaan!" she rasped, sure she had lost him, his light snuffed out by Enlil's will.

But as the attack on her mind receded, Juaan's continued presence washed across her senses. He was crouched to the ground, gasping, but even as Nyri watched, he straightened to his full height, wiping the blood from his nose as he lifted his chin in defiance. "We are more than the mockery you consider us to be," he said. "And it is you, Lord Enlil, who is doomed to die here."

Enlil hissed as he stepped back. "So, you have mastered your power, *enkidu.*"

"So it would seem," Juaan said grimly.

The Sky God's eyes narrowed. "You think yourself great enough to defeat me?"

"I guess we're about to find out." And Juaan swept forward. Enlil met his attack, striking out with his spear, but Juaan was not foolish enough to meet such a blow with his own. He twisted the below the shining weapon, using his momentum to slide along the ground and, with blinding speed, let the sharpened antler tips of the *arshu* flash out, slicing across the legs of the Sky God before he straightened out of the attack on the other side, blood dripping from his weapon as tattered pieces of glimmering cloth fluttered to the ground.

Nyri thought Enlil's scream of fury would burst her ears.

Juaan did not wait for his enemy to recover. Nyri could feel the rush of his blood as if it were her own, the sing of his heart as he lost himself to the dance, swinging, cutting, out-maneuvering the golden being he strove to defeat, the thought of her forefront in his mind, fueling his determination.

Enlil's face was a distorted mask of hatred as he tried and failed to strike down the man who dared to face him. Blood poured from several wounds that Juaan had inflicted. The Sky God had the physical power, but the raknari warrior possessed the combat skill that he did not. With Enlil stripped of his crushing mental advantage and devastating weapons, the fight was an even one.

A handful of men, emboldened by the Sky God's failure to kill the man before him, rushed to tip the balance against the Lord of the Skies. It was a fatal move. The golden being flexed his will and all those rushing to Juaan's side convulsed, their eyes rolling back into their heads before they collapsed upon the ground. Only Juaan remained fighting, resisting the invisible attacks from his mind even as the blood poured from his nose.

Her mate had been right. He was the only one who stood a chance at defeating Enlil.

But that chance was waning. Exhaustion began to tell on Juaan's limbs from carrying the fight alone. Nyri felt the quiver of his muscles under his flint-like will to keep moving, keep fighting until he could land the killing blow.

Enlil sensed it, too. Triumph gleamed in his eyes as he unleashed another invisible attack upon Juaan. Nyri saw her mate flinch and gasp. Or maybe the gasp was hers as the pain ricocheted through their bond. It took all of Juaan's concentration to prevent the god from ripping his mind to pieces, and he was still for a heartbeat too long.

Letting loose a howl of victory that drowned out even Nyri's scream of denial, the shining spear flashing out, smashing Juaan's weapon in two. Only Juaan's honed reflexes saved him from the same fate. But he could not avoid the long hand that snaked out to grab him by the furs and lift him into the air.

"You are strong, *enkidu*. I will admit that. But still no more than a mortal animal." Enlil growled into Juaan's face as he extended his other hand and placed it over his chest. "Ninmah's weaknesses have betrayed you, and I thank An every day that I had the wisdom to order them. Goodbye, *enkidu*."

Juaan grunted as his heart stuttered.

"No, no." Nyri struggling against Bahari and Selima's combined grip. "Let me go, he's going to kill him!"

Juaan was resisting with all his might, drawing on the power of the Great Spirit of KI to combat the invasion into his body, holding the Sky God's attack on his heart at bay by a breath. But it was not enough. It was only a matter of time before Juaan's strength gave out, and Enlil knew it.

She could not lose him now. They had come so far, suffered so much. Nyri threw all of her own energy through the bond she shared with Juaan, adding it to his strength, spitting through her teeth with the effort. She dug her fingers into the blackened ground, drawing on the power of the earth to push back the energy that did not belong. Enlil's advance halted. The Sky God snarled, doubling his efforts to crush Juaan's heart, pushing back.

It was then that another flame burst to life inside Nyriaana. A third presence joined itself to the struggle. Indomitably, it burned, singing through Nyriaana's veins, rushing through her.

This time, true fear flashed across the Lord of the Skies' face as he was confronted with a combined power greater than his own. Heartbeat by heartbeat, his invisible invasion was pushed back, reversed. The Sky God's own strange heart laboured under the pressure being exerted on it.

Nyri closed her eyes, drawing all she could from the Great Spirit. Enlil's life force stuttered.

And then the pressure from the god's mind shattered. Nyriaana stumbled mentally as the wall she had been pushing against abruptly vanished. Wrenching her eyes open, Nyri was in time to see Enlil release his grip on Juaan's furs, letting him tumble to the ground. The tall being wavered on his feet, his golden face twitching.

Her confusion lasted only until she saw the flash of red. Like fire. Eldrax stood behind the Sky God. As Nyri watched, he drove his long knife into Enlil's back for a second time, then a third, and again until the Lord of the Skies toppled to his knees, dark blood gushing from the wounds.

"I told you your time was over," the Red Bear drawled as he limped around to face the Sky God. "The last thing you will see is my feet as you bow to the saviour of mankind."

Enlil coughed, blood spewing from his mouth as he did so. "Saviour of mankind?" A wet laugh. "There is no saviour for you, *savage.* You were bred to plunder and destroy. I will cleanse—"

Nyri never got to hear the rest of the Sky God's words. With a disdainful sneer, Eldrax caught the golden being about the neck and twisted, snapping it between his thick arms.

The blue eyes went blank as Enlil toppled lifeless to the ground.

Nyri did not stop to think. Shaking loose from a stunned

Bahari and Selima, she darted forward. She had eyes only for Juaan as he struggled to rise from the ground, his face ashen.

She never reached him. Eldrax caught Nyri by the furs and yanked her to his side. "Oh no, you're not going to escape me again, witch."

"Eldrax," Juaan rasped. He staggered to his feet, his legs shaking beneath him with the effort that it took. "Let her go."

Eldrax's fingers dug painfully into Nyri's back. "I think not. I have been looking forward to this day, Khalvir. I have defeated the Sky Gods themselves. I have saved us all, just as I always promised. And now I will take whatever I please. And she pleases me." He swept his fallen battle club from the ground and swung it in challenge. "But you are welcome to try to take her back."

Fire flashed in Juaan's green eyes.

"No, Juaan, don't," Nyri denied. He was spent, he would not survive another fight.

"Shut up, witch!" Eldrax shook her. "I will have my revenge upon this traitor and finally take what is mine over his pathetic…"

Eldrax choked off, the air strangling in his throat as Juaan advanced upon him, his face tight with the effort it took. Sweat dripped from his brow. "No. I am no longer Khalvir, Eldrax, and you are no longer any match for me. Leave me and mine in peace and I may yet let you live."

Eldrax's black eyes bulged as Juaan continued to block the functions of his body, keeping him alive only by one beat of his heart and the next. Blood gathered in the corners of the Red Bear's eyes.

"Let. My. *Ankida.* Go." Juaan bit out every word.

Eldrax's mortal terror rippled through Nyri as he flung her to the ground.

The rest happened too fast for Nyri to comprehend. One moment, Eldrax was choking, surrendering to Juaan's greater strength; the next Juaan flinched, his concentration shattering as something unseen struck him hard in the throat. Nyri's hand flew to her own neck, the painful sting echoing through their bond.

Eldrax roared back to full strength as Juaan dropped to his knees, green eyes unfocusing. Sweeping his bloody knife from the ground, the Red Bear caught him by the hair and wrenched his head back, exposing Juaan's jugular. "I will enjoy this," he hissed.

A broken spear was in Nyri's hand before she was even aware of moving. No thought existed. Blind with fury, she lunged for Eldrax's unprotected back, stabbing the sharpened flint tip deep between his ribs, driving it home, yearning for the strength to reach the black heart.

She did not have it. The haft ripped from her hands as Eldrax grunted and swung around, surprise on his pale face as he looked down at the broken spear haft protruding from his body, then at her. "Witch." He staggered forward. Nyri backed away, glaring up at the man who had tormented her for her entire life.

Hatred twisted the Red Bear's features. The knife was still in his hand as he lunged for her. Nyri watched him close the distance as though in slow motion, knowing she would never be fast enough to escape his last blood-maddened charge.

Selima knocked Nyri aside. His target removed, Eldrax

overbalanced and fell to his knees.

"You," he rasped around the blood spilling from his mouth. He tried to rise again.

"Oh no, father." Cool as a mountain stream, the red-haired girl stepped to the Red Bear's side and plucked the knife from his weakening grip. Her eyes flicked to Nyri, who tensed in the face of the deadly intent carved into the pale features. But the dark promise was not for her. Selima turned back to her dying father.

The light in Eldrax's eyes was fading, but they sparked briefly as they beheld his daughter standing before him. "M-mother?" he whispered, reaching up to touch Selima's cheek with his bloody fingers. "F-forgive—"

The knife flashed out, loosing a river of red.

"Never!" Selima spat as Eldrax's black presence gushed from existence. Her father's body toppled to the ground next to that of the Sky God he had striven for so long to defeat.

Nyri tore her gaze away from the sight. The pain in her neck was growing. Pain that was not her own.

"Juaan!" she gasped. Locating her limbs, she staggered to her feet and rushed to his side.

"Nyri, Nyri, Nyriaana," he breathed as he collapsed back into her arms. Shudders ran through his entire body.

Nyri's hands went to his neck. A long *vaash* barb was protruding from his skin. She ripped it away. The world tilted. Purple liquid oozed from the wound. "Oh no. No, Juaan. No." She cast about, seeking aid, but found her sight blocked by a leaf clad body. She looked straight up into dark indigo eyes gleaming in triumph as they gazed down at Juaan's stricken form.

"I promised, I promised I would kill you one day, Forbidden," Daajir said.

31

Smoke and Ash

"Nyriaana!" Kyaati was at her side, grasping her around the shoulders. "Nyriaana?"

"D-Daajir?" This was a dream. Daajir was dead. He could not be here ripping her heart away.

Only he was.

The vision of him remained solid, sneering down on her as Juaan shook in her arms, the insidious toxin seeping through his body.

"Galahir!" Kyaati shrieked.

Numb, Nyri watched as the familiar form of Galahir sprinted into view, Bahari at his side. Together, they tackled Daajir to the ground, heedless of his furious protests.

"Nyri?" Another familiar voice, another presence she had never thought to feel again.

"Baarias?" Nyri was becoming detached from reality, her pain, Juaan's pain, merging. Everything was happening too fast.

"Yes, dear one, I am here."

"Baarias!" she cried, reaching for and catching hold of his

hand. "Help."

"There is no help for him," Daajir laughed, still struggling in Galahir's and Bahari's grip. "I made sure of that!"

"Witch!" Kikima was at Bahari's side. Her amber eyes burned as she snatched Bahari's hunting knife from his waist and smashed the butt into the side of Daajir's head. He fell limp in the Cro men's hands.

Juaan convulsed, moaning low in his throat, one hand tangling in Nyri's furs. "Shhh, shhh," she soothed, stroking the hair back from his sweat-slicked brow, feeling the toxin spreading, burning as it went.. "I'm here now. We're both here. Y-you're g-going to be alright," she said. "H-hold on for me, Juaan. Everything is going to be alright."

"Nyri…" His eyes locked on hers with an effort.

"Baarias!"

Her old teacher's face was grim as he pushed away Nyri's hand so he could place his own at Juaan's temples. After a moment, he lifted his gaze. "Nyri…"

"No," she whispered, angered by his defeat, "no, Baarias! Help him! You cannot fail him again now! Help me!"

Baarias closed his eyes briefly, a tear spilling loose, before he nodded and looked to the rest. "Is there…?"

"A couple of shelters remain," Kikima answered. Nyri hated the stricken expression on the other woman's face. Why were they all behaving as if this was the end? This was not the end. She would not allow it. Juaan would be healed. Enlil was dead. Eldrax was dead. Their fight was over. They could live their lives in peace now. Together at last.

"I'll watch him," Bahari told Galahir as the bigger man released his grip on the unconscious Daajir and approached

Juaan, understanding what was needed.

Nyri hissed as Galahir stooped to remove Juaan from her grip.

"Nyriaana!" Kyaati admonished.

"Let Galahir carry him, Nyri," Baarias commanded gently. "You are causing him more pain by keeping him here."

Kyaati pulled Nyri away as Galahir lifted Juaan carefully into his thick arms. Agony lashed through Nyri as Juaan gated a cry, his skin flaming at the slightest contact. The green eyes were open slightly, the pupils dilated as he tried to focus.

"*Ankida?*" he whispered as Galahir strode along, bearing him to one of the few surviving shelters left in the flattened camp.

Nyri pulled away from Kyaati and ran along at Galahir's side, unable to bear any space between them. She clutched onto the one hand she could reach. "I'm not going anywhere, Juaan," she choked.

The journey to the shelter seemed to take a long time, Nyri feeling every flare and burn of Juaan's suffering, but at last the hide walls protected her from the sight of the death and despair left in Enlil's wake. Only the scent of scorched flesh and ash lingered in the still air.

Kyaati and Kikima rushed to gather the piles of scattered furs, heaping them at the centre of the space for Galahir to lay Juaan upon. "It's good to see you again, my brother," Galahir murmured. "Hold on, the witch healer is here. If he can bring me back from being smashed by a Watcher, he will have you on your feet before Utu is risen."

Kyaati caught her mate around the shoulders, her face pale as she tugged on him. "Come, my love," she said. "W-we have to leave them alone now." Galahir frowned up in confusion at Kyaati's tremulous tone, but allowed himself to be led away. Kyaati paused at the entrance to the shelter. "Nyri, I—" she swallowed. Her grief and guilt filled the space. "Just know that I am here."

Before Nyri could scream at her, tell her to stop behaving as though Juaan was already dead, her tribe-sister disappeared through the billowing hide curtains.

Baarias crouched on the other side of Nyri.

"Tell me what needs to be done, Baarias," she said. "Tell me!"

"Ease his pain as best you can," he said wearily. "I will see what I can do."

The task gave Nyri a rock to cling to. One small focus to keep her from spiralling out of control. She banished the memories of what she knew of this poison. It was *not* incurable. She had Baarias with her. She had newfound skills of her own. Together, they would reverse the damage the toxins were inflicting.

Plunging all of her will into killing Juaan's pain, Nyri blocked all else out. It was difficult. Her stomach turned over as she detected the damage Daajir's weapon had already wrought, degrading, slowly melting away the tissues of its victim. Juaan was slowly, invisibly bleeding out from the inside as his nerves were seared away. *Baarias will save him. We will save him,* she chanted over and over in her head. If she considered any other outcome, she would be lost. Redoubling her efforts, Nyri was rewarded as she felt Juaan uncoil beneath her hands, his breath becoming easier as the shuddering eased. The agony leaking through their bond receded. "Nyri," he whispered, seeking her hand with shaking fingers. Panic shot through Nyri at the frailty of his grip. She gripped on for both of them, taking his hand in both of hers.

Nyri, Juaan's voice echoed around her mind. *It's—*

No! She cut him off, denying what she heard in the tone of his thoughts. *Don't you dare say goodbye to me.*

Baarias was working fast. Sweat dripped from her old teacher's brow. In her mind's eye, Nyri watched his actions, analysing every skill he was bringing to bear against the spread of the toxins. He was trying for her, but Nyri could taste the bitter flavour of his thoughts. Baarias knew his efforts were doomed.

And that is why you are failing! Nyri snapped. Keeping one part of her mind on numbing the searing pain, she threw the rest of herself into aiding Baarias, mimicking his actions with single-minded determination. She was not going into this already defeated. She was going to win!

She dragged energy from the Great Spirit, digging in. But whatever she tried in order to purge the invasion only exacerbated the problem. The toxins sped up, eating through vital connections, breaking down life's pathways. Nyri gritted her teeth, pouring more and more of her energy into every trial, anything she could think of. Despite her effort to block the pain from Juaan's consciousness, her doomed attempts to heal him kept breaking through. He twisted on the furs, hissing through his teeth until she relented, only to convulse again when she tried a different attack. Nyri began to tremble from exhaustion, but she fought on.

"Nyri."

She ignored Baarias. He had ceased his efforts long before.

Nyri doubled hers, refusing to yield against the blackness now playing around the edges of her vision.

"Nyri."

No. She dashed herself against this killer invading her *ankida's* body, stealing him from her, heartbeat by heartbeat, spilling out and solidifying his blood in its wake. His heart laboured.

"Nyri!" This time Baarias' voice was sharp. "Stop! It's no use! If you keep going, you'll kill yourself. You'll kill the both of you!" Somehow, Nyri knew he was not talking about her and Juaan. Baarias knew of the precious secret she carried. "You are just causing more suffering. It is time to stop."

Nyri, please. Juaan arched off the furs under the onslaught of her last desperate effort. *Please!* Insidious, unstoppable, the toxins burned on.

Nyri let out a wailing sob and fell back. Baarias caught her by the shoulders.

"Daajir made the weapon for this purpose," he murmured. "I am sorry, Nyri. There is nothing to be done. I have tried. I have tried many times."

Nyri did not hear much of Baarias' words as she stared at the centre of her world, suffering on a tattered pile of furs before her, his body being destroyed from the inside out. Only one word flared in the flames of her mind.

Daajir.

Ripping away from Baarias, she fled from the shelter. Kyaati and Galahir were waiting a respectful distance away. She bolted past them. They fell back from the look on her face. Her target came into view. Daajir was recovering from the blow that Kikima had dealt him, blinking his eyes open as Bahari kept him under spear point.

"Get away, Bahari," Nyri hissed, hardly recognising the sound that came from her mouth to be her own voice. But Nyriaana did not exist anymore. She lay dying upon the pile of dirty furs right next to Juaan.

Bahari hesitated until Nyri levelled her gaze at him. He paled visibly and backed away a step. As soon as he did, Nyriaana swept down upon Daajir like an avenging falcon. She could have asked Bahari to plunge his spear right through this murderer's heart. She could have grabbed one of the many weapons littering the battlefield and killed him herself, slowly, tortuously. But such physical punishments were fleeting. And Nyri did not want Daajir's suffering to be brief. She wanted him to know intimately the torment she would live with for the rest of her life.

There was no Kamaali present to perform the *zykeil* ritual safely, but Nyri was beyond caring for such details. Grabbing Daajir around the head with both hands, she dug her thumbs into his temples.

His eyes widened as he read her intent. "N-n—"

She did not give him a chance to struggle, Nyri unleashed the full force of her will upon his mind, pouring out all of her fury, all of her grief, the future he had stolen from her, the sense of being cut adrift, staring into a hole of blackness that would never end.

She was screaming into his face as she bore down upon him, ripping his mind apart with her unskilled transference, but she did not relent. She relished the sight of Daajir's face twisting into madness, locked forever in this moment of torment that he had caused. His scream echoed hers when Nyri finally released him, letting him crumple to the ground.

552

Weeping and writhing, he clawed at his face, trying to block the torturous thoughts and emotions she had forced upon him. He was incoherent in his cries.

Nyri stood above him, detached, watching the physical representation of her heart on the ground.

"Should I kill him now?" Bahari was staring at Daajir, his face more frightened than it had been when he fought the Watcher who took his hand.

"No." Nyri still did not recognise the voice that spoke. Daajir got on his hands and knees and began to crawl away, a river of incomprehensible speech and sobs gushing from his mouth. "Leave him. If he's lucky, a *grishnaa* might find him and end his miserable life. Goodbye, Daajir."

Nyri turned her back on her former kinsman. She would not see him again.

Nyriaana. The world swam before her eyes. She staggered as she felt one half of her whole slipping away. He was calling for her.

Juaan. She stumbled forward, almost blind, as she made her way back towards the shelter. The scent of smoke and ash on the breeze was fitting, for that was all that remained of her soul.

Nyri pushed her way back through the entrance to the shelter. Baarias was kneeling next to Juaan, gripping one twitching hand as he leaned close over him.

"Forgive me, sister-son," he was murmuring. "For being blinded by hate and fear. You deserved so much more. I should have… I should have been there for you, too."

Nyri did not hear Juaan's response. His voice was too faint, but the tears flowed down her old teacher's face as he squeezed the hand in his. "Rest easy, my son. I promise I

553

will take care of them. I will protect them with my life as I should have protected your mother. Farewell."

Baarias rose, releasing Juaan's hand as he came towards Nyri. He did not say a word or ask where she had been. He just squeezed her shoulder, letting some of his strength flow into her, before disappearing outside and leaving them alone.

Nyri. Juaan's hand groped the furs at his side, searching. Now that Baarias had gone, the pain had returned in full force. He twitched upon the furs as the killer in his body seared through his veins. Nyri fell at his side, snatching his hand up in hers, fighting the agony away with all her strength and only partially succeeding.

Juaan sighed, lifting her hand to his cheek and pressing it there. Nyri flinched at how cold his skin felt. He was shivering in the fire. Nyri laid down upon the tattered furs next to him, curling her body around his, lending him her warmth. She clung to every heartbeat, every vibration of life. If she could breathe for him, she would.

"Will you stay with me, Juaan?" He had always promised. He had promised.

"To the end," he whispered.

A wave of pain went through them as the toxin flared, moving deeper. Juaan keened, gripping onto Nyri as he hissed through his teeth. Nyri choked, throwing more of her energy into blocking it out. It didn't work, but she could not stop.

"Nyri," he gasped, "Don't. Y-you heard Baarias. There is only one thing you c-can do for me now." He placed one of her hands over his heart. "Please."

Horror ripped through her as she comprehended his

silent request. She ripped her hand away. "N-no, no please, you cannot not ask that of me!"

"Nyri, I-I do not want to spend days watching you suffer. Y-you cannot keep this up." She felt him tug on the energy she was expending to keep the full force of the toxin's effects at bay.

"No."

"You must. For me. F-for him." His free hand shifted to her abdomen. "I am already lost, my *ankida*. You have to set me free." Another wave of agony cracked through Nyri's waning effort.

Nyri broke apart. Gripping onto his furs, she buried her face in his chest and wailed out her denials. But no matter how much she wept, no matter how much she twisted and turned in the face of reality and the unfairness of it all, she could not escape. The spark of life within her stuttered under its father's hand. If she did not let go, she would be left with nothing.

Nyri gulped on the air. "B-but we've had so little time," she wept. "It's not enough. Not enough."

"Nyriaana, l-look at me," Juaan said, lifting her chin towards him. "These days with you have been the h-happiest I have known. My life has been f-filled with pain and darkness, but I was made better for the love you gave me. I-it was all I could ever a-ask for."

He grasped her face in both hands, looking hard into her eyes as though trying to burn the memory of her there. Nyri realised his sight was fading. "Never let your light go out. For I w-will follow it. I can never truly leave you." He replaced her hand on his chest and captured her lips with his. *Please. I am not afraid, my love, for you are here.*

555

Nyri sobbed into the kiss. Tangling her free fingers in his hair, she entwined her energy with his as he reached out to encompass her, binding himself around her heart and thoughts. Their essences glowed together, caressing, loving; all of his treasured memories passing through their mind's eye, hers now to take forward. Joy and peace surrounded each one. He sighed. *Let this be my last moment.*

Another wave of pain was building, already threatening to rip the moment away. There was no choice, no time to think. Drowning in tears, Nyri reached for the Great Spirit of KI and curled her fingers over his heart. She did not let him feel it as she plunged the energy inwards, stilling the vital beat within.

The ravaged body beneath her shuddered once, fighting her for a moment, then grew quiescent, the tortured shivers melting away as the great weight of death dropped it back into the furs. Juaan's last breath sighed past her cheek. She felt his relief, his gratitude and his boundless love for her fading past her soul, a last lingering kiss of benediction.

Goodbye, Nyri, Nyri, Nyriaana.

* * *

32

The Eagle and the Snake

nlil's consciousness awoke. He immediately knew that he wasn't alone in his bodiless mind. His brother was there, waiting for him.

With the destruction of the Ti'Amat's power source, Enki had been freed from his confines in Irkalla.

Have you come to gloat? Enlil thought.

No. Enki's voice echoed through his mind, as powerful as he remembered before Enlil had imprisoned him thirty millennia ago.

Save your pity! Enlil snapped. *You brought me to this fate.*

No, brother. You brought this upon yourself. My Lullu Amelu have earned their right to exist as free beings in the cosmos. What more do they have to do to prove themselves to you?

Enlil laughed. His brother was truly insane. *Earned the right? They have earned nothing. They will only ever abuse what they have been gifted. They are nothing more than the base animal you used to create them, veiled in the mask of the divine; worse, for they have the intelligence to bend their primitive urges in cruel and imaginative ways.*

The only comfort I draw is knowing that within them lie the seeds of their own downfall. We bred them to follow blindly; we bred them to plunder, to always thirst for more and feel nothing for the land they stand upon. They will reap their own destruction. Taking and taking until all that remains is a husk of what once was; left with nothing more than dust at their feet.

Enlil had the satisfaction of detecting a shiver of concern in Enki's consciousness before he banished it. *It is a potential fate,* his brother replied. *But they also possess the ability to evolve. They are passionate beings and will defend what they love fiercely, as you have just discovered to your demise, brother. One day, I have faith that they will surpass us.*

Fear flared inside Enlil. *No,* he swore. *They will never rise to spread their darkness. I will always be there, dividing them further in language and belief until they tear each other apart. Hate, violence and greed drive them. I will not have to do much. To unleash them on the universe would be the gravest of sins. If they become powerful, I will drown their civilisations in flood and flame. The Lord of the Skies will prevail.*

Anger flared in Enki's thoughts in the face of Enlil's promise. *Perhaps,* he thought, *but each time you lay them low, I will be there to teach them to rise again. A snake, you always named me? Then look well, brother, wherever man advances, the serpent will appear and you will know you have failed yet again.*

All sense of brotherhood evaporated with each of their vows, distancing them. The space between filled with a stark promise.

Then let it begin, Enlil said. *We will see at the end of days who these creatures truly are.*

Indeed, we will. Enki's voice faded. *Until then, brother.*

THE EAGLE AND THE SNAKE

* * *

33

Passing of an Era

ive days later.

F Kyaati travelled alongside Galahir as they made their way across the plains. It had been a quiet journey, filled with somber reflection. So much had changed in the last days, it was hard to comprehend. The Sky God had been vanquished, the Peoples of the land were finally free, free of taboo, free of fear, free to love. Even the domination of Eldrax was at an end. The clans he had subjugated could go back to living in peace.

But they had no leaders. All the old Chiefs had been killed many seasons ago to be replaced by Eldrax's most loyal warriors. Galahir had been the only leader the men had looked to since the battle for their survival had ended. With the death of Eldrax, her mate was now Chief of both the Eagle Clan and the remnants of the Hunting Bear. With the merging of the two tribes, Galahir was in command of the largest family on the Plains.

There were many who had wanted to stay under his

protection, still fearful of the surviving Watchers who had fled the battle following the destruction of their master's power. The scouts had not sighted them. No one knew what holes they had crept into, or when and if they might strike again. But one territory could not support all the clans combined. And so Galahir had travelled with the other tribes, escorting them back to their old territories, appointing men he could trust to be wise Chiefs to guide and protect.

Alok and the Thals had travelled with the Cro on their journey back to their *etuti sagkal,* as they called it. Along the way, Alok had explained the concept of *trade* to Galahir, revealing a lifestyle in which all clans could exist together without the need for stealing and bloodshed. Her mate had taken the learning to heart and Kyaati had been present at Galahir's side when he gathered his appointed Chiefs together, vowing to share in the bounties of the land with them all and receiving oaths for the same in return.

Kyaati's heart had swelled with pride at the sight of her mate ushering in a new time of peace and understanding between the Peoples of the Plains.

It was the happy surface of their new existence. But under that surface, Kyaati knew it would take a long time for the wounds of the past to heal. So much had been lost. So many bodies to bury. Kyaati had forced herself to look into the faces of all those who had sacrificed their lives before they were veiled forever. She would honour them with remembering before the world forgot. It would take a long time for the scent of freshly dug earth to leave her senses.

Only one face had been missing from the fallen. The one she would have relished seeing in its lifeless state. That

561

of the Lord Enlil. But the body of the Sky God had been nowhere to be found. It had disappeared, seemingly into thin air, when the men had come to bury it.

Kyaati shuddered.

The last three unburied bodies were being dragged on litters behind the ever dwindling procession on the journey south, those of Imaani, the wolf Nekelmu, and of Daajir. Once the remaining Cro tribes had been escorted back to their own territories, Kyaati, Galahir and the Ninkuraaja who travelled with them, would return to the southern forests to Cast the bodies of their fallen brethren to the river as per tradition. Uma had wished it for her *ankida*.

Kyaati had mixed feelings about giving Daajir the honour of a customary Cast off. Scouts had found his broken body two days following his murder of Juaan. He had thrown himself from a cliff to relieve himself of the torment of living with Nyriaana's pain.

Nyriaana. Kyaati's heart contracted sharply. Her tribe-sister had cut herself off from everyone since the loss of Juaan, a living husk drifting through her existence. Kyaati knew that pain and would have done anything to spare Nyriaana, to ease her suffering. But she also knew there was nothing anyone could say or do for her. Not yet. Her loss was too recent, too raw.

It would take many blinks of Ninsiku before her friend found a spark of interest in life again. Until then, Baarias was watching her closely, making sure she put food in her mouth and sipped water, keeping her alive until she herself found reason to live again.

Not for the first time, a crushing sense of responsibility rose up to strangle Kyaati's thoughts. She shouldn't have left. She deserved to face every last bit of the suffering she had caused. *She* had been the one to bring Daajir. If she had not… Kyaati dug her nails into her palms, adding another set of crescent cuts to her already abused flesh.

Galahir had tried to convince her it was not her fault, but Kyaati could not escape the burden of her guilt. She did not know if she ever would.

She should not have left, but Galahir had needed her, too. The heavy responsibility of easing the Cro clans into their new lives had kept him busy, but Kyaati could sense his heartbreak at the loss of his oldest friend. He felt alone and adrift without those he had always looked to for leadership. It would take a long time for Galahir to accept that he was the leader now and could trust his own judgement. He had needed her support on this journey to the south and so Kyaati had departed at his side.

"Is this the place?" Bahari's voice broke into Kyaati's brooding, bringing her to the present. The Cro man was looking to Galahir, who nodded solemnly.

"This is a rich game trail. He should be set to rest here." Galahir let out a sharp whistle, signalling the bearers of Nekelmu's litter. Galahir indicated a place near a grassy bank and the men busied themselves digging a hole in which to lay the magnificent wolf. They worked tirelessly, their work made easier by the thawing earth, and Nekelmu's resting place was dug before the shadows shifted towards the east.

Galahir himself lifted the broken body of the great alpha wolf and laid him in the grave, his nose towards the prevailing wind. "This wolf saved my life," he announced to their followers. "His kind are henceforth to be honoured among man, forever welcome at our firesides should they choose to grace us with their company." He saluted the black form with his spear. "Farewell, Brother under Utu," he murmured, throwing the first of the soil back on top of the wolf.

Once the soil had been replaced, it was time for other partings. Nekelmu's chosen resting place also marked the boundary of the most southerly of all the known Cro clans. As the Pronghorns shouldered their supplies, readying to return to their camp and their women, they looked to their new leader.

Bahari's shoulders lifted as he sucked in a steadying breath under their expectant regard. The young man's uncertainty was obvious. He had spent almost his entire life removed from his birth People, raised by Thals. Now he found himself chosen by Galahir to lead this small but proud Cro clan of the south.

Kyaati graced him with an encouraging smile, soothing the energies around him. He would make a fine and strong Chief. Alok himself had blessed Galahir's decision.

Only one person remained unhappy. Kikima shifted at Kyaati's elbow. As had become usual, the half-Deni woman was not far from her side, but Kyaati suspected Kikima had another reason for accompanying her on this journey south. She and Bahari had spent much time in each other's company, sharing the hardships and triumphs, joys and sorrows of the last days, and it had not been hard to see their burgeoning relationship had only grown deeper. Kyaati could sense her friend's intense sorrow at this last parting.

She reached out to squeeze Kikima's hand in support as Alok clasped his honour son by the arm in farewell and recognition of a fellow Chief. No words needed to be spoken between them as Bahari took up his new mantel and stepped back from his adoptive father with his head held high. He came before Kyaati next. "It has been an honour knowing Dryads," he said. "I sorrow for Nyriaana."

Kyaati's throat was suddenly too thick to allow speech. She dipped her head.

Bahari reached into his furs and then pressed an object into Kyaati's hand. "Give this gift to her when she is ready?" He looked to Kyaati for her agreement. "Too soon to give now."

Kyaati glanced down at the object Bahari had pressed on her and swallowed. It was a pendant with a wolf's head carved out of a green stone. A stone the exact shade of…

"It match Jade Wolf's eyes," he said. "For her to remember."

Kyaati closed her fist around the cool stone. "I promise," she whispered.

"Thank you," he said. "Eron be with you, Kyaati." He then lifted his face to the tall woman at her side. His proud bearing slipped; suddenly shy, he asked: "Kikima. Come with me?"

Kikima's shock flashed across Kyaati's higher senses. "C-come with you, but—"

Bahari caught hold of her hand as she took a step back. "I no know Cro custom well and you not known me long," he said. "But… need a trusted friend to guide me true. Need… you." He ducked his head upon this last admittance, flushing.

Kyaati could have sworn she heard Kikima's heart thud, but she shook her head. "Bahari…"

Bahari looked crestfallen. "What wrong?"

"Bahari, you hardly know me. You don't know—I can't…"

her hands went to her abdomen in an unconscious motion. Kyaati tasted her friend's guilt, her unhappiness at concealing her secret from this man. She dropped her proud head. "I need to tell you."

Bahari settled his hand over hers. "Not fool, Kikima," he said. "I know."

Kikima's head snapped up. "Then... h-how can you...?" she trailed off.

Bahari frowned. "Child not responsible for sins of father in Thal tradition. I Chief now," he said. "Your child live in peace under my protection. I no reject you, Kikima. Come with me?" he asked again.

Tears spilled from Kikima's amber eyes, but still she hesitated, her gaze flicking between Kyaati and the man asking for her company. Loyalty warring with her heart's desire.

"Don't you dare even think of refusing him," Kyaati said, stamping down her own grief at the thought of parting from the woman who had become her closest confidant. "Go, Kikima" she said. "There has been so little joy in these last days, so much stolen. It would lighten my heart to see at least one of my family happy. Bahari needs you. Go with him with all of my blessing." Halima had raised Kikima to become a matriarch. Now Kyaati knew that destiny would be fulfilled by Bahari's side.

"Thank you." Kikima snatched Kyaati up into a fierce embrace. "I will miss you, my matriarch."

Kyaati laughed through her own tears. "This is not goodbye," she sniffed. "We will see each other often."

"I promise," Kikima responded, before releasing her. The half-Deni girl then stood to her full height, dipping her chin once to Kyaati in respect, before turning and walking away east towards her new life at Bahari's side.

Clutching Galahir's arm for support, Kyaati watched them go until they passed out of her range of sight.

"It time we returned to our *etuti sagkal*, also," Alok said, calling Kyaati's attention back around. "Our path now takes us west of yours."

Galahir inclined his head. "May the Light Bringer always shine upon you."

Alok bowed low, whistling a signal for his People to follow. He then paused, looking back. "Girl!" he called to the red-headed figure standing unobtrusively at the rear of Galahir's now small procession. "You come with me now."

Selima blanched and backed away uncertainly from his sudden demand.

Alok's gaze softened. "No fear me, girl. You heard my son. Child not responsible for sins of father in Thal custom. Join my *imrua*. Baarias told me you skilled healer. Need such talent with herds returning. And you blood of my dear Nen. In you, I see her beloved face. I honour her by taking good care."

A wary hope kindled in Selima's eyes, a single tear escaping as Alok promised to take care of her. There was no hesitation as she left the remnants of her father's clan behind and moved to the Thal leader's side. She met Kyaati's gaze briefly as she passed and dipped her chin. Kyaati paused for a moment before returning the gesture. She still wasn't sure if she fully forgave the girl for her past actions, but she hoped with the proper regard and guidance, Selima would grow beyond what her father had thus far made her.

The Thals departed, leaving Kyaati's band with one last

duty to perform: to return to the forests of her birth. Behind her, all of her People, except for Baarias and Nyriaana, waited between the ranks of Galahir's best warriors. Their eyes sought the dark line of their ancestral home, now visible in the distance. Relief was evident on their faces. Kyaati could understand their longing. The vast openness of the Plains took a long time to adjust to.

The journey took the rest of the day and the shadows were lengthening by the time they reached the border of their homeland. Kyaati led them inside, the Cro now falling into line between her People, still wary of the dangers the forest presented and looking to the Ninkuraaja for guidance.

Darkness was complete when they reached the *eshaara* grove, the din of the night creatures singing all around them. Too loud, Kyaati thought with a sad smile.

"Aardn?" Pelaan called. Kyaati's father cast around, searching for the Elder who had remained behind, but only silence answered his call.

"Over here," Umaa's voice was dead as she pointed into the undergrowth at the edge of the grove. Kyaati followed Pelaan to Umaa's side. There lay Aardn, her frozen mouth stained with the juice of night berries. Kyaati heaved a sigh, feeling the sting of yet another loss.

"Why?" she asked.

Her father shrugged heavily. "She knew she had lost us. After a lifetime of doing what she thought was right to preserve us, what did she have to live for once we were gone?"

Kyaati's heart squeezed with pity and guilt as she looked down into the pale face. *I'm sorry*, she thought.

"It was not your fault, Kyaati," Pelaan pressed her shoulder.

"She chose her path. We will give her a proper Casting with the others." Together, they lifted the Elder's body and placed her next to Daajir.

"We will remain here for the night," Pelaan announced, "and observe the fast before the Casting in the morning. Galahir, you and your warriors may stay in the *akaab* tree," he waved them towards Baarias' old home, all the chambers in the vast trunk at ground level. "Nothing will harm you there."

Galahir bowed his thanks and led his weary men towards the embrace of the tree.

"Blessings, father," Kyaati bid Pelaan a good night before following her mate. The Cro were already rolling themselves into their furs and settling to sleep in the piles of old leaves that still littered the ground, such was their exhaustion. Kyaati's own feet were dragging as she moved to Galahir's side and lay down beside him.

He immediately caught her in his arms and held her close, burying his face in the crook of her neck as Kyaati laid Elhaari on the ground beside them, fast asleep in his furs. She could feel her mate's turbulent emotions, so many raging just beneath his control, but overlaying them all, she sensed his thankfulness. They and their son had survived. They were alive, and they were together when so many others had been denied that privilege.

Kyaati gripped his hand, allowing nothing but her own gratitude to permeate the moment.

"Do you think your People will remain here?" Galahir asked after a long moment.

"I don't know," Kyaati said. "Such a change so fast is a lot to embrace." She sighed. She could not force them to leave if that was what they decided. "We will have to see what the morning brings."

"Hmmm," was Galahir's only response as he drifted towards sleep.

Putting thoughts of the following day out of her head, Kyaati closed her eyes. Cradled in the familiar red gold walls and scent of an *eshaara* tree filling her senses, she was asleep within moments.

* * *

"Go in peace and in the light of Ninmah."

Three rafts rested on the bank of the river as dawn broke over the forest, Pelaan standing at their head as he spoke the ritual words. Each remaining member of the tribe moved forward to set aglow the *girru* moss surrounding the dead, Ninkuraaja and Cro alike, honouring the souls of those passed.

Kyaati touched the moss at Imaani's and Aardn's heads, but did not approach Daajir's raft. Her father gave her a reproachful look, but she ignored it. She would not honour the murderer who had destroyed Nyriaana, leaving her with the shards of a broken heart that the passing of the seasons would blunt, but never truly mend.

Umaa clutched Imaani's cold hand to the bitter end, wading out into the waters of the river next to her lost *ankida* until the current became too strong and the river swept him away in a reflection of how the Great Spirit had swept up his soul.

Pelaan waded out to her before her knees buckled under the weight of her grief, tucking her under his arm as he guided her safely back to shore.

The rafts passed out of sight and a pregnant silence fell over the gathered witnesses. The reason for returning to the southern forests had been completed. Now the Ninkuraaja stood at the facing a new and uncertain future.

"Come," Kyaati prompted. "It is time to leave."

The red-gold faces turned towards her, but no one spoke. To Kyaati's dismay, a couple actively stepped back. "No," Raanya spoke. "We fought the evil and now it is done. It is time for us to live in peace. In our home. Why do we need to return to the Cro and their savage ways?" She eyed the fur-clad men standing behind Kyaati.

Kyaati sighed. "Because we are needed." Even as she spoke the words, she felt the truth of them in her heart. "You all heard what Enlil said. Man was created to plunder and destroy, and what he said was true—for the Cro. But not the Ninkuraaja. Ninmah made us differently. Enlil overlooked that.

"Fate might have turned against us, closing the path to the world our People might have made, but we cannot give up. If we do not go now, if we stay and perish here in this forest, then there is no hope for KI or his Children. We have to share our knowledge and the wisdom we have been taught, passing our Gift to the babes to come." She lifted Elhaari in his sling. "It might not be enough, but in some small way, we must live on."

Leaves rustled as her People shifted uncertainly. Kyaati held her breath. She could not force them to choose the path of survival. They had to come to the decision on their own.

It was Umaa who came first. Her face ravaged by grief, she approached Kyaati. "I choose to live. I will not allow Imaani's sacrifice to stand for nothing," she said before joining the Cro in Kyaati's shadow.

Pelaan was next, pride shining in his eyes as he looked into her face. The rest followed in her father's wake. Not one soul chose to stay. As the last of her tribe came to her side, Kyaati felt a rush, a swirling of triumph and hope from the Great Spirit of KI himself. And then there was a voice. Bodiless, it resonating through her body. Her heart leaped as her head whipped around, fearing to see Enlil standing in the trees. But while this voice had the same otherworldly power of the Lord of the Skies, the tone was different.

Well done, daughter, it spoke, before lapsing into silence. Only the birds sang in the empty trees.

Unnerved, Kyaati hurried after her clan as they made their way back towards the Plains.

A whine stopped her. Batai was standing half hidden in the trees. The wolf's yellow eyes held a query, his head tilting as another uncertain whine slid between his teeth. Sighing, Kyaati crouched before him, touching her forehead to his. "Batai," she spoke, burying her hands in his fur. "We cannot stay. For you, we have to embrace another life now, one that might make us enemies for a time. But I vow, one day, I do not know when, we will return." She gestured around at the untouched forest and all the life within. "We will turn back to this, retaking our place among the Children of KI to live in harmony once more. Through us, man will come to understand."

And Kyaati rose to her feet. Touching the wolf's head once in final farewell, she walked away, and did not look back.

* * *

Epilogue

Nyriaana screamed.

"I can't do this," she rasped, panting as the pain subsided, only to rip through her once more; her belly tightening, squeezing.

"Yes, you can." Kyaati was at her shoulders, smoothing her sweaty hair from her brow with cool hands. "And you will."

All around them the trees rustled, restless in expectation as the water babbled close by. All else was still, as though the Great Spirit of KI himself was holding his breath. Nyri had chosen this spot inside the copse, next to the river. The sound of the trees and the flow of the water over stones was a comfort.

This was the place where she and Juaan had spent so many days lying on the banks of the river, when he had still been Khalvir. It had been his favourite place to be alone, the place he had shared with her, the place they had grown to know one another again. She felt closer to him here. An essence of his spirit still lay within the earth and in the trees. She fancied she could almost hear him whispering words of encouragement in her ear.

Nyri cried out again, clutching the jade carving of the

wolf's head in her fist next to her breast.

"The babe is almost here," Baarias' voice eased over the air. "Just one last effort, Nyriaana. When the tightening comes again, push hard!"

Already it was building. Her back arched off the ground as the agony stole her breath. She could not think. Baarias was calling, but she could not hear him. *Juaan, help me!* She cried into the silence of her mind. From the moment she lost him, Nyri had buried their severed bond down deep, knowing the emptiness she would surely feel there would shatter the fragile grip she kept on her sanity. Now, drunk on pain and the herbs Baarias had given her, she reached for the only comfort she wanted. *Juaan.*

Warmth and strength swept through her, like the fluttering of a kiss on her brow, a brief flame flaring in the darkness. *Nyri, Nyri, Nyriaana.*

Juaan? Her eyes wheeled, searching the empty wood. Surely she had imagined it, her mind conjuring the impossible when she needed him most.

"Nyriaana! Now!" Baarias commanded.

Real or imagined, Nyri seized upon the invisible strength, keening through her teeth as the pain crested. On and on it went, greater and greater. She didn't think it would ever stop. Surely she would be torn in two. But then, just when she thought she could give no more—it was over.

The thin cry of an infant filled the air.

Kyaati's sigh of relief rushed past her ear. "You did it, Nyri!" her tribe-sister crowed, cradling her as Nyri collapsed back in exhaustion, her eyes rolling closed.

"A healthy girl!" There was a rustle of leaves. "You have a beautiful daughter, Nyriaana." She could hear the tears in Baarias' voice as something warm and wet was pressed against her. Nyri somehow found the will to open her eyes.

And there she was. "Oh." The soft cry shuddered through Nyri as she beheld the one promise that had kept her breathing since the day Juaan had been taken from her. Her daughter squalled against her skin, needing, soft and helpless. Nyri's dead heart sparked, warmth breaking through the ice that had encased it for so long, splintering it, cracking it apart. It was like breathing again after a lifetime of drowning.

"Oh." She gathered their baby up into her arms, nuzzling the damp, downy fuzz on top of the delicate head. The world shifted, resettling around a new beautiful centre. All hers.

All his.

The flame in the darkness flared stronger. Movement flickered against her periphery. *Juaan?* Nyri lifted her face from her precious bundle.

And he was there.

Insubstantial, ghostly as the breeze, he stood against the trees. The sob caught in her throat. *Oh, Juaan.*

He smiled. *Nyri. Nyri, Nyriaana.* Peace and contentment radiated from his image, sweeping out to encompass her as her trembling lips lifted into an answering smile.

Look, Juaan, I did it, she thought. *Our daughter.*

Behind him, more figures appeared in the dancing shadows. Sefaan, a red-haired Thal woman, a Ninkuraaja female whose features reminded her of both Baarias and Juaan. *Rebaa.* All were gazing at her with the same warmth and pride as Juaan.

You have done well, child, Sefaan's voice whispered through her mind. *Be at peace now.*

"Nyri?" Baarias frowned. "What are you looking at?"

Nyri blinked, and the vision faded, each figure curling out of existence one by one like smoke. She hitched a breath, holding Juaan's gaze until the last. And then he was gone, leaving an empty space between the trees. But the sense of calm and contentment did not leave her. The flame flickered on in the darkness, fading her pain and fears away before it. For he was there.

To the end, she thought to the empty air.

Without answering Baarias, she dropped her gaze to her daughter's perfect face just in time to see her eyes blink open, taking her first look at the world she had been born into. Bittersweet laughter bubbled from Nyriaana's throat as a single tear tracked down her face.

"Just like his," Baarias breathed.

"Yes." Nyri brushed at the soft cheeks, feeling the power radiate from the small body.

"What are you going to name her?" Kyaati asked.

Nyri's smile widened as she gazed into her daughter's green, green eyes. Reaching up to her throat, she lifted the pendant bearing the *enu* seed Sefaan had entrusted to her so long ago, and placed it over her daughter's head, fulfilling her promise at last.

"Ariyaana," Nyri answered. "Her name is Ariyaana."

And somewhere, in the far forests of the south, a new *enu* seed tumbled to the leafy ground.

The End

Not quite ready to leave the world of *The Ancestors Saga?*

Turn the page to discover Chapter One of *Raknari: Khalvir's Lost Years,* and follow Juaan's backstory as he grows from a lost boy with no name to one of the most feared warriors on the prehistoric plains.

Raknari: Chapter One (Awakening)

The boy awoke. His eyes stung and watered as he forced them open. He blinked rapidly in an instinctive attempt to clear his vision. His stomach roiled and he drew a deep breath against it. He wished he hadn't. The air was thick and acrid and a sharp pain in his side jabbed through his chest. He rolled over on to his knees, coughing and retching until his throat felt raw.

Finally, the fit passed, and he sat up. The world turned before his eyes, and the nausea threatened once more.

"Ah!" he groaned, his hand going to his head. A point behind his left ear throbbed painfully. He could feel a lump growing under his bruised skin. When he brought his hand back, his fingers were bloody. The world rolled again.

"You wake?" A rough voiced asked from close by.

Startled, the boy looked up and saw a large man sitting upon a fallen tree. His features were coarse, his forehead was long and sloping, his nose broad and his lips wide. The most striking feature was a mane of fiery red hair. Glinting black eyes glared out from under the heavy brow. A powerful emotion stirred within the boy's heart as he met them. Hate? Fear? Should he hate this man? He frowned. Who was this man? The first fluttering of unease curled through his stomach. Where was he?

"Where you get this?" the stranger interrupted his

579

thoughts, thrusting a long, thick spear towards the boy in his massive fist.

The boy stared at it; like everything else, the object was unfamiliar. He shook his head at the red-haired man, not knowing how to respond.

"Tell me!" The man shot to his feet with a speed belying his bulk. Expression black with fury, he advanced on the boy, raising the butt of the spear high. "Tell me where you got!"

The boy shrank away, terrified. He raised his arms to shield his head but, even as he cowered down, a wave of defiance arose from within. Crying out, he pushed himself to his feet and met the stranger's eyes evenly, chin raised. He would not bow before him.

This action only seemed to madden his attacker more and, with a roar, the big man brought the haft of the spear crashing down. The boy found he could only stand there, watching the weapon as it raced towards his face. He could not have moved, even to save his life.

"Eldrax!" a voice called out. The spear halted a mere breath from the boy's cheek. Letting out a frustrated growl, the red-haired aggressor turned to another of the strange men standing away in the trees. Smoke smouldered from the cracked bark.

Trembling, the boy sank to his knees again as his attacker moved away to speak with the one who had called for his attention. The world continued to swim hazily before his eyes. He tried to clear his thoughts; tried to remember how he had got here while fighting the panic that was threatening to set in. The boy looked around, searching for something familiar, anything that would ground him and offer comfort.

Massive trees surrounded them, almost too huge to be comprehended. Their branches twisted together in a way that was peculiar and yet… oddly familiar. The boy felt the urge to climb into one of them, but had no idea as to why he should want to do that. Trunks blackened and burned, their dead leaves rattled in the breeze. The sight brought an overwhelming wave of sadness. But more than anything else, he was aware of a pain in his chest. It was not the physical pain of his ribs that would heal in time. This pain went deeper. He had lost something. Something important, and its absence had left a hole in his heart. The space at his side yawned. He rubbed his forehead, confused.

The forest was offering no clarity. The boy looked down to study his body. He was dressed in woven leaves. The garments felt tough, leathery, and did not fit well. Too tight. He wondered at that. He looked at the men surrounding him. They were all dressed in thick furs in varying shades of grey and black. His confusion only deepened.

A few of the men's eyes followed him as he stumbled back to his feet and limped forward. The boy knew he could not escape them, and he couldn't even guess why he would want to do that. His vision hazed in and out of focus and he tripped on something heavy and soft. He came down on top of it, catching himself on his hands. His left arm gave out from under him. The elbow felt bruised.

The discomfort was driven from his mind by the blank, dead eyes staring up at him, just a hand's breadth from his own. Letting out a low cry, the boy threw himself back away from the body. A fresh wave of nausea clawed up his throat. Doubling over, he retched again, pain lancing up and down his ribs. He heard laughter break out at his expense.

Gasping and with his hands braced upon his knees, the boy dared to look back at the corpse on the ground. The red-gold skin of the fallen man was pallid in death. His black hair was thrown out around him, framing the expression of horror twisted forever upon his frozen face. He would have been small, perhaps only just reaching above the boy's shoulder had he stood erect. The man's eyes were large and his ears tapered to a subtle point. But the most intriguing feature to the boy was the man's garments. They matched his own.

Had he been a part of this man's People? The boy glanced down at his hands and the hope was immediately dashed. His own skin was a shade darker. It did not match that of the man on the ground. He felt his face, his ears. They tapered, but not to the extent of the dead man's. But nor were they entirely curved like the fur-clad men about him. Their skin colours ranged from pale to very dark. But none had the reddish hint of his own.

"Boy." The gruff command came from behind him. He flinched and turned his head to see the red-haired warrior approaching him. The inexplicable wave of hatred swept over the boy again. "Tell me where others went. I need know."

Others? The boy looked around. *What others?* His lack of an answer aggravated the warrior. A large hand caught him right across the mouth. His lip split as he went down in a heap. Hot tears of anger prickled in the boy's eyes as he sat up and wiped at his bleeding mouth. He glared up at the large man looming over him, forcing his tears away. He would not give this beast the satisfaction of seeing him cry.

"Tell me where went!" the man demanded again, raising

his gnarled hand once more.

"I don't know!" the boy screamed back at him. "I don't know. I don't know!" He put his head in his hands and rocked back and forth. The pain in his skull throbbed. He thought that his head would burst.

"Don't know?" The beast's voice was softer now, uncertainty creeping into his tone. The boy met the black eyes as the warrior appraised him. "What you remember?"

The boy's eyes flickered around, still seeking an answer, but there was nothing, nothing. His panic was rising again, threatening to choke him. The red-haired beast appeared amused by his distress. The black eyes were cruel and without mercy as he laughed in the boy's face. "You no remember anything!" It was not a question. "What your name?" he taunted, pressing, leaning in. "What your name?"

And the boy couldn't answer. He didn't even know his own name. The panic overwhelmed his will, and he broke into helpless sobs before the monster. "I don't know." His head throbbed. The world spun, fading around him once more as he collapsed onto his aching side.

"I don't know!"

Continue reading *Raknari* (*The Ancestors Saga,*
***Khalvir's Lost Years*)**
www.loriholmes.com/raknari

About the Author

Growing up in England and having had a misspent youth devouring everything science fiction and fantasy, Lori enjoys reading and writing books that draw a reader into new and undiscovered worlds with characters that are hard to part with long after the journey comes to an end.

Lori's debut novel, The Forbidden, begins the epic journey into the Ancestors Saga, combining history, mystery and legend to retell a lost chapter in humanity's dark and distant past.

When not lost in the world of The Ancestors Saga, Lori enjoys spending time with her family (3 children, 2 whippets and her husband - it's a busy house!) usually outdoors walking and exploring the great British countryside.

Find out more at www.loriholmes.com

You can connect with me on:

https://www.loriholmes.com

https://www.facebook.com/loriholmesauthor

https://www.amazon.com/-/e/B06XBFF5RR

https://www.bookbub.com/profile/lori-holmes

Also by Lori Holmes

The Ancestors Saga

Book 1, The Forbidden:
www.loriholmes.com/forbidden
Book 2, Daughter of Ninmah:
www.loriholmes.com/ninmah
Companion Novel To Book 2, Captive:
www.loriholmes.com/captive
Book 3, Enemy Tribe
www.loriholmes.com/enemytribe
Book 4, The Last Kamaali:
www.loriholmes.com/kamaali
Raknari: Khalvir's Lost Years (Companion Novel):
www.loriholmes.com/raknari

Printed in Great Britain
by Amazon

23142714R00341